Only Caro's Baby
Good Girls Book Two

Christine Young

Chapter One

Glasgow 1823

Duncan Murray, fifth Earl of Downberry, bored to tears, waited with little anticipation for his birthday gift to arrive. The lady, Caroline, he'd been told was an exceptional beauty as well as a practiced lover. Letty personally recommended her, that according to Torra who supervised the girls now that Letty was wed. He meant to enjoy all this woman's unique charms then send her on her way. When the girl was offered, he'd been more than a bit jaded. Prostitutes weren't usually in his repertoire of dalliances. He was assured since she came from Miss Scarlett's escort service, she was different, safe. He wouldn't have to worry about the pox.

He also understood why his friends along with his brothers visited the escort service on the outskirts of Glasgow. The women there catered to the mental as well as the physical needs of a man. It wasn't just sex they offered. Companionship was the distinguishing mark that separated them. The women would attend balls or the opera if that were the request. Men paid extra to bed them. However, bedding was only allowed if the woman wanted sex. If the woman refused, there could be no argument.

For the longest time, he'd been in a deplorable mood. After his fiancée left him for another more interesting as well as wealthy man, a man with a loftier pedigree than his, he vowed off all women except widows or those he could purchase for the night. No attachments became his new motto. No falling in love came in a close second. He only needed a wife to sire an heir. He had more than enough time for such as that. This lady would do just fine to ease his needs for the evening.

Since that horrible day when the message his fiancée left him was delivered to his door, he spent his time with his head in his financial books. In the last year, he doubled his fortune. The moment he heard the door open, he cringed. In another heartbeat, his butler announced the lady.

He wasn't sure why he cringed. Perhaps it was because there would be nothing between them save sex. Deep inside, despite his promises to himself, he understood on another level he needed more from a woman as he still wished for a wife along with children. Well, this woman wasn't in the running to become his wife.

Now, this was the time of reckoning. This was about sex coupled with carnal delights the two could share, nothing more. He would enjoy her charms then send her on her way.

"Miss Caroline here to see you, Sir."

His longtime butler's voice held a note of scorn. Johnston always showed disdain when he gave in to his baser needs. This occasion was vastly different. After all, today was his birthday. Lately, that had been quite often there was scorn in the butler's words. However, it was rare he brought his women to his home.

This lady was his birthday gift from his brothers as well as his friends.

He was known as a womanizer, also a gambler and reprobate throughout the town even though he wasn't. Having carefully nurtured those sentiments to keep doting mothers with simpering daughters from tagging along behind them, from thinking he was a worthwhile catch. He wasn't. At least he didn't want to be. When it came time to picking his mate, he would find a woman he could control, one who would make no demands on him, a woman who would give him his needed heir.

"Come in," Duncan said as he took the measure of the woman standing in front of him. The female was exceptionally tall for a woman. With her face covered in powder, he could not decipher any semblance of cheekbones. Eyes heavily traced with kohl coupled with rouged cheeks and lips, he almost sent her away. For him, there was no physical attraction. If she possessed an iota of beauty, it was hidden behind layers of face paint she wore. The cape settled on her shoulders, secured by a large pink bow not only concealed her feminine charms but the decoration also signaled his gift was to be unwrapped. He wondered if he would enjoy the unwrapping. At the moment, he didn't believe so.

Why the devil did Torra think this woman would appeal to him? She was nothing like the others Miss Scarlett sent his way. She looked like a painted harlot.

The thought to send her home momentarily crossed his mind again. She didn't say anything. At least she wasn't a chatterbox. He couldn't abide that in a woman. Her eyes were huge ice blue pools of fear. If she meant to make her living as an escort, she was going to have to learn a hell of a lot. Showing terror was not acceptable in her profession. Well hell, she shouldn't be afraid, at least not of him. He never in his entire life hurt a woman. At least he didn't think so.

When his second thought flashed through the mud in his brain, he decided before he sent her away, he would find out what was under all the paint. Maybe, just maybe there was a beautiful woman hidden beneath all that powder, kohl and rouge. Perhaps she possessed a slight smattering of freckles. He adored freckles. He liked to sip on each one before he let his mouth settle over the woman's lips.

"Johnston, bring me a basin along with two pitchers of water."

His command was curt, to the point. There was no reason to question yet he was certain Johnston would do so.

"Sir?" true to form his butler queried with arched eyebrows. "That's a bit unusual even for you."

Duncan shot him an amused grin as his attention drifted back to the woman who stood uneasily near the door shifting from one foot to the other. It appeared she might bolt at the first opportunity. "You heard right. A soft rag also."

With each of her puffy little breaths of air coupled with the shifting of her feet, he was becoming more and more intrigued. Perhaps tonight would ease his boredom. After all she was paid for until dawn.

Duncan's gaze drifted back to the girl. Something about her fascinated him. Enticed some part of him he believed long dead. She just wasn't what he anticipated. Older than he expected when Torra told him about her, she appeared hesitant to speak, even to ply her trade. She hung back by the door as if she thought he might bite. Hell, perhaps he would later on when she was beneath him. Her tiny pink tongue drifted across her bottom lip. He watched mesmerized, sure the motion was not a seductive technique she learned in her profession. Instead, the movement seemed created by nervousness.

After Johnston left the room, Duncan chuckled softly, surprisingly charmed by the situation as well as determined to get to know this woman parading as a prostitute. If she was as Torra hinted, new to the business, the evening might not be over as soon as she presented him with the entire gift, the whole package. His friends paid for the complete night. Perhaps that's how long he would keep her here. That thought brought on more interesting possibilities, rare that he ever spent more than an hour or two in the company of a woman.

"Would you like a drink? Something to sooth those nerves I'm seeing. Don't want you to be jittery."

"What? Oh! Would like the candles doused," she gasped, startled by his question, her eyes wider now than they had been earlier.

Her bottom lip caught beneath even white teeth entranced every male nerve he possessed. Instantly, he wanted his teeth in the same spot, could imagine the soft warmth he would encounter.

"A drink? A glass of wine? Something stronger?"

Amusement lit up his features. Holding back the chuckle took mustering every ounce of control he possessed. He didn't believe she would see the humor. Least of all, he didn't want to douse the candles. He wanted to see all of her.

"Yes, wine would be nice. Don't remember having anything stronger," she said her voice a low sultry purr.

Just as she was taller than most women, her voice was deeper, throatier, sexier. The sound wasn't like smooth whiskey but the vibrations were close.

Once more, he wondered if this was part of the act or her innocence. Could a woman lower her voice to such a degree on purpose? Did some women have voices naturally low and evocative? Some could change the tone for the situation. He detested high trilling feminine voices as well as giggles. Women who giggled incessantly he couldn't abide. "Try brandy then. The burn could be a challenge."

She choked while he watched her swallow. "This is all..." she opened her arms to encompass the room. He caught a glimpse of her scantily clad body. "...a challenge for me," she finished, her voice a breathy sigh.

While she opened her arms the gift she meant to give him, her body, had been slightly revealed. Her generous endowments pleased him. Torra had been right about her body if nothing else. It was possible she could be a dream come true. Once all that horrid paint was washed from her face.

He poured her brandy. After handing the glass to her, he lifted his in a salute. "To challenges then."

Dimples formed on either side of her provocative mouth when she smiled. Making it a mission to kiss those tiny hollows, he grinned back. She sipped, her gaze hovering over the rim of her glass. Her grimace sent a small chuckle to his lips.

"It burns." She set it down on a table before smoothing her hands down the cloak covering her. "What do we do now?"

"Wait until Johnston finishes interrupting us with delicacies to tempt our pallets. He will do so, until he understands it is well past time for him to make himself scarce," he spoke softly as he strode toward her. "After that we will find numerous ways to enjoy ourselves. What do you think? Would you like to enjoy me?"

"Delicacies?" she queried breathlessly as he wished to see more of her. "Enjoy ourselves? You? Y-you have to get r-rid of the c-candles."

"Sit, relax for a few minutes. As I said before, I'm sure my butler will spend as much time interrupting our dalliance as he can. When we get to know each other intimately, I want you all to myself." He bent close to her; his lips very close to her cheek. "He doesn't approve, you know."

"Oh, not many would." She sat, as if she could distance herself from him, her legs crossed over each other. "Approve."

The cape's opening revealed long legs; naked, shapely legs. For a woman, well-muscled legs that left him even more intrigued about the lady along with what exactly he would find beneath the gown. This woman, Caro, was not your average courtesan. As with most women, there were hidden depths to be uncovered. He meant to be the man to uncover Caro's secrets. Well, he wanted to uncover her breasts first then her woman's charms; after that all her secrets.

"More than you would think."

Two trays of food along with the basin as well as pitchers of water he requested were set on one of the tables. Johnston stopped on his way out to add logs to the fire. Duncan stifled his laughter. The man had been with him for the last ten years. Johnston undoubtedly knew him better than he did himself. At times the stoic butler acted as if he was his father.

Ah, but that had been a lifetime ago. It seemed he'd always been on his own, always in charge. Well, he did have a mother, one who adored him as well as his three brothers and his father. When he shook himself from his thoughts, he saw she was sipping the brandy.

"Tell me something about yourself."

He relaxed on the chair spreading his arms across the back. His fingers trailing lightly along the pink cloak, they stopped at the bow. He would untie that damn bow soon.

A few drops of brandy spewed from her too painted lips. She covered her mouth with a hand. To his delight some of the obtrusive color disappeared. "Sorry," she murmured as she wiped brandy from her chin. "Didn't' expect a question such as that one. Didn't think you would want to know anything about me. Assumed we would, well we would then that would be that. What would you like to know?"

Sporting a wide grin, he handed her a napkin.

"First of all, what brings you to this position where you are selling your body? While I don't mind purchasing the use of your womanly charms, there is something about you that is..." Leaning forward, his fingers in a steeple beneath his chin "Something is telling me this is not anything you've done often or at all. Why is that? You're different."

The quick tilt of her chin spoke volumes to him. The regal bearing set off another round of questions he had no answers for. He was sure she wanted to tell him to mind his business then she'd mind hers. For some reason he couldn't fathom, he wanted to learn everything there was to know about this woman.

This evening would not prove boring. No, not if it continued as it began. There would be nothing to put him to sleep. He found he looked forward to what the night would give even if he had to douse the candles.

No, intriguing and enticing might be adequate terms. In her

feigned innocence, even to the fact she wanted no light she was charming.

"I'd like an answer," he persisted determined to hear a few intricate words even if he was sure they would all be lies.

The cape covering her rose and fell several times with the deep breaths she inhaled. Her eyes seemed to cross as she thought about the question or perhaps the answer. At least it appeared she was thinking. It also appeared she didn't want to enlighten him.

She lifted her shoulders now. "It's quite simple. Why do most women sell themselves? I'm sure it's not for the enjoyment of a man's body. That's not possible."

Amused, he decided at least this one time she would discover how wrong she was. "Don't believe you've answered my question. At least I'm not sure what is simple along with what is not. You're not here because you want to enjoy my body. Why are you here? I certainly would like to enjoy yours."

Caro sucked in a deep breath of air as her face took on a delightful shade of pink. Her eyes blazed with emotions he wanted to tap into. "A change of subject would be nice."

"You mean to prevaricate."

"I wouldn't think a man of your standing, your reputation would understand that word. Or is it just something you toss out because you've heard it before?" Her composure seemingly regained, she smiled sweetly, the dimples showing delightfully on either side of her lips.

Air hissed into his lungs. She was right. It was past time for a change of subject. Eventually, he would discover what brought her to his home, willing to gift him with the luscious curves she possessed as well as the silken heat of her core. She was his for the entire evening. He meant to make use of all the hours his friends paid for. Overjoyed, he didn't react on his first impulse to send her home.

"Before we begin, I'm going to see what is below the paint on your face. Sex for me is not enjoyable when I can't see the woman beneath me as she actually is. I don't want to taste the powder and rough when I kiss you. I need to taste the woman. What do you taste like?"

The jerk of her body surprised him while she squinted at him. The basin of water he held caught her attention. That small chin he wanted to get closer to tilted upward in defiance. Her dimples winked at him asking for his ardent attention.

"You, you," she swallowed. "What are you going to do with that?" she asked, a shaking finger pointed at the water then at him.

He slanted her a laughing grin. "Are you afraid of water? No, I'm certain you are not. So, I will answer your question. I intend to wash your face as well as the large crests of your breasts, your nipples to be precise. I'm sure Torra painted them as well. Did she? We'll see what else the women colored after I've swept all the goop from your face. Do sit still now. This will be over before you know it." He tried for a nonthreatening tone. Nonetheless, her body tightened with the first words.

The rapid switch from sitting to standing caused the brandy to slosh in her glass, small drops sliding down the outside. "You're not touching me." Her indignation was totally out of character for a purchased whore.

He arched a brow, studying her thoughtfully. "Supposed my touching you was why you were here. You've had a change of heart?" He paused a few seconds, "I mean to spend the night touching as well as tasting every delectably delicious part of you."

He was suddenly hiding his annoyance behind his teeth. What the devil did she intend? She wouldn't find additional coin in her purse if she left now. Surely, she must understand that simple fact.

The flush covering what he could see of her sent his heart pounding double-time. Everything she did or said belied her ability for this job she undertook. What secrets did this lady keep? By the time morning arrived and she left, he hoped to have uncovered at least one or more of her mysteries.

"You could wash yourself. However, I decided it would be more enjoyable for me to do the job."

"No! Blow out the candle first."

"You refuse?" He stood over her now that she sat back on the oversized chair near the fire. "There will be no payment. No enjoyment of this man's body for you. The only way we will make it through the night will be my way if you wish to be paid. Do you wish to go away empty handed?"

For several seconds she turned her head away. He heard the heavy intake of air as she struggled with a decision she shouldn't have to make. Kissing the line of her chin to the small lobe of her ear would be enjoyable. Exploring his way down her neck to spots still covered by the innocuous bow as well as the cape would prove pleasurable. He quite enjoyed the tick of her jaw while she thought about what he said.

"I'm resigned. What do you want me to do?"

"Nothing, nothing at all. Sip the rest of your brandy or down it all in one gulp. I'll be happy to pour you more. Whatever you like. All you need to do is sit motionless then enjoy yourself. I'm going to remove the makeup now."

Moving slowly, as he watched the skittish creature in front of him, Duncan dipped the soft cloth in the water that he poured into the basin. Before he touched the cloth to her cheek, one finger found the pulse at the base of her neck. With the tiny caress the spot jumped, leapt to life. It seemed Caro's passion was raw and deep. She might not think she wanted to be here. Her body did.

Using small strokes of the damp cloth he swept her face with the rose scented water. For a moment he thought it odd that Johnston would have brought scented water, rose or anything else. When one small section was left devoid of paint, he placed a kiss, tasted her flesh, sipped the softness he encountered. With every caress upon her skin, her pulse bounced even more. With each kiss a soft purring sound floated from her slightly parted lips.

He was well pleased by her face now that there was no makeup to cover her. Beautiful. His heart thundered in anticipation of the ensuing hours with this ever-intriguing lady. Her passion ran hot and deep.

When he ran the cloth across her lips, she closed her eyes. Several times, he stroked her mouth. She parted for him, her tongue touching her top lip. This was unadulterated torture. What the devil was he doing to himself? Now, her every action screamed out her experience with men. To Duncan, she was truly an enigma. One moment her innocence bounded out at him, the next the practiced courtesan.

His breath drew inside, raggedly, slowly. A fine sheen of moisture coated his forehead. Nevertheless, he meant to linger, to entice raw desire from this woman who didn't believe pleasure could be had with a man's body. What the devil were her experiences? She would discover her delight tonight with this male form. He would find his pleasure with hers.

When he was satisfied with her face, he knelt in front of her, his hands framing her lovely features. "Do you want a kiss or do you wish to continue the bath?"

Her eyelashes flew open. "A-a kiss? N-no...why?"

The color of her eyes changed from ice-blue to sky blue before darkening another shade. "You want to proceed to the end without accomplishing the beginning, the foreplay? The foreplay can be as much fun as the thrusting and groaning as well as all the exertion that makes a man bone-weary as well as sweaty. We both know how difficult that can be."

This time instead of color painting her face, she turned white as snow. Something else to discover about his puzzling Caro tonight, why did a woman selling her body turn white at the mention of explicit sex?

"Start at the beginning, yes. Yes, you are right, it's most likely the best course. The beginning. No, should never begin at the end," she whispered her voice paper-thin. "We will kiss."

"That's what I thought you would say." Slowly, he bent close to her, felt the almost nonexistent puffs of air brush lightly across his face. Her breath smelled of mint. Would she taste of mint or the brandy she drank? Both. Exploring the soft bottom lip that seemed to call to him, he swept his tongue across the moistness slicking it further, wetting the plump fullness. Her mouth was damp and enticing more than sultry, beckoning him for extra attention, which he was pleased to give. "Now, would you like to proceed the same way with me? A few tender kisses, you could learn about my lips, taste me as I've tasted you."

"That was a kiss? she asked him her doubt clearly visible in the changing color of her eyes. "I thought..."

"What did you think?"

Her eyes widened perceptibly. No words were forthcoming.

So, why doubt? If she was what she pretended to be she would know the truth. Wouldn't have to ask. "A partial one. Not complete by anyone's standard except perhaps a virgin." Tossing those words to her played into his need to discover who she was along with her true reason for volunteering to be his birthday gift. By her admission, she was new to the escort business. Perhaps her circumstances changed so dramatically she was forced into this life.

Perhaps not.

She might just be a damn fine actress.

"Should we continue?"

"What comes next?"

Caro appeared determined now. Maybe the determination lay in the fact she didn't want to give anymore of herself away to him.

"Why don't you tell me? What do you believe the next step to be?" For his purposes he thought the question brilliant. The food on the tray tempted him to take a slight diversion. There were two slices of cake he believed were meant to pass for his birthday cake as well as a variety of foods destined to delight anyone as well as restore energy for the night to come. If one is to exert energy, one must replenish it.

"Do you have cake? For your birthday?"

She moistened her slightly red lips. They weren't swollen, not yet. Soon they would be. Time to do so was elusive so far as he searched for answers to the puzzle she presented.

"I have you for my birthday, all night. Why don't we both pick something? Cake later when we are exhausted."

With a berry between two fingers, he smoothed the piece of fruit across her bottom lip, back and forth slowly as her gaze traveled the same path. Her breath hitched inside. A broken sound tore through her. The tip of her tongue brushed one finger. "Open *lassie*. Taste what is tempting you."

She did.

He placed the berry on her tongue, exploring the soft inside lining of her bottom lip, tracing the sharp edge of her teeth. "Bite me."

He found himself grinning like a besotted fool when she followed his command. She bit down. Not hard, though with enough force to send a myriad of shock waves to his tortured groin. When her teeth closed around him, she gazed at him questioning.

Duncan picked up her hand. Did the same to each finger, sucking the tip into his mouth before biting gently. The breath she inhaled wavered, shaking as her breasts rose and fell beneath the pink cloak, her agitation clear.

One hand behind her neck, he drew her closer. His lips slanted across hers while his tongue swept between her lips in the same manner as the berry. He was enchanted when she opened for him, when her teeth closed gently over his tongue. They played together. The dance of tongues so different from anything he experienced with any woman before her. Her hands fell upon his shoulders, nails biting into him, unexpectedly pulling him closer. Delicious raw emotions sprung from her, charming him. She was warm and pliant beneath his fingers, everything a man could want.

"Enough foreplay for now. Did Torra paint your nipples?" He stared at her hard while wondering if she would answer with the truth. He detested the paint courtesans used on their body. Before they were intimate, he would rid her of all the paint despite her apparent discomfort.

Her fingers fumbled with the bow on her cape. He stopped her. "I will unwrap you when the time is right. After all you are my birthday present. You need to answer me. Keep in mind I can tell when you lie. Your expressive eyes tell me the truth."

He realized the expression drifting across her face with each question rendered her an open book.

She didn't answer with words slowly nodding. He liked it that she was not a woman who jabbered incessantly. Yet it would be nice if she could find a way to speak a word or two.

"You *ken* I will have to fix that."

Again, she pushed her head up then down before she inhaled a deep breath of air. Realizing this was not easy for her, he tried to be as gentle as he could. He would wash every intimate part of her. He would do his best not to look. Quickly, he unfastened the front of her gown. She was naked beneath. Her nipples were rouged garishly. He could see Torra laughing at him. Perhaps this was meant to be a joke, either that it was meant to convince him she was practiced at her profession. Soon enough he would discover the truth.

"T-the candle..."

Impatiently he stared at her. With a long huff of air, he blew out the closest candle. "The rest will stay." He didn't like the fact her body was cast in shadows.

Duncan saw no humor. He supposed he could have waited. He didn't want to wait. When the time was right, when he orchestrated her seduction to his satisfaction, he meant to have her come to him in her most natural state, naked from the top of her head to the tips her toes without one tiny bit of paint covering her.

For her part, Caro's backbone was inflexible, her chin tilted royally. Her eyes were shut tight. The rigidity caused the rounded globes to be pushed outward and up. Her nipples tightened charmingly. As gently as he could manage, he cleaned them then refastened the gown, which dipped low enough to reveal the coral around each nipple.

"Is there anywhere else Torra painted?" He didn't have to ask the question, as he was certain he knew the answer. For his birthday, Torra would have gone all out to please him. What Torra and most prostitutes didn't know was that most men...possibly he was wrong. The ghastly painting of intimate parts of the female body didn't please him. He'd never thought he was vastly different from the majority of men. When he tasted a woman, he needed to savor her essence not makeup, not powder and rouge.

Her nod coupled with the look of despair sent him into a tailspin. The last thing he wanted to do was make her more embarrassed than she already was.

Well hell.

She was an escort. What did she think when she entered into his home? When he purchased her? Caro must understand what would be expected of her. What was she doing here if she didn't want to be intimate with him?

"I'm going to cleanse the paint from you. If you like, you can close your eyes and pretend I'm not looking at you, touching you. After that we will proceed normally."

"Wh-what is that? Normal? Sir, one more candle?"

"Duncan," he reminded her then did her bidding creating more shadows. Well hell!

"T-thank y-you."

"Since this is your first time as an escort, whatever we do will be the normal for you. Now spread your beautiful white legs for me. This small task will be over with before you even know it has begun. I will be very gentle with you. I won't look either. Will that make you feel better? Or...you can cleanse yourself." Truly, he didn't care.

"I," she swallowed, "I doubt that."

"Do you want to do this yourself? I'll turn around. However, in time I will see all of you. What would you like?"

"You..."

He didn't understand why she chose to have him do something she was having such a devilishly hard time with. Yet she voiced her wishes.

She did spread her legs. He knelt where she opened for him. Her tiny hands rested on his shoulders. He was disappointed when she moved them. She did close her eyes. Her fingers gripped the edge of the chair she was sitting on so tightly her knuckles turned white. When he touched the hot, swollen feminine folds with the cool rag, she flinched. He felt the tightening of her muscles as her legs closed around his shoulders. Finishing as quickly as he could, he tugged what there was of her dress to cover her.

"Now." He dropped the cloth into the basin of dirty water. "That wasn't so bad now was it, Caro?"

"Humiliating, embarrassing..." she answered so very softly. When she looked at him, her eyes wide, "My name is Caroline."

He gave no credence to her comment. She was Caro to him. No other name would do. "It is all done. In just a moment, we can proceed to the unwrapping of my gift." He pulled the cord that would bring Johnston to this room.

"Sir?" he asked after a few seconds that led Duncan to think the man was standing outside the door.

"Take the dirty water then bring me another basin along with a pitcher of fresh water. We might have need of more water later this evening. After that you are excused for the night."

"Food too?" Duncan asked Caro as he waited for Johnston.

"If you be wanting me to lose my meal on you well then yes," she murmured looking at him, her eyes still wide blue pools that seemed to question him at every turn.

All the earlier passion that blazed in her eyes vanished. He didn't like that. Well, there was nothing to do about it now except find a way to retrieve the desire, create more than she ever knew before from any man.

"Perhaps you should wait until the embarrassment has worn off."

"Is it going to do that? Wear off?" she asked as her fingers made intricate patterns in the cloak.

More wine would surely work to relax her. Yet the brandy was stronger, potent. A drunken birthday present was not to his liking. He wanted her cognizant as well as willing when he pushed inside her. Perhaps they should proceed with the unveiling then her state, inebriated or not, wouldn't matter quite as much.

"For you, I'm not too sure. Where you are concerned along with each turn of events, you leave me guessing. You present quite the puzzle to me, one I would dearly love to solve."

"Is it that hard to understand after what you did?" Her voice was growing stronger.

"You are deliciously deceptive. Yes, it is hard to comprehend how a woman in your line of work, even newly arrived at the profession would become so embarrassed that her face flamed when a man touches her intimately."

It seemed to Duncan this woman had never been with a man. The thought of being her first left him in confusion. This evening was to be about him not a virgin prostitute or otherwise. On the other hand, the situation enthralled him. He'd never been any woman's first lover.

How to proceed?

His experience included widows mostly. He never kept a mistress simply because his needs weren't that great. He didn't want the added expense along with the headaches or the drama. Except for his ex-fiancée, women didn't keep his attention for more than a few months.

Eager to move forward he smiled at her. "It's time for your unveiling." He held out a hand to help her stand.

~ * ~

An encouraging smile on his face, Duncan kept his hand held toward her. Thoughts of fleeing crossed her mind with lightning speed. The stakes were too high for her to do that. Suddenly, a wave of guilt shuddered inside. She was about to steal something from this man, something precious. Indeed, from everything she heard about him, the earl wouldn't give a damn.

He was a fine-looking man.

Looking at him, Caroline caught her lip beneath her teeth. After she first entered the room, he loosened his cravat. Now the once intricately folded piece of cloth lay on the floor near the window where he'd been standing. His fine white lawn shirt was partially unfastened. He was a rake. The brogue, which deepened as the evening passed, gave her reason to pat herself on the back at her choice. He was not highly intelligent. That fact stood in her favor. He'd almost done her bidding. He doused two of the four candles. She kept her fingers crossed that he would put out the rest. She didn't believe he would. The sinking feeling entered her that she would have to accept the shadows instead of complete darkness.

Now, in front of her, his confidence pulsed through him. He was so sure of himself. Broad of shoulder, tall, long legs with well-muscled thighs. His jaw was firm, strong came to mind his lips full as well as tempting. That thought surprised her. This man knew as well as understood what he was about. Numerous times she had to tell herself this was what she wanted. A baby, it was the only way she would ever have the chance of a child of her own. For her, he was the perfect specimen. As a bluestocking, she was never courted, always had her nose in a book. Until she realized unless she changed her priorities, she would never hold a child of hers in her arms. It was Torra who suggested this. Told her it would be the perfect solution. She could have a child. He would never know. The secret would be theirs to keep.

When the man asked her why she was here, she almost blurted out the true reason. That would have been foolish. He would have kicked her out. By her calculations, this was the best day in her cycle with the possibility to conceive. She would have sex with this man once then never look back. She understood the biology of a woman's body. This would only take once. Duncan would never *ken* the truth. According to Torra, he was as far from intelligent as a man could get. He would be the perfect biological father for her baby girl. The last thing she wanted was to have a girl who was like her, uninterested in anything except knowledge, unable to do anything but read as well as research whatever struck her as interesting.

"Unveiling?" He repeated, one of his perfectly sculpted sandy eyebrows arched upward. "Tonight? Would you like that? I would. I want to see what is packaged beneath that beguiling pink bow."

She swept her sweaty palms down the pink cape before placing her hand into his trying to push her thoughts as well as fears from her head. In no time, she knew she would be naked. What he'd done earlier would mean nothing in the scope of what was about to come the rest of the evening.

"Yes, tonight, will you blow out all the candles please," she squeaked, truly so nervous she thought she might jump from her skin. The need to get this over with then go home was prevalent in her overstressed mind. If she could continue the pretense that brought her here, after tonight she would be increasing. It was all she wanted.

"Good then, we're in agreement. The two candles will remain. For a few minutes, I was afraid you would run from me. I will be gentle." His amused smile sent a bombardment of question into her head.

To her amazement he did blow out the candles. To her chagrin, brilliant moonlight lit the room. "Gentle?" she queried thinking he had already been gentle. That first fact didn't change the other fact. Already he'd seen as well as touched her places no one except her mother had ever seen. That when she was a *wee* babe.

"Very gentle." Slowly, he untied the horrendous pink bow Torra dressed her in with Honey's suggestion. The satin fabric slid along her flesh sending ribbons of vibrations into her core. Caroline held her breath, the sensation so erotic she nearly lost her breath. He'd barely done anything to her.

The two women argued about just how much they should do to

entice Duncan. They argued about what he liked as well as what he didn't like. Neither one ever slept with him. All their reasoning was based on other men they'd been with. For that matter, Honey wasn't an escort. She was a first-floor maid at the escort service started by Letty. Letty was wed. Her given name was Scarlett. She rarely visited the house. Torra ran it now. Her mind seemed to be rattling around in a befuddled mess.

She jerked when his lips touched the back of her neck. His teeth grazed a sensitive spot. Caroline didn't know when he moved from in front of her to behind her. What little was left of her mind deserted her when earlier he sucked a newly cleaned nipple into his mouth. Her mind vanished totally when he cleaned her in the most intimate spot on her body. She wondered what he would do next.

"Relax, sweet *lassie*. No reason to tense up on me. Won't be doin' anything you won't be enjoyin'."

His voice was a throaty masculine purr, his Scottish brogue deepening so much the sound seemed to resonate from deep inside.

Good, his intelligence level slipped another notch.

The exploration of her neck, the back of it, surprised her so she very nearly soared from her skin. Expectations as to how the evening would proceed were beyond her. Torra told her very little. Strange quivering began in that intimate spot he cleansed traveling higher to explode in spasms unlike anything she'd ever felt before. Her body jerked when his teeth closed over her earlobe. Her breath hitched in the back of her throat. A fragmented sound tore from her mouth.

"No need for jitters," he murmured softly while his moist tongue explored then delved inside her ear leaving her in need of what she didn't *ken*.

The movement tender, surprisingly erotic, he brought the cloak down her arms. His hands were slightly calloused where they skimmed over freshly bared skin. The small sound of pleasure unexpectedly escaping her lips surprised her, shocked her more each time she heard the muted noise.

"N-not jittery." She needed to deny her fear more for herself than for Duncan. He wouldn't believe what she told him except she had to believe she wasn't afraid.

His chuckle sent a bolt of new sensations shimmering through her. He turned her while the cloak hit the ground. One finger traced a path along the low-cut corsage that revealed more than the fabric concealed. Her nipple tightened when his fingertip grazed the thinly veiled surface. Surely, she didn't understand why Torra insisted on a gown such as this one.

Baby.

You're doing this for a baby. Don't forget what is at stake. Whatever you do don't let him know you've never been with a man before. When he is finished, it won't matter. The deed will be done.

Baby...for the baby.

You do remember your stealing his sperm.

I'm not going to think about that.

"What is it then?" His lips followed the path of his fingers as one hand slid up her leg, encountering nothing to heed its upward progress. "Very naughty. But I already knew that."

Both Torra and Honey insisted she wear nothing beneath the gown. When he cleaned the horrid makeup from her, he'd not been surprised to see she wore nothing save the gown.

Naughty?

"Hot, just hot and..."

She moistened her lips, unable not unwilling to tell him what he did to her as well as how he made her feel. Dazed, she realized the sensations were nothing she'd ever felt before. When she told Torra she wanted a baby, she had no idea anything like this would happen. Taken aback by the sound of his masculine chuckle, she tried to push away from him.

"*Nay*, do not worry about the laughter you heard. I was pleased that you are enjoying my man's body. Very pleased you are hot, you say? Are you slick with desire for me? Shall I see?"

"Has naught to do with my enjoying yours. It seems your fingers are delving into places I've never thought of then making me feel things I don't understand." Immediately, she understood she said too much. She changed the tenor of the conversation. "I like the way your hands as well as your mouth on me make me feel."

For too many seconds, his hands ceased their movement. His dark brown eyes narrowed, his brows furrowing together as if puzzled. She wanted to know what was in his mind.

"You're enjoying my manly hands? Is that not enjoying my body too?" he finally queried.

Before she could form a thought or reply, his lips enclosed hers framed hers, moistened them with his teeth and tongue sensuously played. Warmth spiraled within sending myriads of shock waves, pulsing thoroughly within. Remembering the last time he kissed her, she opened for him, felt his enthusiastic exploration bone deep. Heard the purr move in ribbons from her core to travel outward. His hands cupped her bottom drawing her closer. She felt him hard and pulsing next to her belly.

"I am, though I *dinnae ken* what you're about or what all this means." Her whispered words were absorbed into his mouth.

With her tongue she ventured inside his, thrilled by the damp heat she encountered as she learned more about the man who would sire her child. The wildly stimulating sensations were drugging, intoxicating. "Don't stop."

"I don't intend to do anything of the sort, at least not until we're both sated, exhausted as well. Not until I send you home in the morning," he murmured, his warm brandy scented breath whispered across her cheek.

Cool air suddenly caressed her. When she looked to see what was happening her breasts were barred to his view. His lips closed over one tight peak, sucked and laved until she cried out. After a short pause, he continued, slowly as each movement continued one into the other. Her fingers curled into his hair. He was so warm, his body hot to her touch. The stubble of a day's growth, brushed across her bared flesh sending waves of exciting shivers coursing through her.

"I-I don't believe I can stand any longer."

Her knees were so weak and wobbly. Her body trembled against his. He bundled her into his arms. Within seconds he set her on his bed. In an attempt to distance herself from the pulsing rush of newfound feelings, she pushed against the headboard. Her gaze riveted on his mouth, slick with moisture, wetness that came from her mouth.

20

Grinning, he slipped from his shirt letting the cloth stay where it landed on the floor. For the longest time, she stared at his lips slowly moving lower. Suddenly, her avid gaze dropped to where his hands were unfastening his trousers. When her scrutiny shot to his eyes, mocking laughter shimmered there. She gasped in a swift breath of air, filling her lungs for a moment before she let the air whoosh out. She was about to see her first naked man, the father of her child. Her breath stalled then stuttered to an abrupt halt.

Caroline found herself doing as well as saying everything she was told not to. Sandy hair covered his upper chest then narrowing as it trailed down to the band of his trousers. His stomach was hard, rippling with muscle, so unlike the softness of her belly. She discovered she had a raw and slightly desperate need to see him naked. Heat flew to her cheeks at the unexpected notion.

"You want to enjoy this view for a few more minutes or should I continue disrobing?" he queried as he strode closer.

It didn't seem he wanted to wait for an answer. Sitting on the bed next to her, her bared breasts swaying with the movement, he pulled off his boots. The thud when they hit the floor told her that his trousers would soon follow.

"I believe I would like to watch you. If you don't mind."

She ran her tongue across her lips, moistening them. She didn't know why she wanted that, yet she felt certain there was a solid reason somehow grounded in logic, which at the moment she no longer possessed. One she could not refute without more information. "I did like the kiss too. I like to touch you although I haven't done that much, touching of you."

"Of course, you realize I also want to see you with nothing covering the sweet, so very saucy charms you've been hiding from me. Would you like to take your gown off or would you like me to do the favor?"

She sipped air, frantic for something she didn't understand. "It is halfway already. Actually, there was not much of it to begin with."

"Ah, I see, you think we are going to be doin' this halfway? That is not my nature. I need to be learnin' everything about you, be touching

21

and caressing every silken part of you, not just half of you, *lass*. Half is to be so unsatisfyin'," he spoke blandly as if the words meant nothing.

"I like the way you look. Can I touch you?"

At her blatant words, words she didn't understand where they came from, she was surprised at the low very masculine sound that rumbled from his chest. Half chuckle, half groan she had no idea how to interpret the sound.

His fists clenched then unclenched several times while his eyes sparked dangerously hot. "Believe me when I say this. At the moment, this *verra* moment that is all I can think of, your hands upon me exploring the differences between us. Hell, I *cannae* believe I'm saying this to a woman who has been as well used as you have been."

Caroline gritted her teeth at his words that suddenly changed the tender feelings she was having for him to something more sordid even though what he projected about her was exactly what she intended for him to believe. When he came down upon the bed, his huge body lay between her legs. She felt the quickening his presence induced. Sucked in dry air, coughed.

A few seconds later all rational thought left her. His lips were everywhere, learning exploring and enticing her generating a magical enchantment. Her body spun, spiraled before coiling uncontrollably to a place she never before knew existed until tonight. The gown slipped downward farther as he sought to reveal more of her body to his questing gaze.

"Lift your hips, Caro," he whispered close to her ear creating shivering warmth, moisture from his warm breath floating across her cheek.

She did so then felt the weight of his body against hers, felt the pulse of his arousal. "I like the way you feel," she told him without thought, as it seemed they were so close she felt his heartbeat.

"As do I like the bountiful curves of your breasts pushed against my chest." It seemed then all his attention was centered between her breasts and her lips. All she could do was hold on to him as he sent her body into a breathtaking ride of mounting ecstasy. Desire vibrated, shimmering between them as if they were as one.

She wanted to tell him she was truly enjoying his manly body. She couldn't speak. His hands traveled lower, traced a path along the curve of her hips, lower to spread his fingers across her belly. Small sounds ripped from her as they moved together in silent rhythm. She responded wildly, her hips arching in a mad attempt to reach out for more and more.

Emptiness brought her eyes to open. When she saw him next, he was naked. His blatant masculinity stole her breath. Torra explained to her that his penis would not appear as the paintings and statues she'd seen in museums. In many of the anatomy texts she read, this was also explained. Nothing, none of her research prepared her for this sight. "You're magnificent..."

"Do you be likin' what you see, sweet *lassie?*" His grin seemed to stretch from one ear to the other.

"I did not expect this. I cannot seem to catch my breath. You're more breathtaking than I expected." His body was certainly much more than she anticipated.

"You can close your mouth anytime," he chuckled.

He came down on top of her again, his hands pushing wayward strands of hair from her face. Now nothing existed between them save air. The palms of Duncan's hands were hot as they continued downward to explore along her inner thigh. "I'm going to finish what we started this evening then we can decide how to proceed later. You be turnin' out to be a sweet birthday gift after all. Mayhap the sweetest I've ever received."

Once more his hands touched upon her everywhere. It seemed to her there was nowhere his agile fingers did not stroke. She was wrong though. Surprising her, he caressed her most intimately, spreading her, entering into her with a finger then a second. Uncontrollably, her hips arched upward with sensual ecstasy, spiraled tightly in the new evocative sensations he initiated in her. Without mercy, he continued to taunt and tease her until spasms engulfed, took over her body with wave after carnal wave of delicious pleasure.

"Duncan!" she cried out his name as ripples of pleasure pulsed and soared until she was heaving, coiling tightly against him pushing.

She found she lost all earthly control of herself. It seemed to her a power not of her own took charge of her body. He soothed her with

23

whispered words she couldn't understand. Stroked her tenderly in ways that didn't incite the same magical enchantment as he had before. Slowly, her body found peace at his soothing hands.

"Are we done?" she sighed softly running her nails along his back, feeling the quivering of his muscles as she did so. "I did like what you did."

"Not by a long shot, sweet *lassie*. I *dinnae ken* why you might think we are finished here," he said as once again he began the tender assault on her senses. Heat rose, spiraled hotter then hotter still. He nipped. He kissed. His tongue swept her with tender molten flicks of moisture. She twisted again reaching for that elusive place he guided her to earlier.

Once again, he spoke of things she should know about. She didn't.

This time he did not take as long to bring her to that point where she was purring for him, needing the potent end to the lovemaking. Wishing only to feel the continuous rhythm that stretched from him into her then back again. She wondered why she felt no pain. Why he did not seem to be satisfied as she was before he began anew. Torra told her with the first joining there would be pain.

His sex jutted against her. His rod touched her, probed intimately. She didn't recall that before, that feel as his penis slowly slid inside her, expanding, pressing hurtling her to a new height. This was different from the first time. The heated glide of his body inside her most intimately was hot and hard, filling her, stretching her. He was part of her, buried deep inside. She realized then that he brought her to a most shattering place without actually giving her his sperm. That was what she wanted, what she needed was his sperm. They had to make a baby this time. There would be no more chances for her. Duncan was the perfect specimen of a man to be the father of her child.

He thrust hard, was suddenly deep inside her. She froze crying out with the searing pain. Tears slid down her cheeks, slipped over her jaw. She'd never imagined this, never thought it would...it would hurt so damn much. Her nails bit into his shoulders while she clung desperately to him as if that sole action would end the agony.

It seemed he also froze. "Hush, sweetheart. The pain will go away.

I never...well hell...the thought did cross my mind. You were so damn innocent. On the other hand, you provoked and enticed just as a trained courtesan would. Asking might have been appropriate. Telling might have been better."

"Torra told me it would hurt this time, only this time. I never thought it would be so bad," she spoke softly, more tears slipping from her eyes. "Torra never told me that I should tell you." She stole a deep breath of air, catching the masculine sent of him. Inexplicably, she arched against him as if she wanted more.

"You should have trusted me. Why didn't you say something?" He braced his forearms at her sides. His eyes appeared warm and gentle, seemingly concerned for her.

Her top teeth closed over her lip. There was no answer to his question. If she told, he would have sent her home. The risk was too high. As of this moment, she didn't think he'd gifted her with his seed.

Slowly, he began to move within. A sound broke from her throat, shattering her nerves. His fingers roamed along her, his lips found purchase on hers. She arched as she felt the length of him inside, moving, swiftly taking her higher and higher back to that wild bliss he brought her to before. He kissed her again and again as his steel-hard penis moved deep and strong inside her core. Felt the tremors. Knew there would be more this time. He would gift her with what she wanted.

"Duncan!"

He absorbed his name into his mouth, caught the cry with the same air as their kiss shared.

Heard the deep masculine groan as his body convulsed into hers. "Caro, sweet, sweet *lassie*."

He fell upon her, his weight closing over her until he braced himself on his forearms. Deep inside her, his hard body pressing against hers, he gently pushed damp tendrils of hair from her face.

"I didn't think you would believe me," she murmured as his fingers entwined with hers slowly rhythmically soothing the emotions that were brimming within.

"You're right of course. I would have thought it another ploy that I would have to figure out at a later date. We should eat now since we have all night to be together."

"Eat?" she queried slipping her tongue along her mouth leaving dampness where his lips had been.

"Yes, eat," he chuckled lightly grazing her chin with his teeth, "unless you still believe you might lose the contents of your stomach. Come let's see what Johnston brought us." He withdrew from her then.

The loss of his warmth surprised her. Caroline realized she liked the way he felt deep inside, as if he was part of her. "There is the cake?"

"Ah, Caro, that's the second time you mentioned cake. Do you like your sweets at the cost of all else?" He was chuckling, laughing at her. "Something else you haven't told me about yourself?"

She found she didn't care. "I do. Believe I'd rather eat cake than most anything except perhaps chocolate." When she realized what she said, heat flamed her cheeks. She couldn't help but lift her shoulders in an attempt to apologize. "It's a weakness."

His knuckles grazed the heated spots on her face then down her neck to the tops of her breasts. His lips followed suit, caressing her slowly, gliding along tender white flesh. Suddenly, he placed a quick kiss to her lips.

"Cake it is then."

He rose. She watched him. In all his splendor, his strides were long and fluid. His buttocks tight and firm, his hips were narrow as she let her gaze wander to the width of his shoulders. If she had a boy, he would be magnificent in form. It would be his mind she would have to worry about. She wouldn't have trouble teaching him all he needed to learn. After all, she didn't believe Duncan was stupid, just not possessing a brilliant level of intelligence. He was normal. With all her heart she yearned for normal brainpower.

He brought one slice back. Seemed to see the disappointment in her eyes. "We'll save the second piece for later."

"Later?" She thought she would be returning home now that his seed was inside her.

"In the morning. You are being paid for all night unless you displeased me. So far, you've been delightful. I count myself a lucky man."

"Displeased you? Delightful?" She was a ninny, a pinhead of the worst sort. Of course, she understood she would be here for the evening. She agreed to that and more if the contract she signed was legal.

He fed her a bite. It was chocolate cake, the creamy vanilla icing delicious. She could eat all the icing.

"Are you a little parrot now?" he queried opening his mouth so she could also feed him.

She brushed his lips with the icing, wanting suddenly to taste the spot, to see if the sweetness of the icing was sweeter on his lips.

"Go ahead," he told her bending close as if he understood what she'd been thinking.

She pushed away from the bed, settling her lips on his, her tongue sucking the icing from him. He reciprocated. This kiss seemed to go on and on continuous, never ending. She found she wanted him again and again as she drank each caress.

The night exploded around her. They made love then ate again. He took her in different ways until she wondered if she didn't know everything about what a man and woman did in the intimate privacy of their bedroom. He was delicious. His touch sensuous. She found she slept in his arms. Was surprised when sunshine woke her. The day was bright. She was certain she would have his baby.

"It's time for me to go home," she whispered wondering if he was awake or not.

One callused hand held her breast, toyed with the hardened tip as she also wondered how she would live without seeing this man again. Somehow in this short time, he became important to her. Well, he would be the father of her child, a child he would never know. Guilt swamped her. She stole from him. Stole his sperm. *Nay*, he gave his donations willingly.

No promises

Unexpectedly, he was inside her, moving slowly then faster and harder. She was ready for him, hot and slick with what he called her cream or her honey. Together they moved as one. He found the swollen knot that brought so much rapture, massaged until she was crying out, tiny feminine sounds rippling from deep within to be released into the daylight.

"Not yet." His teeth scraped along her neck, his fingers playing with a taut nipple. He thrust harder and faster until once more the delicious ecstasy of the moment took control of her body. He held her until she breathed easy.

"I have to leave."

His home was near the university. She couldn't be seen departing in the morning. For her new child's sake, she had her reputation to consider. The story of her pregnancy already forming in her head, it was true she would have explaining to do. The explanation would have to be sound. The trip she planned to Edinburgh for the duration of her pregnancy already set in motion. It was all so simple as she intended to tell anyone who questioned as well as all who did not. It was a cousin's child. She died in childbirth. The poor baby had no father to take care of the *wee bairn*. She was all the babe would have in its life.

"Stay for breakfast." He placed more gentle kisses along her neck. Turned her so he had better access to all the erotic parts of her he coaxed so sweetly. In the back of her throat, she moaned unable to stop the sound.

"Can't." Caroline rose from the bed, covers draped around her.

Her body wrapped in fabric for his last look. She would not see him again. Even though pangs of regret shot through her heart, it was the only way.

It seemed he didn't mean to protest her departure further. At least he understood. This was for the best.

Then it seemed he did not. "Why?"

Another question she couldn't answer. Ignoring him, she found her clothing along with the cape. Tempted to ask if she would see him again, curbed her tongue against something so foolish.

"At least let me order you a carriage. Johnston will take you home. Wouldn't want you to hire one."

She nodded. That was a splendid idea.

A few minutes later Johnston knocked on the door. "Sir?"

"Will you take Caro to Letty's home, please?"

He still lay in the bed, the sheets pooling at his waist. Looking at him she heated, her cheeks flaming. Her virgin's blood was on those sheets. After the first time he cleaned her blood as well as his sperm from her legs.

At the open door, Caroline stopped, smiled. "Happy birthday, Duncan. Hope you had a good night. I certainly did."

~ * ~

Caroline waited on the front porch of Scarlett's home until Duncan's carriage pulled away then rumbled down the street. She drew in a long deep breath, held the air inside her lungs until she could hold it no longer believing with all her heart her mission was accomplished successfully. In a couple of weeks, she would know if she was increasing. If that was true, which she believed it to be, the rest of her plan would be put into action.

Once the carriage disappeared around the corner, she strode across the street to her home. Her two-story home was comfortable. She liked its location as well as the surrounding atmosphere. While she could afford a townhouse in the city, she much preferred living on the outskirts. She had a garden along with the peace and quiet she craved. Her roses could be tended to easily and without explanation as to what she was actually attempting to accomplish.

She smiled, satisfied. This all came about, her chance to have a baby, because of chocolate cookies and a borrowed cup of flour.

Slipping inside the home, she left the cloak with the wicked pink bow on the coat stand. Her one servant was up, pattering about in the kitchen. "Louisa, will you heat up water. I'll take a bath in the first-floor bedroom then I plan on sleeping for a few hours."

She was exhausted. He kept her up most of the night. After what she did with the earl, she had to be pregnant and carrying her child. She smiled. Her hand resting on her flat belly, her dream of having a child would finally come true.

She ran upstairs, found a nightdress to slip on after the bath. As for the garish gown she wore to Duncan's home, she would either burn it or give it back to Torra. Made no difference to her except she never wanted to see the horrid thing again not even to relive the beauty of the night she spent with a man who gave her so much pleasure, a man she would never see again. Before last night, she never thought sex could be so delightful.

But then what did she know about sex.

Nothing.

Well past noon Caroline rose giving up on the sleep she sought. She was too excited. Torra along with Honey and Muira, three of her friends from the escort service across the street, would want to know what transpired, if she was successful as well. The two women would be knocking at her door soon to hear all the details, details, the intimate particulars she didn't plan to share. Settling her hands on her belly again she gave in to the urge to smirk. She had to be pregnant. Her child would be inside, growing. The number of times he planted his seed inside her one of those cunning little sperm cells must have found the waiting egg.

The timing was perfect.

The man was perfect in every way. Closing her eyes, she held the gown to her bosom. He did touch and kiss her everywhere. She was also a bit sore from her activities last night.

She couldn't have asked for anything more. Rapidly, she dressed. Found her way to the kitchen where Louisa left a sandwich for her. She discovered she was famished. The glass of lemonade, which was also left, was mouthwatering. She ate it all as if she hadn't eaten in a week. She reminded herself she wasn't eating for two at least, not yet.

The knock on her back door didn't surprise her. Both Honey and Torra stood on the porch, expectant smiles on their beautiful faces. They were trying to peer around the yellow lace curtains. She smiled and waved wondering what happened to Muira.

"How did it go?" Torra asked breathless as she strode into the kitchen, Honey behind her. "Are you increasing even as we speak?" She winked at her before taking a place at the table.

"Tea?" she asked unwilling to divulge too much too soon. For some reason she had this need to prolong the story as well as savor her evening close to her heart. It was her story, private as well. The events of last night seemed so very intimate, not meant to share. She wanted to cherish every precious memory. After all this was when her child was conceived. She would never forget the night.

"Caroline..." Honey was impatiently tapping her foot. "Don't be so obtuse. You know neither one of us has one iota of patience. We need to learn everything that happened, now."

"Tell us."

"Where is Muira?"

"Didn't feel well."

That wasn't going to happen.

"Tea first then we'll talk." Caroline couldn't help the joy bubbling up inside her. She hummed as she heated the water. A plate of scones was set out. The tea poured.

She was most assuredly pregnant.

"Well?" It seemed Torra waited long enough. "Did our mission contemplated, planned as well over a borrowed cup of flour turn out to be successful?"

"I'm increasing. After..." Heat rose to her cheeks. "I have to be. All went as planned. Duncan was flawless. The timing was textbook."

She recalled her surprise visit to Letty's home over a month ago requesting a cup of flour for the cookies she was baking. At that time, she told Torra how much she wanted a baby. Torra swore she had a way to help her. Together and with Honey's assistance they conceived a plan. Last night the intrigue was successful.

"After?" Honey laughed as she bit into a scone slathered with berry jam.

"He had sex with me, more than once, well...all night if you must know. We didn't sleep except perhaps the last hour I was there."

Torra told her she knew of the flawless person for her. A man, who was not all that bright, wasn't at all brilliant at any rate, perhaps of adequate intelligence. So, if she did have a girl child, the poor darling wouldn't take after her. She would never end up a bluestocking with her nose in a book every hour of every day.

"He was insatiable then?" Torra asked seeming to know the answer ahead of time. "He liked you a lot. Most men will send the escort home after a few hours. Since your carriage rolled up just short of six this morning, I assume he kept you for your money's worth."

Heat suffused her cheeks. "It seemed so. He wasn't put off that I was a virgin. Just presumed I had some rotten luck. Because of the misfortune was forced to sell my body. Only asked me a few times why I was here. That was before anything happened between us. As you've probably guessed, I didn't answer."

"So, he has no idea all you wanted from the encounter was a baby, a child you meant to keep from him. He would have anticipated you used precautions to keep that very thing from happening. Real escorts *ken* how to prevent a child. Your man would know that."

The blush grew hotter. "No idea."

Caroline felt as if all her wishes were fulfilled last night. She would never see Duncan again. The thought was unnerving since she would enjoy another night like that with him. A small pang of guilt swept inside at the thought she was keeping all knowledge of his child from him. If he ever discovered her ruse, he might be angry furiously so. He might seek retribution.

She did not think of that.

He wasn't going to discover the deception.

"Best you keep it that way. One never knows what a man will do if he ascertains he has a child, was duped as well, in addition lied to. Duncan Murray has tons of money as well as power. Since he does have the resources, he could make your life miserable if he wished," Honey said her voice soft, suddenly tinged with sorrow. "Perhaps we didn't think this through entirely. There could be repercussions we didn't think of." Honey reached out her hand to touch as well as give reassurance to Caro.

"In two weeks, I should know for sure. When that happens, I'll leave for Edinburgh. When I return, he'll have no reason to encounter me or to discover the existence of the child. In any case if that materializes, I will say I adopted the *bairn* and do not know who the father is. At least that is my story. It will have to be believed. If for some reason he discovers the truth, he will have no options left to him. It would be my word against his."

"The plan is risky."

"I wouldn't want to be wearing your shoes if he ever determines the truth," Torra told her as she sat back in her chair. "I've heard he can be ruthless to his enemies."

If that occurred, she would want to be wearing her shoes either.

"What will do if you aren't with child?" Honey challenged. "Are you willing to do the same with another man?"

Coldness engulfed her even while her stomach curdled at the thought of his discovering her treachery. She didn't ever want to do what she did last night with another man. That just wouldn't, *nay* couldn't happen. She could enjoyably repeat the process with Duncan however. More time with him would not be wise though. He might guess at her intentions if she spent another evening with him. She was a terrible liar. He would see through her lies then insist on the truth.

"Suppose I would have to find a way to see him again. There would have to be..." She was shaking her head thoroughly confused. His seed had to take root inside her. The scheduling was impeccable. Her monthlies were always on time. There was never any deviation.

"There is always a means. You know very well we have connections. I'll help you any way possible." Torra reached out holding her hands within hers.

"I'm pregnant I know I am."

I have to be.

Chapter Two

After his encounter with the virgin escort, Duncan had trouble thinking of anything except the way she felt in his arms, the way she tasted along with twin dimples on either side of her mouth. He wanted to see her again, hold and kiss her, howl with the pleasure her raw passion gave him. Two weeks passed. Then another. Finally, time was on his side. He had a free day. One where there were no business meetings that couldn't be avoided or clients he had to see. Several times he sent Johnston to the house where she was supposed to live, inquiring about her.

Johnston would always come back empty handed telling him she wasn't there.

Torra always told him she didn't know where Caroline lived or even her last name. Caroline worked that first night then deserted them. Torra was no more pleased than he was. Indeed, she was furious with the little chit for abandoning them.

"I lined up several jobs for her. She refused them all. Ungrateful little bitch," Torra would mumble as she closed the door in his face.

Duncan was beside himself with the thought he might never see his Caro again. The feeling was strange, even more bizarre than he could believe possible while he realized he thought of her as his. He never felt the need to see a woman a second time. Somehow in that one, solitary night Caro managed to burrow into the shell he always encapsulated himself in. He spent night and day thinking about her.

The softness of her body.

The way she purred when he stroked and caressed her. The disjointed sound that always caught in her throat when he sucked her breast deep into his mouth while his teeth toyed with the hard tight tip.

Her scream of delight when he brought her to her release was ever-present in his memory. He had to see her again, make love all night long. If he could just have her one more time, she would be out of his mind. If so, he could forget her in the process move on with his life.

Raising his hand to knock at the door of Letty's home, he hoped this visit would prove more fruitful than the previous visits. Before the door opened, he heard a scurrying of footsteps as well as a few muffled words. The back door banged shut.

The ensuing silence felt eerie, unnerving. It appeared to him he stumbled on something clandestine. This wasn't at all what he expected as the strange situation left him with questions he didn't know how to ask. It seemed the ladies had secrets they didn't want a visitor to learn. Ah well, he doubted if the scrambling and whispered words had anything to do with his Caro. The devil, thinking about her again aroused him.

Had him wanting her desperately.

His brothers called him out daily as to his surliness. He wasn't used to finding himself in a constant state of arousal. Truly, this was all too new to him. He discovered he didn't want anyone except Caro. Another woman would never replace her in his bed. He had to have her one more time...maybe two...perhaps even more than three.

Honey opened the door. A brilliant smile plastered on her face. "Duncan, so nice to see you again. What can we do for you? Another escort perhaps?" Her words poured unnaturally from her. Indeed, the woman hid something as she looked as if she tried to peer around him.

"May I come in?" he asked as he looked over his shoulder catching a fleeting glimpse of calico darting across the street. "What was that?" He stepped away from the door intent on discovery. His gaze was focused on the slim ankles rushing up the steps to another house.

Honey peered around him, "Just our neighbor. She never wants anyone to see her leaving the house. You understand why of course. She comes occasionally either to borrow a cup of flour or to return one. Sometimes she brings chocolate cookies. It wouldn't be good for her reputation if she were to be seen coming and going from this place. You understand why, of course."

"Flour?" he asked his mind reeling as he was shaking his head. "That woman comes here to borrow flour? An escort service? Seems damned strange."

"Or sugar, or butter, or...she likes cookies, especially chocolate," Honey blurted then turned red.

Caro has a sweet tooth. Somehow, he couldn't envision her baking cookies. She was sultry, provocative as well as enticing in every way. *Nay*, she would never bake cookies although she would certainly enjoy eating them.

She moved aside to give him entrance into the house. Torra walked from the kitchen. "Duncan. How nice to see you again. To what do we owe this visit?"

"Have you heard anything from Caro?" he asked the question realizing the answer was most likely no just as it always was.

There would be no change in her status even though he hoped to hear something different. Desperation at never finding this woman nearly sent him to his knees. It was only his determination that kept him going.

"She hasn't been here since that night of your rendezvous with her. She seems to be a private lady. She didn't even return for her pay. She earned the entire sum. You must have been enamored of her to keep her until the early morning hour."

He was more than enamored. He had to taste her again to inhale her sweet scent of roses as well as woman. Once with Caro wasn't going to last him a lifetime. "Yes, I'd like to see her again. If you can tell me how to find her, I would forever be grateful," he told the two women as he followed them into the drawing room. "Can you arrange it?" Duncan found he was holding his breath. "I will hand her the groats personally."

The two ladies looked at each other for a moment. "Don't see how as we don't know how to get in contact with her. She never left us an address where she could be reached. She would have to come here looking for work. Would you like us to send a message to you if she does come back?"

"Don't think she will though," Honey pointed out the obvious.

With a hefty sigh, Torra said, looking at Honey, "No, what's it been? Three weeks? We haven't heard a word from her."

"I have to find her. Didn't she say something, anything that might tell me where she lives, a clue perhaps, a name, a last name? A friend or a companion she might have in common with either of you? How did she find out about the service in the first place? You must have asked her that question. I know you it's your policy to extensively interview the men. Don't you do the same with the women?"

"No, nothing. She didn't mention one person or a last name. Poor thing, don't believe she has anyone. We rarely interview the women we hire. It's too invasive. They all have secrets they don't want to share. We don't like to pry into their past. With space as well as time, they usually reveal their truth."

Duncan wasn't sure he believed her. The house must ask some questions of the women since they spouted the utmost discretion. Honey brought him a brandy. For several moments he stared at the glass, swirling the amber contents, hoping the burn would help him ease the arousal pulsing against the fabric of his trousers. The thought was purely wishful. He knew nothing or no one save his Caro could ever work that particular miracle.

"Would your neighbor know anything? The one across the street who brings you cookies?" he asked realizing the lady must be in as well as out of the house on a regular basis. "I could walk across the street and ask."

"No!" Both ladies shouted.

The resounding 'no' uttered by both ladies struck a chord he meant to discover more about. It seemed perhaps that might be his best course of action. These two ladies were obviously hiding something from him. Perhaps the lady across the street knew more about his elusive Caro than Torra and Honey were willing to admit.

"Why?"

He meant to get to the bottom of this sooner than later. His grin widened as they stared at each other both open mouthed. Both women's eyes appeared to cross simultaneously.

"At best she is reclusive. Doesn't like visitors. She would not be pleased if we allowed you that transgression. Might not bake us any more cookies," Torra said her voice becoming whisper thin. "In any case, she would not talk to you. She would not even open the door to you."

"She's afraid of men," Honey added as what appeared to be an afterthought. "No, you don't want to go over there and frighten her. She wouldn't have anything to say that would help you discover the whereabouts of your lady friend."

"In any case as I said before she wouldn't open the door for you. It would be a waste of your time as well as energy to walk across the street," Torra said one hand on her chest as if she tried to hold in the air she breathed.

"I see."

He didn't see anything at all. He would set some of his men watching the house night and day. His gut was telling him strange things about this reclusive neighbor of theirs. Getting to the bottom of this was essential. Anger began to simmer. He didn't like deception. This reeked of trickery.

After finishing the brandy, he set the glass on the table. "I'm going now. Make sure if you hear anything about Caro, you let me know. Send a message immediately."

They wouldn't. He was sure of that fact. After he left, he strode across the street. The two ladies were peering out the window watching him joined then by a third. Ah, Muira showed herself. Perhaps he should visit with that lady too. He chuckled softly to himself, knowing he was on to something. This reclusive lady might give him the lead he sought.

He knocked on the door. Heard nothing. Didn't expect to have the door opened welcoming him after what the women told him. Curious, he stepped around the house. The backyard was well kept. All types of flowers grew there but mostly roses. Some were of the most amazing and different colors. A stilted breath of air whispered from his lungs.

It seemed to him this antisocial lady was involved with grafting roses. His brother at the university might shed some light on this woman. If he was right about what he was looking at, she was very good at it. He recalled then the soft scent of roses that came with Caro.

He told himself it didn't mean anything.

Could be a coincidence.

Or not.

When he turned to look at the home again, on the second floor a curtain was pulled back. He couldn't see the face though he knew the lady watched him. Wasn't sure why he smiled.

No coincidence there. He supposed if a stranger were walking around his backyard, he'd be watching the man or woman. No, he'd confront the person learn what they wanted. No way in hell would he hide.

Well damn, he wasn't a lady. She could hardly have the nerve to provoke him. That could be dangerous.

With new thoughts swirling in his head, he set off for home. He was supposed to meet his brothers for dinner at his house. Cook was making the most exceptional meal. At least that was what Francois told him this morning. His brothers would undoubtedly have something to say about his obsession with lady Caro going on three weeks.

The devil, he'd even lost weight.

He would have to find her soon.

Ah, back to his brothers, Evan, Fletcher and Gordon. They were all carefree rakes. Lucky devils, they didn't have any responsibilities save the ones they created for themselves. While he had his share of dalliances, he could never have been considered a rake.

Evan worked at the university, involved with the biology laboratory. He would have to make it a point to quiz him on the grafting of roses as well as question him if he knew anyone who might be involved with that particular hobby. Evan, although he denied it, was the most brilliant of all the siblings. He was a genius, again the man would not admit to the fact.

Fletcher involved himself in more liberal and abstract pursuits such as philosophy. He was well versed in just about every past philosopher who ever wrote a book. Gordon, at twenty-five, had not settled down to one pursuit of interest. He spent his time flitting from one concentration to another.

All his brothers sought him out for investment advice as he had a knack with money as well as numbers. He could easily double a fortune in a year. Had done so for each of his brothers several times. They were all rich as Midas. None of them needed to work yet they all did.

When he strode up the steps to the townhouse, he realized they were all there ahead of him. He should never have told them about his birthday gift. Of course, they asked having bought the woman for him. Evan told him he was too stuffy and needed a lady who could set his imagination on a new course. They all wanted to know what happened that night. Told them he didn't kiss and tell. What happened the evening in question was nobody's business except his and the lady's.

Now he was besotted with a virgin escort who he couldn't find. They would tease him with the knowledge if he let on how desperate he was to have her in his arms again.

Love-struck fool that he was.

When he stepped into the drawing room Fletcher handed him a full glass of brandy. "Found your birthday gift yet?"

The smirk on Fletcher's face irritated him. Whether or not he found Caro was no business of his.

Duncan slanted him a deep scowl before deciding he would go along with them. After all they were right. He was obsessed with finding the woman. "Not yet. I will though. Going to set someone to the task since I don't have the time to follow any leads." That was the major part of the problem. There were no leads. He would hire someone who could figure this out. How could one lady be so hard to find? So damn mysterious? The escort service was the one as well as the only clue he had to go on.

"We could buy you a second gift to get your mind off the first," Gordon said while Evan stared out the window clearly immersed in other thoughts besides the lady who took control of his senses.

"Do you know anyone at the university who is involved with the grafting of roses?" Duncan supposed now was as good as any time to start the conversation that might lead him to Caro.

"Not quite my line of work," Evan said thoughtfully. "I can always inquire."

"She would be in your department if she was employed there. So, do you know of anyone?"

"I might. There is a woman who lectures every once in a while. Don't know her name though. In her particular field she is regarded highly," Evan told him turning from the window then rocking back on his heels, his hands clasped behind his back. "I believe for this woman the grafting of roses is more of a hobby than a science. Don't know if she is using what she learns for a particular purpose. One hobby she is very good at by the way. Heard she has a degree in literature as well as botany. Brilliant lady."

Duncan felt as if he was left to pry any scrap of information from his brother. "Can you find out?"

At the news Evan imparted, he found himself disappointed. A woman, an escort would never have two university degrees. This lady he bedded was no bluestocking. She was passionate beyond anyone he'd ever known. In his arms, she responded as no other woman ever had.

"What's this lady got to do with your beautiful escort?" Gordon asked one dark eyebrow arched upward. "Escorts don't tend to have degrees."

"Doubt if there is anything. My gut, however, is telling me she might know something that will help me find my birthday present. Since I need to find Caro, I'll go to any means necessary. Honey and Torra are lying through their teeth about the lady across the street as well as Caro. Muira won't put in an appearance while I'm in the vicinity."

"They are?" Evan asked. Then with a slight lift to his shoulders, "What can you expect?"

"Suppose not the truth," Duncan shrugged thinking he deserved the truth. His brothers paid quite a bit of money for his one night with her. A little honesty would go a long way.

"Caro, you say is the lady's name. Do you know her last? That would help narrow down the list of women who are escorts." Evan seemed to be mulling over the name. "It's not quite right. You don't think for a moment this lady who came to you as an escort for the night, a woman we paid to give her body to you, could be grafting roses? Would have two degrees?"

"Caroline. No, that would be a ridiculous assumption. I'm not prone to believe the absurd." He drew in a ragged breath feeling as if his hunt for the elusive woman would never bear fruit. Every possible clue stopped in a dead end. A place that was not acceptable to him. Somewhere there had to be a path that would lead directly to her. He would discover her trail. After all he did have the necessary resources to do just that.

"So, what brought up the notion of grafting roses," Gordon asked sipping at his drink while he stared at him as if he had a hole in his head. "Did one of Scarlett's ladies mention it?"

"A woman across the street from Scarlett's is obviously grafting roses. In her backyard one can see all colors and sorts of the plants. The flowers are magnificent and unusual. She was staring at me through a partially open curtain from the second floor."

"You walked into her backyard?" Evan asked sounding appalled. "Our stuffy earl, actually did something daring? In search of a whore?"

"I did. She's not a whore."

He wasn't going to feel one iota of guilt from his brothers. He also wasn't going to spend more time talking about this woman with them. They couldn't help him. Evan possibly could lend assistance, however, he didn't seem to be enamored of the idea.

"When are you going to visit the crofters?" Gordon asked, changing the subject to something he was sure his brother considered more important than finding the whereabouts of a woman they would consider a bit of muslin. "I'll go with you. Been bored lately. Need something to set my mind to."

"Since the university ball is in a week, I'd better go tomorrow. It's time to collect the rent although I loathe doing the chore."

"Yes, I would too if I possessed your fortune," Fletcher said laughing. "Collecting money from poor farmers who cultivate your land. Diabolical notion. Totally out of line."

"Not as if the three of you don't have so much wealth you couldn't spend it all in a lifetime," Duncan shot back feeling irritated with the discussion.

It was time to move on to something else.

"You've more."

"They insist on paying rent. If I don't charge them enough, they complain they aren't being treated right. They tell me they are working the land to feed their families not gain untold wealth. Don't know what to do about them." Duncan stuffed his hands into the pockets of his trousers.

"It's pride talking," Evan said grinning.

"They don't want Murray charity. Can't say that I blame them.

You well know you've invested for some of them clearly improving their lot. To wound their pride even more you've not charged them one groat for your financial services. They owe you their loyalty as well as the rent on the land they borrow."

"They love you," Gordon laughed. "Don't know how you do that? Everyone loves you except your escort who doesn't seem to want to see you again, let alone love you."

"Torra told me she didn't take the money."

That fact bothered him immensely. He thought she agreed to the job because she fell on hard times. The words came from her lips. That was another fact that didn't line up with his thoughts about his beautiful elusive lady. She lied to him at least once that he knew of. What else was she lying about?

"I still don't want to charge them anything. I don't want to give up the land either. It seems to be a stalemate I cannot undo. In any case, I need to go tomorrow or they'll all be riding here to make their monthly payment."

His thoughts continued churning, desperate for a momentary diversion.

"Back to the ball. It is a fundraiser, as you well know as well as a bestowing of honors for the most outstanding scientists of the year. We need to make this a gala affair." He was thinking perhaps Evan could make sure the rose lady received an invitation. He could also send one to Letty's house in case the woman appeared again. This time, however, if that happened, he wanted to be the one to escort her. He meant to make that fact undeniably clear. If Caro accepted the invitation, she was to attend with him. For her, there was no choice.

"You have that look on your face," Fletcher said as he reached for an appetizer. "You've got a million ideas zooming around in your head. Out with them. I've got this feeling you're about to embarrass us."

"What look is that little brother?" Evan asked with a manly chuckle as if he knew full well what Fletcher was saying.

"That you are the cat who swallowed the canary," Gordon put in for his older brother seeming to notice that look as well.

"What are you thinking behind that all-knowing grin?" Duncan asked getting back into the conversation. "It wouldn't be something about the rose lady, would it?"

"It might."

"Are you going to make me pull out every word?" he asked, realizing this could indeed give him an introduction to a woman who might know something about his Caro.

"Perhaps."

Duncan waved a hand in the air, his impatience getting the best of him. He hadn't seen her for three weeks. He wanted every one of those days back. Now his brothers played games with him.

"What is it you were thinking?"

"The rose lady, at least the one at the university, is up for an award. It will be bestowed upon her the night of the ball. She will undoubtedly be there to receive richly deserved acclaim. Reclusive or not you will find a way to speak with her. Perhaps all you seek will be granted to you that night."

The weight on his shoulders seemed to slip off with his brother's words. He had a week to wait. Of course, he understood meeting Miss Rose might not help him with his search for Caro. On the other hand, the meeting might prove more than helpful.

He grinned, satisfied with the night before it was over. Perhaps he would have sweet dreams instead of the hellish ones where he never saw her again.

"Dinner is served," Johnston was at the doorway. "However, you have a guest. Miss Torra is here to see you. Should I waylay dinner or would you like to invite her to join us?"

This unusual visit could be the answer to all his prayers. "Hold dinner. I'll see her in my office. I'm sure she would refuse anyway."

Duncan strode to the back of the house where his office was located. He poured a brandy for both of them before sitting on an overstuffed chair facing the fire.

Duncan heard the swish of her skirts as she walked into the room. Felt her hesitancy.

"Close the door. I'm sure this is meant to be a private conversation."

He hoped she would confess about knowing the identity of Caro. Hoped he would no longer have to pursue this. Caught the scent of her flowery perfume. "There is a drink. Sit down. I assume you've come to tell me something about Caro."

"Yes, nonetheless it wasn't what you are hoping for."

"What might that be?"

"There is no doubt in my mind you want to see her again. Caroline doesn't return the sentiment. One night with you was enough for her. At least that is what she says. She won't become a mistress to you. Also, she prays you will stop trying to find her."

He laughed, solid laughter, hooting laughter emanating from his lips. The last way he thought of her was as a mistress. Actually, he hadn't had time to think of her in any specific light whatsoever. Until she encountered him, she was as innocent as any woman could be. She sold herself. Didn't take the money. For what purpose? The reason was something he would discover. It now seemed obvious to him, that for Caro the night was meant to be one time only. He would have to figure out a way to disavow her of that notion.

Well hell he had to find her first.

"Don't want her as a mistress. She couldn't pass the interview. Besides, I don't keep mistresses...too much drama."

He laughed realizing the message coming from Torra meant Caro was as good as caught. Finding her now would not be nearly as difficult.

"You want to see her again."

"Yes!" His fist landed hard on the table. "You know I do."

Bloody eyes but this was inane. Now that he understood Torra could reach Caro, he would set spies around Letty's home. Nothing would get past him. Caro would be his in a matter of time. He could wait.

"You don't want to wed her." Torra continued in a vein he disliked.

"I don't," he agreed with the woman.

"That in and of itself will either make Caroline your mistress or your whore. She won't become either. It's best you don't see her again. I've said my piece." Torra stood smoothing her skirts with her hands, the look in her eyes unreadable.

She had indeed. His gut turned sour. He was no closer to finding out her true identity than he had been three weeks ago. Hitting himself against the side of his head as if the act would help him understand, he swore as he watched Torra leave.

He meant to find a way. Nothing Torra said just now would make him give up on his quest.

~ * ~

"I'm not pregnant. How could that have happened?" Caroline sat at the table with Torra and Honey fighting back tears, moisture clogging her throat. She drew in a long, deep, shaky breath understanding she would have to find a way to see Duncan again. She'd been so positive, so certain that it would only take one time. She was never late. She wasn't this time either. Now, she wasn't at all sure what to do. What if she couldn't have children?

All this would have been for naught.

Her hopes and dreams were squashed. Torra and Honey gave her courage to see her dream fulfilled where she'd had none.

When she thought of that night, she would always recall Duncan, his teasing smile, his hesitation at first because of the garish paint on her face. A gentle man introduced her to the physical side of love. She would never forget him or all the different ways he made her feel.

"Are you sure?" Torra asked seeming to plant a few seeds of doubt in her head. "Sometimes..."

Caroline's shoulders shook even while she tried to nod an affirmative. "I bled, not much but sometimes..." She wasn't truly comfortable sharing such intimate details of her body. These two women understood as no others would. Who else could she confide in?

"While first appearances tend to suggest you didn't conceive, you do need to see the man again, privately. I wouldn't be jumping to conclusions. It is still possible," Torra said softly trying to give encouragement where it was obvious she had no hope. "I've heard of women having one or two monthly flows after conception. As that is not the norm, it happens."

"You still have to see him again. There is no other choice for you if you truly want that child you've been imagining all these years." Honey put the words out there again. "Need to make certain you don't give up on your dream. It's obvious by the number of times he's come here asking for an address, the man is smitten with you. He will be more than happy to have the opportunity to share his seed with you."

"When though?" Caroline paced, worrying her hands. She stopped at the window looking at her home across the street. The risks were great, the reward greater. The tiny puff of air she blew out ruffled a strand of hair that fell free from the tight bun she wore.

"One week," Torra said patting her hands together, "at the university ball, the fund raiser. Surely you must have heard about it. You work there. I'm sure he will be more than happy to see you, perhaps set up an assignation."

"Only lecture about grafting roses coupled with a few theories about how character traits are passed on that have yet to be proven. I like to think about the possibilities, about what different children will look like. They won't hire me full time though. Men rarely if ever give women a chance to prove themselves. These men at the university are no different."

"I suppose you're one of those geniuses who are trying to prove said theories," Honey said grinning. "I still remember the day I met you. You were writing. What were the letters, advice messages?"

"Yes, I was working on my advice column for the Glasgow Herald. A little ironic don't you think, a spinster, bluestocking giving advice on love? Now, at least, I have people to get advice from also. It was so ironic a woman with no love experience was telling women how they should act as well as react to the men in their lives."

"When I came knocking at your door, we didn't even know each other. I needed a cup of flour. You poured out your heart to me," Torra spoke softly.

"After I told you my tale of woe, I handed you a batch of freshly baked chocolate cookies. You've supplied me with all kinds of things to keep the goodies coming your way. Sometimes I get restless. Baking gives me a way to think while I figure out what I want to do next."

Caroline wanted to avoid thinking about her pathetic theories. Her choice of a man to sire her baby revolved around her thoughts about principal factors in humans as well as how they coupled with lesser factors. How two parents provided the information that would eventually make up the characteristics of their child. For her, the man's intelligence had to be questionable. Duncan's was.

"Even if Duncan is not so bright, my child could still be more like me than him. I don't want that. If it's a girl, I want her to be normal, just like all the beautiful women who stroll in the parks on a man's arm, who wed and have children. The young ladies who are courted by dashing beaus."

"Who don't have a unique idea in their pretty little heads. Maybe a person somewhere between you and Duncan in intelligence might be more befitting," Torra said, her grin widening, as she seemed to be thinking about the possibilities.

"I have to conceive first," she whispered with a half sigh, half moan of despair. "It hasn't happened yet. What if..." She couldn't bare thinking about the what ifs plaguing her head.

Torra was drumming her fingers on the rim of her teacup apparently thinking before she said. "Back to the ball. You most likely have an invitation waiting somewhere for you to pick up."

"One gold embossed invite is sitting on my desk as we speak. Why would we expect Duncan to be there? Does he have something to do with the university?" she asked wondering where all this was leading.

This ball was held once a year specifically as a fundraiser for the school. She couldn't conceive one reason why Duncan Murray would be in attendance. Of course, she'd never gone before. Never been nominated for an award.

"Pretty much everything. The earl donates to the university every year as well as sponsoring two scholarships. His brother Evan is a professor, believe another brother also teaches there."

"The earl?" She didn't *ken* the man she slept with to father a child was an earl. "He has intelligent brothers?" Fear slipped into her belly. Here it was, more what ifs to curse her.

"Yes," Torra said flatly as if she was speaking to a child with no

48

understanding of the world, "The Earl of Downberry. That's who you slept with. That night was his birthday. You were his gift from his brothers who think he is far too stuffy and responsible."

Well, she supposed that supposition fit. The look on her face, she realized, was one of total surprise. She had not suspected anything like this. From time-to-time gossip revolved around the man along with the endowments he gave certain departments at the school. Never equated the man she wanted to sire her baby to one and the same as the one with the groats. She began to have second as well as third thoughts.

"I didn't realize Duncan Murray was that earl." Her heart raced at the idea. "If he has all this money to give away, how can he lack intelligence?"

She was suddenly petrified this man was not what she thought him to be. That night, with their conversation, his Scottish brogue deepened. She joyfully thought his intelligence dropped lower and lower with each word he uttered."

"Well, if one listens to gossip, it is said two of his younger brothers received the bulk of the intelligence in the family. Perhaps he inherited the money and the siblings know how to invest it wisely. Your earl is only known as a playboy as well as being irresponsible."

"Yes," she swallowed the lump of terror lodged in her throat. "Yes," she repeated thinking that must be so.

Just because some of the siblings were brilliant it didn't mean all would be as intelligent. Instead of fear, she suddenly felt sorry for the man. What would it be like to grow up so inferior to younger brothers that they had to invest your money for you?

"Regardless, the earl always gives away all the awards. It will be fun for you. You can figure out a way to seduce him into his bed when you get there. I would love to see the look on his face when you step forward to receive the honor. He will have no idea how to proceed."

"He will be tongue tied."

"Frozen in time." They all giggled.

"Suppose I'll need a few pointers on seducing. It didn't go so well last time. Everything the two of you thought he would like, he denied. He washed all the paint off before he would kiss me."

"All the paint?" Honey asked wide-eyed with speculation. "Even the..."

"All of it."

The memory of those first moments when she believed her best course of action was to run out the door burned in her mind. When he washed her face, then her nipples, he created a fire that seemed to sweep from him into her in a continuing circle. She shuddered as her body reacted to her memory.

"Your nipples?" Torra asked. "Well, I certainly wish we didn't rouge your most intimate parts. Did he?"

"He asked me," she told them. "I had to tell him the truth. He would have discovered the lie. The humiliation was very nearly my undoing. I'm positive if he hadn't been so gentle, even caring, I would have run from the room screaming. The scene was even more humiliating when he did so after he took my virginity."

"Well, back to the ball. It's in one week. Do you have anything appropriate to wear?" Honey stood as if she was more than ready to stride across the street to peruse her closet.

"No, nothing. I've never attended before. I'm up for one of the awards this year. It's one of the least...well...don't know how to explain it. It wasn't an important award, not one based on genius or creativity."

"Any award sounds wonderful to me. Never received an award before. I would frame it then hang it on the wall. What is it?" Torra asked as they both stood looking as if they were of the same mind without speaking. "We've got to get you to the dressmakers pronto."

"Not important, not at all in the scope of all the discoveries made during the year. They like my roses. Call me the rose lady and since many can't remember my name, they started calling me Rose. I won't be accepting the ridiculous award. Too humiliating to be singled out in that manner when I yearn for so much more." A soft sight of air followed, one she didn't mean to let go of. "If it were something important, I would be there smiling."

"Your earl will be handing you your award," Honey said softly. "You want to look your best when you accept. You can't just not go get the dang piece of paper. That would be terrible."

"Not going to humiliate myself by walking on to the stage as well as accepting something that isn't worth the parchment it's written on."

That was one thing she was adamant about. It wouldn't happen. Nothing would change her mind. She wanted an award for something with meaning. Had a burning need to prove her ideas on how traits were passed from parents to their children. She didn't have a research lab or the funding for such an endeavor. All Caroline had were her guesses coupled with her observations. No one would trust in her ideas enough to fund her research.

"Your reasoning eludes me," Torra spoke with conviction. "If I had one tiny speck of your abilities in addition your creativity, I would run onto that stage arms wide open to eagerly accept the confirmation I mattered. Now, I'm not feeling sorry for myself. I *ken* who I am. You should not feel sorry for yourself either."

"What they are extending to me is thank you for the numerous times I've been a guest lecturer for the biology department, nothing more. They ask whenever they can't find someone prestigious to come talk. Perhaps in the future I'll stick to my advice column. Since they won't give me a chance, I should turn them down. My articles are what pays the bills."

She touched her hand to her stomach wondering about Torra's words. Was she pregnant? If she knew, she wouldn't need to attend the ball, as she'd much prefer to remain in hiding. Just the thought of seeing Duncan again seemed to unravel every coherent thought in her head. The feelings were something she didn't understand, not one tiny little bit.

"Now, you're just feeling sorry for yourself. You don't do it well. We need to take a carriage to the dressmakers so you've got something decent to wear," Honey said reaching out for Caroline's hand. "You're going to the ball. Whether or not you accept the award, is of course up to you. Accepting would give you a chance to meet the man again."

"He would know who I am."

"True. That wouldn't be so bad. Would it?"

Torra must have understood the look on her face. She reached out to hold her hands in hers. "Don't you worry. This time we won't dress you as if you're his escort posing as a harlot. The gown will be tasteful. I see you in a dark blue very fashionable gown with all the trimmings. Honey, what do you think?"

"I do believe dark blue would suit you well. Make sure the bodice is low enough to entice but not to label." Miss Scarlett waltzed into the room, Robert Munroe the marquis of Stonebridge better known as Bobby right behind her. "And... if the gentleman sitting beneath a tree down the road is any indication, the house is being watched. I suggest you take the marquis' carriage instead of ours if you don't wish to be followed."

"What makes you think the man is watching us?" Torra stood striding to the window to see what she could see.

"Gut instinct," Bobby said softly. "The man is not watching Letty's home but the one across the street most likely." He turned to her. "Caroline, is there anyone who would want to know your every move?"

"Wouldn't have the vaguest notion," Caroline murmured following Torra to the window. "I don't have enemies if that's what you're asking. Except for these ladies don't have friends either."

"Now," Letty poured herself a cup of tea while Bobby helped himself to a brandy, "we've heard a few things even though we haven't been in town. Seems the Earl of Downberry is looking for a certain escort who came from this place. He doesn't believe you ladies are telling him the truth about her or her whereabouts. What do you say? Truth or not? He has the power to ruin us if he wishes. I wouldn't like that."

"I didn't want him to know who I was," Caroline spoke up even though her stomach turned sour. "Your ladies are only saying what I've asked them to say. I'll make sure Duncan understands if it becomes necessary. He's not going to ruin the best friends I've ever had."

"Don't suppose it's any of my business as to the specifics. Nevertheless, I do need to know if he abused you in any way," Letty said, as she seemed to study her from head to toe.

"No!" Her gasp of air coupled with the explosive word startled her. She gulped for a bit of air. "No, he treated me very well. Did nothing that wouldn't be expected of an escort."

"You're not an escort," Letty said softly.

"How did you find out?" Caroline wondered who would have spread rumors.

Who knew about the night except Duncan and of course herself?

After adding milk and lemon to her tea, Scarlett sipped thoughtfully. She appeared attentive. Caroline was sure Scarlett was mulling over what she should and shouldn't say to her.

With a lift of her shoulders, "Even though I'm not here most of the time, this is my business. Torra runs the day to day, however, this house is still my responsibility. It would not do my reputation a favor to learn that my girls are being abused, mentally or physically or my customers for that matter. If a lie has been perpetrated, I want to know about it. The lie will have to be dealt with."

"I..." Caroline was left with a loss for words. She did not lie except perhaps by omission. At the moment since she didn't know if she conceived, there was nothing to tell. "Are you implying?"

Scarlett waved her hand in the air dismissing the question. "A man wants to know beforehand if what he has purchased is what he is going to get. Don't believe Duncan Murray received what he expected. That again is none of my business. It is, however, speculation. There has been talk."

"I pleased him, if that's what you're asking."

Caroline stiffened resenting the insinuation even though it was true. Neither Letty nor Duncan would have any idea what she intended. They never would.

"Did you now?" Scarlett sat back, her hands wrapped around the cup, her eyes narrowed on her. "That is good. Now, however, you don't want to see him again nor do you want to receive further work from this house. Tell me. What is that all about? You are leaving a wealth of information to guess work." Letty sat forward. "I don't like to guess. Dealing in truths rather than half-truths is better for everyone."

"All true, I'm just not in need of the money. I thought over what happened, what I did and decided being an escort didn't suit," she whispered into the stuffy air, air that seemed to be closing in around her. All her lies would be discovered. She would pay for her crime against Duncan. What she didn't know was how.

Scarlett leaned forward, "May I ask why?"

"You can ask," she murmured turning away so as not to feel the intense scrutiny of her eyes. Heat scalded her cheeks as memories flooded her head.

"You won't tell me."

"No, my reasons are private to me. Why I chose what I did is no one's concern but mine." No, no, no... this woman knew. She had to surmise or she wouldn't be staring at her so.

"Perhaps it is also Duncan's." Her eyebrows arched in supposition. "He seems to be interested in you, more than a little interested. He's spending time along with money to find you."

Caroline understood the woman saw into her very soul. What she did was Duncan's concern although she wasn't going to tell him anything. *This baby is nobody's baby but mine!* Even though the thought was premature, she meant to make it happen.

"I don't see how. True, I slept with him. Spent the entire night in his bed. Do I owe the man anything else? I was bought and paid for. One night, the entire night was what he bought. The man has no other rights. What makes him believe he can be so highhanded?"

Scarlett sighed. The look on her face plainly said she wasn't getting anywhere with the questioning. "No, you're correct. You owe him nothing. You were bought and paid for. He has no hold over you. There is also no reason for him to expect to see you again unless both of you want to do so. Seems this quest of you by Duncan is one sided. Go on, ladies. Caroline needs a ball gown." After a short pause, "Wait."

"You snagged an invitation to the university ball. How? Did Torra get you one?"

Caroline felt the color drain from her face. This question was too unnerving. It would reveal more about her than she wanted anyone in this household besides Torra, Honey, as well as Muria to know. She played with the fabric of her gown before meeting Scarlett's gaze, never before feeling quite so uncertain.

"How I received the invitation is no concern of yours. Rest assured it did not come from your ladies. They did nothing wrong. Nor did I come by it through nefarious purposes."

"That may be. Why would you want to meet this man now when you've been avoiding him for three weeks?"

Before she thought this through, she blurted, "He has something I need. Want."

"I'm sure all you need do is send a message to his townhouse that you want to see him. I'm also certain he will be pleased to give whatever it is he has back. He would deliver it to you himself," Letty said, appearing to understand more than she was letting on.

"Come, we need to get the ball gown." Torra appeared with Honey in tow. "We will use your suggestion and take the marquis' carriage." Torra grasped Caroline by the arm, tugging her up then toward the carriage entrance.

With that said the two ladies hustled her from the house then into the waiting carriage. "Get down." Torra pushed her head so low Caroline thought she would wind up on the floor.

"Don't want whoever is spying on you to see you. Wouldn't do at all to have him follow you to the dressmakers," Honey said with a little giggle that sounded more like apprehension than humor.

Once they were past the spy, Torra let her up. She brushed hair from her eyes. "Does it matter if that man follows me to a dressmaker? What is more important is if he follows us back, if he sees me walk into my house. I'll be done for. The earl will know where to find me. That can't happen. It's fine if I see him one more time. Nonetheless, he can't under any circumstances learn who I am or where I live." She was already done for.

Caroline was torn. This was just too soon to make plans. She'd like to flee to Edinburgh today. With her luck this spy of Duncan's would follow her to the city. She didn't *ken* how to get out of this mess. Now with Scarlett at the house, Torra and Honey would have fewer opportunities to help out. Scarlett would tell anyone inquiring about her where she lived, doubt it not.

An hour passed while it seemed they were no closer to concluding with the dressmaker than they were when they first walked into the store. She needed to finish with this. At home she had work to do. Her column was due in two days. She didn't have one clue how to answer the question. The woman wanted to know if she could kick her husband out of the bedroom if she was angry with him for something he'd done. She wanted him to sleep on the couch until he apologized. Caroline believed that to be a perfect solution to the trouble between the couple. What did she know?

Caroline wanted to just blurt out that the man had no right to her unless he was good and kind. The law didn't agree with her. Once married the man owned her as well as everything she previously possessed. She tried to come up with something witty, except wit eluded her.

"Hush," Both Torra and Honey were inside the dressing room, their eyes seeming to cross. "He's out there."

"Who?"

"You've got to be quiet," Honey whispered. She held one finger to her lips for emphasis. "It's the earl. He is sitting out there pretty as you please looking at fashion plates. Doesn't appear to be going anywhere soon. Lady Robina even gave him a glass of brandy."

"I can't see him."

Actually, Caroline didn't understand any of this. Couldn't comprehend why he sought her so diligently. He had her sweating. True, she wanted to see him one more time, needed to have him make love to her, in one week not today. Today would do her no good. Nor would sex happen at the dressmakers unless he found a way to accomplish the deed in the dressing room. At the crazy thought, heat flushed her face.

"No, you can't. Nevertheless, if he wants to, he can wait you out. Seems our spy hightailed it back to the earl. After that the blasted man told him where you were. Using the other carriage must not have been a very good decoy."

"Perhaps you should pretend you want to see him. Be brave, go out there and talk to him."

"No."

"We can try to sneak you out the back door," Torra suggested as she looked wistfully toward the door.

"He most likely has his spy there waiting for that very thing. If he followed me here, I'm sure he wouldn't leave something like that to chance." Caroline was feeling more depressed with each passing second.

"Brazen it out. You don't have to admit to anything. Don't have to tell him where you live. Don't have to give him anything you don't want to. Your life is yours to do with as you please. Be stubborn, we both know you can."

"Obviously, he knows where I live."

A wave of guilt swept through her. This wasn't the first time she felt that remorse. If she had her way, she was stealing from him, stealing something he would never be aware of. He would have expected her to use precautions. She was after all an escort.

"So, why doesn't he do anything about it? Why hasn't he come to see you?" Honey challenged, her hands fisted on her hips.

"Probably waiting for me to do something stupid," she sighed. "Do you think he'll wait until it's closing time to leave?"

"That's only a few minutes away. Don't believe you've any options. At least none that are good."

"Look at it this way. You've got an absolutely lovely gown to wear to the ball. You know you want to go, will have to see him again. Why not one more time before the celebration? You do have to figure out how to end up in his bed again. Maybe if you talk to the man, it will give you some ideas. Inevitably, seeing you will give him ideas."

"Just not now. Not while I'm feeling as if I'm taking something from him. I've some heavy thinking to do."

"He knows what can come of having sex. If he didn't use precautions then I'm sure he doesn't care about possible repercussions," Honey told her. "If the rumors are true, he probably has bastards all over town. What is one more?"

"She's an escort. He would believe she took insurances," Torra said bluntly, reminding Caroline once more she was stealing from the man.

Shame was not something she dealt with very well. "What if he asks me something I can't answer?"

She had visions of him following her to her house. Wanting her right then. It was too soon. She couldn't see him for another week. Lord, but her pulse raced. She could barely inhale or think a coherent thought. She remembered how it felt when he was deep inside her.

This wasn't good, not good at all.

What to do?

She decided she would brazen the situation out. The ladies, her friends in this crazy endeavor, the ones who planted the seed into her muddled head that she could dupe someone into siring a child with her had already hightailed it out of the dressing room. With her luck they most undoubtedly left her to fend for herself. She was alone in a dire situation. She sucked in a long breath of perfume-scented air. Sneezed.

With what little courage she possessed, she left the dressing room hoping for the best outcome possible.

"Duncan? Whatever are you doing here?"

She stepped into the main room; her heart lodged in her throat. Her fingers were a sweaty mess. She tried to smile. Tried desperately for a breath of air. Caught nothing to help her out.

"What do you think I'm doing here?" he asked as his grin widened.

His eyes traveled the length of her then back. He looked at her as if he wanted to devour her. "Much more stunning than the pink cloak although I did like the big pink bow at your neck signifying you were my gift. Untying the bow was delightful."

His voice along with his words thrummed with sexual overtones. He stared at her bosom then her mouth.

She didn't think she could breathe. Once again, she tugged in air that didn't want to find its way into her lungs. She thought of her theft. All coherent thoughts left her muddled brain that seemed to be filled with sand. The last remaining rays of the day filtered in through the window where he was standing. The light slanted across his broad shoulders. Vivid memories of the way the man looked that night before he turned out all the lights. She had not wanted him to see her even though he stroked and kissed every part of her.

One of his perfectly arched earl eyebrows rose upward. "Nothing to say? I'm sure you and your friends figured it all out when you were whispering in the dressing room."

"Figured what out?" Her voice wobbled as did her knees. She had no idea what he was talking about.

Terrified, feeling her eyes widen, she stepped back. She shouldn't be alone with this man. He was too dangerous for her. Torra and Honey should be somewhere close by. Where the devil did the two ladies get themselves off to? Her gut told her they deserted her. She wondered what exactly the earl offered them so they would be compelled to abandon her.

"If you're looking for your friends, they've discarded you. Left you for me. I didn't object when they said their goodbyes then told me you were dressing and would be right out, wanting to see me. Did you, Caro? Did you want to see me? Can't help but think they lied to me since you've been avoiding me for weeks now. You wouldn't let them tell me where you lived. That was not well done of you, Caro."

Shaking her head, still moving back, *Nay, nay, nay* they wouldn't do such a thing. They had though. They were nowhere in sight. How could they leave her to his mercy? She understood why. He must have threatened the escort service. While the two of them were loyal to her, that loyalty went only so far.

"It truly wasn't their fault. I terrified them into leaving you behind. They had no other choice." He smirked as if pleased with himself. "I'm a powerful man. I have ability to ruin lives if I so choose."

"You threatened them?"

"Not in so many words."

"There is always a choice," she murmured studying the floor and the rug as well as the toes of her shoes. "They didn't have to give in to whatever you told them."

"Why don't you want to see me? Hurt my feelings you know. A man doesn't like to believe a woman isn't as enamored of him as he is of her. The night we had together could be recreated. I would like that. Would you?"

"Enamored?" Her heart forgot what it was supposed to do. "Recreated?" That was her intention so she could steal from him. "Would I?" Thievery was never a good idea. "You would?"

"Yes." He was staring at her, gazing at her lips as if he wanted to consume them just as he'd done that night three weeks ago. "Why wait? Why not generate new memories? We could begin here in the dressing room then continue in the carriage, perhaps even the bed in your home. There are so many different places we could experiment with."

Experiment?

"It was only one time."

She realized the falseness of her words as she watched his smile spread across his face. Knew there would be at least one more time but in a week, not now.

"Once? My, although our recollections of that evening are not the same, I must admit you disappoint me. We came together intimately more than once. Although I didn't count it must have been more than four times. What do you think, Caro? Was it five or maybe six times?"

Her eyes crossed. She had no idea how many times he came inside her. "Yes, one night. Why do you want to see me, an escort, again? I'm nothing to you. Will never be anything except a dalliance. I'm not good enough for an earl. I don't want to be an escort." Good lord she was rambling.

"Because I enjoyed you more than I can put to words. Enjoyed you more than I have any other woman in my life. Don't say no to me, Caro. I want to see you on a regular basis."

~ * ~

Upstairs Letty snuggled into Bobby's arms as she traced the line of dark hair past his naval to more intimate spots. His hand closed over hers as he chuckled softly sending ribbons of soft sultry pleasure through her.

"If you want to talk that is not the way to go about it," he laughed holding her hand in his, bringing her fingers to his lips to place tender kisses on her knuckles then the palm. "I'm not complaining mind you. It will be the third time this evening. Mayhap we should put some food in our bellies so we have the strength to continue in this vein. We can have that conversation that has you nearly foaming at the mouth when we are sated in both ways."

"I'm not foaming," she told him wishing he wasn't right about his assessment of her seething emotions. She feared for her business. Knew the girls needed this income to survive.

"Just a turn of phrase. So, what has you so curious about Caroline Kenworth? We were only going to stay the night. I'll wager now you intend to stay the week so we can attend a ball that will bore both of us to tears. Am I wrong?"

"No, you're never wrong about my feelings. I am boiling. Want to understand what is driving Caroline, also what she is not telling us. There are secrets between those three ladies I'd like to uncover. They work for me. I deserve to understand the entire situation as the act enfolds or even before it does."

"Sure, the facts will all come out in time. Secrets have a way of doing just that." Bobby stood. Even after a year of marriage, Letty loved the way he looked. He was all sinew and muscle, muscle that rippled when he walked. He was hers. She never thought to be so lucky.

She loved to hear his words when he reverted back to his street cockney. He spent most of his life in the bowels of London. Knew he was born of titled parents. Was taken from them when too young to do anything to change his circumstances. He did everything he set his mind to, even transforming himself to a man of means. If it had not been for Brett MacLachlan falling in love with Piper who was really the daughter of the notorious London Duchess, he would still be breaking into the wealthy homes in the city.

They were both outcasts. She supposed that was why she recognized a kindred spirit in Bobby. "Why do you think Caroline is so different from most women. She does have a story to tell. I wonder what it is. She has lived across the street from us for as long as I can remember. Never once has she spoken to the ladies or me. Why now?"

"You don't know?" he asked seemingly surprised at his wife. "You are usually more astute about people."

"No, I can't figure it out."

"She is a bluestocking, a spinster. I'm sure she buries herself in her books. Don't think she wants to be but doesn't *ken* any other way of life. She is reaching out in some way. It's our purpose here to discover what it is she wants. Why she became an escort for one night. Perhaps even help her achieve her goals."

"A bluestocking," Letty pondered that for a few seconds. "She's never had a beau. It seems she's always lived in the home across from us. I wonder how old she is."

"Most likely not. Her type usually does not attract men simply because she is too intelligent for most of the male species. She scares men with her acumen. Doesn't mean she doesn't want what most women want," Bobby sat down on the bed with the tray of food that had been left in the room.

The realization came to her in a burst of laughter. "She wanted to lose her virginity. Torra and Honey picked out a man for her they knew would be gentle with her. She wanted to know what happens between a man and a woman. Caroline was willing to risk her reputation for one night in a man's arms."

"Doubt if that's the only reason, however. A woman like that wouldn't care about something so blasé as her maidenhead. There is something else she might want. I'm assuming she has work that pays well accompanied by her independence. So, think about what you do know. What exactly would a woman of her type still want that she doesn't have? She doesn't believe any man will ever be interested enough in her to wed her" He sipped the wine he just poured. "It is a good place to start. I'm sure you have some ideas."

"What are the facts?" Letty began mulling over everything Bobby said as well as what she discovered today from Torra and Honey. "Do you think we can make a few guesses that might just lead us to something pertinent?"

"I believe we can. To begin with, she slept with him once or perhaps numerous times in one night," Bobby listed the first one, his grin still endearing to Letty.

"She pleased him. At least that's what she says. Did he please her? I wonder."

"Her pleasing him must be true because it's increasingly evident he wants to see her again," Bobby went on to say as he popped a grape into Letty's soft pink mouth. "Chew over the facts for a moment."

After a second or two, Letty swallowed the grape. "We can only assume so. At first, she didn't want to see him."

"Maybe she still doesn't."

"No, I believe she does. Somehow, she managed to finagle an invitation to a celebration of our most intelligent and esteemed professors exactly four weeks from the night they slept together." A few wayward thoughts started to form in Letty's head. "There must be something about the four weeks."

"What I'm thinking doesn't make a lot of sense," she tapped her fingers on his chest, "but then again it might."

Bobby leaned against the headboard. The crystal glass holding his wine rested on his hard belly. She had an urge to forget all this conjecture. Letty wanted his arms around her, needed to feel him deep inside. She pushed the wayward thoughts from her brain hoping to discover Caroline's ruse.

"Caroline would know her time. She might also *ken* the best part of the month to have his seed take root. If for some reason, she didn't, both Torra and Honey could tell her."

Letty felt a moment of compassion for the woman, a woman who wanted something so badly she was willing to give up her pride and humiliate herself in the process.

"So, you think Caroline wants a baby, the earl's baby. Why would she want the father of her child to be a man whose sole purpose in life is to chase bits of muslin and gamble?" Bobby asked seeming for the first time in the conversation to be baffled.

"He does like to make money. I hear he is quite handy with increasing his groats," Letty said thoughtfully. "Don't believe for a moment she cares about his fortune. I also don't believe the rumors about Duncan Monroe. In other circles I've heard he's quite the stoic, very rarely goes out unless it is to go out of his way to plant the seeds of his reputation and watch them grow. I've heard he doesn't like or respect match making mamas."

"Hmm...since his seed didn't find a permanent spot in her womb the first time, she plans on trying a second," Bobby speculated, his grin spreading across his face.

"If she is still planning on the same time of the month, I'll wager she is already increasing. Sometimes it's hard to tell. Some women still bleed for the first or second month after conceiving. That might be something she doesn't know. Think we should let the earl in on her plans?"

"No."

'Of course not, it would be more fun to watch this play out. Couples need to figure out these things on their own. They are not a couple." Letty wagered it wouldn't take the earl long to realize Caroline carried his baby. When that happened, Caroline would most likely be in for the biggest surprise of her life.

If she was right about the earl, including his reputation, he wouldn't be pleased by the news. The earl was known to be ruthless when he was crossed. In this the woman he seemed to desperately want, thwarted him.

Chapter Three

Duncan was pleased, very pleased with his endeavors. "Either I'm taking you home or you are walking. It's quite the distance to your house. Blisters would be the prominent feature on your feet if you did so. If you refuse to take advantage of my carriage, I'll have to have the transport follow along next to you to make sure you stay safe. Obviously, I wouldn't want to risk anything happening to you. That would be a complete waste of my time as well as yours. You will except my generous offer now, won't you?"

"You're a cad."

The ensuing blush pleased him.

He watched her bosom heave, remembered the taste of her, the slightly vanilla and chocolate scent he encountered when he prowled her body over the course of the night. The fragrant scent of roses lingered in her hair. While her agitation bothered him, he did enjoy the effect it had on her body. Loved to watch the movement of her breasts beneath the fabric of the gown she wore. If she would allow him to do so, he would kiss her again while he took her home. Practicing restraint would be paramount in his head during the ride. He wasn't going to toss her skirts in the vehicle even though he suggested that very thing. He was an earl after all, a pillar of the community. He was stuffy as well as stoic. The last thing he wanted was to put a shift in his reputation.

He had pride.

He also meant to set up another time to meet her. If she would accept the proffered invite, he had an invitation to the university ball in his breast pocket. He would give it to her tonight. Insist she attend with him. He wanted to be seen by all his friends and colleagues with Caro on his arm.

"That is what I'm known for, my way with women, numerous

women. Once you've spent some time with me, you might feel different though."

He spent years gaining that reputation so he could be left to himself. Telling Caro that fact would not be wise.

"A gambler?"

"True, it is in my nature. I'm also lucky. I only bet on sure things. I rarely if ever lose."

He was betting on Caro, his Caro. She was far from a sure thing, but he meant to change that by manipulating her to his will, giving her choices she could not refuse. Now that he knew where she lived, he would hound her until she came around to his way of thinking.

"A womanizer?"

"You did enjoy the night in my arms, did you not? If I was not practiced in the art of love, you would not have found ecstasy beneath me, atop me and..." he asked blandly watching her eyes darken while her beautiful cheeks blossomed with soft shades of pink.

She did find immense pleasure with him; the perception was true. At this instant in time if he didn't miss his guess, she wanted him perhaps not as desperately as he wanted her. Getting her to admit anything of that nature would be difficult.

She looked away for a moment. He didn't believe she could think of anything else to say to the banter he was indulging in with her. The idea pleased him. He was tired of the insults even though until now it was his intent to make sure the good mothers of Glasgow understood those things about him.

His ploy worked.

Perhaps too well, he wasn't what she thought him to be.

"I'd like an answer. Did you or did you not enjoy your time with me?"

He touched the small of her back, leading her from the shop. He saw the dark blue gown she was having made. A wave of jealousy swamped him. She was going to escort someone else if he didn't miss his guess. He wasn't going to allow that to happen.

She stared at her toes then met his gaze. "I did."

Her embarrassment acute, the color on her cheeks deepened

turning fiery now.

He liked what he saw. "Good to see your honesty hasn't deserted you. That gown, the one you were having made up? Are you escorting someone somewhere?"

Curiosity coupled with possessiveness was not something he was used to dealing with. In all his adult life, he could not recall the feeling of jealousy.

Her sharp indrawn breath of air surprised him. She stopped. "No."

"Good. Hope that's true. Wouldn't want to discover the opposite. I'd have to do something about that if I did. You see, for the time being, you are mine, Caro. Now that I've found you, no one else will be seeing you."

He deepened the brogue, watching her smile grow. Why? It was something to discover when more time could be spent with her.

His driver brought the stairs to the carriage. He helped her into the well-sprung vehicle he invested in, as comfort was important. When he rode somewhere, he wanted a smooth ride not to be bounced along until his teeth chattered. Four white, perfectly matched horses pulled the carriage.

"You've no business prying into my life." Her nose tilted into the air as her voice took on a defensive note. "Yet you continue to assume things about me you should not. You haven't respected my wish not to see you. Here you are, insinuating yourself into my life. Telling me that I'm yours. That, Sir, is a blatant lie."

That was something else to take note of. She was proud, confident as well. "Don't suppose I do or have assumed things. In the near future, I intend to make that my right as well as my concern. Caro, I want to learn everything about you. You could take these moments to tell me something I don't know."

He sat down opposite. His forearms rested on his thighs. Before he left to enter the dressmaker's shop, he gave his driver the order to meander around the city, as he needed time with the lady who would accompany him.

"We don't have a future," she bit out too quickly he suspected by the change of expression on her lovely face. "There is nothing between us we have in common."

A lie this time on her part. There was so very much they had in common. Meant to have so much more. "Oh, but we do. I mean to see to our future as well as everything we both like. For now, relax. Would you enjoy going somewhere to eat?" Reaching into his pocket he pulled out his gold watch. "Devilishly close to dinner time. Do you prefer to eat late or early? We could go to my place," he paused, watching the subtle play of emotions across her endearingly lovely face. "Or...we could go to yours."

"I'm not hungry. Please take me home." Her back stiffened perceptibly at his mention of dinner at his home. He understood she would not do that again. Doing so might be a grave mistake.

Not until I find out what purpose the gown is meant for.

"When it feels right to take you home, if I'm satisfied with your answer to all my questions. After you've told me why you're purchasing such an expensive gown. Do you have the groats or is Miss Scarlett paying for the gown? I would know. Where do plan to wear the high-priced creation?"

She clearly bristled at his suggestion Miss Scarlett might be paying for the convection. Earlier she answered that question. "Not that it's any of your affair, I have the groats," she gritted out impatiently her teeth clenched together in obvious disdain. "More than I need to buy a gown, lavish or otherwise."

"How?"

He leaned forward, his forearms once more resting on his thighs, his long fingers very close to her hands.

She pulled back, her eyes flashing sparks. He enjoyed that side of her. "What do you do to earn your living? I heard you turned down the money that was meant for you after that night we spent together. I would learn the truth. If you need funds, I've more than enough to help out. You shouldn't have to sell your body in order to eat. In fact," he paused as if thinking, struggling with the notion in his head, "I forbid it."

His gaze riveted on her. He picked up her hands in his, wound his fingers through hers. She looked at them. Her breath left her. He moved his fingers along the inner softness of her fingers. She shuddered. He felt the quivering surge from her into him. With delicious thoughts of her pending arousal, beneath his trousers he hardened.

"I...you forbid...how dare you?" Her tiny pink tongue moved slowly across her full bottom lip. Her mouth opened inviting him inside. More than anything he wanted to be inside her. He remembered her taste, the sweet scent of her woman's body. How her heat surrounded him. Felt the rhythmic pulses before her climax. Wanted more, "I," she began again as her gaze seemed riveted on his mouth, "write a column for the Herald."

For a moment he thought her claim amusing, that perhaps she played him for a fool. On further thought he believed it to be entirely possible. "A column, about what?" Her heated shivers moved enticingly in what seemed to be continuous moment from her into him then back.

A broken sound slipped from her parted lips. He brought her hands to his mouth, kissed the back. Traced the palms of her hands with the tips of his fingers. She closed her eyes. He saw her swallow. Saw the rapid beating of her pulse at the base of her neck. Liked what he saw. She delighted him. He would taste her again before he reached her home.

"Stop." In all its subtlety her whisper said please keep doing what you're doing to me. Her purr of contentment begged for additional caresses. He meant to hold back what she was asking. He needed to hear her beg for him to continue not to arrest his actions.

Vividly, he remembered how her lush body coiled and arched beneath his. Recalled their joining as he continued to coax her. While she was still innocent in so many ways, he now absorbed her passion, reveling in the sweet honesty. With him, she was no innocent maiden.

He could never get enough of her.

"What is it you do all those hours you spend at home? Do you entertain lovers?"

She jerked at his insinuation. Her eyes flashed angrily. Tried to remove her hands from his hold. He wasn't going to allow any break in contact, not until he was satisfied with her answer.

"I write," she blurted. "Please, Duncan, don't do this to me. I can't..."

His fingertips trailed slowly up her arm before retracing his path down to her wrist. "What do you write, Caro? I'm curious. Thought you were honest. Don't understand why you want me to stop something you so clearly enjoy. Lying to me will never get you what you want."

Her eyes darkened until the ice blue heated to dusky passion.

"Come sit by me. Tell me everything you do during your day."

He tugged slightly, surprised when she came to him so easily. He settled her across his thighs. His hands searched, exploring, as he delighted in the ensuing shivering response.

"My story would bore you."

Once again, her tongue passed across her sweetly curved lips a small purr rippling from her parted mouth. A dewy sheen of moisture tempted him to taste. This woman captivated him in every way possible.

Gently, he set her so his hands could roam wherever he desired. For a moment only, she squirmed. "Nothing about you bores me, Caro. I've this incessant need to learn about you from the tips of your darling toes to the top of your head. Want to discover more about you than I learned three weeks ago. You must understand what I know about you just isn't enough." He moved her hair aside so he could explore behind her ear.

"An advice column," she murmured in a soft squeak when his teeth touched upon her ear then bit gently. "You cannot."

"I can." He continued knowing at the moment she was his. It did not take much coaxing for his Caro to give over to her emotions the sweetly raw passion that ignited her. She blossomed so very beautifully.

"Please."

He grinned wondering about her comment. "Advice? About what?"

If his Caro was indeed the rose lady, perhaps she wrote about grafting roses. She might have a wealth of information for gardeners. Yes, the column must be about gardening. He'd make sure to take a look tonight when he got home. He had a copy of today's Glasgow Herald sitting on the end table by his sofa in the drawing room.

"Love." She sighed as his lips continued his coaxing explorations along her neck then across her collarbone. Her breasts rose then fell. It seemed she struggled for air just as he was doing the same.

Love?

He almost roared with laughter. Kept the chuckle behind his teeth believing she would not want his humor at her expense. He couldn't, however, help the ensuing question.

"What does an innocent *lass* such as you know about love?"

She did take offense as he felt her stiffen. He should have never brokered the subject in light of the headway he was making with the coaxing, seduction of Caro. He wanted her now, in the carriage, hell, wherever they were, he wanted to toss her skirts, fill her with himself. Her long sigh led him to believe perhaps that she understood he was not making fun of her.

"Nothing. You are right in your assumptions. I don't *ken* anything about love although I've a vivid imagination. I listen to people as well. Torra, Muira along with Honey are a wealth of information when they speak of their clients. Well, not Honey." When she touched his chin with a fingertip, she closed her eyes coupled with a soft purr of contentment. "Honey doesn't do those things. She's afraid of men."

The tiny caress gave his heart a jump. Duncan decided the step backward he thought he took did not happen. "Nothing, perhaps you should learn a bit more about men as well as love before you give advice. I can teach you even help you with the column if you're willing to ask. A male's viewpoint might help give your advice a different edge, new insight into problems of the lovelorn."

He meant to find her column in the Herald and read what her advice entailed. His curiosity about her as well as what motivated her simmered bone deep. He still didn't understand why she came to him three weeks ago. Now, a driving force inside him demanded he discover the truth. Why did this lady give away her virginity to a man she didn't know?

Now, his mouth was so close to hers, he felt her sweet mint scented breath across his cheek. Tasting her right now would be divine. He wanted to be inside her more now than a second ago. He would have to wait until she accepted him into her life.

Sensuously, her lips parted in silent and probably unknowing invitation. Closing the distance, he settled his mouth on hers, experienced the moist glide of her tongue as she met his advance with a gentle advance of her own making. She opened farther for him as she made another tiny constricted sound in the back of her throat. His hand rested beneath her breast. Enjoyed its weight as well as the soft curve on the back of his hand. Longed to turn his hand over then cup the sweetness she seemed to be offering.

He gave her time to move away or tell him no. She didn't. He waited for her, smiling as she moved her head back a short distance the look in her eyes questioning. It seemed she wanted to say something although it appeared she didn't know what the words should be.

"Did you like the kiss, *lass*?" he asked as he continued with caution.

"A kiss? Was that a..."

"Kiss, not like I would like to give you. You have me sweating and wondering if for some reason you didn't enjoy my kisses the other night. Tell me, do you want another kiss like that or no?" Duncan prayed she wouldn't tell him no. Prayed too she would give herself to him again.

"You should take me home." Her fingernails were biting into his shoulder as she moved on, his legs searching he thought for the possible fulfillment of what he purposely created inside her. Ah, his Caro was a passionate woman. Unknowingly, she seemed to be spreading her legs for him. She could be his at any moment.

"Not until you answer my question."

"What question?" she murmured, her eyes glazed over with the raw hunger he understood he generated in her.

"A lie, sweet *lass*, it's not right to lie to your lover about kisses. He needs to know what you like."

"Please..."

"Please what? Come inside the sultry warmth you gifted me with three weeks ago. Take what you're offering now; your gently parted lips only to have you rebuke me time and again. I wouldn't appreciate your doing so, Caro. Don't tell me no if you want to say yes. Don't hide from me ever again."

"Yes," she sighed into his mouth as he took what he wanted along with what she gifted him with.

He planned to have her beneath him again and maybe on top. As soon as she wanted him as desperately as he wanted her, she would be his. He would be hers. Somehow, he would make her aroused to a point she would lead them both into a new bout of lovemaking. Arouse her until she was as frantic with her need, as he was.

He was beyond frenzied.

He groaned wondering how on earth he was going to wait for her to reach that point of no return. The very place where he was now. She was soft curves next to his hard planes. Her scent was vanilla and chocolate reminding him of her self-proclaimed sweet tooth. All he was going to do today was kiss her, place his lips and tongue on as many spots she would allow. Next time he got her alone she would beg him.

If that didn't happen, he would beg her.

His kisses continued as he swept his tongue into the sultry warmth of her mouth. She returned all that he did with such heated passion that he groaned desperate for more of Caro. She returned and returned all that he gave. Nirvana is where she took him. His body shuddered as his sex leapt, hardened and pulsed to find her heat along with the dewy moisture between her legs.

The ties to her gown were easy to pull. Before he left her at her doorstep, he needed to sample more of her. Desired to refresh his mind of the charms she possessed that left him craving her in the middle of the night. Wanting her during the day. Thinking of her in the middle of the afternoon. In all his adult life he never felt this way about a woman.

Simply put, he could not get enough of his Caro.

When the corsage of her gown fell to her waist, he tasted the taut hard nub thrusting upward. Pulled and sucked until her breast filled his mouth. Until her tiny hums aroused so thoroughly, he thought he might explode. She cried out for him as he turned his attention to the other succulent globe.

Somewhere between the first tentative, teasing kisses and the unveiling of her breasts his hand settled on the bare flesh of her thigh, sweeping higher with each kiss. He had not meant to take this not-so-subtle coaxing to this point. Yet...

He was within a hand span of her slick wet heat, a place where he would discover beyond any doubt he might have if she was aroused so completely he could take her here, in the carriage. Was so close to giving her the ecstasy her questing hips sought, her body desired. She arched her back, thrusting her breasts closer to his mouth. Shudders swept from her into him. He caught each movement with one of his own, calculated to send her higher with each practiced caress.

His fingers closed over her woman's mound, parted the hotly swollen folds guarding the entrance to her velvet sheathe. He would pull back again and again until she agreed to everything he asked.

"You are ready for me, Sweet *Lassie*."

His thumb found the silken pearl, touched and caressed until her breaths came in shallow pants. He slipped a finger then another into the tightness he yearned to experience more intimately, moved slowly then faster as she met him movement for movement.

The carriage rolled to a stop. He froze, realizing the two hours he told his driver he needed came to what seemed like an abrupt halt. The man would be at the door in a second, opening the exit, setting the steps for her.

Quickly, he left all thoughts of further seduction behind. The bodice of her gown covered her even though it wasn't laced. "I'm sorry," he whispered. "Seems we've reached your home."

"Home?" she asked, her voice a seductive sultry rumble as she'd fallen under the spell he expertly wove.

Her eyes glazed over. Her lips moist with the residue of his tongue. She had the look of a woman who was nearly sated. He would leave her that way; give her nothing more until she answered all his questions.

"You're home. Unless you want me to come inside and finish what we started, I'm going to leave."

"Home? I thought..."

"We were going to mine. You never told me that was what you wanted. We can always go there now. Well, that is where I'm going. If you say yes, you'll be in my bed for the rest of the night. Tell me now." It was exactly what he wanted even though he was positive she would refuse the invitation. He could wait.

"No, no... n-no..."

It seemed she was gaining more of her senses with each passing second.

This was for the best, would suit his final plans more if he left her in this state of sensual arousal. He didn't know how he was going to do that, leave her. Caro was a blinding need in his soul.

They were at the door, his hand on her elbow as if the shattering collision of their bodies along with the raw passion between them had not just taken place during the carriage ride.

From his breast pocket he pulled out the invitation he meant to use to bring her to him again. It would be a week of not seeing Caro. He gathered his wits about him, telling himself he always prided himself with his control. It seemed where this woman was concerned, he had no control no restraint. She represented raw carnal passion in his blood.

"This is for you." He handed her the invitation. "I want you to be there, Caro. It's a ball, a fundraiser for the university. I'm sure that gown you were having made will suit."

"I..." Her soft pink tongue swept across her lips an erotic invitation.

"Take it. Don't tell me no. If you're not there, I'll send Johnston to get you."

The devil, what would he do if she didn't show up. He would send Johnston in any case. He just gave her fair warning. If she didn't want to go, she could end up anywhere or nowhere. He could find her. She seemed to unravel his brain, leave him sweating with his need for her. He was too damn close to pushing her inside her door then finding the nearest table to fill her with his member. Wanted to hear her scream his name as he remembered from his birthday evening that seemed a lifetime ago.

Her hand did close around the invitation. She brought it to her lips, her eyes seeming to say yes even when he was sure she would tell him no.

"Thank you," she spoke softly, her words barely audible.

His heart leapt. "Does that mean you're going to attend? Do you want me to send a carriage to pick you up? I could pick you up, come along with the carriage. There is so much to do."

"Probably." She turned toward him, her eyes alight with

something he thought might be humor then the shimmer vanished.

Her fingertip touched his mouth. Unable to stop himself he opened, touched the tip with his tongue. When she didn't draw away, he bit gently.

That shattered sound he was coming to realize was her ensuing passion sprang softly from her. He sucked the finger deeper. Still unable to stop he held her hand, did the same to each of her fingers until she leaned into him. This couldn't continue unless she agreed to seeing him inside her home.

"Should I help you inside?"

The devil but he shouldn't. If he did, maybe this time she would allow him to look at her body, see the silken curves he kissed so many times. Three weeks ago, she had him blow out all the candles as well as turn off the gas lighting. All he had was the wonderful moonlight. It wasn't enough. His imagination worked overtime. He yearned to see her naked white flesh in full sunlight.

"That wouldn't be wise or prudent."

Well, she was right about that. The wisdom wouldn't stop him if she could verbally agree to another night of pleasure.

"One more kiss then I'll see you at the ball. Johnston will pick you up. I won't take no for an answer."

"I can get there on my own. Don't need to be beholding to you, to any man." Her words were still breathy and very soft. "Can't be beholding to you, a man. It's not right."

Well hell. That's exactly the way he needed her, under his thumb. "Of course you can, although I want the pleasure of seeing you home."

"Pleasure..." she sighed again seemingly oblivious to everything except his touch.

What was it about this woman who had him aroused within an instant of seeing her? She wasn't his type. She was too old, too independent. He needed his women drawing on his every word. His Caro wasn't like that. She was intelligent. At times possessed a smart mouth, which he found quite intriguing. She didn't bore him. That in itself was different making her unique in his eyes. The English would call her incomparable.

It made no difference to him. He supposed he would eventually grow tired of her as he did every other woman he met except his previous fiancée who grew bored with him.

Until that time when tediousness set in, he meant to enjoy Caro. The devil, he still didn't know her last name. If she was the rose lady, someone at the university would know. If she was the rose lady, she would have an invitation to the ball. So, since she excepted his she must not be.

He felt a tiny wave of disappointment.

Just a tiny one.

Her hands rested on his shoulders. She was standing on tiptoes to receive the goodnight kiss he offered. He touched the tip of her nose with his lips. Kissed along her eyebrows before smoothing them with his thumbs. Her eyes were closed so he settled small kisses on the lids.

She pressed against him, once again her body responding to his tender persuading. He groaned wondering at the sensibility of leaving her. She was aroused. Ready to take him inside her. Her tight satin core would be hot, swelled, as well as dripping with moisture.

He was a patient man.

Known for his control.

The reminder didn't ease his problem. It seemed to him when Caro was involved, he possessed no control what so ever. This joining would be postponed until she begged him. He was determined to see this through. While it was obvious to him she wanted him now, she wasn't begging.

Deciding against the kiss, a full-blown kiss, he brushed his lips across hers intending to say goodnight.

"It appears we got here just in time."

A slow grumble erupted from deep inside as he kept the sound hidden. Caro stiffened in his arms seeming to have a similar reaction to the two ladies descending on them. Two women who were chattering nonstop, grating on his nerves.

"You weren't planning on letting him into the house, were you?" Torra asked as she barged her way between the passionate couple. "You *ken* just how unwise something like that would be."

"I..."

He had the audacity to grin clearly enjoying her look of chagrin as well as the crossing of her gorgeous eyes that were once again ice-blue. However, the passion didn't vanish. The frosty glare was meant for the ladies not him. If he guessed right, she was about to offer him a drink. She would have allowed him inside her house as well as her supple body.

"Goodnight kisses nothing more. I hope Caro is not telling tales about us."

He turned his gaze her way, noting that if her eyes had not been crossed before they were totally in that position now.

"Someone needs to chaperone the two of you," Honey told him indignantly as if Caro had not paraded in front of him as a willing escort.

The women understood what the two lovers did together three weeks ago had been anything but innocent.

The door closed on his nose.

Duncan hooted with laughter. Everything he needed to know about this lady was coming into place. True, he still didn't know what affair the ball gown was meant for. Nor had he learned why she came to him three weeks ago gifting him with her innocence.

He would.

~ * ~

"What do you think you were doing?" Torra pushed her into the drawing room. "Sit. Tell us everything he did. Did he threaten you? Your brain must be musty with dust. Clear it out. Where that man is concerned you've got to think straight or all your plans will be for naught."

Caroline wasn't at all sure what was happening to her or if she even needed to explain this to her friends. The pair of them understood exactly what they did. They stopped the two of them from making love. She turned her outrage on the pair. "How dare you act holier than thou? The two of you abandoned me. Left me to fend for myself. What was I supposed to do? Walk home? I had no recourse except to accept the ride Duncan offered."

"It was either leave you with a man you needed to sleep with again or risk Scarlett losing her reputation, the house along with everything she owns. While she is wealthy on her own, we need this income." Torra waved her arms in the air before pointing across the street continuing her rant. "She could have lost her business. You do know he threatened. We made the best choice we could on the spur of the moment. I've never been one to think fast on my feet. Didn't have one idea how to respond to that man. He's too devious by far."

Honey lifted her slender shoulders, her eyes narrowing. "Neither can I, think fast."

She understood. Nonetheless, the man was not supposed to be intelligent or devious. That would take mind power. "He told me he threatened you in not so many words. I didn't *ken* what he could possibly hold over the two of you. Scarlett, you say?"

She was horrified he would do something like that. Horrified he would think it, let alone deliver on the intimidation. What would he do if he ever found out about the baby? Her stomach churned. Real fear flooded her. She was beginning to believe he was a dangerous man that he was not at all what he seemed on first inspection.

"This is our livelihood. We couldn't stand by and see what we've worked so hard to accomplish ruined even though Scarlett doesn't need the money. This escort service is our home as well as our means to independence. Two more girls arrived just last week. Two more who need homes, shelter and food. There will be more who come our way. A body can make money betting on that fact. First and foremost, we can't allow anything to happen to this business."

"They also need someone to care for them. At the moment the ladies are healing. Living on the streets takes a lot out of a person," Torra said appearing to relive her harder days when she was one of the many who made their way day by day.

The hunger she endured was still vivid in her mind. If she had not been starving, she would have never given herself to just any man who was willing to pay for her body.

All they said was true. With what she knew as a terrified giggle, Caroline went on to tell her friends. "He offered to help me with my advice column. I didn't know what to say or do. He nearly seduced me in the carriage. It doesn't seem to take much sweet-talking for me to fall into his plans. Could have taken me right then if he wanted to do so. For some reason he didn't want me then. That scares me. What if he doesn't want me again? I'll never conceive."

"Why did he stop?"

The heat he generated still throbbed, pulsed in vulnerable places she didn't want to name. "I *dinnae ken*."

Her arousal was bone deep, experienced through the most feminine parts of her. She needed him to satisfy her now not in a week. He was gone.

"Perhaps we should have not barged in on the two of you. He might have gone inside with her," Honey said thoughtfully. "If you aren't already with child, you still might have conceived. Understand in a week the timing would be for the best, nevertheless, conception might be also possible before then as well as after."

For a moment Caroline thought that too. "No, I'm content you stopped him. Told me he wanted me to beg for him. I don't want to do that. I won't beg. No matter how hard he tries to bend me to his will, I won't plead. After the ball, I won't see the man again. Don't want to be left with the knowledge I beseeched a man to make love to me. The notion would hurt too much."

"Through his machinations he'll end up entreating you for sex. Men are like that. They sometimes believe they can control women through sex. It usually backfires. Men lose all rational thought when they are about to bed a woman, especially one as lovely as you are."

"You wanted him though. Would it have been so bad if you let him make love to you tonight? Maybe your calculations about the best time to conceive aren't correct for your body," Torra told her while she brought her a glass of wine.

"This is all too new to me. This arousal stuff, a man's needs as well as a woman's leaves me baffled. When I wish to tell him no, my body says something entirely different." She looked up forcing back the moisture in her eyes. "There is the guilt too, you know. When I speculate about what I'm doing, deep feelings of remorse course through me. I can make excuse after excuse about my actions. The justifications don't change the reality here. I'm stealing his sperm. I'm a thief. Making a baby without his knowledge, a child I intend to raise as my own never even telling him he is a father. I even plan on lying to him if he discovers the child."

Torra took her hands into hers. "Do you think the man cares about babies? He must have sired dozens of children over the years. There is no gossip I've heard that he's never claimed even one. All he wants from you is the sex nothing more. You've no reason to feel remorse."

"Me neither," Honey echoed the opinion. "Heard lots of talk about him before I left the place where I was living. Nothing about him claiming a bastard as his or giving support despite the fact he is most assuredly the wealthiest man in Scotland."

"Any of the gossip good?" Caroline asked wishing this would end soon. Praying she could escape to Edinburgh until she gave birth. Of course, she needed to conceive first.

Honey took a moment to think, "Actually, most of the gossip was good. He seems to be able to gamble and in the process wins thousands of pounds. Those who invested with his company always made money."

"What does he gamble on?" Caroline asked wondering once more about the man's truthful intelligence fearing once again, she might have made a horrible mistake. Today in the carriage he did not seem to lack intelligence. While he didn't appear to be on the same level as she was, he wasn't stupid.

"Don't have the foggiest notion."

"Back to the matter at hand," Torra brought them back to the present reality. "Still doesn't change the fact now does it? If he's only had sex with women in the business, he would *ken* they took safeguards. He wouldn't worry about withdrawing or using a condom. Would always feel the responsibility was in the woman's hands. Rumor has it he stays away from debutants as well as virgins. Dallies mostly with very young widows who would also understand how to keep from conceiving."

"Except for one," Honey pointed out blandly.

Caroline felt the sting of her actions all the way to her soul. This was not something she was proud of in any way. Still, she wouldn't change anything. She wanted her baby.

"You don't mean to tell him, do you?" Honey gulped her wine as if her decision had a major effect on her.

Much to her chagrin coupled with the devastation of her values she could not. "No. I won't tell him, ever. He will never know he sired a child. The point is mute as it stands now. I need to conceive first."

"Good girl. We've worked and planned this for too long to give up then start being honest with the earl. That just won't do. Won't do at all. Can't let him learn about your tawdry little secret. Although I doubt if he would care, especially since you won't be asking for anything in return."

"No, I won't give up my child. This baby is nobody's baby but mine." She spoke fiercely from the heart.

The earl had everything he wanted whenever he wanted it. Could have a child anytime he chose. This one was hers. Damn his soul. To hell with him!

Torra drummed her fingers on the table, her blue-gray eyes studying her intensely. "You've made up your mind about something. Out with it. We need to know everything so we can be forewarned."

"It's true. I do feel guilty. I'm not going to let that emotion rule my mind. This child is mine. The Earl of Downberry be damned. I won't change my mind about anything we've talked about so the two of you have nothing to fear."

"That's what I want to hear. You understand of course Honey and I will do all in our power to help you. Believe after the ball next week we will have to make plans to spirit you away for a while until you figure out if you're carrying his child, the heir apparent. You certainly cannot stay here where he can get to you while he sees you increase. He would know then. While we doubt if he will care, one never knows how a man will react."

"Now, why did you have to toss that title out? The *bairn* will be a girl, no heir apparent, no claim to the title. He won't care if I keep the child since girls have little to no value when it comes to heirs."

Oh, how she knew that for the truth. She wasn't worth the time her father spent to sire her. True, he did continue to give her a monthly allowance, one she invested.

An amazing man invested her money for her. It seemed yearly she doubled her fortune. The man appeared to understand what would make a good deal as well as when to sell and buy. Actually, her father put her in touch with the company. Now, she sent part of her monthly earnings their way to be invested. She had more money than she needed. More than she knew what to do with. The advice column was merely something she did to keep from being bored to tears. Her passion was discovering more about character traits in humans as well as how they are passed down to the next generation. That's why she looked to the university for respect. She sought a grant along with a lab to do her research. She aspired to uncover mysteries.

Everything in her life seemed to be falling into place. Except for Duncan Murray. It appeared as if he wanted to pursue her, to what ends? He continued to surprise her. After his birthday party, she seriously doubted she would ever see him again.

"It's the truth of the titled," Torra said as she looked from Honey to Caroline then back. "You will be lucky if the *wee* one is indeed a girl. She won't be coveted, as a boy would be. So, we will keep our fingers crossed that the *wee* one is indeed of the female persuasion."

"That's the truth of it. I know firsthand," Caroline murmured wondering how much of her sob story she should tell these ladies.

There was nothing about her past she regretted. Now that she was going to have a baby all her own, she was blissfully happy. Without these women, her dream would have never come to pass.

"You do?" Honey jumped in to the conversation at hand sounding curious. "As do I. Could we possibly share a similar tale?"

The soft whisper of a laugh left Caroline breathless. "Another woman abandoned because she was a girl. I was the first-born. My father is a duke. He had no use for me, a mere female in a male dominated society. He gave no love only monetary things."

"A lofty title. My father is a marquis. Even though I was a bastard, I could remain under his roof if that was what I wanted. It wasn't. He belittled me at every turn. Unwillingly, I left only to find worse circumstances. Miss Scarlett found me, offered me work. All I do is clean. Told Scarlett I didn't want to service any one or even escort a man to a ball or lend company for dinner. Didn't want my reputation besmirched any more than it already was. No one truly knows the extent of what I was made to do. I'm beginning to learn a woman's reputation doesn't mean much in this man's world. It's whatever the man she is with wants to make it."

"For me, I wanted a child more than a reputation. Didn't care if the repercussions came back to haunt my father. If anyone deserves to be embarrassed by his daughter, the duke does. I'll never say his name even though he doesn't warrant the respect I give the man."

She understood the bitterness was bone deep. The ladies heard everything she felt in the tone of her voice. It was, of course, another reason why she wanted a girl. A girl she could make sure reaped the benefit of her knowledge. She could give the child everything that was lacking in her life. Because of her investments, she was independent. It was a state she cherished in this male dominated world. Not only did she own this small cottage on the outskirts of Glasgow, she also owned a townhouse in Edinburgh.

First hand, she understood the limitations placed on a female. Knew that if she were a man, she would have the coveted position at the university she wanted. If she weren't female, she wouldn't be writing advice columns in the Glasgow Herald. No, she would have her research facility at the university and she would be funded. Caroline wanted to make sure her little girl would have everything she ever wanted. Every night she prayed the *lass* would not be a bluestocking.

"My God, I never realized," Torra said, as she seemed to ponder the knowledge. "Does Scarlett know who your father is?"

Caroline studied the two women carefully. Understood their relationship changed at that moment. She hoped it was for the better. Suddenly, she was no longer the woman who lived across the street who baked cookies.

"She does. I told her everything, even the part where my father could ruin her if he wanted. The thing of it is the man doesn't care enough about me to expend the energy to that end. It's not as if Scarlett works here. Scarlett married Bobby so..."

"Bobby has more power than your father. He knows people who

he could call in favors from if the man tried to hurt his wife. He knows disreputable people who would be more than pleased to come to our aid if Bobby asked," Torra said thoughtfully. "At least the two of you are respectable," she laughed softly as she turned her attention to Caroline.

"I'm no longer respectable now, am I?" Caroline did laugh then.

Respectability was something she never thought was worth an effort. Either you were a decent person or you were not. If you slept with a man or not, the fact shouldn't carry shame. The world should treat men and women the same.

It didn't.

Perhaps with time the world with its rules and assumptions would change.

She wasn't about to hold her breath in anticipation.

"Well, if either of you knew my sordid history you would swoon," Torra told them, her eyes darkening as if she recalled bitter times. "There are no lofty titles in my history. Just a despicable past, one I once was ashamed of. Because of Scarlett as well as the Duke of Southcliff, I no longer feel the dishonor along with the humiliation that was so much a part of my life. The two of them gave me reasons to live."

"I don't swoon," both ladies said laughing, Caroline hoping to brighten the sudden downturn in the conversation. "Tell us your history. What brought you to Scarlett's doorstep?"

"As I just said, I've no titled father in my life. Don't even *ken* who my father is. My mother, bless her soul, died when I was thirteen. When she was alive, we didn't have much. However, we did have food as well as a table to eat it on. She provided for us the best she could."

"I'm sorry. What I've been through is nothing. I understand that," Caroline said with conviction.

She disliked her father with a passion. Nonetheless...growing up she'd had every convenience a child would want. Even now, her father checked in on her to see if she needed anything. While he didn't love her, he would always provide for her if she asked. She no longer asked anything from the man.

"How did Miss Scarlett find you?" Honey asked reaching her hand out to enclose Torra's within hers.

There was moisture in Torra's eyes, spiking her dark lashes. Caroline was sure the story would bring tears to her eyes also. Rumors abounded about Scarlett's home, her escort service. Scarlett gave all the things Torra needed without asking questions, allowed each woman to find her way then make choices that were right and sound.

"It seems like a lifetime ago. I found a man who would feed me. I promised to do whatever he asked in return he would make sure I had food to eat as well as clothes to wear. Didn't even care if I had a roof over my head. By the time I met him, I'd slept outside for four years, rummaged in the garbage for something to eat. Survival is what the man offered. In return he pimped me out to anyone who would pay. Most were wealthy gentlemen, aristocrats who were bored with their wives. So, the clothes he provided were the finest money could buy. After all, he meant to impress. As a business man, he wanted his clients to return for more of me."

"Once my father had his heir plus one, he didn't care as much about my mother. He spent more time away from home. Was no longer in her bed every night. Secretly, I think she was happy about that. You might have slept with my father on occasion," Caroline said, a broken sound in the back of her throat. She had no reason to cry. Despite her objections moisture swamped her.

"Mine as well," Honey said her voice filled with a wistful note as if she wished her life had been different. "He was the same. Don't believe he ever loved my mother. She was just there so he could have his heir. If I ever marry, I will only wed for love. Nothing else will do."

Reaching out to touch Torra's hand, Caroline asked, "How did you get away from that awful man?"

Torra sat back a wan smile on her face. "Suppose that's where the Duke of Southcliff comes into the picture. His name is Leslie Stewart. He's the one who first changed my life, Letty next by giving me a chance."

"The Duck of Southcliff is not so much a friend of my father's. They must not be much alike. Do go on," Caroline said.

"It seems the man who pimped me out was Leslie's enemy. He sought revenge. Somehow, he managed to kidnap both Leslie's sister as well as his wife. When the duke rescued his wife and sister, he also rescued me. It seems he knew of Miss Scarlett. Had even used the service a few times before he wed. He found if he arrived places with an escort, the debutants with their mama's left him alone. Anyway, he talked to Scarlett for me. The rest of my story you all know."

"No, my father didn't like Leslie Stewart. Looked down his long nose at the man. Said he was a spy. Told me I should always stay away from men like him, dangerous men even though he worked for the government."

"He was, or is," Torra agreed with her assessment. "The general who I worked for said the duke took a woman from him, kidnapped her right out from under his nose. He was angry."

"Rescued?" Caroline asked. "Was he pimping that lady out also?"

"I heard as much."

"Seems this duke likes to rescue ladies," Honey mused thoughtfully. "When your earl discovers you stole his sperm, you might need some rescuing of your own. Perhaps you could seek out the Duke of Southcliff."

Caroline was all too aware of that probable fact. "You should all be going. I've work to do. A column sitting on my desk as we speak that needs my attention as well as the roses in the back yard." She stood, waiting for the two ladies to leave. "Thank you for your help with my dress. Should I let him pick me up?"

Being obligated to him was a fact she wasn't yet willing to contend with. He would send a message. She could refuse. However, she did intend to sleep with him again. Whether she stayed the night or not was up to him. His man would bring her home in the morning or whenever the earl finished with her. This time she would conceive.

At this point she wasn't at all sure what she wanted. No, that wasn't entirely true she wanted his baby. She didn't want him to learn about the child. Other than that...

"If you need anything, you know where we live," Honey walked from the kitchen and out the back door, Torra following.

She watched them go. Thinking right now about love advice was impossible. Her column would just have to wait until she could think of something besides Duncan along with the way he made her feel.

The latest question, the one her editor insisted she read as well as answer was beyond her to be diplomatic. Her boss always insisted on diplomacy. Glory, what would she say?

I came home early from shopping and found my husband in the drawing room with a naked woman. He was naked also. He smiled at me as if it was the most natural thing in the world. I think he's done this before I didn't ken what to do. What should I tell him?

Good Lord, the devil, she should just tell him she's asking the first solicitor she can find to file for divorce. If the woman did that, she'd most likely be left with nothing. She couldn't very well give that advice. Well, if it was her, she would tell the man to go to hell and never return. She would do it too. Her situation was different. She had the funds as well as the means to support herself. She didn't need a man for anything...well...except his sperm. All she needed was Duncan's sperm to take root in her body.

Another interesting question: *My friend, at least I thought she was a friend, told me she put a curse on me. She said if I didn't stop sleeping with my husband, I'd be sterile. I don't believe in the black arts. Now I'm worried she might actually be able to do something like that. I do want another child. What should I do? Forget what she said or stop sleeping with my husband?*

Then the one: *I was rejected by my fiancé because he saw me with the horse breeder. He thought there was something going on. He didn't even ask me why I was with him. The encounter was platonic. I just had a question before I married him that needed answering. Is there anything I can do to get my fiancé back?*

How would some woman know if another slept with her husband or not? Perhaps she should ask the earl for help. He was definitely more experienced, more worldly than she was. His perspective might be quite different from hers. Maybe he wouldn't be quite so jaded when it came to doling out advice.

Caroline poured herself a glass of brandy. Downed it in one gulp. She decided she needed a few moments alone in her garden where she could smell the roses.

After all, she was the rose lady. The men at the university called her Rose because they couldn't be bothered to find out or even remember her name. Duncan was handing out the awards at the gala. If she accepted, he would discover her last name.

Caroline Kenworth, the daughter of the Duke of Rothmore. She wondered if the two knew each other. She thought they might. If they did...

Just as she told Torra and Honey, she wasn't going to accept the award. He wouldn't discover her name. Even if he did, he might not put the two together.

Glory, but he might.

Where would she be then?

Outside, the scent of roses clung to the air. Her favorite yellow rose, the tops of the petals tipped in pink, bloomed bountifully. The bush overflowed with blossoms. Bent over, she ran the velvet smooth petals along her cheek then down her neck. They were soft as baby's skin. She was sure of that even though she'd never held a baby in her arms or felt any part of one. Her baby brother came along when she was two, the next baby boy two days after she turned four. By that time, she understood her father's feelings about her. She lost interest in her siblings as they arrived. After her each one was male. All told there were six boys behind her.

As she studied the tiny prick of blood on her finger, she did smile even though it was fleeting. One of her objectives in the grafting was to develop a rose bush with fewer thorns. So far, she'd been unsuccessful even though she was sure the feat was possible. She just didn't know how to proceed. She thought of using the pollen. Wasn't sure exactly how to do that. She read everything she could find.

Walking around the front of the house carrying a basket of cut roses to put in vases, a young boy approached.

"Message from the earl for you."

Already? "From the earl?" she queried wondering what he was doing. She accepted the message, tipped the young man.

"He wants a reply."

Of course, he would.

Caro,

Saturday night, Johnston will be at your front door at eight o'clock sharp to bring you to the ball. Don't forget the invitation. I'll be waiting for you there. Remember, I don't take no for an answer. If you don't show up, I'll come get you personally.

Yours, Duncan.

A small ripple of laughter followed her reading of his message. "Tell him I accept the offered ride. Tell the earl also, that I'm looking forward to the ball." *As well as the night after.*

She found that she was looking toward Saturday with pleasure. After she left her father's home, starting out on her own, balls had not been part of her life. She did miss dancing even though as she grew older, she spent most of her time watching.

It would be Saturday before she could blink. She would be sure a baby grew inside her womb. She would have to leave, never see Duncan again. She didn't like that thought, no, not at all.

~ * ~

Two hours until Johnston was to arrive. Caroline closed her eyes. Tried to breathe deeply several times. The air seemed to catch in her throat, only tiny sips traveling all the way to her lungs. For her at least tonight, relaxing was impossible. The strain of her undertaking weighed her down. Perhaps she should stay home. If she did something so preposterous, he would undoubtedly show up on her doorstep. He did say as much. She didn't have to let him in the house. He wouldn't go away until she opened the door for him so he could find out why she lied. At the ball she was afraid someone would recognize her. Her father could be in attendance. He often gave to fundraisers especially if they were for a good cause. The university fit that bill.

"Just what are you brooding about?" Torra asked as she held out a bath sheet for her.

"What do you think?"

"The baby you will conceive tonight?" Honey interjected with a giggle. "That is, if you haven't already."

"No and yes. I'm having second along with third thoughts about going. Not sure it's the wisest choice I've ever made. I should just be content with the fact I managed to deceive the poor man once. To do it a second time is reprehensible." Guilt bore her down.

Torra's eyebrows arched in speculation, "The earl a poor man? You are the first, I'm sure to call him that. He is rich as Midas in too many ways to count."

"In any case you have to go. You don't want all your worrying and wishing to go for naught. You've got this second chance at what you want most in life. You will take it. You know you have to do so."

"Don't back down now that all your dreams are about to come true."

Beneath the bath sheet her hands rested on her flat belly. How long did it take to show? "I won't."

The two words held little conviction. Backing down was exactly what she wanted for herself at this moment.

"Are we going to have to go along with you just to make sure you don't turn around and run as soon as you walk inside the townhouse's ballroom?" Honey chuckled seeming to think her statement was amusing.

"No, it seems I need more backbone, doesn't it? I will go. However, if it doesn't happen this time, I'm not going back for a third try. I'll just mark this one up to fate coupled with the fact I'm not meant to have a baby." She slipped into her chemise and petticoats. "How long does it take to show?"

"The baby to show?" Torra laughed softly her smile sincere. "Way more than a month for you, maybe longer. You're tall and slim. You might barely be sporting a baby bump in three to four months. Every woman is different. Since this is your first it might take even longer."

She found herself nodding her head as if she understood everything Torra told her.

"Let's get you ready. Your hair and everything else is going to take some time. Do you have any jewelry you can wear?" Torra asked. "I would think a duke's daughter should have something."

"When I left, I didn't take anything with me. Didn't want father to think I stole from him even though there were pieces that were given to me. They were mine."

"Then you'll go unadorned. Perhaps that is even better for your purpose. Less to remove when the time comes."

Two feminine giggles followed that comment. Caroline didn't see anything amusing.

Precisely at eight o'clock Johnston arrived. He opened the door to the earl's carriage as the vehicle pulled up in front of her house. She wiped her sweaty palms on her dress, all the while wishing the man was bringing her home instead of taking her there.

Caroline didn't want to admit to the fact. She was terrified. Her hand pressed at her throat, she waited.

He set the stairs down then helped her inside. The ride to the townhouse was slow, very quiet, too nerve wracking. She didn't have anything to say to this man who looked at her with disapproval.

She wanted to yell.

Needed to tell him she wasn't a whore or an expensive escort. But she was. No, she was worse than that. She was a thief, a sperm thief. That was even worse.

Johnston escorted her to the ballroom. Quickly, she slipped inside not wanting to be seen, least of all to be introduced. Finding a place in the shadows she watched the proceedings.

Handsome as ever Duncan stood in front of the assemblage announcing then handing out the awards. His voice was strong just as he was powerful in other ways. She didn't want to think about what they would be doing in a few hours if she got her way.

She couldn't help but think. Her's was the last award to be given. When he began to describe the award then announce her name, she backed farther into the darkness. All she wished for at the moment was to vanish from sight.

"The rose award goes, of course, to the rose lady, Annie Kenworth."

Every one turned to look, to see who was going to accept the not so coveted award. She didn't move. She didn't know why someone chose to use her middle name on the award. She would have to think about that.

"Annie Kenworth?" he questioned still searching the room for movement. "Ah, well, she will be able to pick it up at the university at her convenience. Seems the lady in question didn't want to share her expertise tonight with the rest of the scholars."

He must have seen something. She must have moved. His gaze riveted on her, pierced bone deep. Her breath jammed in her throat. He strode forward, the intent in his movements obvious. Her body froze. Simmering flames seemed to leap from him into her. Heat licked at her, scorching her even from the great distance between them. Her hand rose to her throat while she gulped air. Everything seemed to move in slow motion yet at dizzying speed.

When he reached her, he tugged her into his arms. She gasped in startled surprise. "Duncan?"

"Hush now. Don't say a word. You know I want you...bad."

Chapter Four

"Duncan!"

Ignoring the yell, he swept her over his shoulder, her rear in the air for everyone to see. His hands placed strategically on the small of her back to keep her in place. He wanted to move them lower, stroke and caress to his heart's content. He wanted to cup her adorable backside in his hands. Later, once there was privacy for them, he would do just that.

"Hush. Easy now, don't wiggle now."

He strode further into the darkness away from the patrons of the ball, away from the constant chatter, farther from the music and dancing. Now, anticipating what was to come, he rushed down the narrow servants' stairs to the floor below. He couldn't wait to have her. The entire week he stayed away from her home to make this night sweeter. Perhaps he shouldn't have done that. He didn't think he could wait another second.

Well hell.

It was too damn much. Beneath the skirt of her gown, he ran his hand along the silken flesh of her leg until he reached the waistband of her underwear. Pulled. Let them drop on the steps. Thinking he would retrieve them later. The petticoats found a similar demise. Unable to wait a second longer he squeezed her softly rounded fanny.

"Duncan?" she squeaked while he caressed and teased tender flesh. She twisted. "What? You can't do this now. Not on the stairs." The soft cadence of her voice told him she didn't seem to object too strenuously.

He liked the way his name sounded coming from her lips. Enjoyed the soft breathy sound. So feminine it made his teeth ache. He squeezed again. She wriggled against his shoulder.

His breath ruffled into his lungs with a soft tug then changed to fast and hard. Expectation was killing him, swamping his innards.

94

Beneath his perfectly tailored elegant clothes, he was steel hard. She writhed on his shoulder. He prayed she was as stimulated as he was. He heard steady footsteps following in their wake. The door to the master chamber swung open. Behind him he shut then locked the heavy oak barrier. He was so stirred he thought he would explode. He would if he didn't have her soon. Waiting for the evening had been unbearable. Now she was his. The wait was no longer.

He leaned against the entrance to the master suite, his blood pumping furiously hammering beneath his chest.

"Wrap those pretty white legs around me, sweetheart."

She did. His mouth found hers hard and demanding. His questing fingers found their way beneath her corsage, fondling and toying with the stiffened pink nipples. Her breasts were perfect for him. He wanted to taste them, suck them deep inside his mouth. Later. He slipped his tongue inside her moist warmth while he unfastened his trousers.

"Duncan?"

Her soft throaty use of his name again left him panting as if he was an untried youth with his first female conquest. With patience he didn't think he had, he tested her readiness. Slipped a finger then two inside her sweet core the vibrations he found inside seemed to kiss his fingers. She was hot, wet and throbbing in anticipation of the sensual joining yet to come. He felt sure she wanted him as much as he needed her. She was ready, panting with her desire.

"Now," he told her.

His tongue thrust deeply into her mouth just as he drove his member deep into her. He felt the spasms jerk and quiver around him as her hot core kissed and caressed his shaft. Knew when she lost control of her body.

"Duncan!" She cried out his name as he left his seed inside her.

Sated, now he didn't understand how he could have taken her so quickly. Next time he would move with the slow measured speed he was known for. Undeniably, he was a good lover, not an untried boy. She would beg him for her release. Her head rested on the hollow of his shoulder.

"Duncan," she sighed quietly. "I..."

The pounding on the door throbbed against his back. The threat of intrusion kept her from finishing her statement. He wanted to know what it was she meant to say.

The incessant knocking continued. He slipped his tongue between her soft moist lips. "The devil but that was amazing." He stroked his hand along her back all the while ignoring his brothers who were beating on the door and yelling that he had to get back to the ball. Asking him what the hell he was doing and thinking running off with the lady in blue.

The lady in blue.

He would always know her as the lady in blue. He had guests. Responsibilities awaited him upstairs. He could dally later. No, damn it!

Damn his responsibilities to hell.

As far as he was concerned there was only one guest he wanted to entertain, *the lady in blue.* His brothers could amuse everyone else. That guest was in his arms, her long legs wrapped around him while he was still deep inside her. He meant to continue to amuse himself on his big bed. This time he would taste every part of her, lick everywhere.

"Go to the devil!" he told his brothers. "I'm busy."

"Open the damn door!" Evan yelled at them. "The scandal of this will come back to haunt you. Us. If you don't make an appearance soon, there will be people milling around the front doors by morning wanting to get the scoop on the earl's new bed mate. Your plaything, is that what you want? Hell, you left all her frilly underwear on the steps!"

"Not on your life. I've been waiting all week to hold this woman in my arms. Don't care about scandal."

He was striding with her to the bed. Quickly, he set her down then flipped her over so she was lying on her stomach. If he remembered correctly, he liked her back as much as her front. Well, almost as much. "You've got too damn many clothes on to suit me."

This time he meant to take the loving slow. He wanted to make love to her leisurely so he could prove he wasn't a rutting stoat. Show her he had finesse. He tore off his carefully tied cravat before he slipped out of his frockcoat and unfastened his shirt.

"Damn it, Duncan. Open up. What are we going to tell the guests?"

The question came from Gordon, the youngest and the most naïve of all of them. Hell, there wasn't one thing naïve about any of his brothers.

"Tell them I found the woman I want to spend the night with. Tell them to enjoy themselves as I am. Tell them to eat and drink until the tables are empty. I won't be down."

When he heard the retreating footsteps, his attention turned to Caro and the long row of buttons down her back. Gently, he kissed her nape. "You came. I was beginning to think you weren't going to make it. Was thinking that I was going to have to go fetch you. If I did that, we would not have left your home. Which would have suited me just fine. As you probably can tell I've only your luscious body, every inch of it on my mind."

One fastener came undone. One kiss to her back. He ran his hands through her hair dislodging everything that held it in place. She moaned, the soft sound seeming to emanate from the back of her throat.

Another button. Another tender kiss. A ragged sip of oxygen. A soft mew of contentment.

So it went as he reveled in the tender soft flesh he encountered. Her hips moved, begging him. She hummed and sighed. A strangled sound broke in the back of her throat.

"I hope you don't decide to make an appearance later. I wouldn't be able to go with you. You've made a mess of my hair as well as my gown. I can't breathe. My heart is thundering against my ribs."

Bloody eyes, he did rip a couple of buttons in his haste. He would pay the repair bill. "No, not tonight. Tonight, it is just you and me. I found the week to be insufferably long too long. Seems the bit of foreplay in the carriage from the dressmakers left me aroused as well as ready for you. I've been in that state ever since. The moment I saw you..."

Bloody hell, the moment he saw her he couldn't wait another second. He acted the obsessed fool. No, more appropriately, he acted the rutting stoat. Waiting another few hours to bury himself in her soft heated warmth should not have been that difficult. He would have liked to dance with her. "We were lucky I made it to the bedroom before I plunged inside you. Almost stopped on the stairs. Brothers would have found us."

She shivered.

As he kissed and nipped his way down her back, she groaned, whimpered as well as vibrated with raw passion. Her breath wedged in her throat, making a different noise. His teeth grazed her delectable butt. He felt her responses flow into him to settle deep in his belly then his groin. With each passing second, he was more aroused, more in need, harder than steel. Moonlight was the only light in the room. When they entered, the small space was dark. Thank God for the soft light. He would have regretted not seeing this much of her. This was not enough to see of her. For some reason his Caro didn't like the light. The beams slanted across the whiteness of her back and buttocks. Lightly, he kissed her there then squeezed when his finger could no longer resist the sweetest temptation. By the time he finished undressing her, he brought her to that place of ecstasy twice. He only kissed her once. Once was not nearly enough.

"Not yet, Caro. With you I want to appreciate the moments between us. We need to proceed at a turtle's pace if that is possible."

Truly, he didn't believe he could move that slowly. When he entered her, it wasn't to be. Even with his stillness, even though he didn't move, she leapt mindlessly into the inferno coiling around him, sucking him ever deeper into her sultry core. Her desire rose. Her slick heat pulsated around his member, caressing as well as kissing his length.

"I can't stop...can't do this slowly." Her breath panted from her. She closed her eyes appearing to concentrate on holding back. "I'm trying..."

"Just one more minute, sweetheart. Savor the moment."

Another hitched sound spilled from her lips. Feminine sounds of pleasure crashed from her, embodied her.

When he touched the silken knot in the moisture-laden crevice between her thighs, she shuddered, quivered, coiling tight. "If you want this to be slow, don't..." Her voice was a thin veil of inflamed need. "Don't touch me there."

The devil, he wanted to taste her there where his fingers were, where his rod connected with her. Next time. All that she felt flowed into him then it seemed back to her in silver ribbons of enchanting ecstasy. Their movements were continuous as if they were one body. He became part of her. He felt the moment she lost control, gave herself over to the pleasure, the raging delight.

"Duncan!" He absorbed his name into his mouth, as she could wait no longer for the ensuing ecstasy. Wildly, she was moving with him, against him, pushing him.

He thrust hard, spilling his seed into her again. She lay against him, trembling as the sensations still seemed to wreak havoc in her small frame, her breasts damp with a soft sheen of moisture from the proprietorship of his mouth moved with her shuddering. While he stroked her back, he murmured silliness to her.

He could not get enough of this woman. She was a driving force in his soul. Passion should be her middle name or perhaps her last. He wanted her again. Possibly this next time they could savor each second instead of dashing to the end before the loving barely began.

Thoughts of a lifetime with her surfaced, yet for some reason he didn't think she would consider marriage. He wasn't sure why. Conceivably it was because of the way she held herself aloof from him. Perhaps he just didn't know her well enough. He wanted to learn everything about her.

He rolled over with her in his arms. His rod was still deep inside. They made love several more times. He tasted her. She tasted of woman. Smelled of chocolate and vanilla with a soft lingering scent of roses. He was pleased.

He sat. The bell cord was beside the bed. With a tug he summoned Johnston.

"Keep yourself beneath the covers." He grinned at her thinking of her breasts as well as other sensuous parts of her.

A moment later Johnston arrived with a tray of food and drink. "Sir." He nodded stiffly. "The ball continues downstairs. People are talking about you along with your lady friend. What the revelers are saying is not nice. You would not appreciate the words of condemnation." His look of censure was for him not his Caro, thank goodness. All he could see was the mahogany strands of hair peeking out from behind the quilt. If he didn't get Johnston out of here soon, she would surely smother.

He waved a hand in the air. "It will continue just fine without me.

I've already done my obligatory service. The awards all handed out...except for Miss Kenworth's. I've no obvious reason to remain in attendance. As you well know I don't care what people say about me. Never have cared. Never will."

Johnston nodded toward Caro with a loud hrmph. "Other than the fact two hundred of Glasgow's most elite citizens watched as you hauled a woman over your shoulder from the ballroom. Many are speculating that the two of you are ensconced in this very room. That you are lovers."

"They would be correct now, wouldn't they?" He grinned popping one of the sweet delicacies provided for the fete into his mouth while he thought Caro would love the chocolate ones. He preferred the fruit filled tarts. She would love the ones coated with chocolate and filled with a chocolate cream. When he ordered the delicacies, he specifically asked for the sweetest of the sweet confections. He thought of coating her lips with the chocolate cream then other delicate parts of her. He wanted to lick and taste. Perhaps he should let her lick them from his body. His was a delightful idea.

When the door closed and they were left alone once more he grinned at her as she slowly peaked from the covers. Her eyes were huge pools of blue. She enchanted him, charmed every male sinew of his body.

"Yes, you can come out now."

He chuckled watching her rise from beneath the solid covering. Once she sat with her back against the headboard, she pulled a sheet over her breasts then kept it secured beneath her arms.

"Are those chocolate tarts I'm smelling?"

She leaned over his arm then reached for one. Her sheet slipped from its semi-secure spot revealing a delicately shaped breast. She pulled it back.

"They are."

Duncan watched fascinated as she slowly looked at the morsel, sniffed it then closed her eyes as if savoring the sight or perhaps the scent. "I thought you'd want to eat it." He paused for several seconds. "You don't have to keep yourself covered."

"Oh, I do. But...but the chocolate has to be cherished, every aspect of it." She nibbled the edges before sampling a larger piece. "I think I could eat all of them right now. I won't though. Must save some to enjoy later." With wide eyes peering at him between strands of hair, "Will there be a later? If not, I'm going to eat every one of them."

Of course there would be a later. He meant to keep her in his bed the rest of the night. "Good, because we will need more as the evening progresses to keep our strength up." Everything about Caro amused and delighted him. "Wine?" He held up the bottle.

"Yes, there is nothing better than red wine and chocolate." She sat back sighing, seeming to do so with great pleasure, her face a mask of contentment. After he handed her the glass of wine, she sipped adoringly, her eyes closed, a smile on her kiss-swollen lips. He had to taste them again. He was a besotted fool. He wished she wasn't bathed in shadows. Yearned to see all of her with light shining on her silken flesh.

He didn't remember kissing her enough to make them swell from his ardent attention. What he did remember was the exploding climaxes he never felt with any other woman. After another glass of wine as well as more chocolate, he asked. "What is your last name?" It was something he felt a burning need to learn. He was sure she wouldn't say. That brought more curiosity into play. Why would a woman not wish to disclose her last name? His brows drew together. "Is it Kenworth?"

Her tiny gasp surprised him. The stiffening of her shoulders went along with the swift intake of air as well as his guess.

"No."

It appeared she tried to disguise the truth.

That was too quick. He would look into that, her last name. He had men who could uncover everything anyone wanted to keep secret. Before the next week was over, he would know her every secret. What she wasn't willing to tell him, he meant to discover on his own. Since she purchased a home, it would be child's play for him to discover her mysteries.

"What do you do all day?" she asked, her voice soft, her gaze riveting on his lips as if she meant to twist his thoughts in a different direction.

He lifted his shoulders unwilling to tell her more than necessary, just enough he hoped to assuage her curiosity. "Shuffle papers." It was the truth. He did spend most of his days going through correspondence.

"That must be intriguing," she murmured staring at him over the rim of her crystal glass.

"It can be." He did find his work fascinating. Not as fascinating as he found his Caro. "For a while I thought you were the rose lady." He tossed the notion out to her just to see if he got another response.

She tilted her head appearing confused at his suggestion. "The rose lady? Who is that?"

"Yes, the woman who was to receive the last award but didn't show up, Annie Kenworth. Some people at the university can't seem to remember her name. So, they dubbed her the rose lady."

"I..." She ran her tiny moist tongue across her bottom lip.

Crease lines formed above her eyebrows. She delighted him to no end.

It was apparent to him; she ran his comments through her head, thinking of ways to defuel his assumption. With his thumb he smoothed the creases. He wondered if she tried to seduce or she didn't know what she was doing. The women from Letty's escort service must have tutored her in the ways of seduction. She would *ken* a movement such as that might serve to change the subject. He wasn't going to allow it, at least not while they were still filling their bellies with sweet delicacies.

"I?"

"I am no scientist even though I do love my roses. The rose lady must be important at the university to receive something so prestigious, an award. I've never received an award of any sort," she spoke softly her eyes lowered as if she studied the wine in her glass.

"All the awards are prestigious except perhaps that one. It was simply meant as a thank you for her lectures, the giving of her time. She fills a much-needed gap in the lecture circuit. There was nothing exceptional, no newfound research to change the world accomplished by the lady. The woman comes in to lecture on the grafting of roses when the dean of science can find no one else to fill the schedule."

He saw the narrowing of her eyes, wondered at the simmering anger he read there. If he didn't miss his guess, she was furious.

"Why give the award at all if it is nothing special? Wouldn't the woman think it a travesty? I *ken* why she didn't want to acknowledge the worthless scrap of paper. I've heard all the other men who are gifted with an award are also granted money to continue their research. Perhaps she should be treated equally." The tone in her voice intrigued him with curiosity.

For a moment he felt taken aback at her unreasonable outrage. "You've heard right."

He tapped a finger on his glass still searching for some reason for her unusual answers coupled with the intensity of her comments. Would she lie to him since she didn't want to answer his question about her last name?

"What do you like to do for fun?" Flirtatiously she winked at him her body position changing dramatically as if she wished to cover her fury.

Again, it seemed she meant to twist the subject from the rose lady. "Fun?"

He never truly considered anything like that. Fun wasn't something he had time for during the day. He supposed the time he spent with his Caro could be labeled as fun.

"You know, things you like to do when you are not shuffling papers at your office." She finished her wine before she eyed another chocolate confection.

"Those things."

"Yes."

She reached for another chocolate tart. He selected a lemon one with powdered sugar on top.

Slowly, he licked the lemon, savoring the delicious flavor. He wanted to do the same to her breasts. Their flavor would be tastier, he was sure. Perhaps he should coat her nipples with the lemon filling. Deep in the back of his throat he groaned at the very idea.

"I enjoy riding my stallion. Do you ride?"

He was being suggestive. However, she didn't take the bait. The devil, he craved for her to ride him.

"Not for a very long time. Before I left home, I had a mare. She was brown with four white stockings." Surprisingly, she looked stunned.

It seemed to Duncan she said something she didn't want to give away. "Before you left home. Can I assume that is another question you don't mean to answer?"

She smiled at him then. After pouring more wine she sipped, her lips on the crystal suggestive. She closed her eyes. With her tongue she pushed at her top lip.

"We could go riding. My stallion is pure black. He's powerful, difficult to control. I wouldn't want you to ride him though. I know I've a mare in my stables that will be suitable for you."

"I fell off my father's stallion." She shuddered. "I thought I could ride the beast. Was forbidden not to."

"You disobeyed your father often?"

Her smile was impish. "Whenever I could. He was a tyrant."

He meant to ignore her answer. When he thought on what she told him, she did strike him as a woman who would do what she wanted when she wanted to do so. "You aren't strong enough to control a mount such as that. He would have to be gentled first."

He took the glass from her hand. Set it on the nearby table. His hands on her waist he lifted her so she straddled him. "You can mount this stallion if you like. You can even gentle me if that is possible. I'll let you take charge of the ride, do whatever you would like. You are most definitely strong enough to control me."

The look she shot him was filled with both innocence as well as the very realization of what he wanted. "Duncan?"

"I won't allow you to fall off."

He throbbed against the hot, slick dampness he encountered between her slim legs. Her breasts filled his hands. Gently, he squeezed. Decided to taste. Thought to run the lemon of his tart on one nipple then suck the creaminess off, suck and nibble until she whimpered and moaned, until she cried out his name. She was so damn passionate. The fire raged and flamed inside her with little provocation.

"You want me to mount you?" she queried her voice breaking as she asked him, her eyes wider than he'd ever seen them.

"Whatever you like? It's up to you. Do believe we would both find the riding exceptionally fun. What do you like to do for your personal enjoyment?" He decided this riding of his member was more exciting than the other type of riding.

She bent over him, touching him, licking the hard tip of his nipple. A groan of pure male ecstasy rumbled up from deep in his chest. His hands settled around her waist, lifting again. The tip of his rod encountered the wet entrance to her center.

The moist hot tip of her tongue swept across her lips. "I think I like to do this too. Enjoy the control, what little there is of it," the words tumbled softly from her mouth. "I like to feel you deep inside me."

Another groan he couldn't stop lurched forth. She said the most provoking words. "Sit on me, *Lass*."

Slowly, she lowered herself on his shaft. Her tiny hot center tightened around his length. She pleased him. Oh, did she ever please him.

Caro caught her bottom lip beneath her teeth. She rose then lowered herself. Her eyes crossed as her small head fell back. He understood she would reach the peak of her desire sooner than he wanted her to. Figuring out how to slow her climax down was beyond his abilities. Everything about her delighted him. It took only a well-placed kiss to set her on a path of no return. This was heaven. His hands behind her back, he brought her lower. Her breasts tasted just as he expected. He gave attention to both alternating from one to the other as she tried to move on him. Sucking them deep into his mouth, nipping and licking, he grinned as he heard the soft female mews of pleasure with each caress of his tongue. As he held her still, he felt her frustration build.

With patience he didn't know he possessed, he kept her from moving on him. Instead, she arched her body, coiled as she fought against his strength to ride him harder and faster. He would be in control. He would decide when she climaxed. He held her body tight to him, refusing to allow her movement.

Ha!

She reached that point of no return without his male consent. Her head thrown back she was flushed with the heat. "Duncan!" she cried out again, screaming her pleasure. The pulsating of her beautiful body brought his own release as he emptied himself deep inside her.

Caro fell against him. He stroked her tangled hair. Held a strand to his nose to drink in the persistent scent of roses. It was the only part of her that didn't smell of chocolate and vanilla. No, her hair carried the delicate scent of roses. For a fleeting moment he thought about protection. Reminded himself Torra would have schooled her in the art. There was nothing to worry about. She would not conceive.

He realized suddenly he would like Caro to increase from his seed. Feasibly he should see if that was something she might also want. If he had a bastard, he would legitimize the child. His son or daughter would carry his last name. He made a mental point of asking her later. At the moment there were more urgent needs to see to.

They didn't sleep for the longest time. Eating and drinking until they were satisfied, they would make love again. It was a cycle he repeated for the night. Repeated until she could keep her eyes open no longer. She yawned, a hand against her mouth. He would need to let her sleep.

They had much to talk about.

In the morning, he would have Johnston see her home. In the afternoon he would take her riding. Before that he would set one of his men to ferret out as much information about Miss Caroline as could be discovered. Her last name would be nice to know. He couldn't be positive Caroline was her first name. The more he knew about her the easier it would be to deal with her and whatever whim possessed her to keep her identify a secret from him.

When the morning light of dawn crept through the window, she still slept. He supposed she needed it since he kept her up until the *wee* hours of dawn. Her column would be the first thing they did when he brought her home. For the first time, she would hear a man's opinion.

He wanted to make love to her again.

Instead, he rang for a bath. Perhaps they would find the moment this afternoon.

~ * ~

She woke to his kiss. His mouth was soft, on her forehead. When she looked at him at the way his brows were drawn together, she instantly understood something was terribly wrong. "What is it?" She touched his face. The stubble from a day's growth rasped across her fingertip. Felt the tension in his jaw. Saw the not-so-subtle tick of his muscle.

"As soon as you dress and eat, we will leave. Would you like a bath? There is hot water waiting for you. I'll be back in ten minutes."

His voice was brusque, curt as well. She wondered at the change a morning could bring.

He didn't give her a chance to answer his question. She did want a bath. Would love to have something other than her ball gown to wear home. Knew that wouldn't happen. Her hand rested hopefully on her belly. With any luck she would be pregnant. In about three months according to Torra, she would begin to show perhaps sooner if she conceived the first time. His seed was perfect for her child. When he explained to her he spent his days shuffling papers, the news delighted her. He was no professor at the university as his two brothers were. He was far from being a genius. His days were spent sorting papers, a task anyone could perform. It was probably something his brothers gave him to keep him busy or perhaps give him the feeling of self-worth.

She enjoyed his Scottish brogue. Understood no learned or intellectual man in this era would speak in anything but unaccented English. It seemed the only time he spoke with the brogue was when he was aroused. The thought gave her a moment's pause.

When he returned in ten minutes, she was dressed. He set a tray of food on the table. Standing back, leaning on the door where he took her first last night, he smiled at her.

"You should eat unless you wish to return home now. I did so earlier."

He stood at the window, looking down on the front of the house. His hands behind his back, he rocked on the balls of his feet, swearing softly as he did so. Now, his hands were stuffed into his trouser pockets as if he wasn't quite sure what to do with them.

"I'll eat. I'm sure there is nothing so good waiting and prepared for me at my place." She watched waiting for him to tell her what had him so agitated. Having never seen him in this type of mood, she worried somewhat. Unable to resist asking, "What has you swearing beneath your breath? You look as if every nerve is stretched to the breaking point."

"My brothers were correct in their assumptions last night. I was too caught up with pleasuring you as well as myself that I was unwilling to listen. I don't regret anything we did. Do you?" He turned to regard her, his brows creased as if expecting a negative answer.

"I don't recall what they said through the door. Probably wasn't paying too much attention. It seemed you had other ideas as did I."

She broke off a piece of bacon, chewed thoughtfully studying the soon to be father of her unborn child. She was pleased with her choice. If she had a boy instead of a girl, she hoped the little one would look just like his daddy. By far he was the most handsome man she'd ever come across.

He turned, waving his hand in the air before sweeping it through his sandy colored hair. "Doesn't matter. I would have carried on in the same manner if I'd listened. Simply put, Caro, I can't seem to resist you. Don't want to either."

"What manner was that?" she teased slathering a large piece of freshly baked bread with butter and honey. Her stomach grumbled asking for more food.

"I'm hurt that you don't remember the fun we had last night. Speaking of fun, I'm taking you riding this afternoon. Do you recall agreeing to the outing?" He held up his hands to ward off her refusal. "No, the normal type of riding. I've the perfect mare for you."

"No." She'd never agree to something so outlandish that he'd discover exactly who she was. She didn't dare do anything else with this man outlandish or otherwise. Didn't dare begin to care more for him than she did now. It wasn't fair of him to expect anything more than what happened last night. Sex with him certainly couldn't happen again.

"No?" He arched a sandy brow upward. "Why ever not? Riding through the park sounds like a perfectly acceptable past time to me. Don't you want to do acceptable activities?"

She wanted to smile. The task was difficult. She endeavored to keep the grin behind her teeth. He had this way of arching one, just one eyebrow when he questioned her choice of words. One day last week after the carriage ride, she spent at least ten minutes trying to do the very thing, arch one brow. Nothing worked for her.

"How do you do that?" she asked as once again she tried to arch just one of her eyebrows.

"What? Don't start changing the subject on me. Why won't you ride?"

He paced the room, stopping occasionally to glower at her before he stomped to the window to scowl at whatever was going on below.

The answer was truly very simple. "If I'm to put food on my plate, I have to work."

Besides, if they rode then he would find some way to stay at her home. If he did so, he would make love to her again. She wouldn't stop him. She was incapable of such a feat.

"I can make sure you have all the food you can eat." His voice was solemnly persistent.

She searched for an underlying meaning. Flushed to the tips of her toes, she swallowed hard. "You misunderstand my feelings for you, Duncan. While I enjoyed last night as well as the one before that, I won't be your mistress. Will not let you keep me in style or otherwise until you grow bored. Won't allow you into my bed whenever doing so pleases you."

She tried desperately to sound blasé. Didn't believe her words or her tone were issued in the manner she intended.

"Never said anything about your being my mistress. You presume too much. Never possessed a mistress. Never will. More trouble than they are worth. Our relationship would be one of mutual satisfaction. The title of lovers would be more apropos. You would never be bound to my whims. If you wish to say no, then that would always be acceptable."

Well, perhaps she did presume more than she should. "What is it you actually intend if not keeping me as a mistress? I could only assume that your intention of feeding me meant just that, unless of course, you mean to come to my residence to cook my meals. I'm an abominable cook. Could always use a good chef. Although the cook I have in my employ is acceptable."

He paused thinking, as if he tried to figure out what he did truly mean. Without saying more, he walked to the window again his hands grasped behind his back. "We need to leave secretly or as secretly as one can under the circumstances. I would like to see you this afternoon. If not to ride perhaps I could help you with your column. Give you a man's perspective. Would you like that?"

"I would thoroughly enjoy a man's perspective." A long breath of air shimmied from her lungs in a deep sigh. "If I gave in and let you help me, we both know that I would get nothing accomplished. You would take me to my bedroom or perhaps you would choose to have me in front of the fireplace or on the dining room table. In any case the where doesn't matter. It's the what that we have to be aware of. I have to work to feed myself, to pay the mortgage as well as my other bills."

"You think I have no control?" He laughed long and deep, a laugh emitted straight from the belly.

"Perhaps it is just me. Where you are concerned, it seems I've none. The way you look at me melts my insides turns them into liquid heat. Why the feeling is as if I've eaten butter on bacon. What's a mere woman to do in such circumstances, I ask?"

"What else do you feel?"

He stepped closer, closer than she wanted. His knuckles brushed against her cheek for a quick second before he returned his attention to the lawn below.

"What are you watching in your front yard?" Curiosity spurred her to see for herself. She rose, walking to stand by him.

"Snakes milling around, waiting for their pray might be an appropriate description of what I see below. If I fail to protect you, they will rake you over the coals."

His gruff voice surprised her. She didn't understand why she needed protection.

"What is there to damage? I care not for a nonexistent reputation. I won't attend galas or fetes. Your world is not mine. I owe no one an explanation as to my actions. It has been that way for years."

Ah, but if he ever discovered her ruse, she would certainly owe him one.

"What if I want you in mine?" he snarled surprising her. "What if

I don't want your person undermined?"

This man might be more dangerous than she presumed. He could not possibly want a commoner for a wife. He turned down her mistaken notion he wanted her for his mistress. "You have no say in what world I'm part of. I enjoy what I do. That's all that is necessary for you to understand. Don't want to be a part of all this opulence."

Indeed, years ago she ran from more lavishness than this. If he kept seeing her, it would not be long until he realized she was a genius. Would not be long when he would come to understand she didn't fit in his world even though she came from lineage higher than his. He would no longer want her in any way.

"I'm not letting you go. We should speak of this later. Need to see you safely home first." He stopped when the knock on the door caught his attention.

"I've the cloak you asked for." Johnston stepped into the room with the garment, his expression grim. "You do realize you brought this on yourself, Sir."

"You want to hide me while we race through the milling snakes," she laughed softly thinking about these people.

If they knew the truth of what she was about, if they understood the identity of her father...there would be more vipers down below asking questions.

"Yes," his short and abrupt reply obvious and curt to her ears. "I want to protect you."

These two men did not interact as servant and employer should. "Suppose it might be a good idea," she conceded.

True, someone out there might recognize her. When and if her father discovered this dalliance, there would be a different kind of hell to wage. Duncan would pay even though he was not the aggressor nor did he deserve the wrath her father could bring down upon his head. She reconciled herself to the fact she didn't need her father's groats or anyone else's a long time ago. Had more than enough of her own. Her investments were in more than capable hands.

He took the cape from Johnston's hands. Fastened it, he secured the fabric around her shoulders before pulling the hood over her head. He smiled at her. Touched the tip of his finger to her chin.

"You should look down. Don't want anyone to see your face. Could be detrimental to our escape."

"That hardly matters since no one knows who I am."

She hoped and prayed no one in Duncan's front yard could identify her. More than a year passed since she saw her father longer than that since she lived with him. It would be hard to place her as the duke's daughter although not impossible.

"You can't be sure of that. We will go through the main rooms then to a side door. There is an entrance to the carriage house we can take without going outside." He held out his hand. "Come. The cloak is for some accidental happening we've no control over."

Down the steps to the first floor his gait was hurried though not so fast she couldn't keep up with him. After they were both safely inside the vehicle, the doors to the exit opened, slowly the carriage began to move.

"Will they follow us?" she asked as she made a tiny slit in the curtain and peered outside. She didn't want to think about walking through these people to get to her front door.

"I'm sure if any one of them has a buggy or a horse, they will follow the carriage. I could think of no possible diversion to send them in a different direction. You said you didn't care if you were discovered. The problem is that I care about you, about the repercussions. Your name might be smeared in the Herald. If that occurred, you could lose that job you say you need to pay your bills."

His last words hit home, giving her unease at the thought. They sat in silence as the big carriage with the earl's emblem on the side trundled through the streets of Glasgow to her home. At least, she thought that was where they were headed. He might have other ideas though. The inkling he would take her someplace else sent a lump to her belly.

What to do if he did?

"You are taking me home?" she queried noting the hesitancy in her voice. She didn't want to show fear.

When he answered in the affirmative, the pounding of her heart eased slightly. Home? Actually, that could be anywhere he considered home. With the heady feeling of relief, she emitted when she finally saw Scarlett's home then her own caused him to smile.

"What, you didn't believe me?" he arched a supercilious eyebrow heavenward. "I wouldn't lie to you. Will never lie to you. I promise this."

Deciding to be honest, "After our earlier conversation, I had a few doubts."

"With good reason. Taking you to my country home to keep you safe did cross my mind. I rejected the idea simply because I want to keep you happy. In your home you will be safe enough once the furor dies down. However, if I were you, I'd think more than once before I stepped a foot outside your door for the next few days. Who knows how long they will stay? I am hoping they will disappear when I leave. The snakes need to leave you alone. Since they don't know who you are, they will sink their fangs into me."

"If I do step outside?"

She didn't want to fear for her life. Didn't want to feel confined to the inside of her home. A home was not intended to be a prison. "Are you leaving?" Caroline was no longer sure of anything.

"They will hound you with questions. Would you rather I take you from the city? Very few would follow. My manor house has a gated entrance. They would have to scale the wall to get inside. I've also men who would be dispatched to keep them where they belong."

He leaned forward, taking her hands into his. They were cold. He warmed them. She felt the power inside the man, the protective nature.

"I'm going to walk with you. I'll even stay inside for a short time. You did say you had work. Tell me you understand."

Nodding, she stared at him wondering at the easy trouble she could find. A month ago, no one knew her. She didn't have a care in the world. Well, except for the advice column she had no business writing. It seemed, however, people loved her opinions on how to act when confronted with troubling situations with the opposite sex. So, why was she having so many difficulties in dissuading Duncan?

Because I care for the man.

Because he makes me explode with delight.

She cared more for the man than she wanted to admit. Deep inside she understood her feelings for him were more than the amazing sex they had together. Guilt simmered deep in the pit of her belly. She was a robber of the worst sort. The devil, if he ever discovered her deception, no her deceptions. In her mind there was definitely more than one lie. She tried to swallow the huge lump of guilt forming in her throat.

A sinking feeling of discovery flooded her, drowned her in horrific thoughts. Secrets always had an uncanny way of being discovered. They could become nightmares. Somehow her gut told her he would learn what she was up to. Torra and Honey told her he would never forgive her if her trickery came to light. They cautioned her that this idea of hers might not be well thought out. Cautioned her to reconsider. Told her it might well backfire.

Well hell and damnation.

It was far too late to reconsider. She wanted the baby. Her baby, no one else's. This baby she prayed she carried would never be Duncan's. He would never know about the child.

The carriage stopped. The driver opened the door, placing the stairs for her to use. Duncan leapt to the ground extending his hand for her. Around her questions were shouted.

She wanted to cover her ears.

"Who is the chit?"

"Did you sleep with her before last night?"

"Is she going to become your new mistress?"

"Why was she at the ball?"

"Some say she's a good horizontal. Is she?"

The lewd and outrageous questions continued nonstop as Duncan wrapped his arm around her waist drawing her as close as he could. Unable to stand the horrible words, she covered her ears with her hands. Silently, they hurried to her front door. In his arms she trembled. Heat swept through her. Suddenly, she understood her life might never be the same.

She did this to herself.

How to fix it?

Close to her ear, he whispered, "Try not to pay attention to them. I'm not going to leave you here alone. We should have gone to the country. Fewer would have followed. Only the most blood thirsty of the serpents would have dared go that far for the story. A sordid tale people will forget about in time. All they need is another scandal of some sort to have them dashing in a new direction."

"I don't see how what the two of us do together can be an interesting story. I'm nobody. There is no reason for anyone to care."

He looked away for a moment, pinching the bridge of his nose between two fingers. "Unfortunately, I'm not. It's not so much who we are. It's what I did last night at the ball, a ball that was a fundraiser for the university. I acted a complete ass. If we'd stayed, danced a few dances, sipped some punch before we disappeared no one would have noticed. That is the story. They are all wondering, after so many years, what woman caught my attention so intensely that I would forgo decorum to create a scandal of this magnitude. It seems when you are near me, I can think of only one thing."

"Who are you really?" Inside, she turned in his arms. He shut the door with a violent bang. "I'd like to know the truth."

"Just a man who wants you so desperately that I cannot think straight. I can barely breathe when I first see you. My heart forgets it is supposed to beat to keep me alive. For the love of God, I've never felt this way before. What is it about you that has me acting in ways I've never behaved in my entire life? This is not my true nature." His breath rushed out raggedly.

She yearned to console him, instead she blurted her feelings. "God help me. You do the same to me. I don't know what it is. Unlike you, I don't have experience in *amour*. Though somehow, I *ken* this is different."

Immediately, she regretted her words. She could not take them back.

With no hesitation as if he felt now exactly the way he just described to her, his mouth crushed down upon hers as his tongue thrust inside. Deep in the back recesses of her throat she whimpered while she wound her hands around his neck then pushed her body as close as she could next to his. Dear God, but this was something she couldn't say no to. She was desperate to feel him become part of her. She wanted to take his penis into her mouth, until he howled with his pleasure.

If he thought he lost control, he had no idea what happened to her. When she was with him, when he looked at her, she couldn't form a coherent thought. Couldn't breathe. When he kissed her, she spun wildly into erotic and magical places that seemed to be her imagination. When she lost all control, she knew everything that was happening to her was very real.

She pushed away as she regained her senses understanding this ill-fated relationship between them should not be encouraged. "Don't."

Heavy breaths attempting to make their way from her lungs caused her to pause. "We can't. If you stay, if you continue in this vein, you won't leave. I won't get my work finished. More rumors will start. The scandal will continue until we are both devastated."

The devil, she was so aroused she didn't think she could work now. She wanted to feel his penis deep inside her vagina. Needed the feel of his weight covering her while he kissed her everywhere.

He swept his hands through already disheveled hair. "I'll leave..."

He turned from her then turned back, "Bloody blessed hell." He lifted her in his arms, his hands tightening around her buttocks, squeezing. "I find I cannot leave. At least not yet, not until I taste you one more time. This is insane."

"No!" She pushed from him, her finger touching her lips where his mouth had been seconds before. "You have to go. I'm serious. I cannot dally with you. The column is due first thing in the morning. It will take time to calm myself. At the moment I'm shaking so hard I will not be able to stand."

"If you allow me, I'll take you to the highest high then I will calm you. Will soothe all your shuddering nerves. I can leave then before we are tempted again or I can stay and help you as I would prefer."

"No." Her voice was certainly calmer than she expected. She sipped in a tiny breath of air.

"Very well, are you going to take your advice to the paper? You can't. You know that don't you?"

Suddenly, she realized what he was asking of her. If she left the house, they would follow. They would discover just exactly who she was.

Because she was reclusive in nature, the paper always sent a messenger to take her column. She would not have to leave her home for any reason.

"No, they send someone to pick it up."

"Thank God," he murmured as he gently touched her cheek with his knuckles. "With great difficulty, I'll leave now. You can finish your work. I won't come back this afternoon for a ride. Don't suppose that would be prudent under the circumstances. Although a different kind of ride than the one I planned would be possible."

His grin was wicked. Last month she would not have understood what he alluded to.

Today, at his words, heat rose to her cheeks precipitously understanding what type of ride he was speaking of. "Thank you..."

She closed her eyes wishing she didn't have responsibilities. Wishing he loved her. The thought stopped her cold. No man would ever love her. She was too strange, too different, far too intelligent. A bluestocking was how men described her. The name was not meant to be complimentary. Men wanted women who didn't have an intelligent thought in their pretty little heads. She wasn't like that.

For a moment he looked away. "I'm going to be out of town for a few weeks. I have to go to London on business. Don't actually know how many weeks. Depends on things along with what transpires. If you need anything, send a missive to Johnston. He's not really a bad sort. He likes you. Thinks I'm taking advantage of you, which I am. He will come to help you. Do you understand? No matter what you've endured in the past or what you might think today, you're not by yourself."

She nodded while watching him leave. Her heart lodged in her throat as she understood what she'd done to this man with her selfishness. Nothing would change. She was going to depart. She had to never see him again. Escape somewhere he would never find her. Sobs tore through her as she watched the Earl of Downberry's carriage sprint swiftly from her home. In the process he was leaving her for the rest of her life.

Caroline wrapped her arms around her body. Tears flowed, dripped from her chin as she realized she would never see the love of her life again.

She would never see him again.

Her love?

~ * ~

The next morning, she sent the column to her editor. Unable to go outside, she began packing essentials beginning with her clothing. The townhouse in Edinburgh was purchased a little over a month ago with her escape from Glasgow in mind. It was furnished and waiting for her. A trunk of clothing would be sufficient. As she increased, she would purchase more.

All she had to do now was wait until the pack of reporters dwindled from her front lawn. There weren't many now. She assumed the majority of them followed Duncan to the city. Surely, they wouldn't shadow him all the way to London. Certainly, they would have to let this scandal die a natural death.

She rested her hand on her belly. In two weeks' time she would know if she carried his child. Would know if her immoral plot to steal his sperm worked. At this instant in time, she didn't like herself very well. Over the next years she'd have to learn to live with the depravity. When she held her little girl in her arms, she would know peace for the first time in too many years to count.

He might look for her. When she thought about that, she doubted he would do so. She was just a woman who graced his bed two wonderful nights. At least she thought they were truly amazing. She hoped he thought the same. Perhaps she didn't hope that. If he did, he might not let her go so easily as she prayed.

The fact that Duncan left for London played nicely into her hands. She meant to take advantage of his absence. Originally, she didn't plan on leaving until she knew if she conceived. At this point she needed to capitalize on any good fortune that came her way.

If she found she needed something more, she would have to buy it in Edinburgh. She didn't dare risk asking the ladies to help her out. Duncan was crafty. He might put a man on them in hopes of finding her. If he did want to find her, which in her mind was still dubious, she would need to take care. He threatened their livelihood once to find her. He might do so again. His scruples seemed to be nil. He was ruthless, a characteristic she didn't see before.

Still, she needed to proceed as if he would look for her. Caution needed to be at the forefront of her mind. The paper she worked for would be more than willing to give him an address if he asked.

What the devil had she started? One domino after another fell, each piece dooming her. Quitting work at the Glasgow Herald was her only option. She wished she'd thought of it this morning. A message could have been sent along with her column. The prudent and logical action would be to disappear with no trace left behind. She wouldn't give anyone her address, especially not the ladies across the street.

Duncan Murray had the means to hire men to find her. She understood his wealth was impressive. Her life was unraveling at the seams even though she was about to have what she'd dreamed of for the longest time.

Looking out the window, she longed for one last walk in the rose garden. That was something she would miss. The next eight to nine months would feel like a veritable lifetime. She prayed then that the time to wait would only be eight months.

Wicked shivers of fear swept down her spine. If he did look for her, there were too many ways to count for him to find her. He could ask questions at the paper. Even if they didn't have an address to give him, she used her name to sign all the documents when she purchased her new home. The bright spot was the fact he didn't know her last name. With the proper resources, discovering her name wouldn't take him more than a ride to the paper.

He wouldn't know she went to Edinburgh. Maybe she should have settled on a quiet village somewhere in the highlands. She didn't suppose it was too late to change her plans. No, it would be easier to lose herself in the city.

More people.

More houses.

Well, she still didn't believe he would waste energy on looking for her. She was worrying herself for no reason.

"You home?"

It was Torra at the back door. She supposed Honey was a few steps behind. When she opened the door, the two women literally tumbled inside giggling, chattering as they swept by her.

"All this ruckus," Honey said laughing as she quickly let the door slam in a reporter's face. "You and the earl must have had one wild night. What happened?"

"He was incorrigible." Amusement at the ladies' comments lightened her spirits. "Yes, it was a wild night. One I will affectionately remember for the rest of my life."

Her hands dropped to her belly. She hoped Duncan would look on the evening fondly.

"Incorrigible, you say," Torra poured herself a cup of tea before helping herself to a scone. She winked at her, smiling an all-knowing smile. "That sounds absolutely decadent."

"You and your earl were on the front page. Said he had you hiked over his shoulder as he disappeared down the steps to the second floor. There was even an artist's rendition of what transpired. Is it true?" Honey asked with wide-eyed disbelief. "In some ways that's very romantic."

Caroline felt the heat of her blush. In some ways the act was more barbaric than romantic. She sucked in a ragged breath. "That part, yes. Don't know what else was said. Once he saw me, he didn't give me a moment to breathe." She couldn't tell them everything, especially not the way she responded to him. Wanton was the only description that leapt to her mind.

Filled with lust, they both were.

"See your starting to pack up. Isn't that a bit premature?" Torra was watching her closely. "Thought you would wait two weeks before you left long enough to know the truth."

She felt the urgent need to be away from Glasgow today. The carriage to take her to the city would be here tomorrow morning. "He's away in London on business. Duncan didn't know how long he'd be gone. As persistent as he is, there might not be another time to leave quietly. This way there will be no protest. He will return. If he cares to come see me, he will discover I'm no longer living here."

"Of course, you don't even know if he'll look for you," Honey reminded her thoughtfully. "What are you taking with you?"

"Mostly just my clothes. I've decided the best course of action is to quit the paper. Don't need the money. If he did search, he could get my address from the Herald. Can't risk that. The townhouse is furnished. Most everything else can all stay here."

"If he wants to, he'll find you. Won't be too hard. With his resources..." Torra let the rest of the sentence hang.

She was sure Torra was trying to tell her even though his intelligence level wasn't equal to hers, he would find her. The resources were his, to employ men to discover where she was.

"He won't look."

She didn't truly believe that statement, not after the way he acted last night then into the morning when he wanted to stay with her, make love to her again.

Today the last kiss he gave her was hard as well as demanding. He wanted her then and there. It was only her ardent no that stopped him from tossing her skirts. At the time she was sure he would back her up against a wall, just as he did last night.

"You're deluding yourself if you mean to believe that nonsense. As sure as I'm sitting here, that man will look for you," Honey told her. "You must hide well if you don't want him to discover your subterfuge."

"Most assuredly," Torra agreed while she tapped a slim finger on her chin, as was her habit. "It's pride, a man's pride is at stake. He'll search until he finds you. What he does after that is anyone's guess."

"Best you figure out a diplomatic way to tell him you're breeding and your condition is with his child. Not only did you not bother to tell him, but you moved keeping him from discovering that fact in the normal way," Honey said, her voice soft as if she just understood some of the repercussions awaiting Caroline.

"I don't see how he can find one inconspicuous woman in a city that size." Caroline was deluding herself. She knew that for the truth it was. All he had to do was use his resources whatever they were. She was positive he could also call-in favors if not from his brothers, then his friends.

"You could take a ship to America. He might not think to look for you there," Torra gave her opinion, one she might want to take.

She tossed her a lofty smile as if she understood the impossibility of such a trip.

"Don't you think, even if he doesn't find you, that it's a bit convenient for you to show up back in Glasgow nine months after you disappear carrying a *wee* babe on your arm? What if the child looks just like him? He would suspect," Honey said all the time she was shaking her head.

"What then?" Torra asked.

"He's not smart enough to figure all that out or put the pieces together. I'm not worried. He won't be able to put two and two together to come up with a baby."

Caroline pulled out dishes then put them back. She walked into the main room then back. She fluffed a pillow then repeated the process with the other ones.

"Don't think a man has to be that smart to realize the woman's belly he's been plowing has a child inside. He *kens* you were a virgin a short month ago. As far as knows he's been your only lover."

She sucked in a deep breath of air. "If I don't believe this will work, I'll go crazy. This baby is mine. Only mine. He won't find me, he won't. He's not going to take this child from me. I won't allow that to happen." She had to convince herself.

"We have talked about the consequences. You are aware if he discovers what you are about, he can tear the *wee* one right from your arms."

Torra set her hand on top of Caroline's, as if that gesture would lend comfort.

"He won't." Her confidence was slowly being ripped from her just as the child would be if Duncan discovered the scam.

"The two of you will continue to help me."

She needed assurances from them. This was all too much right now to handle.

"Lie for you?" Torra asked with a note of disdain. "We can't lie if he threatens Miss Scarlett. This is our livelihood. I'm certain for sure that I don't have to remind you; it's all we have. If he does that, you'll have to take your chances with him. Who knows those chances might benefit you as well as the babe?"

"I've already asked too much of the two of you, Scarlett as well. Do what you must to protect yourselves. You won't have my address so you can't give me away."

Caroline watched as the ladies she called friend walked from her home, battling their way through the last remaining reporters circling the house.

The horrible feeling in her gut told her they were most likely correct in their assumptions. She was naïve to think for a second if he wanted to find her, he wouldn't. She was gambling on the fact he wouldn't look.

Taking her chances was still her only option. She supposed she could plead ignorance. Tell him she didn't know what she did would give her a baby. No, she would never lower herself that far. Something so absurd wasn't in her nature to lie about. Eventually, if he found her, she would speak the truth.

Chapter Five

Duncan Murray's fist crashed on the solid cherry wood desk in his office. The man he hired to find Caro jumped at the impact. He didn't believe he'd ever, in his entire life, been this angry. She left him, disappeared with no trace. This man was here to find her.

Caro was gone, vanished. His heart hammered.

What the devil happened to her?

He went to her home to see her as soon as he returned from London. No lights shone in her house. He knocked. Beat on the door. Still, she didn't answer.

His business took him six weeks instead of the two he hoped it would take. Those days were the longest of his entire life. Part of the reason it took so long was because he couldn't stop thinking about her; her breasts, her tongue inside him, his member inside her. He hadn't been able to concentrate on the figures that were put in front of him. The only figure he saw was Caro's. Damn the disturbing woman and how she affected him. He couldn't even work.

Well hell.

"She left me! Ran off to God knows where when I wasn't looking. Why the devil did she do that? She never mentioned she was moving."

He was beside himself with worry then raging fury. Why should she talk to him? She didn't owe him an explanation. When he found her, he was damn well going to change that fact. In every way he meant to make her his no matter the consequences. She wouldn't run from him ever again.

"You want me to find her then bring her back?" the man, Daniel was his name, asked. "She shouldn't be too hard to find. You've given me enough information to start. She works at the Glasgow Herald. I'm certain her editor knows her last name. After that it should be one hell of an easy task to locate the little witch."

"No. Want you to find her then tell me where she is. I'm going to confront her where she is the most vulnerable. Where hopefully she doesn't have a soul to support her."

He found himself pacing, swearing beneath his breath. Surprising her would be interesting. The thought of no one but him to support her took an astounding leap in his mind. If she thought she was independent, she would soon find out how vulnerable he would make her.

First thing he did when he returned from London was to go see her. It was after eight o'clock in the evening. All the way home, he'd been thinking about her soft sultry warmth. How she would invite him inside her body. Over and over again, he relived those moments of anticipation.

After he discovered her home empty. He stomped absentmindedly around her house attempting to think. When he knocked on Scarlett's door, no one answered. He knew he could brow beat the women into giving him her address. He didn't want to threaten them again. He would if he had to do so.

Hell, all he thought about the last six weeks was holding her in his arms, kissing her, hearing the soft female noises she made when he loved her. He spent those six weeks in a state of semi-arousal. They were the longest bloody weeks of his life.

The second time he visited Scarlett's home in order to ask more questions, the ladies stalled when he asked them where she was, why she'd gone. It took threats to get them to reveal anything. When they did, when Torra finally revealed Caro's intentions, he lost what little sanity he possessed. Fury raged deep inside his entire body until he shook with the raging emotions. He still wasn't positive they told him everything. Probably revealed only the most sordid details.

He wasn't about to let her get away with any of this. Find her he would if he had to tear all of Edinburgh apart. That wouldn't be necessary. There were ways to discover exactly where she lived. Daniel was a good investigator. He gave the man enough intelligence for a good start. In time her trail would he hot. He would be there to find out truths she didn't want to share with him.

Discovery would take time.

Well hell, he wanted her now. This instant.

Torra begrudgingly told him all Caro wanted from him was his seed. She wanted a baby, his baby.

Why the devil did she pick him for her pilfering? The ladies failed to tell him why. His fist landed on his desk once more. In one swift move he swept his desk free of the clutter. His gut churned sourly. He'd eaten very little in days.

Torra also told him she left before she knew if she carried his child. She had to know by now. Christ, he had been in London six bloody weeks passed the ball. Then more time to find her and other business to conclude. She would be ten weeks along or she could be at fourteen weeks. Just because she bled slightly after their first joining didn't mean she wasn't increasing. Thinking of her lies, he was shaking with the simmering dark anger encompassing him. He wanted to throttle her then make love. Was any part of her passion real?

He needed sex with the lovely little harlot, hot and as fast as they could come together.

She wasn't going to get away with this act of selfishness. The nerve it must have taken to come to him that first time. A virgin, bloody eyes, he stole the innocence of an untried woman. She was old though. On the shelf. How the devil was he supposed to know she was innocent?

All trussed up in the cloak. The pink bow around her neck calling to him. The garish dress beneath the cloak. Her nipples as well as her most intimate feminine petals rouged as if he would like that as if she was actually a whore. The rouge was Torra's doing.

Nothing about that night had been normal.

"Start at the newspaper. She still has to be working. Caroline Kenworth, that's her name. Finally, he got an answer to that question. The last name started more thinking. He knew that name. Had a bad gut feeling about the ringing her newly discovered name started in his ears.

Couldn't be though. There was no way she could be the daughter of the Duke of Rothmore. The man was ruthless. If what he just learned about her was true, so was she.

Days turned into another week then another. Daniel discovered her address in the city. Until now, he couldn't get away from his work.

The time wasn't all wasted. His manor house was cleaned and decorated; a room prepared for the baby. He purchased a special license then contacted a minister in Edinburgh. The first thing he was going to do, after he made love with her, was marry her. This baby she was carrying would not be a bastard. If she thought to deny him, he'd keep her in his bed until she agreed.

The laughter coming from the back of his throat was not light hearted. Humor in this situation didn't exist. Some of his anger over the ensuing weeks changed to a low simmering boil ready to erupt at a moment's notice. Still, thoughts of her coupled with what she planned burned deep. He no longer felt the raging lust when he thought of her. How she reacted to his commands would dictate the rest of his life. He had a wealth of questions that needed to be answered. Daniel found the answer to a few.

When he reached her residence in the city, she wasn't home. The maid let him inside. Apparently, Caro gave no instructions that he wasn't to be admitted. Did she believe he wouldn't look for her? She was too intelligent to make that mistake. Every man would search for his child as well as the woman who stole his seed. When he thought about that, he felt violated, used in the worst way. He'd assumed the ladies at Miss Scarlett's place would have instructed her in the ways not to conceive.

He found the brandy then poured himself a generous amount. Too restless to sit, he paced. When he finally heard the door open, he smiled. She was his now.

"Caro?"

She dropped her packages, her eyes wide. The small pink tongue he enjoyed playing with slid across her bottom lip. He watched the pulse at the base of her throat leap. Her small hand, one that stroked so tenderly that brought him so much pleasure, flew to her neck.

Good, she was reacting either in fear or her blood was pounding because she wanted him. He decided it was most likely a bit of both. Fear was a good emotion for her to feel at the moment, although he didn't want it to continue for too long. She would need to know what he meant to take from her.

"Duncan?" her voice wavered softly as he took in her essence, chocolate and vanilla with a rose flavor. "You're here."

He should have brought pastries. "You look surprised to see me. Didn't you think I would look for you?"

His gaze ran over her swollen body as he decided she must have conceived the first time they met each other. She had to be more than three months along much more. He would watch over her now. See that she did everything right. He felt a huge wave of protectiveness surge through him along with satisfaction. He wasn't sure if it was for her or his child growing inside her. A bit of both he decided.

Her answer was not forthcoming. Instead, she picked up the lost packages. As if nothing untoward happened, she set them on a table by the door. When she returned, she started arranging the pillows. Picked one up, plumped the softness then set it in a different spot. Did the same with another then another.

"Sit down, Caro. Watching you is exhausting me."

He kept the chuckle behind his teeth as he wondered if this was something she did when she was nervous. He needed her to be nervous. It probably wasn't good for the baby.

Well hell.

Sitting now and playing with the fabric of her skirt, she didn't look at him when she spoke, "Why are you here?"

"Tea?" he asked. "The maid brought a pot in about ten minutes ago. It should still be hot."

"No. Why are you here?"

He leaned negligently on the corner of the fireplace before setting one booted foot on the hearth. Sipping his brandy, looking at her unable to get his fill, then in a slow lazy bland tone, "I contemplate you must know the answer. If you think about your words, the question was nothing but stupid."

He focused his gaze pointedly on the slight swell of her belly. She did hide her pregnancy well. He knew her body. Had touched every part of her, kissed and nibbled his way to every delicious curve. She could hide nothing from him.

He saw her slightly larger breasts heave as she inhaled a sudden deep breath of air. Her fingers at her temples, she massaged. "Enlighten me."

"You are going to play games? Now?" The sting of anger he'd been trying to tamp down for several weeks rose to new heights. "Truly, Caro, you do not wish to toy with me. Not in my present mood. I'm not going to let you get away with anything."

Her face was slowly losing color. She rubbed her arms, with what appeared as a desperate lift to her slight shoulders. "I cannot guess your wishes. Last time I saw you..." She moistened her lips. "Last time I saw you, you single handedly created a giant scandal. In the process you involved me. I had to leave Glasgow to get away from the reporters, the snakes as you labeled them."

For some strange reason the all-consuming lust he felt for this woman was now tempered. Yes, while he still wanted her, needed to be buried deep inside her, he understood he could wait until this conversation played out. He would sleep with her tonight. The evening would be delightful. He would wed her tomorrow. As soon as the ceremony was finished, they would be on their way to his country home. She would stay there until the child was born, forever if he had his way. He didn't intend to let her out of his sight.

Well, that was the plan. What to do if she refused to wed him? Ah, he'd already given that annoying prospect further consideration. Plus, there was always the child to use to his benefit.

"If you want to be obtuse well then..." He paused as he emptied his glass then poured another. "I came for my child."

At the mention of the baby, she swayed closing her eyes. Spilling brandy, he reached her before she fell to the floor. Swiftly, he set the glass down then swept her into his arms.

Duncan felt fear rush through him. He had not intended to intimidate her into fainting. It must be the pregnancy. With Caro settled on his lap, he stroked her back, murmured to her. Her cheek rested against his chest. Protectiveness assailed him. He wanted her to wake. Needed her to yell at him. Wanted her to howl. Had not expected this state of oblivion to occur.

She moaned softly.

He felt the cad.

The soft moan wasn't the same as when he pleasured her, when he brought her to such heights that she couldn't think. No, this was different. The tenor of the sound scared him. He startled her. It was too much too fast. Calmly, he should have explained to her his plans. Tell her she would have no say in what would happen next.

This time the sound moving softly from her lips was whisper thin. She was recovering. She would wake up soon. He would tell her what he wanted, what they would do. She would agree with all his plans because she had no choice or say in the matter. He planned the scenario meticulously.

He wouldn't take her now. He wasn't a randy stoat. He would give her time to adjust to the unwanted surprise he gifted her with in her drawing room. He was patient.

"Duncan? What happened?"

"You fainted in my arms. When I first saw you, I wasn't sure if you still lusted after my man's body. You must." He grinned then, pleased with her recovery.

"What child?"

It seemed she remembered why she fainted. She meant to play this game to the bitter end. His hand rested on her belly, explored. She flinched. "My baby and yours of course. That's why I'm here. Stealing my sperm was not good of you, Caro. I decided to claim what is mine."

He hoped she wouldn't continue to deny what was as plain as day. He would be forced to show her how her body was increasing. Not only her belly was larger but also her breasts had grown. For emphasis, he moved his hand on her slightly swollen belly.

"I don't know what you're talking about."

She tried to push away from him. He held her fast. Allowing her to escape him was not part of his scheme.

His hand caressed her belly keeping her still. She hissed in a quick breath of air. He continued to stroke her there thinking how nice it would be to feel his babe move beneath his hand. Feeling that wonderful movement would come later.

"Caro, I know you stole my sperm. Know just about everything you plotted against me. Understand how you used my man's body to get what you wanted. Your goal comes with a price. Me."

She laughed. The sound was delicate though it also held a note of fear. That same terror he saw before she fainted. "What makes you think I know anything about a baby?"

She still meant to deny the obvious.

He stroked her belly again, cupped the curve beneath his palm. His hand rose to one breast then the top of her corsage. Gently he tugged. The tip of one breast spilled out. He closed his hand on the rounded globe. Her moan of pleasure this time pleased him. He held back. He meant to wait until after they ate to make love to his soon to be wife.

She would not deny him.

"I would show you except I would have to remove all your clothing. I would like that. However, I would much prefer to wait until after dinner. You see, I know you're increasing. I kissed your breasts, touched your flat belly. They've changed to accommodate my child. You're larger in all those beautiful spots that pleased me so very much."

"Why are you here?" she asked, a breathy voice whispered into the air. "What is it you want from me?"

"Do you agree there is a child or do you want to continue this falsehood you're perpetrating? The dance of words between us cannot continue."

He brushed his knuckles across her cheek. This was quiet nice sitting with her on his lap. Amazingly, he still found he could wait to have her. He hoped this amazing feat of his continued until they were ready to retire for bed.

"I want to raise our child. Since he will need a mother, we will wed tomorrow. Murrays don't have bastards. I have the special license."

"No."

"Truly, you don't have a choice, Caro. I will ruin your friends, friends who lied to me just as you've done if you continue to say no. Do you want to see Torra and Honey tossed out on the streets again to fend for themselves? While Scarlett doesn't need the business, it does give her pride in the fact the escort flourishes."

"I don't believe you. You're not that kind of person. You would never ruin them." She tilted her chin in the air. "You're not vindictive."

Like your father?

"Would you care to test that assumption? I guarantee you that you won't like the end game if you challenge me. No one challenges me and wins."

This was a side he hadn't seen before, this person who sought so diligently to lie even when she was defeated. He realized he knew very little about her. She was an enigma. About all he did know other than the fact she was intelligent was what he learned the two nights he spent with her. She did have an appetite for sex. He hoped this appetite was just with him.

"I would do anything, even ruin two not so innocent women to get what I want. Caro, I want you and the baby. Don't ever doubt me. It's a package deal. We will spend tonight together. Tomorrow we will wed. After that we will be on our way to my home in the country. You will stay there. We will live there most of the year. I can do business from home. By the way, I arranged to have the questions for your column sent to my residence. You can keep working if you like.

"No."

"Yes, all of that."

"You can't dictate to me."

"Of course I can. I already have. You will be pleased with this arrangement." He didn't want to argue with her any longer. She didn't understand. "My son will not be born a bastard. He will be born at my home. He will have my name."

"Girl."

Duncan thought he should change tactics. His lust grew, as the argument reached no acceptable conclusion. All he could think of was kissing her. If he did, they might not eat. Perhaps he could control himself to one time with her. He was aroused, near to bursting from his trousers. She was sitting on him. Her woman's petals were so close. He could unfasten...

He swallowed hard. Setting her aside he stood in front of her, watching the delicate play of emotions cross her face. She wanted him.

Extending his hand, "Come, we will have food brought..."

"Dinner is ready just as you ordered." The maid who let him into the house earlier stood in the doorway.

He smiled at her look of chagrin. "Good, are you hungry, Caro? I find I'm famished for two things. Mean to satisfy both hungers before the night is over."

He smirked as he changed his mind once more. They would eat in the dining room where it was infinitely less dangerous.

Color returned to her face. She accepted the proffered hand as he escorted her to the dining room.

The food was delicious as well as the wine. He found he was hungrier than he thought.

"You must eat. There is a little one growing in your womb who needs nourishment probably more than you. Don't care if it's a boy or a girl. If you keep insisting it's a girl well, I'll have to give my encouragement that the child is a boy. What do you think? We could make a wager."

"You can't possibly want to marry me." She placed a piece of baked potato in her mouth, chewing slowly.

"I wouldn't do anything I don't want. Especially marry a woman I don't want. Never in my adult life have I done something that doesn't suit me. We will wed tomorrow then we will do well together. You will be my wife in the duration, have my children. We will have more than one. How many children would you like, Caro? Perhaps an even dozen?"

"No one has ever wanted me. Why you?"

The voice he heard didn't sound like his Caro. He knew enough about her father to understand the man only wanted boys. Daniel, his investigator, discovered the fact she left home when she was only sixteen. She lived in the house across from Scarlett's since then. She was an independent woman. She made her way with little help from her father. He knew how much the duke gave her because during the course of his investigation he learned that over the years he invested the monthly allowance for her. He increased her savings every year. He chuckled softly. The groats were all his now. She had no means to set out on her own. Before he arrived in Edinburgh, he made sure of that.

He would have to tread lightly while informing her about his acquisitions that affected her to her detriment.

"Well, that is no longer the case. I know about your father. More than I should. More than I ever wanted to learn. Know this Caro, I care about you."

She choked on water. Tears spiked her lashes. "This is all too sudden. It is only the child that has you here. I would let you see her any time you wished. You don't have to marry me."

He found he was growing impatient with her stubbornness. He waved a hand in the air, "No, that won't do. No, it won't do at all. Come now, I believe there is dessert to eat. Your favorite. Do you think our little boy will enjoy sweets as much as his mother?"

She glared at him.

He barked a shout of laughter. He loved her obstinacy. They would suit well.

They finished the meal. "Would you like a small glass of sherry before we retire. I know I would like brandy. Oh, possibly with the *wee* one growing inside you, drinking alcohol might not be such a prudent idea. Always wondered about that. What do you think?"

"Should stick with tea I suppose."

She followed him. That surprised him. They sat for a while watching the flames in the fireplace. At least he was watching the fire, thinking of the inferno he wanted to create inside Caro. Clearly nervous, she plucked at her skirts. Her tea grew cold. It seemed perhaps he should take her to bed. That didn't feel right just yet. For a strange reason he didn't understand, he didn't want to rush her. He wanted her to come to him so very willing that she would turn to liquid heat in his arms. The way things looked right now that wasn't going to happen.

He didn't understand this waiting. Didn't understand why she seemed to hold herself in check. By the glazing over of her eyes, she wanted him. Everything today had been a surprise to her. Perhaps that was why. Caro most likely didn't expect to ever see him again. If that was the case, she was foolish to believe so.

In her bedroom she paused, lowered her lashes as if she became timid. For the longest time she seemed to study the hem of her gown.

"What is it? You suddenly shy?"

He had a hard time believing after what they shared at the ball as well as his birthday, she would be wary of him or what they did together.

She looked at him. Her tears were very real. Moisture splayed on her lashes appearing as diamonds when the moonlight caught them. She brushed the moisture away with the backs of her hands.

Well hell, this was not the way he wanted to start this relationship. Seemed too one-sided for him. "Tell me what's wrong. I can help, you know."

He grimaced. The command could have been broached a bit softer. He didn't mean his query to be an order. The words, the tone, sounded every bit the command.

"You've no idea." She sniffed continuing to avoid looking at him.

That was the truth. "That's why I asked. You've never been this reluctant. No, perhaps the first time, the first two minutes you were shy. After that..."

She turned from him, struggling a bit with the buttons. "Can we take this a bit slower? You know. I've a lot of adjustments to make in my mind. I didn't expect to see you here today. Not that I don't appreciate the offer of marriage, I always believed two people would love each other before they committed to living their lives together."

He thought if they took this any slower dawn would be here before he got her out of the gown. "I've tasted every part of you, Caro. Loved you in too many different ways to count. Why?"

She ran her hands across the slight swell of her belly. Realization hit him in the gut.

"I'm fat. I'm not the same. Even with no light..."

"You're beautiful. Why on earth would a pregnant woman think she is fat? It's beyond me. You carry my child. There is a beautiful, wonderful human being living inside you."

For a moment before he reached the right conclusion, he thought she truly believed they should love each other first. Under this circumstance and after what she did, he didn't know if love was possible. While he wanted both Caro as well as his child, the reason wasn't because he loved her.

Boy or girl, he did love the baby.

"Tonight, let me love every part of you, touch you, kiss you. I want to see as well as feel how your body has changed. I want to be with you when it changes even more."

Puling her into his arms, he kissed her hard and deep. He'd thought to take this slow. It would take all the strength he possessed to do so. What little control he had when she walked into her home vanished while they dined. Still, she held back the passion he knew first hand she possessed. She held herself away from him. He didn't like that fact.

"You..."

"I?"

"No, Duncan, this just isn't right. Making love to you right now isn't the same."

Anger found its way to the forefront of his mind. He couldn't let what she did go. "What wasn't right was stealing my sperm. You pretended and lied to me. You're right this is honest. Do you know how to do honest?"

"You're angry."

"Furiously so." Inadvertently, he found that in venting his anger he was calming himself. To some degree he understood what drove her. Understanding was not excepting.

"We should wait until we are wed."

~ * ~

"No!"

"Tomorrow is only one night between us. Surely you can do without sex for one night. I would sleep alone this evening."

She'd never seen him so angry. The veins in his neck throbbed and bulged. True, she'd never seen him except when he lusted after her. What they felt was lust, powerful hunger nothing more. With a force she couldn't deny, she felt it still.

He stepped toward her, his hands clasped behind his back, as it appeared he struggled to keep them there. The look on his face told her he wanted to throttle her. He wouldn't. She was almost sure of that fact.

Almost.

"Do you..." he stepped closer.

The scent of his anger filled her. He was all male, graceful, so sleek and powerful. He could take what he wanted. She didn't want this, not with his rage separating them. His brows were tightly drawn together leaving a furious crease in the middle of his forehead. "Do you have any idea how I felt when I discovered you missing? You couldn't even be bothered to leave a message."

She stepped back, afraid of meeting head on with this furious man. As she found herself shaking her head, she did wonder how he felt. "You went to see me? We only had two nights together. We weren't even friends. I didn't believe I had an obligation to inform you about my whereabouts."

She did. She almost forgot about the child.

"Almost to the minute I returned from London. I stopped at my townhouse to take a quick bath then change clothes after what had seen a full day of travel. I needed to see you, hold you in my arms. I was desperate to be with you again."

"You did?" she squeaked as his hands rested on her trembling shoulders, his fingers digging in until he suddenly let his hands drop away.

He seemed to change his mind. He set them back. Pulled her closer until only a thin layer of air separated them.

"The house was dark. I was afraid something terrible happened to you. I ran around the perimeter knocking on the back door along with the windows." His fingers tightened on her shoulders. She wanted to run. There was nowhere to run or hide for that matter. She tried to swallow the lump of terror lodged in her aching throat.

Caroline didn't know what to say to that bit of nonsense. No one, least of all her father or even this man truly cared what happened to her. This man she knew for two marvelous nights told her he cared. Ha! What she believed was that his caring was all about the baby. When he returned, he wouldn't have known about the baby.

"Liar..."

Her voice was too soft, too weak to carry any weight. Oh, how she wanted to believe him. Needed to know that someone appreciated what happened to her.

"In that you're wrong. Don't understand the way I feel about you. One moment furious then the next needing to take you into my arms, you have my entire body shaking. Sometimes when I think about what you, along with what you've done, I want to hit something."

He jabbed his fingers into his hair, leaving it rakishly disheveled. She wanted to run her fingers through the length, feel the silken texture.

In his hold she flinched. "Never has anyone even been concerned about what happened to me from one moment to the next," she blurted then regretted the words. Pity was not something she wanted him to feel for her. "I don't expect you to do so. What I don't want you to do is pretend something you don't feel. I don't want you in my bed when you're furious with me."

"You won't dictate this relationship." His fiercely potent anger reappeared. "You will do as I say."

"I will fight you. I'm not going to marry you tomorrow. No matter how autocratic you believe you are, you do need my consent."

Once again, she announced her feelings even while understanding he would have a way to make her give her consent. At the moment she didn't know what it was.

"What will you do then? If you choose not to wed?" A feral smile grew on his handsome features. "Where will you go?"

She didn't like the expression she read on his face. He must have a way to force her into this hasty and unwanted marriage that she didn't know about. Understood he had the means as well as the power to make her life difficult if she refused. She reminded herself he wasn't vindictive. Maybe all he wanted now was revenge, to trap her in a loveless marriage. Ah, but no, he would also be trapped.

"I have the money to live on my own. I'll continue as I've been doing for the last eleven years." Saying the words, she suddenly felt more secure.

"No, no you don't. In that belief you are wrong," his voice was soft. She no longer heard anger in the tone but victory. "I wasn't going to bring this up, however you make assumptions that are blatantly false. You underestimated the strength of my rage."

Panic swamped her. She tilted her chin. "Of course I will. I do."

"Let me tell you how it is. You own nothing, Caro. You've no money, not one groat to your name." He gestured with his hands. "I now own this townhouse as well as your home in Glasgow. Neither do you own a home anywhere else. If I decided to rent to you, you have no way to pay me." He paused as his gaze centered on her ever-widening eyes.

"I have enough wealth to purchase a new home. I don't need to work. I've quit my job at the Herald."

"You don't have the funds available to you. You would need to work, however without my approval the Herald won't hire you. I've taken care of everything concerning your finances. You have nothing to call your own except what I will give you."

"What are you saying?" She collapsed on a chair, her body shaking with the news he gave her, her face cold to the touch. Very real fear flooded her. This wasn't possible. He couldn't have acquired everything she owned. It wasn't legal. "I'll fight you in court."

"You could try. Nevertheless, you won't win. With no other choice left to you, you will wed me on the morrow. All your wealth, all you once owned is now in my name. That is why it took an extra week for me to get here to Edinburgh. You have nothing except what I choose to give you," he repeated. "Even your father was convinced you no longer need a monthly allowance. He expects me to wed you, take care of you along with our child. If you choose not to do so, he will be angry as will I. He also doesn't want a bastard in the family. It is the only thing we've ever agreed about."

She stood, her fists clenched so tight her nails gouged into the palms of her hands. She wanted to throw things at him, spit as well as claw his eyes out. Instead, she tossed her lukewarm tea in his face. He swore. The cup hit him on the side of the head, the saucer the middle of his chest. Anger swamped her. She didn't want to believe him. Somehow, she knew he spoke the truth.

"How dare you!"

The book sitting on the end table found its mark. She dodged when he lunged to capture her. Quick steps took her around a chair. She found an unlit candle. It missed his head by the tiniest space.

"I dare anything."

Slowly, he closed the distance.

For a moment, she bent over, breathing hard, inhaling, exhaling, filling her lungs the best she could. She searched for another object. Hands on his slim hips he stood next to her. Didn't touch her. Her back against the wall, she had nowhere to run.

The hard objects were too far from her reach. In any case she knew he wouldn't allow her to toss anything more at him. Grabbing the pillow off a nearby chair, she swung the pillow at his head. He laughed as he caught her hands in his. Her breaths were coming in huge gulps. She couldn't bring enough air into her lungs to sustain life. He pulled her hard to his body, his hands keeping hers behind her back. She was flush against him, felt his arousal hard against her belly.

"Bastard!"

"I repeat how will you go on? You can't live on the streets. I won't allow that. If you don't want to wed me, you must think of something I would agree with."

His lips molded across hers, his tongue finding its way inside. Unwittingly and against her wishes, she opened for him.

This was different, rage and anger from both of them stoking the fire between them. Flames raged out of control. An inferno burst inside. She pushed half-heartedly on his chest, tried to move her mouth away from his. One of his large hands now held her head in place as he ravaged her mouth with his teeth and tongue. His warmth penetrated, enveloped her in sensations so hot and intense there was no way to fight them. For as long as she could, she battled the moan of pleasure trying to escape from between her lips.

Abruptly, he let her go. She stumbled backward. He stared at her for the longest time. She lightly touched her kiss-swollen mouth with the back of her hand, her body trembling from anger as well as the sexual need he fueled.

"Without me, how will you go on?" he asked again.

"You've taken everything?" The realization hit home. He controlled and dictated every facet of her life. "How?"

"I have. You're mine, Caro. The sooner you admit to the fact, the sooner you will be happy."

Defeated, she sunk to the floor. Her arms rested on a table, her head down. She gave into the sobs erupting from her. He took all she was all she ever wanted to be. He owned her. He didn't care about her. If he did, he would never do anything so cruel. Single handedly he stole her independence, the one thing besides the baby growing in her womb she cherished.

"Marry me and I'll make sure you receive a grant at the university to study your roses."

Her head jerked up. Her gaze met his. Fire flamed. "What don't you know about me? How could you confiscate everything without my solicitor contacting me?"

"Your solicitor is a good friend of mine. He agreed that what I planned would be good for you also."

"I don't believe you. He would never...did you threaten him too?"

He sat down beside her stroking her back. "I don't want to hurt you. Just need to make you happy. Knew you would stubbornly protest the marriage. Had to figure out a way to make this...to make it so you would have no choice. My plan was magnificent."

Absorbing the words he spoke, she felt so many raging emotions. He won. Perhaps she could have been persuaded. Instead, he stole all her options. Just like the women at Scarlett's home, she was penniless as well as in a man's power. She couldn't even go to work for Scarlett because he promised to destroy her if the women didn't tell him where she was. What would he do to her if she asked for a job at the escort service?

"Leave me alone," she told him, wishing to be able to forget all that transpired since she came home this afternoon.

All her carefully laid plans burned to ashes in these few moments. In less than a few hours, her independence vanished. Torra warned her something like this might happen. Told her that the man was ruthless.

"Don't believe that's an option. I want you in my bed too damn much. If you are honest with yourself, you want the same thing." He paused watching her for several seconds. "Don't cry. I'm sure it's not good for the babe. Come to bed with me."

She bristled. Sitting up, her fury she was sure evident. Everything was about the *wee bairn* she carried. Selfishly, she needed something to be about her wellbeing as she longed for someone, anyone to care about her, just her. She grit her teeth trying desperately to make her point. Unable to think of the right words, she felt deflated.

"That's where you're wrong, Caro. He is mine too. Just as you are mine." With that said he picked her up from the floor. "You're going to bed, Caro. You look exhausted. There are dark circles beneath your eyes. With my influence, you will take better care of yourself. We will wed in the morning. After the ceremony we will start on our way to my country home."

Gently, he placed her on the bed, left her there while he walked to the basin of water. With the soft cloth he found, he washed her face seeming to rid her of the moisture that slipped down her cheeks.

She wanted to yell at him again.

There were no more words left she could recite.

He won.

She didn't like that feeling. "I won't sleep with you tonight. You can't force me." Belligerence didn't suit her especially when she couldn't back up the words. If he wished it so, he could have her climaxing in seconds. This was what it was. Sex coupled with sensual pleasure was all they had between them. Lust was not enough to sustain a marriage.

Duncan didn't say anything. He brought her a second cup of tea. The drink was warm. It felt good on her throat. She was tired.

"Would you like a fresh pot? Perhaps a little lemon and milk? Heard milk is good for a growing fetus."

Surprised at his choice of words, she blinked wondering anew if he was truly who she thought he was. A stupid man could never have manipulated all her money as he did. Perhaps one of his brother's did the nasty deed with his request.

She had nothing. Despair filled her gut.

"Yes, a new pot would be nice along with the milk and lemon." She meant to stall. "Would like some honey too, please." Perhaps he would leave the room. Maybe he wouldn't return. All she wanted at the moment was to put on her nightgown then crawl into bed.

Alone.

She didn't dare.

He rang for the maid. Of course he wouldn't leave. Shortly the requested drink was in the room along with some chocolate truffles and brandy for him. He waited on her. Treated her with civility she didn't expect, making no demands on her. He was quiet. The throbbing veins on his neck weren't quite so prevalent.

Unnerved by his presence and terrified of what he would do next, she sipped the tea, ate the truffle. Everything was delicious. She found she wanted more. The devil but she didn't remember eating much at dinner. At that time her stomach churned so intensely she didn't think she could keep much in her belly. Between bites she studied him.

When she brought herself from her musings, he was loosening his perfectly tied cravat. The white cloth fell to the floor. Suddenly, his shirt was hanging open, his pants unfastened.

"W-what are you doing?" She knew her eyes were wide. All the lights were on in the room. Before she never actually saw him.

Naked.

His smile was slow, widening as the seconds ticked by. "Getting ready for bed. It's been a long day. Tomorrow will be even longer. I need sleep. Continuing these conversations will only tire you more. I won't have that. As I told you earlier, tonight as well as most every night after, I'm sleeping with my soon to be wife. Believe I'll make sure you travel with me when I need to leave for business trips."

He tugged off his boots. When his fingers found the fastening on his trousers again, she closed her eyes. Swallowed the lump in her throat.

"Truly, Caro, you've seen all of me. I've been deep inside you numerous times, too many to count on two hands. Oh, but I forgot your shyness along with the lights. Should I make sure there is no light in the room save the wonderful moonlight? Do you want the chamber dark?" He left his pants on before he settled next to her on the bed a brandy in his hands.

"I don't want to see you naked now or ever."

The chocolate truffle caught in her throat. She coughed wishing she had not taken that last bite or said those words. The sentiment was useless, the words an outright lie. It seemed he would do what he wanted.

"We will have to do something to change that attitude of yours.

As of this moment I'm not sure what though. Rest assured, I'm not going to remain celibate the entirety of my life or yours. I mean to take good care of you, protect you. You will live a very long time." He took the empty cup from her hands then set it on the table beside him. "It's time for you to get ready for bed. Would you like help? Can you undress without aid?"

If she was a statue, she couldn't have been more frozen. For several seconds she didn't breathe. Her heart seemed to forget to beat. She couldn't do this, couldn't undress in front of him, couldn't lie next to him. He would want her naked.

His voice was calm, terrifyingly calm. "Caro, if you don't undress then slip into whatever you want to wear to bed, I will do it for you. It's past time to retire for the night. In my mind, I've been a very patient man."

"I'll do it," she squeaked, standing too fast.

A wave of dizziness assailed her. She sat back down, her head in her hands.

He cursed a blue streak. "I swear..."

She wanted to laugh. Wasn't that what he'd been doing? "I'm fine," she said too fast as another wave hit her.

She wasn't sure what was wrong. Until tonight there had been no issues. Her midwife told her everything with the babe was coming along just fine. She was fine too. It was the night. A woman didn't have morning sickness at night. No, this must be Duncan sickness.

"Caro?" Abruptly he was kneeling in front of her. His hands held hers. "What is wrong?" He sounded terrified.

She wanted to laugh. Kept the sound behind her teeth. "Don't think anything is wrong. Just tired as you said as well as terrified. Probably hungrier than I thought. You surprised me, stole the breath from me. I've been on tenterhooks for hours expecting the worse. Only to discover the worst was more than I expected."

"I will do it then."

He turned her. Despite her protests, his hands quickly unfastened her clothing.

She held the gown in front of her, shielding herself from his view. He wasn't looking as she suspected. Instead, he stood in front of the armoire searching, she supposed for a nightgown.

When he finally found then pulled one out, he laughed. "When we're wed, I'll purchase something entirely different for you. For tonight this will serve as your temporary shield against my amorous intentions toward you. What do you say? Can you let go of your clothing long enough to slip this over your head? I will make sure the room remains dark. Perhaps you need the chamber darker, black might be to your delight."

He handed it to her. She did as he said while he made sure all the lights were put out. It was dark, pitch black. There was no moon to light the scene since he drew the curtains across the window. She was thankful for that.

With the covers pulled back she slipped beneath. She felt the bed sag on the other side as he too crept under the covers. She stiffened when his big hand closed around her tugging her closer to him. The same hand settled on her belly while he pushed her hair from her neck. His lips touched lightly on her nape.

"I'm still angry at what you did."

"Doesn't matter." His deep voice vibrated against her back. "In time, you will get over your annoyance."

When she shivered, responding to the pureness of his touch, he chuckled softly. "Even though you are furious with me, you still respond sweetly. You're hungry for me, Caro. Can deny the fact all you want. Your body, however, is telling me something entirely different."

He continued to explore, caressing her, tempting her to turn in his arms, to seek greater fulfillment. She tried to deny herself the pleasure. The hand that just a moment ago rested on her belly swept down the length of her leg all the way to her toes. With the return path, her gown rose higher, higher still until he cupped her breast in his hand. Heat traveled to her toes.

He nipped on the lobe of her ear as he set off sparks that flamed higher and higher with each passing second. His tongue explored while his fingers created a more mercurial sensation flooding her.

Dazed by his questing fingers, she tried to keep her sensual response hidden. With a breathy purr then a soft whimpering moan of desire, she understood once more she lost the game he was playing with her.

His swollen member pushed against her. He slipped his leg beneath hers. With a groan, he pushed inside her. She cried out. He held still.

"Hush, just hold back for a moment."

A small wooden sound caught in the back of her throat. She couldn't do that. Her body wanted fulfillment now. Not when he decided it was time. Beside herself the spasms of her release flooded her. Each kiss of her ecstasy licked him brought him to a higher plateau.

"Duncan!" She cried out as his guttural groan resounded with her cry of pleasure in the darkness of the night.

He stroked her back touching on each vertebra. "Sleep now. I promise to keep my hands to myself for the rest of the night."

"I didn't want you to do that." She felt his grin behind her as his lips touched upon her neck once more.

"Make love to you? I'm going to be your husband. You could have said no." His voice was gruff, filled with the pleasure of their joining. "I will make love to you whenever it pleases me or you. All you have to do is ask."

It was almost as if she could see his brow arched upward. Heat from his body comforted her. She didn't know why she fought him. Her stubborn streak got her where she wanted to be. This place she yearned for could also be her downfall. She was still so furious with him she wanted to howl at him. Didn't think she could ever forgive him his impertinent behavior.

She stole his sperm. He stole all her money as well as both her homes. He promised her grant money if she obeyed him. Lord, she didn't need that promise to obey him if she wed him. If she defied him, she would have nothing. If she wed him, he would see all her dreams come true.

How could that be?

Did he have that much power and wealth? Torra mentioned it must be his brothers who were actually behind the genius of the investments. His brothers, all of them would never agree to steal everything from a woman. This was absurd.

His hand rested on the curve of her hip. "Go to sleep, Caro. I know you're thinking wonderful thoughts about our marriage, about sex between us. I'm a good lover. However, as you well know you have to sleep. Tomorrow is an important day."

"You need to stop touching me." Her voice was a soft whimper in the back of her throat. There had to be more between them than the overpowering need for sex.

There was the anger.

~ * ~

After he told her about the loss of her money, he'd not intended to seduce her. When he was close to her, when the sweet scent of chocolate and vanilla invaded his senses, he lost all ability to think. When he looked into those soft blue eyes simmering with her fury, he was a man doomed. He wondered if the rest of his life with her would be the same.

He thought he could control his lust. Well, he did for more hours today as well as this evening than he believed possible. The bed undid him coupled with the prim nightgown that covered her from head to toe. The challenge to get beneath the fabric tempted him until he could no longer resist. When he saw her decked out so primly, all he could think of was touching the silken flesh the material was supposed to conceal. What she didn't realize was the fact that through the thin fabric of her night apparel, he could see the dark outline of her nipples, the curves of her hips and breasts as well as the enticing shadow of her woman's mound.

Now, when his fingers closed around her breast, he felt the beating of her heart, heard the soft whimper of pleasure his touch generated. Stealing her homes as well as every penny she owned had not been easy for him. He could think of no other way to pressure her to see things his way. Taking the child from her was never an option in his mind. The only way he could turn her to his viewpoint was to make her dependent on him. Now though, he felt certain he could find grant money for her research if that was what she wanted. The dean of the university told him she'd tried for several years now to obtain a grant. She was a woman. That fact sealed her fate. Unless he stepped in, there would be no money forthcoming.

Yes, she'd always been refused. He was sure the rejection was because she was female. While he understood the reason, would have gone along with the soundness of the thought until he met Caro. When she came to him in the harlot's costume on his birthday, he never believed she would become important to him. When she climaxed so delightfully in his arms, he'd never thought she was a genius.

After she discovered he was more intelligent than most, she would once again be angry, furiously so. Once more, he would have to weather the tempest of her rage. She couldn't be angry with him. That just wouldn't do. It was not his fault she made assumptions about him without delving into the facts. Perhaps it had been Torra along with Honey who gave her the misinformation. He did have to admit at least to himself he was behind the rumors that set the level of his intelligence into question. He chuckled. Those rumors sent him the best gift of his life.

She pushed back against him, the fascinating curve of her buttocks tight against his arousal. He groaned vowing to himself one time this evening with her was enough. Tomorrow night he would indulge in all the fantasy he harbored for the weeks he spent without her.

He dozed.

When he woke the sun peaked through the window. He rang for a bath as well as food and drink.

He didn't need to wake her for another few hours. For several seemingly timeless seconds he watched her breathe. She was his forever. No matter what she said, the baby was his also. When he made love to her, he forgot what she stole, forgot his fury in discovering her thievery. All he could think of now was their future.

Speedily, he stood then slipped on the robe he set out the night before. After the knock, he opened the door while servants brought in steaming water. Johnston stood just inside the entrance. His face grim once more letting him know what the disapproval of his actions wrought.

"When you are done here, I've set out your clothing in the other room. I assume you wish to give her privacy for her bath."

"You are absolutely right," Duncan said laughing as he watched the man back from the room. It seemed he just noticed Caro's bared shoulder. He wondered if the man ever had fun. Johnston was stuffier than any duke he'd met.

With his bath finished, he padded to the other room to dress. He wasn't going to return to Caro's bedroom. Didn't want to see his bride before the wedding. The early morning view of her soft shoulder he'd kissed last night didn't count.

He whistled. Sent the servants he brought with him scurrying to get the hot water for Caro. An hour later he sent the maid who let him into the house to the bedroom to wake her. Now all he had to do was wait for the preacher. The man said he would be here at ten o'clock sharp. It was eight-thirty now.

Before he left Glasgow, he was sure his brothers as well as Letty along with her friends, Torra and Honey, were invited to the wedding. He hoped they would be here for her. She needed a friendly face in the room.

Satisfyingly, his life stretched in front of him.

He was pleased.

The decisions he made for both of them would suit.

Chapter Six

Torra, along with Honey, arrived a half-hour after nine, Scarlett and Bobby a few minutes after that. His brothers had been waiting for him when he came downstairs. He didn't know of anyone else she might want in attendance. Even asking her father if he would give her away, he was met with instant disdain. To his knowledge there was no one else.

Why would he want to do something as ridiculous as that? Ask her father to give her away? He thought most fathers wanted to see their daughters happily married. The duke didn't give a damn what happened to Caro. When they wed, she would no longer be the duke's responsibility. No, pleasantly, she would be his.

The pieces of the puzzle that made Caro who she was were beginning to fall into place. At this point all he could possibly do was reassure her, give her the self-confidence he understood she lacked. While she put on a brave front, he now appreciated what lingered just below the surface. The reason she didn't believe a man would want her for herself made his job tougher. Deep inside he understood that was the reason she gave herself to him under false pretenses. All the blame went to her father.

In his life he'd never met a woman who appealed to him more. She matched him on every level even while she was his total opposite. Her father was an evil vindictive man who he'd never liked. Made it a point to stay away from him. She had brothers. He figured they were probably cut from the same cloth as the father. Duncan did give the man credit for making sure Caro didn't want for monetary things as he never failed to gift her with a monthly allowance. He supposed to a man such as the duke, possession and power were more important than a person's soul and mental well-being.

The minister arrived ten minutes until ten. His gaze shifted to the upstairs room where his bride would be dressing. Torra and Honey went upstairs as soon as they arrived. Scarlett followed leaving him with Bobby and his brothers. He was terrified she wouldn't appear.

"How did you do it?" Bobby asked as he poured himself a cup of tea. "Didn't think it was possible."

"Don't know about you, nevertheless, I could use a stiff drink about now. Tea seems a bit tepid for my needs."

Well hell, he was nervous, terrified Caro would change her mind. She might try to call his bluff. What he told her though wasn't a bluff. Everything he said about her finances was true. What he didn't say was that he planned to restore everything to her name once he figured out how to make her love him.

"Yes, how did you convince her to marry you?" Fletcher asked with a chuckle coupled with an all-knowing grin.

"I'm not a bad catch," Duncan shot back slightly offended by the offhanded humor. "Many a mother has shoved their simpering daughter my way. It was all I could do to ignore them. Was forced to create a false life so the mothers wouldn't think me suitable."

"Ah, so that's why you always made sure your bad reputation preceded you," Gordon added as he tossed back the rest of his brandy then a wink directed to his siblings. "Maybe we should learn the lesson you wrote expertly. The plan appears sound now that you actually found the woman for you."

"I have to do the same," Evan said with a shrug. "Maybe I should see what Torra will send me on my birthday."

"Not easy getting married. Your circumstances are most unusual. Blackmail wasn't well done of you. I assume that's how you convinced her. Hard to come back from something like that. She might not ever trust you." Bobby set the teacup down. He poured glasses of brandy handing one to Duncan as well as the brothers along with the minister who he thought would surely need one before the morning passed.

He didn't need to be reminded of the black-hearted deed he accomplished too easily. What she did was worse. If he thought for a moment she would agree to the marriage, he would have never jumped through the necessary hoops to rid her of everything she owned. She stole from him. He returned the deception two-fold by taking everything she owned. After he spoke with Torra and Honey, he understood she would not change her plans. He knew to win her compliance she would need to be totally dependent on his whims.

Though he would never hurt her. He offered her her heart's desire. If she truly wanted the grant, she would have the money.

This was what he wanted for so long. No woman fit him as she did. He prayed once again eventually she would come to love him.

"You do know what she did to me." Duncan wasn't sure if Bobby had been told or not.

"I heard." The voice was solemn yet a smile tugged at the corners of his mouth. "Don't want to know how this will all work out. Can't be good for the wedding night. The battle ground between the two of you must be cavernous."

Oh, the wedding night would be wonderful. He had no doubts about carnal pleasure between them. Just as Caro did last night she'd melted in his arms. She would always give of herself. He did know she tried to hold back, tried to keep part of herself from him. He didn't allow her success in that useless endeavor.

"In the end, I'm confident our life together will work out."

He thought of the home in the country. There he would have her to himself for as long as he wanted. Hell, he would plant as many rose bushes as she wished. Thought of the grant money he would gift her with, coupled with how pleased she would be made him grin. Perhaps if he kept her supplied with chocolate truffles, she would forget her anger. He knew all her downfalls, all her guilty pleasures.

"I see they are ready." Bobby pointed to the door where Letty stood.

There was no smile on her face. Her back was stiff. Her expression didn't bode well for the next hour or two.

"She told me what you did." Scarlett's voice was too calm, almost appreciative if he guessed right. "That was a bold move. She didn't deserve to lose everything."

Duncan waited for an explosion of some sort. He did threaten Scarlett's establishment. Scarlett was wise though. She would know it was all bluster to get the ladies to spill the information he needed. The ploy worked very well.

"Since you *ken* what Caro did, then also understand why I reacted as I did. She deserved what I doled out. I've no regrets. I would do the same again if necessary."

He straightened, content the confrontation with Scarlet was at an end, at least for now. His brothers Evan, Fletcher, along with Gordon stood by his side.

"Well, Bobby and I guessed. Decided to let the two of you work the difficulties out on your own. Suppose the two of you are still in the process. Of course, we only guessed about you becoming her sperm benefactor. Never thought you'd break her financially. It was brilliant by all standards. You do plan on giving the money back."

"No comment," he grunted not willing to give his intentions away.

He wasn't about to give over his advantage to a woman who could ruin his plans.

He turned to Evan trying to ignore Scarlett's remarks. "You do have the ring?"

He was met by a speculative lifting of an eyebrow. Sardonically, Evan spoke, "I would never disappoint at such a jubilant time."

He never thought anything would get past Evan. When he turned his attention to Evan then Scarlett who was sitting in front of the fireplace next to Bobby, their nods told him they all knew he'd liquidated all of Caro's assets. The strange thing about it, he didn't see a tinge of disapproval.

Scarlett stood. One by one, Torra first then Honey walked into the room. His breath caught in the back of his throat. This was the day he'd always dreaded, the end of his bachelor days. Now, he was a man well pleased. He was looking forward to the next years of his life.

He smiled, suddenly no longer nervous.

With glee he looked forward to the wedding night. He wondered when if ever she would let him make love to her in a lighted room. The fun would be in the waiting and wondering. In this end he could be patient.

The ceremony seemed to be over before it began. After all he'd asked the minister to make it short. Caro fumbled over the words especially, when she said she would obey him. When that was said, she stared at him, her eyes furiously cold, coldest ice blue he'd ever seen.

Arrogantly lifting his shoulders, he grinned. He didn't care about obedience. He liked the challenge of new thoughts and ideas. She was entitled to her opinions. Wanted a woman who would keep his life interesting. In bed she excited him. Out of the bedroom she matched him intellectually. What more could a man want? The problem was she had no idea how he felt about her.

She would come to understand he wanted only what was best for her, for the two of them, for their unborn child.

His grin widened uncontrollably, his eyes dancing with amusement, understanding she was still processing all he set in motion. Actually, she set everything in motion by stealing his sperm, by not telling him her objectives. Most undoubtedly, she was probably trying to figure out how she could get her money back before she said I do and he kissed her, before the minister pronounced them husband and wife, Mr. and Mrs. Duncan Murray.

Before they signed the papers.

With the witnesses chatting in the drawing room, Duncan poured champagne. He tapped his glass on Caro's then raised his glass in the air, "To the most beautiful bride in the world. She is mine, everything I've always wished for."

He drank deep and long. The champagne was delicious. He wanted more of everything.

While he kept his gaze focused on her, she sipped then graced him with a tenuous smile. She set the glass on the table. He wondered if she would drink the bubbly. After that he wondered if it would be good for the baby. Maybe he should have toasted his new bride with milk.

"There is a wonderful chocolate cake with vanilla icing my magnificent chef Monsieur Dubois made early this morning. There are also all kinds of pastries waiting for your enjoyment. We will cut the cake then be on our way. I do hope all of you stay and enjoy the delicious morsels waiting for you. Drink the champagne. The house is yours to stay in tonight. There are certainly enough rooms. Mr. Johnston will close the townhouse after everyone leaves in the next few days then join me at the country estate."

"I would stay for a while, speak to our guests. If you don't mind too much?" Caro said, her voice shaking.

He wanted to know if nerves or exhaustion caused the shaking. "Ah, indeed, I see you've an eye on some of the sweets. Dubois has packed a basket for us to take with us. I told him to fill it with the sugary confections just for you. However, I'm going to have to insist you eat the meal before you turn your attentions to the desert, which I've come to learn you crave."

"As you wish," she told him meekly while she studied the toes of her cream-colored slippers.

What the devil? He didn't like that. She was no meek woman. *As I wish?* That wasn't the woman he bargained for, the woman he went to great lengths to secure. He expected just the tiniest bit of a confrontation, maybe a lot of argument about his most recent decry. Thinking on it for a few moments, he figured he could raise her temper if he wanted. Feisty was the way he wanted her.

"I'm glad, no, I'm thrilled you're taking seriously the part of your vows where you promised to obey. I've always wanted an obedient wife."

He kept his grin behind his teeth. The simmering heat in her deep blue eyes was more humorous than he could have anticipated. He relished how the anger would turn to passion. He would have to wait even though it would be damn hard.

This was nice, very nice.

"Yes, my husband," she whispered back at him while Scarlett shot Torra and Honey a wicked glance.

Everyone in the room including him understood she was merely playing a game with him. The two of them would learn about their relationship as they proceeded. It would be hot, the flames they generated when they came together in bed fiery, or against the wall or...would rise higher and more intense than the sun. Hopefully the fire would not scorch them. He held out his hand to her, hoping she would walk by him without taking it, in the process throwing out all the meekness she displayed now.

She didn't.

Inwardly, he laughed, meaning to deal with all her

precociousness. She took his hand, smiling exquisitely at him. He saw the wickedness, the enchanting gleam in her startling clear blue eyes promising retribution. The battle would come sooner than he expected. Afterward, she would dissolve in his arms. Once again, he would show her how good sex between them would be.

What Caro didn't understand was that he was one step in front of her. Not too much time passed before they were in his carriage trundling along. His carriage was well-sprung, made for luxury. The ride would not be too uncomfortable for her. At least he didn't think it would.

What did he know?

He wasn't a pregnant woman. It would be a while before they reached the inn. He probably should have found one closer although he was eager to arrive home. Eager to begin the day-to-day marriage that would be the rest of his life, until he stuck his spoon in the wall. Taking more than two days was out of the question. He let the air he inhaled out in a rush realizing once more he wasn't a lady who was increasing. The time sitting might be terribly awkward for her.

No harm was going to come to her or the baby, not if he could do anything to stop it. "Are you hungry?"

She had to be. Last night she barely ate. All that was sent to the room this morning were a few scones.

"Very." She stared at his mouth then her ardent attention dropped to his crotch.

What the devil? He tried to ignore the blatant perusal. Thought better of it as he set his gaze on her lips. Two could play at this game. Her lips were moist, as if she'd just passed her tongue across them. He let his attention settle on her bosom then lower to her softly rounding belly then the juncture of her thighs, the seat of her passion. This time he didn't keep his smile between his teeth when he watched her adjust her position as if their visual play aroused then tempted her. Well, he knew it didn't take much to bring either one of them to inflamed passion.

"Do you want to play with fire? I find I do."

Slowly, she lowered her lashes then looked at him. "I'm hungry. What did your cook pack for us? My stomach is grumbling. I do believe the *wee bairn* is kicking me, trying to tell me it's time for his lunch."

Duncan's heart caught in his throat. "He's kicking?"

She seemed to think better of her word usage. "No, I'm sorry. It's too soon to feel anything like that. I didn't mean..."

He was disappointed. "Soon though?" His question seemed to amuse her.

"Probably, I sincerely don't know."

This time when she looked down, her cheeks turning pink, he understood what she said was contrived. "So, would you like to see what's inside the basket? I'm serious that you need to eat the sandwich before the dessert."

"You do understand how my sweet tooth works, don't you? I most always eat dessert first. If you insist though. I can try to do as you command, my husband." She accepted the sandwich he handed to her with a grimace. "Roast beef."

"Eat all of it then you can have more food. Anything you like." He looked through the contents of the basket. "Afraid there is only wine to drink."

"I will sip just enough to wash down my food."

He wished he'd had the foresight to ask for water. They couldn't have brought milk for her. Tea would have been fine even if it were cold or warm. "I'm sorry. Didn't think about what was packed to drink, just the sweets. Will have to a better job tomorrow thinking of your motherly needs."

They ate. The food was delicious. True to her word, Caro dank only a fraction of what he gave her. She would need water before they reached the inn. The day was warm. She released the buttons at her throat. He felt as if he let her down, both of them down. In the future he would have to think of new ways to see to her needs.

When she fell asleep, he wanted to pull her into his arms. She looked uncomfortable. Hell, he didn't even give her a chance to change her clothing before ushering her to the carriage. She still wore the silk wedding dress he purchased for her. He was damn uncomfortable in his clothes. A pair of soft doeskins and a simple white shirt would have suited him better. He ran his finger around the collar before he loosened the cravat. After that he unfastened the top of his shirt. He felt better. Didn't know what he could do for her.

His eagerness to leave, to have her all to himself did him in. They would stop sooner than he planned. If it took them a week, his home would still be standing when they arrived. Damn his plans. They weren't worth the thought it took to put them together. He didn't usually lack foresight.

As she twisted on the seat in front of him, she groaned. Her head slipped to the side. Startled, she sat up, rubbing the back of her neck. When she stared at him, she looked as if she was in pain. Her eyes were wide deep circles of blue, dark patches of exhaustion beneath.

"You're tired. We'll stop soon. I've changed my mind about our timetable. Come here." He patted the seat beside him, hoping she would do as he asked. He didn't mean for his words to sound like a command. In lieu of the ceremony, he half expected her to say, yes, my husband.

Not giving her a chance to deny his request or pretend submissiveness, he pulled her onto his lap. With his hand gently on her face, he bade her to sleep.

"Duncan," she said her voice wavering on a thin note that for a moment terrified him. "I don't understand why you wanted to marry me. You don't love me. I don't even think you like me. You detest what I did to you. None of what is happening here makes sense to me."

"Don't over think and don't put thoughts into my head that just aren't there. We suit, you and I. We will get along admirably. Two people do not have to love each other to make a success of their marriage."

Every instant he was with her, he was falling in love with her. He admired her. She intrigued and excited him. Damn, he was aroused right now just holding her.

"I would that you loved me."

Well hell, he would that she loved him too, nevertheless he knew that wasn't to be, not after what he did. She would be angry with him for a very long time. Would most likely find little ways to make him pay. Actually, he looked forward to the ensuing skirmishes.

She did move in order to sleep against him. He turned her, massaging her neck and shoulders. Loose strands of hair trailed down from the swept-up hair do. He couldn't resist a light kiss to the back of her neck. Felt the shivery response. Willed himself to good behavior. She was too tired to indulge in lovemaking in a carriage no less. If he succumbed to this raging desire, he would regret doing so.

Gently, he pulled her closer into his arms. "You need to sleep. We'll stop at the next inn. It's about an hour down the road. It will take an extra day to get home. I know the time will be well-spent."

She nodded her head, allowing him to wrap his arm around her. He felt the soft whisper of air sweep slowly from her lips. It had been wrong of him to make so much haste, he belatedly realized. Not being used to thinking of another's feelings was too new to him.

He would learn.

~ * ~

"Wake up, sleepy head," he kissed her on the forehead. "We are here. You can rest all you want once we get to our rooms."

She sat up looking around while pushing hair from her face. He was gazing at her as if he'd never seen her before. With his thumb he caressed her bottom lip.

"It's..." she began as she moved away from him. "I..."

"You're at a loss for words?" he asked as his grin gave a lift to her heart. "That's unusual."

"It is, isn't it?" she laughed softly.

With his wide grin appearing suddenly, it seemed he delighted in the sound, her laughter something that had been lacking since yesterday's revelations.

He was being nice, nicer than she expected. Everything he wanted was his. If he kept his word, everything she wanted, her research grant would be hers. It was a steep price to pay.

"Come, let's get inside. Need to get out of these clothes. I'm sure you would like something else to wear also." He was out of the carriage before she could blink.

He reached inside, his hands on her waist. He lifted her into his arms, his strides long and sure as he headed toward the inn.

"I can walk." She pounded his shoulder even though she accepted the help, enjoying the comfort of his arms around her.

"I love the way you feel in my arms."

Obviously, he didn't listen to her.

"You will have to put me down. You cannot possibly think to do all that needs to be done before we get to our rooms still carrying me." She sounded indignant. She was. "You're embarrassing me." Caroline felt heat stain her cheeks.

"Wouldn't want to do that."

His laughter was not what she expected. She adored his masculine chuckle. "Seems we can't escape scandal anywhere we go. Do you suppose there are reporters here?"

"Don't need to be sarcastic. I am embarrassed. It's not well done of my new husband to make me blush."

She didn't know what to say to get him to put her down. To no avail, she pounded on his shoulder.

"Can do anything I set my mind too. As it happens, I've stayed here numerous times. They've all the information they will need to charge me as well as send me to my rooms. So, don't have to put you down. Should have planned to stop here in the beginning. My mistake of course, simply because I wanted you in my home as soon as possible." He whistled as he walked through the front room. Nodded at the man at the desk. "My usual room, Sean?"

The man nodded.

"Send up food, whatever the special is, my favorite brandy as well as milk. Maybe a pitcher of water. Oh, make sure there is a chocolate desert of some sort included with the meal." Pleased with himself he continued to whistle.

Caro buried her head against his chest, her mortification growing with each word out of his mouth. He knew her too well. Was able to find her weaknesses despite all her precautions.

"I will see to your needs, Caro. Don't ever think you will want for anything. If I'm too obtuse to recognize what you want, tell me. You as well as my child are important to me. Intend to spoil both of you."

"Don't like milk," she mumbled close to his ear. "Would rather have anything except that."

Her breath whispered across his neck. When his arms tightened, she knew he wanted her, remembered the night of the ball when he took her against the closed door. She shuddered.

He whirled, turned back to speak to the man again. "In about an hour send up hot water for a bath." Then to her, "What would you drink?"

Reluctantly, knowing he was right, "I'll try the milk. Could you put chocolate in it? Might make it more palatable."

"Good girl. Perhaps you're right, chocolate in it would do the trick. You will like it then?"

She pushed away long enough for her to see the simmering heat in his eyes. "You know I will."

A tiny mew of desire rippled from her. She knew that look all too well. The quirky wicked smile coupled with the simmering heat of his eyes. He wanted her. He walked back to the desk. "Instead of milk, we'll have hot chocolate."

Seemingly unable to resist the dewy moisture slick on her lips, he kissed her. Touched his tongue inside her mouth. Traced her teeth, sucked the bottom lip into his. When he stopped and she looked up, he was grinning hugely.

Once more he spoke to the man behind the desk. "My new wife. Married her today. Want to make everything perfect for her and the wee *bairn*. She wanted my seed so I gave it to her."

She groaned, hiding her face again. When he reached the room, he juggled her in his arms to reach the handle. "Should have put you over my shoulder. This would have been much easier. Would have had two hands to use."

"Would have hurt the *wee bairn*, you cad," she muttered between clenched teeth. "What were you thinking? How dare you say that to people we don't even know. Do you like embarrassing me?"

"The truth is always best, isn't it? I do enjoy the color on your cheeks." He arched a brow skyward. "I'm a proud papa. Going to tell everyone my good news. No need to keep it secret."

"It isn't their business."

"True, it was a tiny bit of retribution," he told her as he kicked the door shut then turned. "Everything else I told you is true. Besides, I've known Sean for at least ten years."

He let her feet drop. Her toes didn't reach the floor. Before she knew it her legs were wrapped around his big body. His hands cupped her buttocks. She found herself pressed against the wall.

"Remember this? Remember the ball? Apparently, I can't forget. Got to have more of Caro."

Suddenly, he was touching her, caressing her in the most intimate places. She sucked in air. Her body flamed, the dance between them primal, as old as time before time.

"Thought I was supposed to sleep," she closed her eyes absorbing all the ecstasy into her.

"After this. I find I cannot help myself. Sleep later." Her underclothing on the floor, he was deep inside her. Her sultry core giving him easy entrance, kissed him with heat, throbbed drawing him ever deeper. She climaxed in seconds, her body pulsing around him, driving him to push harder and faster until he too joined her in the euphoric sensations.

His forehead rested against hers. "I'm sorry..."

To Caroline he didn't sound the least bit contrite. "You shouldn't say things you don't mean?"

"I do mean the words. It's just...well hell. You make me crazy. When you tempt me with heat-filled eyes, your body oozing against me, I can't resist. The way those eyes of yours shimmer with the promise of sexual ecstasy is irreverent."

She hoped it would always be that way between them. For now, though, she wanted to hang on to her irritation. He made her foolish too, foolish for him. She wasn't going to tell him something he knew.

With her legs still wrapped around him, he walked to the bed. He set her on it, standing back, lust still shimmering deep in his eyes. He fastened his trousers. "Let's get you out of that dress and into something more comfortable. What do you say?"

"Would love to. What do I have to change into?" She didn't know what he brought with them. He told her a trunk was packed. When she looked, she saw no sight of his or her trunk.

With the knock on the door, she hoped it was her belongings. It was along with his.

"Well?" he stepped back, his feral masculine grin wide. "Would you like me to help you pick out something to wear?"

"You can't stay in here when I change my clothes." She watched as he opened the chest for her, pulling out a lavender muslin day dress. "This should suit. Should make you more comfortable," he paused, rummaging a bit farther. "Perhaps your matronly night dress would be better. After we eat, I'm going to leave for a while so you can sleep. You look exhausted to the bone."

"Where are you going?" She sat up straighter thinking she didn't want him to leave her alone. She also didn't want to be in the room with him when he had nothing to do, knowing what would happen between them.

"There's a card game downstairs. Thought I might have some fun, win a bit of change." His smile stretched across his handsome face. "Would you like some pin money since you have none?"

"You did tell me you were a gambler. I suppose you have money to lose. Hope I didn't just get married to a wastrel."

"Ah, Caro, you give me no credit, never have. You've such little faith in me." He sat down beside her tracing her jawline before sliding his finger down her neck to rest at the pulse at the base that was still throbbing uncontrollably. "I've more than enough money. As I told you before, I know how to win. Also know when to stop. Can ferret out cheaters. While I make it a point never to confront a man like that, I will always pull out of a game there is no chance in hell of winning.

Thought you would like privacy before we share the marriage bed. Tonight, we can practice all the ways we've made love, maybe try something new. Would you like that, Caro? I mean to keep you up at least half the night even though I understand you will need more sleep than I."

"I do want privacy." She nodded toward the door, an expectant look on her face. "You will give it to me?"

"Soon as you prove you can unfasten the dress you are wearing." Stepping back, he crossed his arms over his chest. His gaze drifted the length of her while he waited.

She knew her expression fell. Knew he had her where he wanted her. Again. "You are right, husband," she told him meekly. "I cannot do it by myself. Honey fastened them all before the wedding."

He roared, his laughter echoing around the room. "There is my biddable and humble wife. I thought I lost her. It is a welcome change to have her back. Will you keep me guessing as to which wife I will encounter?"

She smiled sweetly, hoping he was actually going to do what he was saying. An ache swept through her. Loss filled her. "No, my husband, I'm still very much with you, humble as well as submissive."

"Come, let me unfasten the gown. As long as you're being meek, obeying my every command or wish, I brought a negligée and robe I want you to wear. It's meant for me to see you better." His masculine chuckle unnerved her.

Hastily, he unfastened her dress then unlaced her corset. While she held the fabric to her breasts, he found the sheer gown and robe he wished her to wear. It was a pale pink confection. It was beautiful. She understood why he wanted her to wear the negligée. He wanted to see all of her. In this she had nothing she could hide from him.

She'd never owned anything such as this, so extravagant as well as revealing.

Before sitting, he rested his hands on the arms of the chair. Even though he looked nonchalant, she knew he watched her. He would make love to her again. They would not be able to stop themselves. He blew out the candles. The room was cloaked in shadows.

Swiftly, she donned the night clothing he gave her. She was clad from neck to her toes, yet if the light had been burning, he could have seen all of her. When the knock on the door sounded, he wrapped a quilt around her shoulders.

Servants entered with food and drink. They were gone in seconds. He lit the candle on the table. Once again, she was alone with her new husband. They ate. The food was delicious. He sipped his brandy. She drank her chocolate milk. She found some left over chocolate truffles in the basket of food that had been sent with them. They were just as good the second time around.

The bath water he ordered was brought into the room. He stood.

"That's my cue to leave."

"The bath is for me?"

"I'll take mine when I return. Sleep," he told her then he vanished, the lock to the door falling into place behind him.

The bath eased her sore muscles. He was correct in assuming the carriage ride drained her of energy aligned with the tension he generated when he informed her of what he did with her finances. All the candles and gaslights she extinguished. The room was dark. Unlike the night before, moonlight drifted through the open window.

She slept.

When she woke, it was to feel his hard body pressed against her, his large, slightly calloused hands exploring her legs, bringing the gown higher just as he'd done the night before. He told her he would make love to her half the night. It was why he insisted she sleep. Restoring her energy was imperative. She didn't want to make love, at least not until he explained to her how much money he lost while gambling.

She knew he'd lost money. Men who gambled also lied. They always lost hard earned money. Her father often lied to his mother although he wasn't a wastrel. Lord, she hoped she didn't just marry a squanderer, a man who had to rely on his brothers to keep him in all the fine things he took advantage of. She felt sorry for his brothers, wondered why they didn't put him on an allowance. He certainly spent a great deal of money at this inn in just one night. Perhaps it was her money he was spending. The thought sent a terrified ripple of apprehension through her. Did he marry her for her money?

They must keep this room for him, perhaps for his entire family. His brothers must pay for the extravagance, the sudden unexpected thought making her feel better.

When his hand cupped her breast, she couldn't help herself, "Duncan. Stop!"

"Don't want to. Been waiting half the night for this. It's our wedding night." He nuzzled her neck, bit and nipped his way to her ear. "You're too damn tempting for that to happen."

Her body stirred heating to a mercuric level. "No, you have to answer one question for me."

"Don't want to." His lips and teeth found her ear. Bit gently. "Don't like questions. Besides, you're the dutiful wife, remember?"

She struggled against his hold, turning she pushed on his chest. "How much did you lose?" she uttered the words wishing this room wasn't so blasted dark so she could see his eyes.

Eyes were the mirrors to the soul. By looking at them she would know if he told the truth. This way his words would mean nothing.

"Won one thousand English pounds. Thought I'd invest the money for you. We could buy the roses you need for your research. Told you that you needed pin money. Now, can we continue with more pleasant endeavors?"

She needed to ask if one of his brothers could invest it instead of him. She felt a traitor just thinking those thoughts.

"Yes, yes, supposed that would actually be a very good idea. What's going to happen to the roses at my old home?"

A stab of sorrow filled her. To Caroline it seemed she had lived there forever. The place across from Letty's was the only place she'd ever been able to call home. When she lived with her father, the duke, she always felt as if she didn't belong.

"You can use them, graft them or whatever you do to the new roses. Don't you want to use the pollen too? Don't actually know what it is you're doing other than the fact I heard your work had something to do with figuring out how and why animals as well as plants have different characteristics." His hand skimmed a leg higher then higher still, until she felt his calloused hand resting on her hip.

She sipped air.

"Yes, you're right."

She supposed that whatever he knew about how characteristics were passed on and what she might be doing with the roses was way over his ability to understand. A man with so little to offer in the way of intelligence would know next to nothing about the passing on of characteristics from one generation to the next as well as what she was trying to prove. Overriding and retreating genes would be beyond his capabilities to understand.

"What is your research about? Why were you refused a grant at the university all these years?"

"Because I'm a woman. You wouldn't understand." Trying to explain her theories to a man with such low intelligence would take a decade or more. No, if she could evade the topic, it would be so much better. She could always go back to his amorous intentions to avoid speaking about her ideas.

"A woman should be given as many opportunities as a man, especially a woman as brilliant as you seem to be. Why don't you try me and see if I can comprehend the tiniest detail?"

"Trust me you won't," she uttered the words suddenly feeling guilt as she watched the slow simmer of anger cross his features.

"Then we can make love now." His fingers closed on a breast, flicking across a hardened peak. "No, perhaps not yet, I want you to explain this to me. Something makes me believe you don't think I'm very smart. If you give me a chance you might be surprised."

She gasped in a breath of air choking while his fingers squeezed the breast they'd been holding and now teasing the nipple with his thumb. "Don't blame me if you don't understand anything. The explanation is complicated. Most people wouldn't understand."

While she tried desperately to put a few coherent thoughts together, he continued to tease her body with promises of more sexual delight.

"You've said as much. I'm not most people." He squeezed again, ran his thumb atop her nipple. "I'm your husband."

She closed her eyes willing words that he would understand to come into play so she could use them. At the moment, she was having a difficult time thinking. "Well, to begin, when two people with blue eyes marry, all their children will have blue eyes. The color of blue will vary, nonetheless the children always have some form of blue eyes."

"That's not hard to understand. Unless of course, the woman cheats on her husband with a man who has brown eyes. If a man doesn't know what you do, he might believe the child is his. That is something to think about."

"Truly, Duncan, don't complicate this more with your wicked thoughts. I'm calling the factor a retreating factor," she told him still trying desperately to put this into words he would understand.

His teasing hands didn't help. Perhaps that had been her problem in writing the papers for the grants. Her hypothesis was too complicated. She needed simplicity to sell it to the dean.

"Why retreating?" he asked as his hand slid down the curve of her hip then lower as he continued to coax a response.

Her hips arched seeming to beg for more, "Because..." she gulped air trying to ignore the simmering flames in order to concentrate on what she tried to say. "Because when a brown eyed person and a blue-eyed person have babies, sometimes the eyes are brown, sometimes they are blue, but most often they are brown."

"I don't understand."

Ha! She knew he wouldn't. "Since most often the occurrence results in a brown eyed child, I'm assuming that the brown factor overrides the blue."

She sounded smug even to herself. This theory made so much sense. She wanted to be able to prove it.

"Which would lead to the conclusion that everyone male or female have two factors for eye color." He second-guessed her theory.

"You're right!" She was shocked, amazed he would come to such a conclusion. "How did you come to that observation?"

His questing fingers delved and parted her in the most delicious ways. "Doesn't it make sense? What other factors can you trace to retreating as well as overriding genes? How would it apply to roses?"

"That's what I'm not sure about."

Maybe that was another reason she'd been denied. There was so much she wasn't sure of. Perhaps she should start with white and red roses.

"So, what other factors can result in this easy reading of the passing on of characteristics?"

"Well, nothing is ever truly easy. While eye color is the simplest there are so many varying shades that it's actually very complicated. Hair color is the same way. There are many more people who have dark brown hair rather than blond or red. Perhaps dark hair overrides the lighter colors."

"You think you could draw similar conclusions? What about green eyes and red hair?" His questing hands settled at the apex of her thighs, parted her, delved deeper thrust inside her vagina.

Her hips bucked as she still tried to hold the exploding passion back. "There," she swallowed hard, sucked in air, "are things like what we call a widow's peak. Few people have one." She sucked in more air. "Oh, God, Duncan."

"Neither of us have a widow's peak. Does that mean our wee *bairn* won't either?"

"Probably not."

"What about ears?"

"What about them?" She was drowning in the flames kissing her where his hands roamed. The devil, but she couldn't think of anything except what his hands were generating.

"So, your ears don't come straight to the side of your head. Mine do. I much prefer yours. Gives me something for my teeth to hold on to. What kind of ears do you think our little lad will have?"

"*Lassie.*"

"What kind of ears?" He tugged on hers while his fingers continued to seduce in the most intimate parts of her.

"I don't know." Her voice was a thin wail. "Never studied anyone's ears before. They are usually covered by hair. How do you know about ears?"

His tongue swirled inside her ear.

"Like everything about a woman's ears," he whispered softly so close to hers. "Like kissing and tasting, swirling my tongue inside while feeling hot feminine shivers of pleasure glide temptingly through her body. Pleasuring a woman, in this case my wife, is all about the arousal."

His penis was inside her then. She climaxed almost the moment he thrust deep inside touching her womb. He held her close, calming her as he ran his hands along her arms then her back.

"Hush, sweeting, you'll be fine. That was only the first time. We've all night to talk about overriding as well as retreating characteristics. I like your feet. What do you think, are there any interesting things to note about feet or the backs of your knees? What about the twin dimples at the base of your spine? We can explore all the intriguing possibilities."

~ * ~

"You've only been back one week. She is in the kitchen again, making a mess. Tell her she cannot go into my kitchen." Monsieur Dubois paced Duncan's office waving his hands in the air. He swore softly beneath his breath. His face was red either from anger or the heat of the kitchen.

"I will talk to her. Actually, you are going to have to live with her in the kitchen." Duncan grinned at him understanding her sweet tooth drove her there.

Her need for sugar seemed insatiable. She loved making cookies.

"Why?" Dubois settled his hands on his hips trying for the words that would convince his employer that his wife had no business in his domain. "Why does she keep tormenting me?"

"She loves her chocolate," Duncan laughed softly thinking about the chocolate bonbons he brought home from the village the other night. Together in bed he fed them to her.

"She makes such a mess." There, he appeared pleased as if that statement would fix his problem. "I cannot create delightful meals if I have to work around dirty baking dishes. She cannot be there."

"She told me when she asked what I thought about her baking that she always cleans up the messes. Did she lie?"

Well, the thought was a pointed question he wasn't going to be able to answer. "No, she didn't lie except the truth of the matter is that she is underfoot." He waved a hand again. "She is always in the way. Not used to having anyone working around me in my kitchen. Don't like bumping into her every time I turn around. When I go to the pantry, I don't' want to have to wait for her to get out."

"You will have to learn. Caro is the lady of the house. Is she there now?"

He wanted to watch her baking. Needed to see her with whatever she was using for ingredients dusted on her pert little nose. He hoped she

170

wasn't particular about getting dirty.

"Yes, she's decided she wants to learn to bake bread. Been there very nearly all day long, trying this and that. Her first try was a big loaf of bread." He had to admit to the earl. "It will do for sandwiches. Dinner will be an hour late tonight because I can't get around her. She is occupying the ovens."

Maybe if he appealed to the earl's stomach, he would set his wife straight on her duties, which surely did not include baking. "Why don't you take her riding? That would help me. I might even be able to produce an edible meal by seven if I'm not dancing around her."

He watched as the earl waved a hand in the air, seeming to beam. "Take the day off. We'll eat what she is making along with whatever else might be left in the kitchen. I believe there should be ham. We can use that loaf of bread."

"She is trying to make bread. It's her second attempt. The first loaf might work. No one has tasted it. That's another thing. The kitchen was filled with smoke. Could barely breathe. Don't want to take the day off," he muttered, "I feel as if I've let you down. Never taken a day off since I've worked for you. Don't want to do it now."

Duncan stood. "Then you deserve the time. Cook a fabulous meal for your wife. I know all your family ever gets are our leftovers. Do something romantic. Maybe a dinner eaten by candlelight, what do you think?"

"I believe a day off won't solve the problem. Yesterday she was making chocolate cookies. The day before she told me she wanted to learn how to make a chocolate desert that has crème in the middle. This won't end with a day off. Until you do something, her exploits in my kitchen will continue."

"Besides evicting her from the kitchen, what would you suggest? If I had something to offer in return, she might not be so disappointed. She so loves to bake."

Dubois seemed to think for the longest time. When he looked up with a ghost of an idea, Duncan saw he was smiling, his emotions changing.

"You've thought of something?" Duncan asked. "As I said earlier,

I don't want to disappoint her. Will not keep her from doing what she loves."

"I never come into work until a little before the noon hour. Could the kitchen be hers until then? If she promised to have everything done and cleaned, I would be pleased to share. She could also pursue her hobby at night after I left."

"Good suggestion. I will run it by her. I'm sure she will be pleased. She can have every morning to bake as long as she is finished by eleven." He paused tapping his finger on the desk in front of him. "Sometimes I keep her in bed until then. Suppose she will just have to forgo baking on those days."

"I hope that satisfies her." Dubois backed from the room, "I hope the lady of the house will bow to your wishes."

"I will miss her cookies. Take the day off. I will see you tomorrow. What exactly is Caro working on now?"

"Once more," he repeated, "She is up to her elbows in bread dough. Another loaf mayhap or something else, I had no idea when I left to talk with you. So upset I was, I didn't ask her."

The earl's wicked grin sent strange thoughts into his head.

Chapter Seven

So, Caro is up to her elbows in bread dough?

The thought delighted him, intrigued him as well. He meant to pursue her vulnerability to his advantage. She would have no hands with which to push him away or try to control what he was about to do. Caro would find herself at his mercy.

He was still irritated with her for her lack of confidence in his abilities to understand her simple ideas. He wasn't stupid as she thought of him. She still hadn't seen the diplomas in his office. He meant to surprise her sometime with the evidence of his acumen. She would be furious with him. It wasn't his fault she came to the wrong conclusion making false assumptions about his lack of aptitude. He couldn't keep the laughter from tumbling out. She would learn though.

For a moment he stared in the direction of the kitchen going over all the wonderful possibilities. His mind was thorough.

When he saw her, he grinned from ear to ear. Dubois had not lied to him. He could have given him more details. Her hands were indeed immersed in sticky bread dough. She had not yet added enough flour so she could knead her concoction. She would finish this loaf of bread after he was finished with her. Ah, but he would not be finished for quite some time.

Her face was dusted with the flour she used, white patches across her lovely cheeks. He locked the two doors to the kitchen before he strode to his wife.

"Duncan?" She paused to push an errant strand of hair from her face with her arm. "You've got that look on your face. Can't you see I'm busy? It's not the time or the place for a dalliance. Someone could walk in on us." She glanced at him. Her look said hands off. "No, I don't want you to do this."

"Sent Dubois home for the day. Locked the doors. No one is here who could walk in on us. You're mine to do with as I please for the rest of the afternoon."

Endless possibilities. He imagined himself deep inside her. Imagined her cry of pleasure. Ah, her lips were moist, pliant.

"Duncan!" she screeched when his lips settled on the back of her neck kissing the length, nibbling where his lips were pressed.

"Let me see. I've had you on the couch in the drawing room, two of the eight bedrooms. I do believe in the kitchen is next on my list."

He was randy as hell just thinking about where his male part was going to visit in the next few minutes. It would not take much to ready her. She was probably dripping wet for him now.

"No."

"It's sounding as if you try to deny me, your husband. What happened to obey? You are supposed to be meek and biddable."

"This is carrying obey too far. Can't you see? I'm baking bread." Her breath rushed out as his hands slipped under her skirt.

He ran his hands along the insides of her legs to the apex. "You can do nothing to stop me, sweeting."

His fingers found tender slick flesh, hot, swollen with just this tiny coaxing. Her underwear slipped to the floor. He picked her up so they would not be wound around her feet.

She was amazing, adorable too. He wished he could see the dimples on either side of her mouth. He would kiss them next time.

Caro was ready for him. Only a few seconds later he was pushing into her, faster and faster as he started to reach his climax.

"Duncan!"

"Ah, I've missed this. We should make love every morning in the kitchen, on the floor, against the door or while you are baking something delectable. Although it is of my opinion there is nothing more delectable and delicious than you. You are my favorite sweet confection. I've spoken with Dubois or should I say he spoke to me. He is not happy that you are getting underfoot in his kitchen so to speak. I do like you under me as well as riding me. We'll have to try that again soon."

She was panting now. He ran his hands along her arms and back to soothe her tattered nerves. His hands grazed her sensitive nipples. She was so predictable. She would tell him no then give all of herself to him.

He was pleased with his wife.

He forgave her for stealing his sperm.

Duncan knew she wanted to ask him what he and the cook talked about. She was too weak with her woman's pleasure for speech. As a patient man he would wait for her to regain her strength. It would not take long. Her recovery was always remarkable.

More minutes passed. She leaned her head against his chest, her breathing slowing.

"We can do this again. Did you like your pinnacle?" It was a man's question. He wanted her to answer. Understood she wouldn't. Needed to hear how good he was.

Finally, "What did you talk to the cook about?"

He would make her wait for the good news. "As soon as the dough has been shaped and cooked, we should go for a ride. Would you like to ride with me?" He had more than one idea here. She would understand both. If anything, she was a brilliant woman.

She tugged in a huge gulp of air. He knew what she was wondering. "Can't possibly do that, ride with you. This won't be done for a great deal of time. Still has to rise twice. I'm wanting to make cinnamon rolls."

"Ah, more sweet stuff for your never-ending sweet tooth. We should stay here in this room. Instead of finding a good mount, we can remain in the kitchen. I wouldn't want boredom to set in while you wait for your dough to swell. While the dough is rising, I can sit on one of the kitchen chairs. You can mount me instead of the horse I've picked out for you. Your pretty parts can swell for me personally. Either ride will pleasure us both. Bring us to ecstasy. What do you think?"

Her hands were still in the dough, his fingers still embracing the curves of her hips, squeezing. He wanted to see her face. The expressions flitting across her beautiful features would tell him so much more than her silence or even the ensuing words if she chose to speak to him.

Then, "I think not. You should leave now." Her voice wavered with a broken sound of her rising passion.

He knew she wanted him again. He grinned.

"I'm bored this afternoon. With nothing to do, no work to set my very agile mind to exploring ways to increase my fortune, I find I'm fighting the tediousness of this afternoon. Isn't that what an obedient wife is for? To ease her husband's world-weariness, give him something to do with his hands? A man needs to have sensitive places for his hands to find purchase."

"Of course, my husband," she purred sweetly, pushing against him. "I would do most anything to ease the dullness of your afternoon. If I did so now, you would become a sticky mess. Bread dough painting places I'm sure you wouldn't want to be covered with. Bread dough is not tasty."

He thought of his member covered in the sticky stuff. Thought if she made cinnamon rolls coupled with the cinnamon, sugar and butter covering his penis, she might kiss the sweetness away. It would be torture and pleasure all at the same time. He wanted to lick the sweet confection from her breasts as well as other parts. He was reminded of the rouge he was supposed to have delighted in his days before marriage.

"Believe my thoughts have run to something more appealing. I'll watch and wait for the best opportunity." With that said he stepped away pushing the sexual beast inside him to the back of his mind. He could let that male animal surface later. While she smoothed her skirts, he enjoyed the tantalizing wiggling of her buttocks as she aroused him with the adorable gesture. He was sure she was ready for him again. What to do?

"No, you should take a ride on your giant black stallion. If you go for a couple of hours, the rolls will be finished, hot and mouthwatering. I'll bring them to the dining room table. We can eat them for dinner since you sent Dubois away before he prepared the last meal of the day."

He wanted her to be his last meal of the day. "How long before the first rising is done?" He did need to relieve tension. A ride of a different sort did sound appealing while he waited to see what pleasures awaited him in the kitchen. He wished she would come with him. Possibly tomorrow.

"An hour or so?" Her words were hesitant as if she wondered what exactly he was up to. "Why?"

"Thought I would leave you in peace until you reach the cinnamon and sugar stage." His ideas were rapidly assuming a character all their own.

"I don't trust you. Don't want the sticky stuff on me. Think I'll stick to a loaf of bread. Plain bread will do just fine."

Well hell, he should never have told her his plans. She guessed his intentions. Definitely, he would have to think of something else to spend his time on or find a way to ignore his wife for the next couple hours.

With flour still dusted on her face, she was so endearing. He wanted to devour her. It didn't seem she was having anything to do with that. Heaving a huge sigh and on the off chances she was lying to him about her bread dough plans, he said, "I'll go riding. As you so nicely put the events of this afternoon in order, I need to find something better to do. My thoughts were a fantasy that was all." He started from the kitchen unlocking the door to the dining room then heading to the back door and stables. "Dubois agreed with me that you can have the kitchen until eleven each morning. After that this room is his."

"That won't do. You almost always keep me in bed that long. I'll never get to use the space as I would like."

"It is the deal. We could always come down at midnight. Whip up something delightful for a bedtime snack. Although you are the snack I enjoy the most."

"You would be with me?" Her censure to that idea was very clear.

"Cooking with my wife would be a pleasant pass time. There is so much you could teach me."

"You *ken verra* well if you followed me here, we would get nothing finished."

He grinned as he stepped out the door. In a few minutes his horse was saddled. He was riding. Fresh pine filled air stung his nostrils. Wind ruffled through his hair. Warm August sun beat down from the sky. He wondered if he would always want his wife as much as he did now. He supposed he would have to wait to find out.

He turned his horse, heading for the frigid loch located on Murray property. Swimming would cool him off until he saw her again, until he thought of her. For some reason it didn't surprise him when his father joined him.

"Saw you from a distance. Thought I'd join you."

Duncan slowed his horse to a walk. "If you're asking about this quarter's financial statement, you'll have to wait. I've been busy with my wife. I am a newlywed, you comprehend." Duncan understood his father and mother were eager to meet his wife. He wasn't ready to share her yet. When they saw how old she was, they would question his reasoning. While he didn't want his son to grow up a bastard, that wasn't the only reason he insisted they wed. His father would want to know it all. Would want to understand why he did something there was no need for him to do. If he didn't want to wed, he could legitimatize his son.

"No, your mother wants to know when she can meet Caroline. Seems you managed to wed a duke's daughter amidst scandal of the worst sort. Surprised your mother, me as well."

His father was right. He'd be the last to deny what had been talked about the duration of his visit to London. Caro must have felt the brunt of the gossip here in Glasgow. Crazy thing was, he didn't believe she cared. She went about her business accepting the fact her true friends didn't care about the thriving gossip and innuendos.

"All you say is true. Caro isn't like anyone else I've ever met."

So very true, he needed to treat her with more respect. Needed to look to her needs as well as protect her from his lust. The problem was she lusted for him as much so protecting her was beyond default.

"Your mother and I figured that out. You've never been a man to treat a woman as you did Caroline. I even chuckled when I saw the rendition in the paper after the university ball."

He was shaking his head at himself as well as his unruly body. Admitting reluctantly to his father, "I can't keep my hands off her. When I look at her, I have to have her. When I think about her..."

"You might not want to hear something like this. I'm going to tell you anyway. I feel the same about your mother. When I met her, even now. However, I never tossed her over my shoulder at a charity ball or any other kind. What you did behind the closed door of your bedroom is ripe with speculation. Has me guessing but also understanding my assumption is correct as is everyone else's."

"You still lust after my mother? No, don't answer that. I'm sure it's more than I want to know. The devil, but I do want to know if I'll feel the same way about Caro when I'm fifty or even seventy-years-old." He didn't want anything concerning their sexual life to change. However, he did want to vanquish his anger at her. Even though he forgave her, he was still angry at the way she handled the situation.

Well hell, she lied to him. Lied to him about his child. He would have to figure a way to get over the lie. Set out to deceive him.

"Yes, and I'm sure you will. A woman such as Caroline comes along only once in a lifetime. Don't mess up your relationship. Come to terms with how you feel about the woman."

"Your words of warning come too late. In too many ways to count I've already done so, messed it up. I had to though. Didn't have a choice. Caro wouldn't have married me if I didn't have something to hold over her head. I took something very dear to her away, leaving her with nothing."

"What did you do?" His father was watching him as if he knew this was dire. It was and he found it amusing.

Duncan wasn't sure but he thought his father was holding his laughter back at his expense. There was nothing funny about the situation he was in now. He hurt Caro deeply. In time, if things changed between them, he would give all he took from her back. She would be pleased to see her savings doubled or tripled.

"Decided to give her tit for tat. She took something from me. So, I returned the sentiment."

"Now that's specific. What did she do to you?"

He did laugh then, roared with it would be a better description. Duncan was sure he must know the answer to his question. His brothers would not have kept Caro's pregnancy a secret. At the wedding it was obvious she was increasing.

"You do *ken* the answer. She stole my sperm."

"You returned this by doing what?"

Needing to explain himself, he said, "Caro doesn't know it, however I'm the man who has invested all her money over the last seven years, since she was eighteen. It was easy for me to transfer all her funds to my name. In addition, I managed to sign both her homes into my name. Having the resources at my disposal the deed was not difficult to accomplish."

"That's down right thievery. Would have been yours by marriage though." His father said the obvious.

He didn't want or need her property or money. "She wouldn't have wed me. Values her independence too much."

The urgent need to defend his actions rose hard and fast. His gut burned while he remembered what she did. The fury he felt at the discovery surfaced anew. "She stole my sperm! Lied to me!"

He needed to hit something. Every time he thought about her thievery his temper escalated.

"A woman can do that? You know what the repercussions of staying inside her were. You should have taken precautions. How is this her fault? It seems to me you know better."

His anger turned to fury. "She presented herself to me as a whore right down to the rouged nipples and other parts. Believed whores took precautions. Didn't know she was pretending. Didn't know she was a virgin. The devil, but she'd never even been kissed."

"Ah, I see. So Caroline Kenworth duped you. That must not sit well with you. Perhaps that's the crux of your problems with her not the fact she conceived from your seed."

Perhaps his father was right. Maybe that's why he'd been so very angry with her when he discovered what she did and why. In his recollection, no man and especially not a female had ever duped him before. His fury also stemmed from the fact she didn't tell him about her condition. A man deserves and needs to know if he has sired a child. It's his right.

"She did," he admitted reluctantly. "Caro wanted the baby. In addition, she wasn't ever going to tell me. She fled to Edinburgh the moment I left for London. Upon her return, she had a story concocted explaining the babe as a cousin's, one who died giving birth."

"She could have done better. There is something missing in this explanation though. Why did she pick you to be the father of her child?

You are a good choice of course but..."

He grit his teeth, fury simmering at the reason. "Another factor in the list of crimes against me. She wanted me for the father because she believes me to be stupid, a dolt, a man who relies on his brothers for his income."

That brought another burst of laughter from his father. "Truly, she believes one of the most brilliant men in all of the British Isles maybe more, is stupid. In my humble opinion, she has a great deal to learn about her husband."

"She does."

"As, I'm sure you do about her. Sounds as if the two of you are both stubborn to the breaking point."

"Well, I've got more to learn about her as well as her convoluted reasoning. At every turn she baffles me. The only thing I'm positive about is her eagerness to have sex with me."

"Why would she want an unintelligent man to be the father of her child? Doesn't make sense."

"To begin with, she is positive this *bairn* in her womb is a *lass*."

"That makes a difference?" his father questioned, one eyebrow arched to the sky.

"Apparently so. She doesn't want her girl to be like her."

He would give anything if he had a girl just like his Caro. He prayed she or he would be more intelligent than either of them.

"Beautiful and intelligent. While I haven't met her, I would assume you would never wed anyone who didn't possess those characteristics. So, tell me again why she wanted the father to be stupid."

His teeth clenched together so tightly his jaw hurt, understanding his anger wasn't going to leave him anytime soon. He couldn't wave it away just by wishing it gone. "It's very simple. At least she thinks it is. Caro doesn't want her female child to be like her. It seems because of her great intelligence she has suffered. Of course, she is a bluestocking. Can't keep her nose out of books. Her father never favored her because of this as well as the fact his first-born was not male. And... because she had no interest in balls or meeting men under circumstances that aren't conducive to actually getting to know someone, she was never courted.

Never even been kissed until me. She can't dance, at least that is what she tells me. Her talents are not inclined toward music."

"So, she was a virgin when you met her. A virgin pretending to be a whore?" That brought more skepticism to his father's words along with more chuckles.

"An escort more appropriately."

"Ah, one of Scarlett's girls."

"Just for that one night. She counted the days between her monthly's, knew when the best time to conceive would be. As it happened that day, the first time was on my birthday. Now, wasn't that convenient? My brothers gave her to me as a gift."

"Must have been for her intentions. She would have had to convince Scarlett." His father's laughter made him realize how foolish he'd been. "If you were the man she wanted to sire her child, she would have found another way. It's apparent to all Glasgow the night of the ball was another perfectly timed attempt to conceive."

"You're right. She didn't think she conceived that first time so she had to try again, the charity ball." He fisted his hands remembering exactly how he felt when he first saw her in the ballroom.

"You played right into her hands."

"True."

"Believe I'm more eager now than before to meet this girl."

"I'm not sure I'm ready for anyone in my family to meet her. My brothers attended the wedding but didn't talk to her. I whisked her off as soon as the ceremony was finished and the cake cut."

Again, he reminded himself that was probably not the best thing to have done. While he was having the devil of a time forgiving her, she was probably faced with the same feelings.

"I'm certainly glad I'm no longer young. Does she know yet how intelligent you are?"

"Not yet. I intend for that to happen soon. Have a burning need to get all the lies as well as assumptions out in the open."

"She'll be angry."

"Furiously so. Nonetheless, she cannot be angry with me. I didn't make the supposition. She was the one who kept secrets. Still she believes

I'm not up to snuff where it concerns the mind. I'm not sure seeing a few diplomas will change her low opinion of my brainpower."

"Since you're headed to the loch with the intention of cooling down, I'll let you go. You've got my mind thinking about your mother. Believe I'll head home. Expect to get an invitation to dinner soon. It's about time she meets the rest of the family."

Duncan watched his father's back as he made his way to the manor home about a mile from his. This was all Murray property. His brothers owned homes nearby also. They would be expecting invitations he wasn't ready to issue.

The frigid swim in the loch cooled his enthusiasm for his wife momentarily. However, when he walked into the kitchen an hour or so later, the lust roared back with a vengeance he couldn't cool. He didn't understand how the sight of her never failed to set him on fire.

Her face was still dusted in flour. At the moment her bodice was unfastened far enough he saw the valley between her breasts. He sipped in as much air as possible. The sweet curves swayed slightly as she turned to see who came into the room. She smiled. The little sip of air he managed to inhale wedged in his throat.

The pan was filled with cinnamon rolls. The breadboard covered in the cinnamon, sugar concoction. He wanted to dip his finger in it then trace her bottom lip with the sweetness he found. After that he wanted to taste her, see if she was as delicious as he expected. Run his tongue along her lips. He could put drops of the sweet stuff on her nipples, lick and sip.

The devil, but he tormented himself. He locked both doors. This was his fantasy. Before the evening was finished, he meant to change the erotic images to reality. She could lick the tasty sugar off any part of his body she chose. After that they would bathe. Perchance he would have her in the bath the two of them would share.

~ * ~

Caroline sucked air when she turned and saw him, standing with his hands on his narrow hips in the middle of the kitchen. When he strode to lock the doors, she knew she was in trouble. Problem was she didn't have a clue about the exact nature of his intentions. Wasn't sure she cared.

"I'm not done," she ventured to say as his steps brought him closer. "With the cinnamon..." She lost all thought processes.

He stopped long enough to grab a chair then bring it next to her. His grin was too wide, too broad as well as too all-knowing. Her heart pounded as she searched for an escape route. She couldn't go anywhere until the rolls finished baking. She needed to clean the area to make Monsieur Dubois happy. The look in his dark brown eyes both terrified her as well as excited her. He would do just as he pleased. Unable to admit to herself, what pleased him would certainly also please her.

He sat down. Reached out to her. She gasped when his large hands settled around her waist. With no effort he lifted her, pushing her legs apart so she straddled him. His intentions were simmering in his dark brown eyes in the scintillating shadows. There was no doubt that he wanted her.

"Do either of your parents have blue eyes?" she blurted as if the question could stop whatever it was he planned.

Her breaths came in short gasps. So hot, she was ready to feel him deep inside her.

"Trying to defer my thoughts to something else are you, Caro?" His questing fingers demolished the fasteners down her front. Earlier, before he spread her legs, he'd rid her of her drawers. She wore nothing beneath her dress. Finding her core didn't seem to be his intent. Her bodice slipped off her shoulders. He ran his hands along her arms as he pushed the fabric to her waist. Her unconfined breasts sprang free, moving slightly with her quivering.

In a daze she watched as he dipped his fingers in the cinnamon and sugar sauce left over from when she cut the cinnamon rolls. He ran the sweetness across her bottom lip with his fingertip. Ecstasy, sensual and fiery shivered through her. His mouth descended on hers, licking, tasting, nipping wherever he found soft flesh. When his tongue swept inside her mouth, she tasted the sweetness too. She felt a driving need to give him the identical treatment.

He did the same to each nipple, spreading the delicacy around her breasts. He licked and nipped the tops, the bottoms, her nipples. It seemed all of her breasts were clothed with the cinnamon-sugar.

"This is better than I thought it would be. I want you to do the same to me."

"What?" Her eyes widened, believing he read her lascivious thoughts.

"Yes, want you to cover my penis with the sultry sweetness, my nipples too. Want you to lick it all off. Then we'll take a bath together. We'll make love in the dark or the light whatever you want." His voice was gruff, throaty with the desire he must feel.

Her breath left her in a scalding rush. "You want me to do what?"

She was shocked with the use of the anatomical name for his manhood. Surprised he knew.

"Surprised that I'm smart enough to know I have a penis? I'm a male. I've known since I could pee."

He sucked more of the sweetness from her breasts continued until she squirmed and shuddered. Until she was arching her back pushing her luscious breasts farther into his mouth. God, he wanted to devour every precious part.

Shudders of pleasure coursed through her. For a moment she thought she would climax before anything else was done between them. She controlled herself. She didn't know how she did so.

"Ah, Caro, the look on your face. I thought...well, I suppose you'll have to wait. Don't want you to reach that place without me." He backed off.

He set her away for a moment, filled kettles with water for them to heat. She didn't think she could wait to get to their room upstairs. Apparently, he didn't either. He pulled out the tub from the scullery. She didn't want to take a bath particularly somewhere they might be seen.

He locked the doors.

Still...

When he returned his trousers were unfastened, his shirt hanging loosely around his slender hips.

Once again, she found she was straddled on his lap. His penis pulsed against her opening. She wanted him inside her, needed to feel the sweet tremors that always ripped through her when he made love to her.

She wasn't sure what they did together could be considered making love. To her it seemed more as if they made lust.

"Do it, Caro. Do what I did to you. Need to feel your sweet little tongue bathe me with the delectable heat of your mouth."

Her hands shaking, she reached to the breadboard, lathered her fingers with the cinnamon-sugar. As he did to her, she spread it across his lips. Savored him, tasted, laved all along his mouth. He tugged her tongue inside. His teeth closed over her. It seemed he still tasted of the sweetness. Trembling began deep inside her core.

He backed off seeming to understand once again she nearly climaxed. "Not yet, Caro. I want you to finish this fantasy of mine. I will not allow you to reach your pleasure too soon."

Now she was on her knees in front of him. His penis covered in cinnamon-sugar. She licked and sucked all of him until there was no more sweetness. Yet his taste was always sweet. The groan of a man well pleased but not yet satisfied rumbled harshly from his belly. His hips jerked as she closed her lips over him.

"Oh...please, Duncan..."

"Pleasure you until you can't walk?"

He set her on the chair. Poured the buckets of water into the large tub. Cooled it a bit. When he returned to her, she was shaking so hard she could barely move. Her body still vibrated with the need it sought from him. He'd never made her wait before. Never caused her to tremble in anticipation. He stripped her. She could not have done it by herself. In his arms he carried her to the tub.

With her in front of him, settled into the water. Soap in hand he washed her, taking special care with her breasts and belly, the sweetly feminine folds between her legs. He would come inside her soon. At least she hoped so.

What he did was deliciously decadent.

"You liked that, Caro? Admit to yourself if not to me." He ran his hands over her breast, belly then between her legs. "I know you did." Found that hidden place that sent spirals of heat quivering within tormenting her until she didn't think she could stand another moment.

She could barely breathe. Her heart pounded. How could he

expect her to talk? "Y-yes...don't think I could live through anything like that again. Duncan..."

His name brought him back to the reality that was his. She was so aroused she would do anything for him.

"Yes, I do *ken* what you need. I like making you wait. It's sinful you come so quickly. I want to make love with my wife. It's not fair you don't give me the chance."

He was playing with her now, toying with all the erotic places that sent her where she could no longer breathe. Where her body bucked and shuddered with need, stilling his fingers just before she met the peak, which she longed for.

Inside her his penis filled her, stretched and heated her. She throbbed unmercifully with the mounting tension he fashioned. Once he moved, thrust inside again and again, her tremors began more quickly than she thought possible.

"Duncan!"

All control of her body vanished. He was hers to command. He did.

With a guttural yell he emptied himself inside her. Water sloshed from the tub across the floor. She couldn't move. Her head rested against his chest. He ran his hands gently along her arms then her back. A soft breath of air whispered from her lips.

He stood. Water sluiced from his naked body. She didn't know how she'd come to this point but she was very glad this was the man she chose to sire her baby girl. Still angry, though, just because he sent her to such heights, she could not easily forgive him his deception.

Without a stitch of clothing on expect for the oven mitt, he pulled the cinnamon rolls from the oven. They smelled delicious. Her mouth watered while her stomach grumbled expectantly.

"Wouldn't want to burn dessert. Are you ready to eat dinner or do you want to make love again? We still have some of the sweet concoction left on the breadboard."

"Yes. That was making lust not love. I want to eat. Don't want to get sticky again."

"It would be love if you could control your unruly women's parts to wait for a while. Most the time you climax just looking at me. Didn't think we would make it to the bath before you erupted in delightful ecstasy." He laughed watching her. Then, "When are you going to let me see you naked? It's dark now. Once again, I can't see you clearly. I find I'm growing impatient. A man should be able to observe his naked wife. Should be able to see her, all of her, the sweetest parts of her. I would spread your legs so I could see the silkiest most honeyed part of you."

"I..." She moistened her lips still tasting the sweetness of his kiss as well as her handiwork. "It would be embarrassing."

"Soon, Caro, I'm going to insist. I'd rather you unveiled yourself without a command from your husband. I've the right. I've been patient. Remember, sweeting, you vowed to obey."

It wasn't as if she didn't want to be naked in front of him. Before she was pregnant, she thought to conceal herself from him because she didn't mean to see him again. The less he saw...she didn't know what she thought. Now, as she grew larger by the day, she didn't want him to see how huge she was. Heat flooded her cheeks. He wouldn't be able to see her embarrassment. For that she was thankful.

"Suppose you do have that right. I will as soon as I can make myself. Conceivably tomorrow or the next day."

She decided for him she would try. He was so magnificent. She would pale in comparison. All her self-doubts surfaced then compounded to make her dizzy with fear.

"Let's get you dressed. I'm famished. This time my hunger is for food, not your delectable little body. Although I'm sure it won't take long to change focus once my belly is filled to satisfaction. I'm proud of you, Caro. Your pleasure didn't erupt as soon as I touched you. You are learning to wait for my command."

She wanted to howl at his audacity. To yell at him that he wasn't any better. He had no endurance. Instead, "You're right, my husband. I'll try to be more patient. Try to take charge of my pleasure so I don't climax too soon. I do so want to please you."

She found his all-masculine smile irritated her. Didn't like it when he spouted obedience in his wife.

While he pulled on his trousers, he watched her sink deeper into the water. "I find the humble, meek woman is not to my taste. You don't mean your words, Caro. What am I to do with you? If you don't mean what you say, you should keep the thoughts behind the sweet curve of your soft lips. It's not well done of you to tell untruths to your husband. I'd rather hear what you sincerely intend."

She heard the laughter in his words. The devil, she would do as she pleased when she pleased. She agreed with him though. Wanted to taunt him for the fun of it. "Yes, my husband." She tried for a wicked smile. "I will learn to forget about this obedience thing I previously thought you were obsessed with. All you need do is tell me how you want me to proceed."

The sudden simmer of his eyes told him it worked to some degree. She understood at that moment she could not control him. He, the male in this household, was in charge. He would decide when and where anything between them happened. His driving urgent need for her body changed nothing between them. It would be different if she didn't want him every minute she was with him.

"Time for you to remove yourself from water that must be growing cold. Don't want you to resemble a prune even though I wouldn't be able to see the lovely wrinkles." He held out his hand to assist her from the bath. Her clothes seemed an eternity away. "Don't worry, at this very moment I want food, not your succulent curves in my mouth against my lips as well as between my teeth. I won't jump on you the moment your breasts touch me, as I watch them sway and bob invitingly. Those sweet jewels you possess that tempt me so are quite lovely."

"Very well, but you can't see me."

She knew he saw the outline of her body. Understood that was what she didn't want him to see. Still, it wasn't the same as seeing her in bright light.

"There is your lovely silhouette," he chuckled softly. "Your curves are increasing by leaps and bounds. Why, I believe you're even larger now than before we made love in the tub."

The cad.

After drying her with dishtowels lingering in places, he would know excited her he helped her dress. With a tray piled high with ham and cheese along with both the loaf of bread she baked including the cinnamon rolls to tempt her sweet tooth accompanied by drinks, they walked upstairs. She hoped the bread was edible. She wasn't at all sure it would be. Didn't know if it would be cooked through. What she did know was that the rolls should be delicious with the entire sweet confection within them. She'd wanted to coat them with vanilla icing. Because Duncan showed up when he did, she didn't have time. The icing most likely would have put more wicked thoughts into his head. He would have made her sticky again. There would have been a second bath.

In his room, he poured himself his usual brandy then her chocolate milk. Truly, she thought she would grow tired of milk. She wanted a glass of wine, just one. While she didn't know if it mattered with only a few months left before the birth, she wasn't going to take the chance. Her *lassie* was going to be perfect, healthy as a stoat. The girl would be normal in intelligence because of her father. Her baby girl would not be anything like her, normalcy in her child's brain was the key to this union.

"I would rather have tea," she muttered feeling the tiniest bit sorry for herself.

She felt resentful. He sired the child. He could do anything he wished, eat anything taking his fancy. It wasn't fair. He never found himself throwing up his breakfast. Would not find himself waddling around unable to see his toes. It wasn't right that he could be the proud male peacock strutting his beautiful feathers while she had to take every precaution while she grew huge and ugly.

"There is something wrong with the milk?" he asked blandly.

"I don't like milk."

"Even chocolate?"

"Do you have the same drink morning noon and night? Maybe I'll try coffee. I've heard a few like the bitter drink. Well?" she queried still feeling a bit obtuse.

She didn't want to be nice. She needed to make him feel some of her pain. Empathy might be better. Somehow felt an argument at the moment would suit her needs perfectly. So, she baited him the best she could.

"Are you feeling neglected? Would you prefer another quick

dalliance before we assuage our other needs? Are your women's soft petals swollen while they wait my entrance?" His gaze swept blatantly over her settling on all the parts of her he liked the best.

She wanted to toss the glass of water she held into his face. "You know nothing," she sputtered.

"Tell me."

"You wouldn't understand."

For a few seconds she turned her back on him. How could a male of the species ever hope to understand how a pregnant woman felt? They couldn't. It would never happen. He didn't have the intelligence to understand. The devil, she wanted a pickle.

"Try me."

He sat back. His hands were placed behind his head as if he waited for her words.

"No, I don't think so, not now while you're looking at me like that. You won't understand a single word nor will you feel compassion at my plight. You have already thought what I'm going through is humorous." She held up her hands. "Don't say it. I know I plotted this very thing. You will just believe I'm feeling sorry for myself."

"Are you?"

"Yes. Wouldn't you if you suddenly became someone you are not."

Unexpectedly, she felt moisture hovering too close to the surface for her likes. She pushed the threatening tears back behind her eyelids. She didn't want him to see her cry. It was because she was pregnant. She hadn't cried since she left her father's home to start a new life on her own.

"You're right. I don't understand. How are you someone you are not?" His question seemed to come from his heart. He appeared honestly concerned for her.

"Look at me. This is not who I am."

She didn't know what else to say to him. It wasn't just her size. Her roses were taken away from her. Torra and Honey could no longer peek in her back door before having tea and a chat. He moved her to the country.

"There is more to this?" While he watched and listened, he fixed a sandwich for her. "You have to eat the meal before dessert or even before you have me again."

For some reason she didn't want dessert. Her cravings changed. Wasn't sure she wanted the food he offered. They did, however, agree on one thing. To keep her growing baby healthy, she needed to eat. She devoured the food. It was wonderful. The chocolate milk was acceptable. She found herself heartily glad that the loaf of bread was baked through. The cinnamon rolls would be mouthwatering.

"I don't care if I have one of the rolls or not. Seems we did have dessert before dinner." The thought of his member coated with the sugary mess brought heat to her cheeks.

"I would work on my column tomorrow with you if you have the time. I do think a man's opinion is important."

She had other reasons for inviting his input. She meant to ask him pertinent questions in regards to their relationship. She needed to understand what motivated him.

He grinned; his smile broad. He was laughing as he spoke. "So, you want me to pretend to be Annie of Ask Annie? Is Annie part of your real name? The award was to go to Annie Kenworth. Were you deceiving all the men at the university by using your middle name?"

She did like the way his eyes twinkled. They darkened now. She understood what that meant. His belly was satisfied. Now, he wanted other parts of his manly body to feel in a similar manner. Problem was those needs were seldom satisfied. His endurance was mind-boggling. His question now stopped her mind from spinning. "Yes, all that."

Her lashes lowered for a second. When she looked at him again, his shirt hung loosely from his shoulders. The muscles of his abdomen rippled when he moved across the room toward her.

"Let's share one. After that I'll ring for a servant. They can put the food away. The kitchen will have to be cleaned in the morning. Cleaning is not your job. One of my, our, servants will do that for you. How are your days going?"

On the big bed he sat down beside her. Fed her a piece of the roll before popping another one into his mouth. She thought the cinnamon-sugar tasted better on him.

"Actually, now that you've asked, I've been bored to tears. Don't have my roses. Don't have anyone to talk to except you. You seem to always be working. I go into the kitchen and torment your cook because he talks to me."

"Do you miss Torra and Honey?" he asked as he continued to share the roll with her.

She did, but it wasn't just that. When she lived in her home, she did things, went places. Had to shop for food. Spoke with the messenger when he brought as well as picked up her columns. She had a life. She did things. Even cleaning house eased the tedium of her days. None of that existed for her now. He chastised her if she lifted a finger even to dust.

"I've nothing to do here. You're right. I miss the ladies. Nonetheless, I also miss doing things, even cleaning. I've nowhere to go. I haven't left the manor since we arrived. Oh!" Her hands slipped to her belly; her smile broad.

"This time it is true. She kicked."

"Our baby boy kicked?"

Hurriedly, she picked up his hand then placed it on her belly. Watched as his eyes widened with awe as the *wee bairn* kicked again.

"Do you feel her?" She wanted to laugh as his eyes seemed to shimmer with pleasure. "It's the first time."

"We aren't hurting him when we make love?"

His question gave her pause but only for a moment. "No, the midwife assured me it was fine as long as I was comfortable with doing so. However, you must have meant making lust. What we do is hardly lovemaking."

"I want to experience everything with you as well as this little one. I need to feel what you are feeling," he murmured, his hand remained on her belly.

"You do? Then I should have sent a bottle of Ipecac to you so you could take some every morning in the process lose your breakfast. Now, how could I put something inside you so you could carry the weight of the baby? None of this is pleasant to anyone unless they are on the outside looking in. Sometimes I sense you are laughing at me. Your amusement at my expense is not well done of you."

He pulled her into his arms for a quick kiss then set a finger on her lips as if he wanted her to be quiet. She didn't want to stop talking.

"Hush, sweeting, is this what you have been peeved about this evening? I would that there was someone for you to talk to."

"You isolated me. We could have remained in the city. Even at your townhouse instead of my home would have been preferable. Torra as well as Honey would have visited." Still pouting she needed a diversion. She wanted to take her disillusionment out on him, who better than the man who caused the feelings.

"The scandal would have continued if we remained in town. This way the gossips have found someone else to turn their censure to."

"May I remind you...?"

"I created it. I *ken* that very well. You needed protection. The distance from the city would give you that."

"No, you needed to hide me away. You were angry. All you could think of was making me pay." She jabbed him in the chest. "In too many ways to count your strategy is working. You made me pay by stealing from me, tit for tat. Now you make me pay by isolating me."

~ * ~

"You saw him." Cora, Duncan's mother asked Sean. "How did he seem? What is she like? Did he tell you anything?"

Sean pulled his naked wife into his arms. Kissed her soundly as he regretted, he would have to wait to make love to her for a second time this evening. He thoroughly comprehended the fact that she needed to understand why there had been no forthcoming dinner invitation from her son. They should have been asked to dinner numerous times. As it was Duncan declined all the invitations Cora sent his way.

"We have to do this now?" Naked he reached for the bottle of wine, topped off his wife's glass before pouring himself a second glass. He would rather explore more possibilities of sensual passion. His conversation with his son got him thinking about his wife beneath him, on top of him and so much more.

"Yes." She told him petulantly, her arms crossed beneath her lovely breasts, ones he wanted to stroke as well as kiss.

Even though a few minutes ago he did savor the taste along with the sweet scent that was uniquely hers, he wanted to do so again. He could never get enough of her, like father like son. He chuckled thoroughly bemused by the situation.

If Caroline and Duncan's relationship turned out to be anything like his and Cora's, his son would have a long happy life with his wife. He drank a gulp. It was heady and aromatic, the flavor brisk. The wine might give him the fortitude to keep his hands off her softness.

"He is angry as, according to Duncan, she is also. They have both done things to each other that are deplorable, however, nothing that has been done can be taken back. Somehow the two of them are going to have to figure out how to mend the chasm that lies between them. Lies along with deceit never result in happiness."

"You can't tease me with those words then expect me not to want to learn the specifics," she told him her beautiful breasts heaving with the words that seemed to make her angry.

He supposed he should tell her what he knew. "I have to have your vow of silence."

"Did Duncan vow you to silence? Did he?" The indignation in her voice was easy to hear. She was tapping his chest with a finger, her eyes flashing retribution.

He brought the lone finger to his lips, sucked the tip inside his mouth bit gently. Smiled when he witnessed her eyes light up with pleasure. "No, he didn't. They are both passionate people. It is my opinion from what I've heard from our son the two of them are well suited. Together they will mend their differences."

"Then what is the matter? Why do you tell me there is a chasm between them?"

She ran one of her small hands along his chest, passed over a nipple before roaming lower to rest on his belly. She teased him even though she wanted him to talk instead of caress and kiss.

He grabbed hold of her hand stopping her even though he didn't want her to end the exploration. He wanted this conversation finished, so he could pursue more pleasurable games with his wife. "If you want answers then you will have to cease and desist this seduction of me. Otherwise..."

"You shouldn't have started this not-so-subtle coaxing of yours," she shot back, her smile broad and all-knowing. She picked up her glass of wine, sipped.

She looked over the rim at him before she blinked a few times. "Go on, darling. Start at the beginning if you please."

"Suppose the problem started before his birthday then escalated from there. Through the months of her pregnancy, the difficulties have not improved. It's all so steeped in deception for both of them. We both understand this behavior is not typical for our Duncan. The anger simmers just below the surface for our son. I believe from his comments it is the same for Caroline."

"We started our lives together with deception, lies of omission if you recall," She reminded him.

"As with our son also, he cannot keep his hands from his new wife. Hence the scandal we all read about in the Glasgow Herald. Suppose I've strayed from the path. The beginning, ah..."

He sipped wishing the tale was done. Just by the way she was looking at him over the rim of her glass he was becoming aroused. Maybe he could stall. It would not take long for them both to climax.

"So, go back to before the birthday some six months ago, I presume."

She turned to see him better he assumed or to provoke him with the sight of her prettily tipped coral breasts. His wife was certainly up to something.

"I believe as he told the story, she was looking for a man of slight to no intelligence to father her child. That in and of itself is the crux of the problem. Duncan resents being thought of as inferior in any way let alone his intelligence."

"What?" Apparently astounded, she blinked a few more times. Her lips parted in silent question.

"Yes, it seems ridiculous that his name came up on the list of most unintelligent eligible bachelors in Glasgow. Nevertheless, his name was at the top of the list. It appears the escorts who she spoke with at Scarlett's place believed the rumors our Duncan so craftily created around his name to keep doting mamas and simpering daughters away from him. The latter was not stupid."

"None of the gossip had anything to do with the level of his intelligence." She sounded indignant that her brilliant son would be labeled as something he was not.

"You're right indeed. Though in this particular case somehow the women equated his rumored escapades with the opposite sex as not being too bright." He laughed supposing their assumptions were not that far off the mark. If a man dallies with many different women, there are all types of repercussions, none of them good. All of them equated with stupidity."

He found himself lost in thought trying to make sense of the conundrum where his son played an integral part. Single handedly he created those rumors to suit his purpose. The fact they backfired was definitely amusing.

She nudged him, "Go on. Why would she want a stupid man to sire her child? This is too preposterous for words. She didn't get what she wanted. I suppose that is why she is angry. Why is Duncan?"

"She doesn't know her baby was sired by a stupendously, brilliant man. So, as you just decided, that is not why she is angry. Duncan thinks she will be even more furious when she discovers that bit of truth he's kept from her. Said he just couldn't find the right time to tell her she's not getting what she bargained for. The problem with all this is that it wasn't his deception. At the time of conception, he had no idea what characteristics she was looking for in a man. He just wanted her more than he needed to breathe."

"Oh my, so that begs the question on both sides. I'm more intrigued than before. Does he love her?"

"Yes, I'm sure of that fact. He doesn't *ken* it yet. So far, the main reason she is furious with our son is because he stole everything she owns right out from under her nose." Sean couldn't help the ensuing chuckle. "The move had to have been crafted skillfully. Our brilliant son could not have managed that feat easily."

"Stole? Our son stole from a woman? He would never do such an outlandish thing. That's preposterous!"

"Stole," he repeated. "It was truthfully quite creative of him. Knew she wouldn't wed him if he didn't do something drastic to bring her to his way of thinking. Didn't want a bastard. He knew he had to find a way to blackmail her, threaten her into his home. To do that, he made her dependent on him. If she didn't wed him, she would find herself on the street or truly working for Miss Scarlett. Because of his influence, Miss Scarlett would never hire her a second time. He understood she would never go to her father with her problem and ask him for help. At that time, he didn't love her though he refused to have his son be born a bastard. I suppose he still wouldn't have married her if there wasn't some other underlying factor.

"I believe it was love at first sight for our son. As we witnessed in the Herald, he can't keep his hands off her. Remind you of someone you know?" Sean winked at her as he fondled her breasts.

She punched him in the chest. "Of course. What happens next? Why is our son so angry he's secluded her at the country home away from all her friends? The isolation must be terrible for her. I'm sure she is not used to finding herself with no one to talk to during the day."

"Did you know she writes an advice column giving guidance about love? Until she encountered our son, seeking a *bairn,* she was a virgin a twenty-five-year-old long in the tooth, bluestocking virgin. Our son impregnated her the first time he slept with her. Well, I guess she calculated the best time for her to conceive."

"There is much more?" Cora was laughing now. Tears ran down her eyes, moisture from her laughter spiked her lashes. "She has well and truly done our son in."

Sean pulled her on top of him. "Give me a break from the tales of our unfortunate son's romantic misadventures. "I'll finish later since I've already given you a taste of what is transpiring just down the road. I need you desperately. It's been an eternity since I've been inside you."

Later, much later, he finished the story.

Chapter Eight

Two days after promising to give the male point of view to the questions she received, he sat in his office impatiently waiting for her. She agreed to come to him, since he was forgoing his endeavors to give aide to her. He didn't actually believe she needed him. It was just that she wanted personal contact outside the bedroom.

However, they both understood there were no guarantees he wouldn't toss her skirts then bury himself as deeply as he could inside her. Because he'd ripped her undergarments when he was so feverish with need, she stopped wearing them. He realized then he'd never made love with her on his desk. He stared at the papers scattered across as he shook his head. If he couldn't control himself, hours would pass before he could sort through the carefully stacked and sorted documents that he would find littered on the floor.

Instantly and against his will, he found himself breathing hard ready for her, the anticipation undoing him one feeble strand at a time. How she single handedly created such intense desire in him with just thoughts of her were beyond him.

In his mind, that was obviously for the best.

When he looked at the clock, he realized she was late. Damn her, she must be doing this for a reason. She must know he would want her the moment he watched her gently swaying hips when she walked into his office. He didn't have the patience to idle away the day. To keep his mind busy, he settled a few piles of documents on the table nearby making space for her. His mind wouldn't let thoughts of her fade. He could see her, legs spread wide while he thrust inside. She would wrap them around his hips. Heard her cry out his name as she always did.

The breath he drew inside his lungs was ragged and harsh with desire banging inside with violent, longing to be unleashed. Unable to think about anything else he sat. Drummed his fingers on the desk. Walked to the sideboard. Poured two fingers of his expensive French brandy. Downed the liquid fire in one gulp.

Where the devil was she?

He roamed the room.

He looked to the wall where his three diplomas were displayed. Grinned. She would learn today he wasn't the stupid lout she thought he was. Wondered at her reaction to the knowledge her child might grow up more intelligent than either of them. He would have to temper his grin when he witnessed the enlightenment shatter her beautiful and usually serene features, tranquil features except when he made lust to her. The last lie he wanted to continue between the two of them was that he was stupid, as he didn't like her not so subtle but numerous innuendos about his lack of brainpower.

The clock chimed three times. She was supposed to be here at two. He was so immersed in his work he didn't notice at first. Thoughts of searching her out crossed his mind. She'd told him she had nothing to do. Why wasn't she here, begging for his companionship? She was bating him on purpose.

He poured more brandy. Paced. Peered out the window to stare at the same scene.

Where the devil was she?

He was just about to race through the house to search her out. His heart thundered fearing something happened. Every breath he stole hurt when the air stabbed into his lungs. Now, his gut ached.

"What are you up to big brother?" Gordon asked as he sauntered into his office grinning from ear to ear. "Mother wants to know why they haven't been invited over for dinner." Gordon paused for a few seconds. "Also needs to understand why you've refused her invitations to come home. Nope, mother doesn't understand. As well you know when mother doesn't understand something, she takes matters into her hands."

Making himself at home, Gordon poured a brandy then sat down in front of his desk. "Do you want a drink?"

"No, not right now."

What he wanted was his brother to vanish and Caro to show

herself. In his mind, he still imagined her on his desk, her devilishly long legs wrapped around him while he savored her sultry core, while the pulsations of her body kissed his penis with voluptuous pleasure.

"You sound as if something is bothering you." The hint of amusement lingered in Gordon's voice. "Trouble with the newly married and expectant couple? Now how could that come to pass?"

"Nothing I plan on telling you about," Duncan grit out all the while his focus lingered on the door leading into the room.

"Don't need to be testy. Now, back to the question at hand. Why?"

"Why what?"

"You are not focusing. Why haven't you invited our parents to meet your bride? They are eager. For that matter you haven't invited me either. I feel a bit disillusioned. Thought you would have wanted to show off your bride."

"Yet here you are." He waved his hand in the air. "Cowards. That's what they are. They sent you instead of coming themselves?" he lifted a skeptical eyebrow. "Their machinations are all a ploy to make me feel guilty. The scheme won't work."

"I haven't refused an invitation by you. Of course, I haven't issued one either. I would be happy to ease the way for our dear parents."

"Don't truly understand why I don't want to see anyone. What I do know is that I still want her for myself. Don't want to share."

That was the truth. Sharing Caro would take all his carefully contained will power.

"Ah, translation, you're afraid you'll embarrass yourself and spirit her off to one of the spare bedrooms before dinner to make love to her. Would Caroline be angry with you if you did something like that? I would think so. Was she furious the first time? Did you have her before you reached the bed?"

Duncan ignored the last question, which was far too close to the truth for comfort. Gordon was taunting him, seeking a reaction he didn't mean to give. "You don't understand or know anything. Caroline has been sick, well, not actually sick but she hasn't been feeling all that well."

"Because of the pregnancy?"

Duncan grabbed onto the excuse, "Yes, it's been hard on her. The symptoms you *ken*. They can be trying. She is in the last few months. So, she is self-conscious about her increasing girth. She will be seven months along in another week or so. How would you feel in her shoes? Would you want to meet your in-laws under less than the best conditions? We weren't wed when she became pregnant." He thought perhaps he managed to get his brother into the proper perspective. Thought also his words were excellent.

He was proud of his creativity.

"What if you're gone on one of your extended business trips and she goes into labor? Don't you think she should have someone close by she can count on?" Gordon asked unemotionally. "If she doesn't meet our parents, she won't know she can go to them. Won't know they will accept the unconventional nature of your marriage."

Gordon had a sound point, so much for his careful reasoning about the dinner invitation. Thoughts of his Caro in labor, giving birth without him near, sent his nerves spiraling. He didn't believe he could bare that. What he did know was that he had to be here when it happened. Would move every obstacle that got in his way to be with her at that time.

His heart flopped when he realized it might only be two months before he held his *bairn* in his hands. A shiver of fear swept down his spine. While childbirth was dangerous for both mother and child, it was seldom one perished. His breath whispered out raggedly.

"What you haven't thought about is the end to all this?" Gordon looked as if he was laughing inside. "Thought you were the brilliant brother."

"I am. What end?" Duncan gritted out between clenched teeth, his mind spinning in erratic circles.

He didn't even know if she'd seen a midwife here in the country. Vaguely, he recalled her mentioning a midwife, couldn't bring what she said to him into focus. Steps needed to be taken. Making sure everything was prepared. The devil but they didn't even have a complete nursery yet. He would have to learn something about babies. Conceivably he didn't. Maybe Caro would do everything. He didn't want her to shoulder the entire burden. It seemed his thoughts split in two different directions shattering all his preconceived notions.

He tried to remember what she told him about the midwife. If she did, he forgot about it in his lust. He needed to control that thirst for her that was never-ending. After she gave birth, he wouldn't be able to make love to his wife for a while. He wondered for how long he would have to abstain. He groaned.

"Think of something you've left off your list of priorities, such as your wife?" Now, it was obvious Gordon was needling him goading him to do as his mother wished.

He wasn't going to squirm under the inquisition.

"Perhaps yes, I'd never tell. It seems Caro and I have a nursery to plan along with a few other things to accomplish in the next two months. Perhaps important concepts we've both overlooked. You should run along." He waved his hands to motion him away. "Caro will be down in a minute. While I doubt if what is ailing her is contagious, one never knows."

"Such as a meeting with our parents. Invite them over for tea. That's innocuous. I'm sure Monsieur Dubois will be happy to provide some of those delicate French pastries he's famous for."

"You're right. A tea would be nice for Caro unless they decide they need to stay for dinner. If that happened it would over tax her. She would be too tired for dinner. We can't have that."

"You just don't know how to share," Gordon accused him. "I suppose wanting one's wife all to himself is not that bad. However, don't you think it will grow boring?"

That was true. He'd never been one to share anything. Caro was not a person to share. She was his.

"You can't keep her locked away forever. Let her out or you'll regret what you are doing. If you don't, she might leave you."

She wouldn't. Caro had nowhere to go. She wanted him just as much as he wanted her, maybe more. Ah when she sucked the cinnamon-sugar from his aroused body, he groaned. His memory worked overtime.

"I see you're thinking of your wife. Not the direction I hoped my words would have taken you." Gordon rose to pour more brandy for himself.

A small noise at the doorway caught his attention. He grinned.

Caro stood framed by the opening. Slowly, she let the sheer robe she wore slip from her shoulders.

"So beautiful," he murmured forgetting his brother must be looking at her also. "I've been waiting for this for what seems forever. I finally get to see all of you in the light of day."

"Good God," Gordon said, his voice no longer bland or filled with humor. "She's beautiful."

The following gasp, the darkening of her eyes sent Duncan reeling. "Close your eyes, Gordon!"

"Not in this life time. I see why you want to keep her to yourself. In your shoes, I would do the same."

Naked, she was racing from the room. Duncan knew she would run to the bedroom. How she would be feeling other than abject mortification was what he didn't comprehend. He was learning he knew very little about the workings of the female mind.

Finally, she opened herself up to him. She showed herself in all her glory in broad daylight. There was no way she would have known Gordon was in his office. Understanding now why she was late; she was trying for the courage to bare herself to him. He didn't think he'd ever been more pleased in his life. Everything was turning out how he wished. Except for the fact his brother witnessed her beauty the same moment as he did.

When he reached the door to their chamber, it was locked. If he didn't act quickly, she might never show herself to him again.

"Caro, open the door. Please." He rested his ear against the wood hoping to hear something. "Please. You're beautiful."

Silence.

Kicking the damn door in was an option. "Caro, I want to come in, talk to you."

"You..."

That was a start. "Open, please." He could always go around, try to come into his room from hers. She would have locked that one too. His only other option was to scale the balcony.

Duncan closed his eyes, "Sweeting. Gordon didn't see any part of you."

That was a damn lie. His brother saw so much of his wife he was drooling. The brandy his bother sipped sputtered from his lips to run down his shirt. There was no way she would ever except an invitation for dinner if Gordon would attend too.

"You can't stay in there forever. I'm so proud of you, of your courage. I understand coming to me naked wasn't easy for you. It was the best gift in the world. I will remember the present forever."

His heart thundered, beat frantically inside his chest. He needed to hold on to her, talk to her.

She wasn't about to make this easy.

Giving up on her opening the door for him, he walked through the hall to the other chamber. She'd even locked the outside door. That was smart. He didn't have nearly the misgivings of kicking in the door between the rooms. In the first place it wasn't necessary.

Racing down the stairs he swept past his brother.

"More trouble?" Laughter followed the question. The twinkle in Gordon's eyes infuriated him.

"Go home, little brother."

"Suppose that invitation won't be coming today."

Duncan focused on the balcony as he raced around the house. Looking up he pinched the bridge of his nose, thinking. A swift breath of air later, he climbed the trellis then landed on the veranda outside his room. As he suspected this door wasn't barred to him. Slowly, he opened it, peering inside to see what awaited him. He didn't see her. Walked into the room to find her curled up on one of the wing chairs by the fireplace sobbing her heart out.

"Caro, please don't cry." He picked her up, holding her close as he settled onto the chair.

"H-he saw me. N-naked. I..."

"I know, sweeting, if there was anything I could do about that I would. Didn't expect him today. His was a surprise visit. Totally unexpected."

"We've never had visitors."

Her tears dampened his shirt. "Don't want anyone except me seeing you without a stitch of clothing on."

It would never serve him well to be angry with his brother. Nonetheless, he was. This should not have happened.

Damn Gordon.

"I wanted to," she gulped air. "I wanted you to...needed to prove to you I trusted you."

"You did just that. I *ken* you trust me with your life." Beneath the quilt she wrapped around her, his hand settled on her swollen belly. In just the last two weeks she'd grown. It seemed when they were wed, there was barely evidence she carried his child. Now, there was no doubt.

"Do you?" she sniffed.

Lightly, he kissed tears from her cheeks. They tasted of salt and Caro as well as all the sweetness that was her. She possessed the most delightful taste coupled with the scent of woman a man could ask for. "I do. By the way, I believe Gordon has left. You could dress and we could go to work on that column of yours or..."

"Or what?" she sounded leery.

"Or, you could let me see you, touch you now in the light of day. I believe that was your intention. Was it not?" He thought of his desk, the cleared space he made just for her. If he didn't do something about this rise of hot raw passion, his efforts would all go to waste.

She nodded, slowly opening up the quilt. When she sat up her bountiful breasts swayed against his shirt. He wasn't going to take her here, like this, after what just happened. What he did mean to do was to stroke her, look at her, memorize every soft curve.

In a way he never thought he was capable of he caressed her, understanding suddenly this was love not lust. He planned to do whatever he could to ease her anger as well as her embarrassment. Giving her back her assets would take time. Never again did he intend to deprive her of anything that was rightfully hers. He would have to figure out a way to make sure they were in her name only, that he couldn't ever claim them again despite how angry she might make him. He would think of a way.

His hands on her waist, he lifted her from him. Set her on the floor so she stood in front of him. "Will you let me look at you, truly look at you? I want to see every part of you."

After she nodded, he let his gaze begin with her eyes, which were slightly red from the tears. Nervously, her tiny pink tongue moistened her generously curved lower lip. His gaze traveling downward, he saw the pulse at the base of her neck leap, as she must have felt his gaze as a whisper of a caress. Dropping down, the tips of her breasts hardened. A rumbled groan left him. He could take her now. She must be hot, swollen, ready to accept his presence inside her woman's body. When his focus fell to her woman's mound, the little mewl he heard was generated by pure feminine desire. He kissed her belly thinking that just below his child grew.

"Should we work on the column or do you want me to make love to you?" His voice was shaky.

He needed to keep his lust from bubbling over. This time he would try to love her as she deserved.

"Right now, I *dinna* think I could think of anything to say. Duncan..." Her voice tumbled out seething with emotions he never heard before.

Her legs were trembling, her knees beginning to cave. Hastily, he bundled her into his arms, striding to the bed with only one purpose, loving his wife.

He fought the urgent need to drive into her. Fought the brimming climax threatening to burst from him. Lovingly, he sweet-talked her. Coaxed her gently. This time, there was no frenzied joining. No undeniable heated rush between them. Unsure how he was able to do it, he seduced her slowly. Kept her body humming for more enchantment, more ecstasy.

She purred.

Mewled softly.

Pleaded with him.

Still, he clung to his sanity as well as his composure, needing to make this loving of Caro last for as long as possible. Beneath him her hips moved begging for him. He ignored the frenzied movement. She arched against him. He disregarded the pleading gesture as he grit his teeth. He was afraid she'd climax before he thrust inside if he didn't slow down. Hell, he didn't want to slow anything down. He was already slower than he'd ever been with her.

"Not yet, sweeting. Patience."

Gently, he turned her onto her stomach. Her derrière beckoned to him. While he'd felt the gently curved flesh, squeezed the rounded cheeks, he'd never seen her in the light of day. The width of her back, he didn't think was bigger than before, unaffected by the swell of her rounded belly. At least by touch it didn't feel larger. He kissed his way up her spine, delighting as her arousal grew higher, higher still with each loving sip of his lips on her flesh. He stayed away from the most erotic caresses, keeping her in need for him. Her passion could explode with the tiniest provocation.

He wanted to avoid that.

Thought he would ignite instead.

Knew the moment he thrust inside her they would both detonate with the delicious sensations of their lust kissed tremors. He understood at this moment, he would never grow tired or bored with her. His marriage would still be like this when they were sixty...as long as they could breathe. There was nothing subtle about his Caro and sex with her.

"Do you want me?"

He brushed hair from one side of her face, touched the exposed ear with the tip of his tongue, swirled, coaxed and teased. He still wanted to take her to this highest peak while she lay on his desk. Ah, another time, he supposed.

"Hmm..." The sensual purr of desire was long and soft, the sweetest music to his ears.

"Tell me, Caro. I won't give you what you're wanting from me unless you tell me." He nipped his way down her neck then laved the spots with his tongue.

"Please..."

"Say the words. Tell me you want me."

"I want you, my husband."

His roar of laughter caught him by surprise. Once again, his not so biddable wife was pretending meekness. She wasn't false about her need for him though. He knew she did want him to finish what they began here.

He was right about the ensuing explosion. Almost to the second he thrust inside her sultry depths she was shuddering with the ecstasy they both sought. In seconds their moisture sheened bodies were recovering, breathing hard, heart pounding.

Turning her so he could rest his hand on her belly, he hoped to feel the *wee bairn* kick. "You are so beautiful, Caro. Don't ever hide yourself from me again. Don't lock me out. I won't stand for it."

Soothingly, he ran his hand along her arm. Kissed her forehead then touched upon her lips. "Promise me."

It seemed she was recovering nicely. "I won't ever do something so stupid as to walk downstairs in the middle of the day naked."

He chuckled softly trying to cease the emotion. "No, I don't suppose you will. Although I will remember forever the way you looked to me. The tiniest bit of fear in your eyes coupled with the courage needed to reveal yourself to me." It seemed he couldn't hold back the ensuing laughter.

She hit him. Punched him hard on the chest. "There is nothing amusing about your brother seeing me without clothing. I won't ever be able to look at him without remembering that moment. What if I had a sister and she saw you naked?"

"You don't?" He was still laughing.

"It's a question for the imagination." She punched him again.

"You will have to give me time for my imagination to recover. I've seen you this way in my mind since you were given to me as my birthday present and nothing my feeble man's brain conjured comes even close to what I'm gazing at now. The human body is a miracle. How could a tiny babe grow so nicely within you? The good lord must be a master engineer."

When he thought of the diplomas on the wall in his office, he wondered if he shouldn't plead fatigue and let her write this week's column on her own. After this debacle he didn't want to give her another shock. Ah, but the lovemaking afterward might well be worth the surprise she was about to receive. If it was as good as this time, he was sure of the fact.

Kissing her full on the mouth, before staring at the length of her body then her mouth, he said, "If you're recovered, let's go to work on that column of yours."

~ * ~

Mortified didn't come close to describing how she felt when she noticed Gordon staring at her his mouth hanging open his eyes wide with what appeared as shock along with disgust. For a few seconds, petrified, she returned his gaze. She gasped a breath of air while she was sure her heart would leap from her chest. When she looked back to Duncan, it didn't appear he realized Gordon was also staring at her. She didn't think her legs would work.

She found they did.

When she reached the bedroom door, she turned the lock behind her entrance hoping not to see her husband for the rest of the day. Knew she couldn't face Duncan, at least not until she had time to think about what happened to her. Her idea of working with him when she was naked had been foolish. She didn't understand what she'd been thinking.

The thought so ludicrous she gave a startled bitter laugh.

Now, she had more hypothetical questions for the advice column. She would need to add them to her fake list of ask Annie's questions. The real questions were answered and sent back with the messenger this morning. She excused her behavior in writing false narratives because she believed this was the only way she could actually rid herself of the resentment she felt for his underhanded deeds.

Tired of the simmering fury seething inside, she needed to let the anger go.

"You never answered. Do you want to work?" He was still stroking her arms making tender forays to different sensitive places on her body. The sensual play of his hands was hard to ignore. "If you don't decide soon, it might well be another five minutes before we dress. Doubt if I can prolong the lovemaking to the extent I just did another time. Doing so fatigued me. I still need my agile man's brain to help you give sound advice."

"I suppose as weak as you are, I should make certain every effort is given to you," she answered cockily belying the mortification still lingering from her encounter with his brother. She rose then, striding from him to wash then find clothing. A little armor in the guise of a gown between them was always nice when dealing with her husband. She would especially need the shield this time. This baiting with questions would help her resolve her issues with the beginning of their marriage. It might make his wrath escalate. At this moment, she didn't care. Perhaps in the distant future she might. Understood her anger issues between them couldn't continue.

Caroline felt the heat of his gaze on her back as she dressed. When she finished, he was still lying negligently on the bed naked. His body was superb. She was a wife well pleased. Backtracking, she should have considered his body when she was searching for the father of her child. What if she chose someone with a sagging belly? Would her child have one too? It was too much to think about. On the other hand, she wanted her little girl to have deep, dark brown eyes just like his.

"Are you coming or are you going to lie abed until dinner? It's not well done of you to spend so much time in the bedroom. You're lack of a work ethic will set a bad example for our child."

"Wouldn't miss this for the world." He stood. His chest was broad, hips narrow sliding into long muscular legs.

She didn't want to look away.

Her mouth watered afraid she would drool.

"Keep staring at me with that warm, blue shimmer in your eyes, we will find ourselves in that bed again or up against the door, perhaps on your hands and knees with me behind you holding on to the lush curves of your hips. Would you like that, Caro?"

Sweat broke out on her forehead. In the back of her throat her breath jammed. Abruptly, she turned from him. "I'll meet you in your office. I've got to pick up the questions."

A few minutes later, her nerves fluttered raggedly when she stepped inside his office. He sat at his desk fully clothed dressed in a casual white shirt and she assumed the buckskins he preferred when at home. She found herself a bit disappointed that he dressed. Watching him naked was an enchanting pastime.

"You're looking at me as if you're seeing me as I was a few

minutes ago."

She looked away as heat stained her face. Heard his masculine chuckle. Well, two could play this game. She intended to meet him head on. "Are you seeing me as I was earlier framed in the doorway wearing nothing?"

"The apparition of you naked in my man's brain is scrumptiously enchanting. It was the sweetest most intoxicating sight of my entire life. I will always remember that image of you. Your naked body outlined in the doorway leading to my office is forever imprinted in my man's brain." He didn't bother to hide his smile behind his teeth. "Shall we strip to nothing then carry on?"

The breath she found she'd been holding left her in a loud gasp. "I think not."

This answering of the questions needed to be perfect. She had to assess the emotions that he sought to hide from her. That would never happen if they were naked. A lot would never come to fruition in that circumstance.

"In this situation, do I get to pretend to be Annie? That was very confusing at the ball. Annie Kenworth won that coveted award though she declined to receive it. Did she ever pick it up from the university? I wonder."

Caroline huffed. Shot him a glare she hoped would put him at a disadvantage even while she understood whole-heartedly the scathing look would not. "It was hardly coveted. No, Annie did not want the damn thing. It was solicitous, made up by males to placate a woman's endeavors. As you well know, I am not stupid, Duncan. I know exactly just how condescending they all were. I was humiliated by the horrid gesture."

His brows drew together creating deep frown lines in his forehead, as he seemed to be thinking. "At the time, I thought the act was nice. Now, knowing you, I suppose you are right. The award, minimal as it was, was meant to placate your very female academic efforts. Nothing more."

A slow slip of air glided from her lips as she gazed at the haughty man sitting in front of her. "You can be Annie if you behave yourself. As soon as you do not, you will have to pay a penalty." She didn't know how that thought darted into her head from out of the blue.

She bemoaned the words as soon as she heard his laughter. Understood she created the humor, as he knew she would be unable to think of a penalty.

"A kiss for every time I misbehave? That would be nice." His hands forming a steeple, he sat back, his grin lascivious.

"I think not. What I do *ken* is that some worthy forfeit will come to mind. This is a column I need to send off in the morning. I won't have the time to redo this if you are not serious."

"Let's get to the task then." He flashed his even white teeth at her, his dark brown eyes still twinkling with amusement.

"Indeed yes, let's get to it."

When she sifted through her papers, her hands shook. The back of her throat parched she longed for a glass of crystal-clear water. She sipped air as she kept her gaze focused on the questions trying to decide which one to ask first. Something that wasn't quite as intimidating as his thievery. Perhaps she should start with her own deceit. No argument they both had misdeeds to account for.

"So, what is the first question? Would you like me to read them? You appear a bit hesitant, perhaps still frazzled from the earlier encounter. Your face is white, Caro. What the devil is wrong? This pallor is not because we made love or the fact my brother gazed at you naked. Is it?"

She started this. A deep breath of air might help. Meant to go through with all the questions. So, she inhaled long and deep, air pulsating into her lungs giving her no more courage than she had before the breath. "Dear Annie," she began, knowing that going for the jugular was not the best course. She would start from the beginning of their journey. She stole a moment of time to look at him. "I have this friend. She wanted a baby more than anything. She was foolish though, understanding she would never have a man look at her in the way men look at women they would like to marry."

"I'm not sure this is a real question," his voice rumbled from his chest and his eyes narrowed as he appeared to scrutinize her his demeanor no longer as relaxed as before. Still, with complete masculine grace, he was sitting back on his chair, his hands behind his head belying her first impression. She supposed the fine lines around his mouth gave his real feelings away.

"Oh, it is. I assure you. They only send me real questions." She held up the stack as if to prove to herself the truth of her words. "We can pick another if you like. I never answer all the questions I've been sent."

"No, do go on. This one seems to be close to home, intriguing. I can already think of several courses to choose from for answers."

"All right then." Her head bobbed up and down in agreement. Her words rattled as she began to speak again. "Now, where was I?"

"This woman's friend wanted to have a baby," he prompted blandly, the expression in his eyes giving nothing away.

"Yes." She scrolled her finger across the questions, searching for the place to continue. "She didn't know what to do so she went to some lady friends who thought she believed could help her with the dilemma she found herself in. They set her up as a birthday present for a man they told her she would like for the father of her child. She presented herself as the gift. However, the woman didn't know if she conceived. Now, she doesn't know what to do?"

His eyes narrowed further as he carefully studied her. He sat forward forearms resting on the desk that was now empty of papers. She thought that strange. His desk was always neatly cluttered.

"Did this woman tell the man she wanted to have his baby? That, of course, is part of the answer. She should have told him before they proceeded to have intercourse."

His word for sex surprised and unnerved her. To hide her shock from him, she looked at what was supposed to be her notes. "It says here that she did not tell him her plans." Her voice wavered as she thought better of pursuing the topic. This was not the best idea. No, the notion was the worst possible.

"So, this woman went as a birthday gift on false pretenses. Did she pretend to be a whore?"

Now his tone was curt. Clearly, she heard the underlying tones of irritation. She knew this would happen. Meant this very thing to help clear the stilted air between them.

Once more she looked at her notes. "An escort who wanted to have sex. She was hired for his use for the night. Also, says she wasn't a whore because she was a virgin."

He sat back again assuming the same negligent pose a salacious smile curling his generous lips. "Let me see if I have this clear. The woman wanted to have sex so she could have a baby. She also had no intention of telling the man about the baby he would have conceived if her plans worked out."

"That's right. What would a man say? What is your point of view?" Not that she didn't already understand his, "Would every man feel the same?"

"Oh..." His voice was a gravely purr, his brows narrowed creating a harsh line. "I believe you know what a man would say. What are you up to, Caro?"

"I want your opinion."

"A man would tell this friend to tell her friend that she should fess up. Tell the man what she did as well as to be prepared for the consequences of the treacherous deed. Stealing sperm was not well done of her."

"What do you think those consequences should be?" She shouldn't pursue this farther. She still didn't believe every man would think the same as he did.

His grin unraveled her farther. "Depends on the man as well as how he feels about the woman. Obviously, he wouldn't want a bastard. However, he also wouldn't want to be forced to wed a woman just because she deceived him."

"Then..." she was more confused than before. "What do I tell her?"

"I believe I answered just now. Just go to him then tell him the truth. She should not steal his sperm. The man should know what the woman he's bedding has planned, no matter how deceptive her actions were." His voice was now a low growl, eyes flashing dangerously.

She'd done everything wrong thinking he would never discover the truth. She ran with his answer. In hindsight he was right of course.

"That is an excellent answer. I will use it. Thank you."

"Why didn't you tell me the truth, Caro? I know this is about us. I'm curious what else you have up your sleeve. Since I'm a gambling man, I'll bet there is a question that has more to do about me. You wanted to get your part out of the way first."

"I didn't tell you because I didn't think you would...would willingly donate your sperm to me. I also didn't think you would care after the fact. Men don't usually claim a whore's baby."

"You've got that part right. If I'd any indication what you were up to, I would have made sure you didn't conceive. After the fact, we both know you are not a whore. So, your "usually" doesn't hold water in this case. Why the second night? Why did you seek me out a second time?"

He'd done her in.

She was expecting the question just not so soon. Didn't mean she liked it. However, she was prepared to answer then ask him one of her own. "I bled," her voice squeaked out, embarrassed to speak of physical parts of a woman's life. It was more information than she wanted to give him. "Because of that I understood I would have to try again. You played into my hands when you gave me the invitation. Knew you wanted me to come see you."

"You didn't need an invitation from me, did you, Annie?"

"No, nevertheless the invite told me you did want to see me again. Never thought you would create a scandal." Her eyes crossed when she thought of what they did, how he tossed her over his shoulder then half way down the stairs from the ballroom, rid her of her underclothing, dropping them on the floor for anyone to find.

"Was there a second question about your friend's friend causing rumors to fly heatedly through the Glasgow nobility?" He jabbed his fingertips on his desk.

"Yes." She looked down then back to him knowing she might come to regret the questions. "Why? Why did you marry me? You didn't have to you know. I was content to be a single mother."

He lifted his broad shoulders even while his eyes were narrowing on her. "You know the answer to that."

"No, no I don't, not truly."

"Didn't want a bastard."

That had always been his succinct reply. Tonight, the truth was what she needed. "Torra told me a man of your station never did anything he didn't want to do. Told me that answer was just an excuse to hide the real reason even though I'm sure it is true in part."

She had not been able to look at him as she held her breath waiting for something she wasn't sure would happen. For some reason, she needed for him to tell her that he cared for her. Never had she ever thought to hear the word sweetly nestled into his sentences though.

"I believe it's time for another ask Annie question. We played this last one to death even so far as diverting to a completely different question. One I don't intend to answer by the way."

She nodded trying to agree with him while she urged the moisture clogging her throat to vanish. "Dear Annie," she began, the lump in her throat growing thicker with each passing second, "before I married, my husband stole everything I own. He transferred my life savings into accounts he possessed. If that wasn't enough, he also found a means to put his name on the titles of two of my homes. What should I do?"

Deep in the back of his throat, he growled his displeasure. "Knew you wouldn't miss a beat. There is nothing she can do, no way to get her money back. A means to retrieve what was stolen from her existed, however it would have cost more than she could afford since she now possesses nothing. She should have chosen her financial advisor more carefully."

For the longest time Caroline couldn't speak. The moisture she was holding back from her eyes threatened to erupt. She'd been so foolish to do this, to put herself in the line of fire. He advised nothing she didn't expect having hashed this over in her genius mind too many times to count. They'd even talked briefly about these incidents standing between them.

"I will write that as sound advice. There is nothing a woman can do when a man takes the notion into his mind to steal from her."

"She could leave him. We've been over this, Caro. Why are you torturing yourself? There is naught you can do. I'll be generous with you. Now that we are wed, you've nothing I don't want to give you. All of the money from your columns is yours. What more do you want?"

"That's one of the reasons I never intended to marry. I liked, no loved, my independence. Why did you take that all from me? I was happy. Would have been happy with my little girl. I didn't need a man to fulfill me."

No longer could she hold back the tears. She turned to run once more from the room, sobs wracking her body until she didn't believe she could breathe. Moisture ran down her cheeks. She stopped turning to shoot sparks at him.

"I don't know. All I do know is that I want my son or daughter to live with me, to be part of my life. Caro."

He walked around the desk until he stood next to her, so close she caught the scent of him, felt his need coupled with the heat of his body encompass her. Sometimes she thought his power would swallow her whole. He would never admit to anything save lust between them. "As long as we are getting this out in the open, there is something else you need to know."

His hands on her shoulders, he walked her toward the wall next to his desk. "Take a look. Once you read them, I've another question to ask Annie."

What she saw caused her breath to snag in her throat while her heart pounded desperately. She swayed, faltering. Might have fallen if he wasn't there to keep her steady. "Tell me what you see?"

She couldn't speak. There was no moisture in her mouth. Didn't want to talk in any case. For several scorching moments, she closed her eyes, letting the implications devour her.

"Caro, you can no longer avoid this. What do you see? The truth is right in front of you. You cannot go back and pick a different father. Even if that were true, I would never allow such a thing."

She swallowed hard forcing all her fears for her child to the pit of her stomach. All she dreaded would come true. "Three diplomas as well as an award stating you graduated summa cum laude."

She wanted to step away except there was nowhere to go. His hands rested on her shoulders holding her in place where she could still see the evidence that caused all her dreams for the *wee bairn* she nurtured inside her to smolder, burn to a charred crisp. She set her hands on her belly dread for the child's future so very real and deep.

After the revelation, her world exploded in front of her, shattering all her dreams of bearing a normal child. She couldn't stop the chills bombarding inside her. Couldn't stop her dreams from crumbling. All she could imagine was the life of her unborn *lass*. The baby girl would be no different than her. She would always be an outcast, a pariah.

The sob she could no longer hold back tore through her throat as he turned her in his arms. "I am not the dolt you thought me to be. Indeed, I happen to be the man who nearly tripled your personal holdings every year. It was brilliant of you to invest the allowance your father gave you. You were a rich woman because of this simple-minded man you chose as the father of your child. The research, or should I say assumptions your friends relayed to you were faulty."

"You should have told me." She couldn't help the absurd accusation from flowing forth. She knew it. By the darkening of his eyes, he knew it.

He laughed out right. Very slowly he spoke seeming to put emphasis on every word. "I was supposed to tell a woman who I thought was a well-paid whore and who was also a birthday gift from my brothers that I wasn't what she thought. That in truth I'm not stupid but brilliant? At the time, I didn't know the direction of your beliefs."

"Y-yes."

His laughter sent fire blazing through her. Nonetheless, it didn't seem he wanted to say anything in return. Instead, he waited as she tried to calm her unraveling nerves.

"That is the most stupid one word to come from a brilliant woman I've ever heard. I'm pleased my children will possess agile minds. Hope they are brilliant human beings, that the light of their minds shines as well as prospers. Hope they find some way to improve mankind."

"She will be different, ridiculed, tormented. I don't want that to happen to her. You wouldn't either if you cared, if you loved her."

"I do love this child growing in your womb put there by my penis, my sperm, the night we had intercourse too many times for my deprived man's brain to remember. Need I speak more exactly? No, I think not. It's a perfect combination. Your egg coupled with my sperm." His hand on her chin he lifted. "Open your eyes, Caro. Look at me." After she did, "I already love our baby, boy or girl. If we have a female child, together we will care for her, give her so much love she'll never feel any of the self-doubt you did growing up. Her life, if the babe is a girl, will be nothing like yours. She will not be ridiculed or tormented. We might have all boys. What then? Would you want them to be lacking in brain power?"

She sniffed leaning into his arms. She did feel better, somewhat. They still had not solved the problems between them. Now, however, she thought she might be able to live with him, accept him as her husband as well as the father of this child. He was her lover. It was true neither could keep their hands to themselves. While his fingers still held her chin to look at him, she watched transfixed as his lips found and parted hers. Watched as he lifted her off her feet. Felt his hardness against her expanded belly.

"I need you, Caro. Do you need me?" It was a man's question filled with arrogance and self-confidence.

The question didn't need an answer. He waited for it though. "Yes..."

"How should we do this? On the floor? The desk is an intriguing idea? Should I carry you upstairs to the bed? Or perhaps against the closed door to my office."

"Lock the door first," she whispered as her thoughts vanished with the passing seconds. Her body heated just thinking about his questions along with the exquisite anticipation.

"Don't want Gordon or another one of my brothers sent on a mission from my mother to interrupt."

"God, no." She didn't need a repeat of today.

"Can't keep doing this the same way." His hands drifted down her belly, pulled her skirts high. His touch upon her sent her whirling, fighting for composure. "We're going to the desk. Do you think you can walk that far? Do I need carry you?" His lips touched provocatively on her ear. His fingers slipped lower to meet hot, swollen flesh between her legs. Her purr was of delight and sensual pleasure followed.

"Don't think so. Not like this."

With that said, he lifted her, carried her to the cleared off spot on his desk. She realized then he planned this. Cool air caressed her bottom just as his feet spread hers. His penis touched upon her. Rubbed provocatively between the folds that were damp with blazing lust. He placed her legs on his shoulders.

The mew of pleasure she held back a second ago erupted when his lips and teeth touched upon her backside.

Ecstasy.

Delight and enchantment.

How the devil could she remain angry with him?

Now with her forearms on the desk, his hands around her hips he plunged inside. His low guttural groan delighted her. She took solace in the fact he still wanted her, seemed to crave her even though she was huge with child, his child, even though she posed those questions to him made him play the part of Annie.

The tremors began slowly before they erupted. Composure was not a characteristic she possessed at the moment.

"Duncan!" Her head rested on his desk between his arms. His hands soothed until she calmed.

"We will have my parents to dinner tomorrow night."

~ * ~

Cora spent the day roaming through her home. Nervous energy boiled through her, twisting her stomach into huge knots. All too well she understood the invitation had been long in coming because her son didn't want them to meet his wife. What was it about this woman that had him hiding her away from family?

In her mind, the question was why. Sean had no explanation except there were conflicts between the two of them that needed to be resolved. She believed there was more to this slight of courtesy. Maybe the woman wasn't pleasant. Perhaps she was a shrew. Eventually, the truth would be evident. For now, she would have to patiently bide her time.

Patience had never been her strong suit. She needed to know everything, yesterday.

So, this woman Duncan wed was possibly as brilliant as he was. According to the tale Sean told, she wanted the father to be the opposite. When she let her son have her way with her, she received more than she bargained for. She married an exceptionally brilliant man.

Cora looked at the ormolu clock ticking its way to seven o'clock. She gazed at her well decorated home. Tried to think of something to do in the interim. There were still two hours to pass before they could leave. She drew in a long deep breath of air. The weather was turning. Temperatures seemed to be dropping. Tomorrow would be clear and frigid. Her grandchild would be born in February some time. Anticipation tickled her fancy. She loved children. Wished she could have had more than four. Sean would have liked that too. It wasn't to be. Now they waited for their first grandchild to enter this world. For that, she couldn't be more pleased.

The footsteps behind her alerted her to the fact she wasn't alone. Perhaps they could find something to do for the next two hours. She smiled when his hands wrapped around her from behind.

He turned her.

"Impatient?" he queried as his lips met hers in a soft, brief kiss. "We should go for a ride."

"What kind of ride are you speaking of, Sean Murray?"

Her laughter felt light and sweet as she thought on her daughter-in-law. They were nearing seven months of the pregnancy. The unlikely couple were wed for several months now.

"Any kind that suits you." His lips found tender spots to tease.

"Believe we should discuss our strategies where it comes to the happy couple," she murmured lightly touching his chin. "Do you think they might have come to a few concessions?"

"If they have, doubt if it has anything to do with the invitation. After what happened when Gordon showed up to plead our case, the two are most likely in a defensive mode. Anything could happen. The boys weren't invited. However, they will be there too. I'm sure Duncan would have thought of that. Don't know if he'll like his brothers traipsing along uninvited. I'm sure Caroline will be mortified to see Gordon again."

She poured Sean a glass of brandy herself sherry. "What

happened?"

"Our youngest son came home yesterday while you were in the village shopping roaring with laughter so hard tears streamed down his face. He was truly quite beside himself."

The tale must be a wild one. "What happened?" she repeated finding herself grinning as widely as her husband.

"Wish you could hear him tell it. Seems Duncan didn't take the time to be angry at his little brother's sightseeing of his personal property. No, he was more concerned about going after his thoroughly mortified and very pregnant wife."

"Sean." Her husband could spend hours on a story just to make her impatient for the end. "Don't do this. What did Gordon do?"

"Oh, neither of our boys did anything wrong, neither did Caroline."

"Then...?"

"Seems Caroline has had a little fetish about Duncan seeing her naked. Until that moment she didn't allow him the coveted view. Seems she always wanted to make love in the dark."

"The devil," she said thoroughly confused. "They've made a child together. He must have seen her sometime."

"Apparently not." Sean let his laughter roar. "She always insisted on the lights being turned off," he repeated his earlier words.

"So, what happened?"

"Not sure of all the facts leading up to the final conclusion of events. Evidently Duncan has been patiently waiting to make love to his wife with all the lights lit in the room."

"You mean they never made love during the daylight hours? I'm having a difficult time believing that."

"Me as well, but this isn't our story to tell. Seems she promised him she would try to be bolder."

"I'm guessing now that she decided to take the opportunity to show herself to Duncan while unknowingly Gordon was at the home visiting."

"Evidently, Duncan was working in his office waiting for her. I know he wanted her to see the diplomas as well as his summa cum laude award for excellence. Perhaps they had an assignation. Who knows?"

"Only Caroline and Duncan. So, what else happened?"

"Gordon arrived to issue the invitation to dinner or plead for one for ourselves. He was standing in the corner of the room. Caroline didn't see him when she stood framed just barely outside the door. She slipped her robe from her shoulders. All her nakedness was there for both men to see."

"She ran."

"Yes, and without the robe."

"When Duncan told his brother to close his eyes he refused. Gordon told me after seeing her in all her glory he understood why his big brother couldn't keep his hands off her. He must have had a pretty good idea what was beneath her clothing."

"I don't know what to say or think," she murmured, feeling a pang of empathy for the dear girl. If that happened to her, she wouldn't want to see anyone in the family either.

"Perhaps we should go now, take a short ride just to use up some time and this restless energy that appears to be ruling you. He is our son. What will he do if we turn up early?"

"What if we see...?"

"Don't you think it would be stupid for the two of them to make the same mistake twice?" Sean lifted that eyebrow that always told her he had something else on his mind.

"Very well, I'll change quickly. Want to take the buggy. This is too important for my clothing and hair to be messed up by the ride."

"Good, the buggy is always conducive to wandering hands. Want you pleading for my manly body by the time we arrive home after the dinner."

"Welcome," Johnston stepped back as they made their way through the foyer. "Your other sons have all arrived before you. Make yourselves comfortable in the drawing room. Help yourself to something to drink."

"Didn't know anyone else was invited," Sean murmured as he peeked into the drawing room, Cora behind him nearly bumping into his back. He already guessed his sons would attend. Nothing could have kept them away. Said as much to his wife.

"Where are Caroline and Duncan?" Cora asked not seeing them. "Surely even if everyone was early one of them would have put in an appearance."

"Can't answer that," Johnston said as he turned his head away. "Believe Monsieur Dubois has dinner prepared now that all of you are here."

The man led the way through the house to the dining room. Succulent French dishes were set out for their consumption.

Johnston bowed. "Please be seated. Duncan would like you to enjoy the dinner."

The meal was served as well as eaten without Duncan or Caroline making an appearance. The entire debacle was not well done of their son. Surely, his new wife would have insisted that she meet her in-laws.

"I can't believe he invited us to dinner and didn't show up himself. The audacity is overwhelming. Where to do you think they are?"

"Hiding upstairs?" Sean questioned grinning. "Under the circumstances of Gordon's viewing this behavior doesn't surprise me."

"No, Evan searched through all the rooms even the bedchamber which was left open for just that reason. They aren't even at the house."

"The meal was delicious," Cora said thoughtfully trying to come to terms with the fact they were deceived.

All thoughts and musings fled when Sean's large hand found its way beneath her skirts.

Chapter Nine

Duncan wasn't pleased when he read the letter, which called him to London. He would have to leave soon. Previously, business always came first. It wasn't within his abilities to put anything in front of his financial pursuits. Whenever he left one month would turn into two. Tonight, on their way to the townhouse in Glasgow, all he could think about was his wife's breasts covered with the cinnamon-sugar. He wanted to relive the moment. Perhaps he could convince her to make the rolls again.

He gazed at his bride, a twinkle in his eyes. "Do you think our plan worked?" Duncan asked as he settled back in the wing chair by the fireplace grinning. He knew he was smirking like a besotted fool as he stared at his wife, so very pleased with this idea of his. To flee dinner with his parents and siblings was brilliant if he did say so himself.

They drove into town to avoid the dinner, Gordon as well as his parents. Caro didn't want to see any of them, not after what happened with his brother. Just looking at him again would bring back memories she didn't want to recall.

Together they decided he would drive her in the buggy to meet his parents tomorrow. Gordon, however, was right in his assessment. She did need to feel comfortable with his parents, God forbid just in case he wasn't around when she gave birth. He wasn't planning on becoming an absentee father.

He didn't like it very much though he would have to go to London again. Even though his trips to the big city were planned, they could also be unpredictable. The thought of sending Evan in his place did cross his mind. He sloughed it off as none of his brothers possessed the creativity to build financial deals that would double or triple their wealth. They told him many times he was too invested in building his empire. Yet that was the way he'd spent all of his adult life.

Rarely did he understand if he was just lucky or he truly did possess some hidden talents. He gambled. Although, he rarely took a risk he wasn't sure of. Those risks so far always paid back handsomely.

"I would have liked to have been a fly on the wall when they discovered we were missing." Caro curled her legs beneath her. "I'm sure your mother will blame our absence on me. She has no reason to think you didn't want to see her. They will dislike me even more now that we ducked out on meeting them."

"As would I, a fly on the wall, novel idea. Dubois promised a magnificent meal. My best wines were brought out along with his finest French cuisine. He was delighted to be able to show off. Believe he told me they were having duck a l'orange along with several other exquisite dishes."

"The expensive French brandy," she added with a half-smile.

He had to admit since the ask Annie confrontation their relationship was less confrontational. During that heated discussion they bridged some gaps that needed airing out. Somehow the vibrant anger seething just below the surface seemed lighter, no longer all consuming. At least it was with him. When he explained to her he intended to go to London, the conversation would probably turn explosive again.

All he could do was to promise her he would be home before she gave birth. God, though, what if she was early? That did happen. There was no set-in stone deadline for these things. He planned to be back a week early. Maybe he should shoot for two weeks before the due date. They did know exactly the date she conceived. That fact should mean there would be no surprises. With babies there were always surprises.

"What are you thinking?" she asked as she seemed to be moving about, uncomfortable on the chair. "I would know."

"That I'm heartily glad we are not eating dinner with my parents. I like the privacy."

Hear about this, he would. Not one of his family members would let it go, at least not until there was something else to take its place. The only good thing about him leaving in two days was his brothers would not taunt him with the deed.

Silence seemed to surround them for a few long moments. When he looked at his wife, he understood how much he cared for her. Maybe it was time to tell her exactly how he felt.

"You didn't eat your peas."

Well, that was innocuous at best. Hardly was saying the words about his intense feelings for his wife. She did deserve to know what was in his head. Well, she never said anything about her thoughts where he was concerned. Maybe she didn't care about him.

"Lately, I don't seem to be too hungry." She slanted him a quizzical look. "Food just doesn't appear appetizing."

The dishes were cleared a while ago. Why he thought of the peas now, he didn't know. Getting into a conversation about what she should eat was not part of his plan. The day after tomorrow he was leaving. Had known for a time now. To introduce her to his parents he would have to put the trip off for another day. Was having second thoughts about dragging her from the dinner plans with his parents.

"Caro." He pulled her onto his lap. His hands rested on the curve of her hips.

"I don't like the expression on your face. What aren't you telling me?"

Idly, he stroked her arm, searching the recesses of his mind for courage to tell her about his plans. Hell, he shouldn't need courage. This was business. She would think he was abandoning her just as her father did. Now that he knew her better, he was coming to understand her fears as well as her lack of self confidence in dealing with men. There were things she needed in her life to make her whole. At this point in time, he was failing to give her those things.

Sucking in a huge breath of air, he placed her hand in his, kissed the knuckles. He blurted, "I'm leaving for London the day after tomorrow."

"No…"

"Afraid so. It's business, Caro. Don't have a choice."

He did though. Just wasn't sure he trusted anyone else to the task. Delegating as well as trusting someone else, even if it was his brothers, was impossible for him.

"How long?" At least she sounded resigned.

He saw moisture creating shimmering diamonds in her lashes. She looked away seemingly unwilling to show her emotions. "What is so important it takes precedence over the birth of your daughter?"

"Son. I'll be back at least a week before you are due. Try for two weeks if I can manage. I promise."

"Bastard..." her voice whispered through her teeth. For a few seconds the word tore into his heart she looked away. "That's why you wanted me to meet your parents. Why the deception? Telling the truth always is the best alternative. Now, I can't understand why we fled the dinner party."

If he was honest with himself, he still didn't want to share her with anyone. Their relationship was still too complicated, too new. Until tonight, in his mind she was just the mother of his unborn child. "Thought you would be embarrassed to see Gordon. Was that all right of me to think of you?" He lifted his shoulders slightly hoping she would buy the outright lie.

"Kind of you to think of me when you're leaving me alone for weeks, perhaps months. What am I supposed to think? That you might care what happened to us?" she said her tone brimming with sarcasm while her hands spanned her belly.

He didn't believe his ploy worked. Sipping his brandy, he watched her over the rim. It wasn't well done of him to leave her. He understood that. By herself, she would be lost in the manor house. He could give her permission to move back to her old home. If she did that, the worry for her would just be too great. Hell, she had Torra and Honey across the street. If she needed anything, they would be there for her. Again, if he was honest with himself, which he wasn't going to be, he didn't want to lose control. The incessant desire to know exactly where she was every minute of every day swamped him until he felt as if he couldn't breathe, at least not satisfactorily. If she were wandering around Glasgow, he wouldn't know where the devil she was.

The incessant pounding on the door had him frowning. "What the devil is that? No one knows we are here."

The truth of his words didn't settle well. It would not have been difficult for his family to figure it out when he wasn't at home to greet them. His brothers would undoubtedly retaliate.

"Seems you have company," she murmured, nervously tugging at her gown where he'd been slipping it from her shoulders.

"They wouldn't dare!"

He knew damn well they would. They would also be just as pleased to interrupt a dalliance with his wife. Probably plan for a repeat performance.

"Seems they did. Are you going to let them in?"

"Do I have a choice? They will continue the relentless pounding until all the neighbors are standing outside on my front lawn caterwauling at my window to stop them. The only way to silence those three is to do as they wish." He stood intending to meet them downstairs.

"Do I need to join you? I'd like to retire to our room. Avoid the conflict if at all possible."

"Yes, unless you want them searching the house for you. When they find you, I won't guarantee they will act the gentleman." No, his brothers might well include Caro in their plans for retribution. He should have expected something like this.

"They are just as bad as you then." She rose smoothing her skirts. "Let's get this over with. Since this is almost the last night I can spend with my husband, I would have preferred to be alone with him."

Her words pleased him. She could never refuse his advances even if she was furious with him. Mayhap she only wanted to be alone with him so she could cosh him over the head with a blunt object. He grinned. The tussle would be fun though. He also knew how the small skirmish would end.

The pounding stopped. Voices echoed up the steps and down the hallway to the bedchamber. "Where are they? Duncan's got some explaining to do, or perhaps fast talking."

That was Evan's distinctive voice. Duncan would recognize it anywhere. He cringed. They weren't going to wait for them to present themselves.

"Upstairs?" Fletcher asked Johnston. "We should wait a few seconds before barging in to their bedroom to see if they come down of their own accord. We could interrupt something. That would be highly inappropriate even for us."

"They both might be naked," Gordon laughed before adding in a loud voice he must be hoping would carry upstairs to their room, "We've brought dinner because the two of you couldn't be bothered to show up for the one you invited us all too. Sometimes your plans don't turn out as they should, big brother. We all expect you to set a better example."

That was Gordon. He watched her cringe. Knew she also recognized his voice. You don't have to go downstairs. I'll understand if you say no."

"As you told me. They won't have it any other way."

Quickly, he pulled her into his arms. His hands rested on the swell of her hips. When he looked into her eyes, they still held the hint of tears. With his thumbs he made gentle strokes across her cheeks. "I *ken* you're not almost crying about confronting my brothers. When I get back from London, I'll make this fiasco up to you. Promise."

He understood she didn't believe in his promise. A new sentiment, guilt, flooded him. Truly he needed to vanquish this unwanted emotion from his head. He had nothing to feel guilty about.

"You don't need to promise anything. Other than the *wee bairn* there is nothing we have between us to hold our lives together. I'll go to my home. Worrying about me would be a waste of time, I'm thinking. After all, when I first conceived, I planned on doing this by myself. The father would always be absent."

"Like hell you will," he grumbled. "You're not going anywhere I don't put you. If you leave the country home, I'll make your life miserable."

Would he? He certainly didn't know if he could do that. This threat of his seemed to be an empty one.

She lifted her chin high, higher than she had any reason to do so. She wasn't going anywhere. *Who will stop her? You won't even be close enough to send someone to retrieve her if she does leave. The locks should all be changed so she would no longer have a key.* He knew she would do what she wished despite what he commanded. He would sell all the furniture in her home. She would have to return to where he put her.

"In this I will do as I please," she spoke softly yet he heard the conviction in her words.

His gut twisted.

The pounding footsteps grew closer. "We need to meet my brothers. We'll discuss this further after they leave. They will burst through that door any second. Not even sure if they'll bother to knock. Are you ready?"

Caro nodded, her face a blank mask. He wanted her to like his family. They were getting off to a rocky start. He offered her his arm. She accepted just as the door flew open.

"Damn, hoped to find the two of you in a compromising position. Both of you have some explaining to do. Mother's feelings were hurt dreadfully." Gordon strode into the room, roaming the exterior as he picked up various objects then set them back where they didn't belong.

Duncan understood the ploy as one to irritate him. "No more than the three of you. Why are you here?" Duncan tried to keep his focus on Caro. Her face was white, ashen. He thought she looked adorable even in her distress. His heart twisted for her.

"We are at your townhouse to make sure your blushing bride has a healthy meal. Dubois was quite upset when he made enough for two more mouths and you didn't show up."

"Dubois knew we wouldn't be there as did Johnston. He always makes more than anyone can eat. Did he take some home to his family? Did the two of you keep him from doing that by bringing a meal here that we will not eat?"

"Are the two of you going to join us downstairs? Or should we stay here and visit?" Evan sat down on one of the wing chairs appearing to take up residence at that spot.

"We were on our way to see you in the drawing room. There was no need to invade our personal space," Caro said as she tried to nudge Duncan toward the door.

Fletcher, bowed low sweeping his arm in the direction of the hallway. "By all means, after you."

Duncan felt the trembling of her body as they walked through the long hallway then down the stairs. He didn't understand why.

Nonetheless it didn't surprise him that his brothers showed up unannounced. In the drawing room Johnston, who had followed them after they left, set out the food the brothers brought with them. The tray was not filled with dinner but dessert.

He grinned thinking of his wife's penchant for the sweets.

She poured brandy around. He filled her teacup, added milk and lemon. She sat, her lips thinned, appearing to wait for her world to explode in madness. Perhaps it already had.

"So," Duncan leaned forward. "Tell me again why the three of you are here. It's not just about mother."

Evan slanted him a full out grin then sifted his hands through his hair. He cleared his throat. "Thought we would offer to go to London in your place. You understand we are all quite capable."

Duncan didn't expect that. No, he had not. His gaze riveted on Caro. A tiny smile formed then she hid it. Ah, she knew him too well. She would understand he could not delegate.

"You all appreciate the fact I've never allowed anyone to see to my business ventures in London. They are all too important."

"What could go wrong?" Gordon asked lifting broad masculine shoulders. "It isn't as if we don't have experience in these things. I thought you taught us everything you know. Are you holding back on us?"

"Everything, and anything could go wrong with the three of you acting on the firm's directive," he gritted out as he sat down next to his wife.

Leaning back, he placed his arm behind her shoulders, let his fingertips touch the tender flesh of her neck. His nails skimmed and floated across her. She shot him a retaliatory glare. He could hardly wait until they were alone. Fire would flame. Tempers would fly, at least hers would. He always immensely enjoyed the scuffles.

"You know we are competent individuals. If you *dinna* trust us, the meetings could be put off a few months. We all know if we lost a few deals because of your absence our pocketbooks wouldn't notice the loss," Gordon said still grinning. "Nothing will happen that we can't fix."

"In case you haven't' noticed your wife will be giving birth before you return," Fletcher pointed out his voice flat. "We all agreed, you have no business leaving her."

"No need to point out the obvious."

She was clearly miffed at him.

He was annoyed at his brothers who were all three of them grinning. "What Caro and I decided is not your concern."

He understood she would now think he had a choice. Something else he would have to figure out how to gain her forgiveness for. He truly did not feel as if there were options.

She stiffened. It seemed her anger was now directed elsewhere. "The three of you don't like me. Well, I'm sorry about that. There is no reason to take this out on your brother. In case you didn't notice, I'm capable of having a baby without a man around. Didn't plan on having one in the first place."

The statement left him reeling, confused. He'd expected the brunt of her fury. Seemed he'd been wrong. She was angry with his recalcitrant siblings, not him. Feasibly they would all eventually share her anger. Honestly, he didn't see himself getting away with this trip to London without a few words spoken between them.

When Evan, Fletcher and Gordon all turned their masculine astonished look on him, he lifted his shoulders. "The three of you probably had no inclination that she planned on doing this by herself. I gallantly stepped in to help with all the necessities. She's been very grateful ever since."

"Yeah, I saw how grateful she was," Gordon said a smirk on his face.

Caro's cheeks heated a delightful shade of pink. He wished he could pull her into his arms, let her hide her face against his chest. His brother's comment was uncalled for, hurtful as well.

Didn't seem she intended to hide. Her chin lifted while her eyes blazed. "As I said, the three of you seem to dislike me. Your cruel words blatantly point that out. I don't care except for your brother's sake. Was it your intention, Gordon, to embarrass me a second time? If it was, you succeeded quite admirably."

"Caro," Gordon spread his arms wide appearing contrite. "I will apologize one thousand times if it makes you feel better. Not used to having a female besides mother in the family. Don't suppose I know how to act in the presence of another lady. My words were meant to embarrass big brother not you. Most of the time he does deserve the humiliation. Though he always gives as good as he gets. Seems you might be following in his footsteps. Even though yours are much smaller."

"We don't dislike you, Caro," Evan began not bothering to hide his grin. "It's just that we don't know you. The dinner was supposed to begin that process. If I recall correctly, you refused to be part of that dinner." He spread his hands wide. "What can I say?"

Duncan crossed his arms over his chest, his gaze slowly perusing one brother then another before studying Caro. He was proud of her. She confronted the men with aplomb even though he understood some of her feelings. Indeed, his Caro was a one of kind woman, unique in so many ways. He felt blessed to have met her.

Fletcher must have decided he needed to be part of the reconciliation. He poured everyone a drink. When he lifted his glass, a toast followed. "Here's to our brother, his wife as well as his yet to be born *bairn*. Welcome to the family."

When Caro didn't drink after the toast, she was met with three sets of frowns. Another issue with his family. They seemed to expect everyone to possess the same values as they had. He cleared his throat to begin the detailed explanation.

Caro beat him to the clarification by making her point. "My not drinking is no rebuff to your welcome to the family toast. Under the circumstances, I appreciate the gesture more than you can possibly know. Before this I believed all of you disliked me. Duncan and I decided that wine along with other spirits would not be good for our unborn child. Came to the conclusion I should stick to drinks that did not contain alcohol. Obviously, all food and drink that goes into my body will also go into the baby's. I would never give a child wine or brandy or…"

"Here, here, we would have never thought of something like that," Gordon told them, his smile broad as he interrupted her explanation. "I suppose she is more intelligent than we've all been led to believe."

"Makes perfect sense," Fletcher agreed with them nodding briefly at her. "I'll remember that when I'm expecting my first child as well as any following offspring."

"First, you have to find a woman who can tolerate you," Evan told him laughing. "Have you given that fact consideration?"

"Seems you're putting the cart before the horse," Gordon said his voice bland. "Just like big brother. Look what it got him."

"A baby along with a wife," Evan pointed out.

"Maybe you should try the escort service," Gordon told Fletcher.

"When was the last girl you courted?" Fletcher asked seemingly on the defensive.

"Don't think I've ever courted a woman. Not ready to settle down, not for a long time."

The conversation went on for a few more hours. He watched Caro yawn. Her head drooped to one side before she jerked awake. He wished she was nestled against him her head resting on his chest. With his decision to leave the day after tomorrow, they had two nights together. By the time his siblings left one of those nights would be gone.

Caro excused herself. He didn't want to let her go to bed without him. If she did, she'd be asleep by the time he crawled in next to her. In her condition, he would never wake her. He shot his brothers a look he hoped told them it was time to leave.

Ignoring the pointed look, Fletcher filled their glasses.

Finally, after another hour passed, "The three of you planning on staying the night?"

"Is that an invitation?" Gordon asked not bothering to hide his intentions. "Since Caro…"

"Caroline," he growled. No one else was going to call her by his pet name. "Caroline to all of you. Got it?"

"Beg your pardon. Caroline is not present to be embarrassed or think we don't like her. You can take our teasing."

"Long past time to end the teasing. Time for the lot of you to retire to your homes, in the process vacating mine. I'd like to go to bed. Tomorrow might prove to be a long day."

"You will take her with you," Gordon paused sending all a devilish grin. "To see mother."

"Obviously, that's why I had a change of plans. While I'm in London, I expect the lot of you to check in on Caro from time to time to make sure she has everything she needs. If anything happens I need to hear about, send a message. Johnston will stay by her side at the country home, however, I would appreciate extra vigilance on your part. Despite the fact I told her no, she might go into Glasgow to her old home."

"What? A wife who doesn't obey? How archaic," Gordon chortled clearly enjoying all that transpired here.

"Since she is used to being independent, I allow her the small idiosyncrasies." Indeed, he enjoyed his Caro more thoroughly when she defied him.

"Don't want anything to happen to the baby?" Evan asked lifting a dark eyebrow in seeming speculation.

"True, don't want Caro to have any problems either."

"You only married her because you didn't want the child to be a bastard. I might have done the same if I cared about the woman. Best you figure out your feelings." Evan's words weren't formed as a question but a statement.

"My feelings don't involve any of you."

He realized the *bairn's* parentage made little difference to him. He married her because he needed her to stay in his life. She was everything to him. Didn't believe he could live without her.

~ * ~

Caroline curled up in the big chair by her fireplace that she loved. Snow fell. Wind howled around the eaves of her home in Glasgow. Torra and Honey left a few hours ago. They visited at least twice a day, sometimes more. Today, she treated them to some chocolate bonbons she learned how to cook from Monsieur Dubois.

The two ladies brought a new girl to visit. Her name was May. Torra said everyone called her Miss May. She didn't know her story. The lady was loath to speak of her past. Just understood the woman's life had been filled with pain until Miss Scarlett took her under her wing, giving her a home as well as a job.

Johnston helped her out by bringing supplies weekly. He was her fatherly mentor giving her advice she didn't agree with. Every time he came by, he begged her to return to the country telling her how angry her husband would be if she wasn't there when he returned.

She supposed she'd heed his advice sometime, just not today. Duncan was due to return in two days if he kept his promise. His letters always explained how much he tried to expedite business although his clients all had other ideas. Told her he wished he was with her. She never told him she moved into Glasgow, figuring what he didn't know wouldn't hurt him. Even though she didn't mention the move, Johnston undoubtedly told the man. He would have felt duty bound.

She felt the first cramping a week ago. Torra told her because this was her first child, she might have early pains. A few of the articles she read mentioned them. Many women had those same sensations early, before the due date. They were false or just getting the baby ready to come into this world. Caro thought it was probably getting her body prepared to bring that babe to the outside who didn't seem so tiny anymore. From everything she read, she knew her body would have to stretch quite a lot for the baby to be born. Contractions were what did the job.

Every book she could find about birthing babies, she read from cover to cover. Went to the university where she found as many articles as she had time to devour. Now, she felt nearly as competent as any midwife. She saw a midwife in Glasgow. If she gave birth at the country home, the woman wouldn't do her any good. The midwife did assure her the baby was healthy and doing just fine. The feeling that she would have to rely on her knowledge flooded her. Johnston certainly wouldn't be of any help. The elderly man would most likely faint dead away.

Dear lord, what if she gave birth at night when no one could fetch the country midwife for her?

The thought of all that could happen twisted, coiling in her belly until she ached. Standing, her hands on her back, she stretched easing the twinges and pains she was feeling. Fears at this point wouldn't do her any good. What would happen would happen.

A cramp more intense than any she felt before seized her. Her knees buckled. Once again, she sat on the chair. Abruptly, she understood if she was going to keep her promise to Duncan, she needed to leave tomorrow morning at first light. It wouldn't do her or the baby any good if she remained closeted by herself in this house. He promised he would be home for her. When he returned, he would go where he expected to find her.

Ten minutes, twenty then an hour passed since her body tensed in pain. Now, she felt nothing except the baby moving inside. She pushed on what she thought must be an elbow or knee to keep it from sticking out. A quick bath would feel good, might help her sleep. Decided to use the huge tub in the scullery instead of the one upstairs. Couldn't possibly haul water up the steps for more privacy.

The bath was heavenly, hot and steamy. Eased her aching back and shoulders.

Startled by dreams of Duncan, she jerked, splashing water onto the floor. She'd slept. Hurriedly, she dried herself then wrapped the towel around her. Finally, in her bed, unable to sleep, wide eyed she stared at the ceiling. True, Duncan wrote a letter every day. He told her how he spent his time.

She didn't want his letters.

Wished for him, his arms around her. Needed to feel the heat emanating from his big body.

Understood she loved him.

Tears formed in her eyes, clogged her throat. She pounded her pillow. Still didn't sleep. It wasn't to be. Felt no more cramping. Decided to put off her return to the country home until the next day. If she sent a message to Johnston to pick her up sometime in the morning, he would be pleased to come for her. Had begged her to return sooner.

Caroline spent the day finishing her column. She visited Torra and Honey. Miss May thanked her for the fresh batch of cookies she brought. Told her how much she would miss her baking when she left. There was another new girl who didn't come to visit with Torra and Honey. Her name was Cybil.

Before dinner that night, she sent a message to Johnston to pick her up by noon, before, if that was more convenient. It wouldn't do for her to arrive after Duncan. Knowing she defied him, he would be angry.

If he held her in his arms, she could deal with his irritation.

The next morning with hugs and kisses from Torra and Honey, Miss May watching a bit from a distance, her hands held in front of her, Johnston helped her into the earl's carriage.

She was going home. During the morning hours she felt a bit of cramping. According to Torra the baby would most likely be born late tomorrow or the next day. Relief that Duncan should be home by then gave her reason to feel confident that all things would go as they should. She decided to wait to tell Johnston of her impending condition not wanting to alarm anyone. When she'd read every word she could find on birthing, she didn't want to act the ninny.

She was afraid though.

Desperately, she wished Duncan would show up. She needed his strength. At this very moment, she didn't care if he was angry or annoyed. She wanted him if for no other reason than to hold her hand and to tell her everything would be fine.

Alone and terrified, her anxiety increased. Tried to calm herself. Reminded herself how much she learned about childbirth. More than anything she didn't want to do this alone.

She cursed his departure. Even though he'd had choices other than to leave, he chose his business ventures over her. When she asked to travel with him, he vehemently denied her.

Even his brothers showed up from time to time, in a group or individually to look in on her, to see how she was doing. To her knowledge they never told Duncan she defied his order to stay in the country. It was amazing to her how much they all looked alike, except for Gordon. Instead of the strong dark foreboding look of the other siblings and the father, his ginger-colored hair was a stark contrast. His features were the masculine version of their mother.

Cora showed up once or twice for tea. She offered her the cookie of the week. Always thought Cora looked at her with suspicion in her eyes. Cora didn't like her. Was at best tolerating her simply because she was the mother of her soon to be first grandchild. All her uncertainties multiplied without Duncan to help her through the rough times. She disliked feeling insecure. The emotion wasn't what she wanted to feel.

"Now she waited for the carriage to reach the country manor house. She didn't know why exactly. She was eager to get home. If all went as planned, she would see Duncan tonight. He would be there for her.

Sometimes things didn't go as planned.

By the time they finally arrived home, she was exhausted as well as irritable. The bumping and swaying didn't sit well with her stomach. A small cramp around the perimeter of her swollen belly startled her. She hadn't felt anything for two days. She decided she didn't want to alarm Johnston, afraid he would panic when confronted with a woman in labor. Everyone told her birthing a baby would take time. Everything she read said labor with the first child could last at least twenty-four hours.

Once she arrived home, she watched Johnston leave for his nearby cottage. Feeling a bit domestic, she began rearranging her garments in the armoire. After that she padded to the kitchen. Dubois knew she was coming. He left a plate in the warming oven. She wasn't hungry. Dubois was not here. She decided it was the perfect time to bake without fear of annoying the cook.

Sorting through her recipes, she found one with tiny chips of chocolate. Humming to herself, she went about her business. In less than an hour, she was eating cookies and drinking chocolate milk. There were two more batches to go into the oven. The first cramp seized her when she pulled the second batch of cookies from the oven. Some of the accounts she read said she should time the contractions. It was nine o'clock.

Sleepily, she yawned.

By nine-thirty all the cookies were baked. About then she had another contraction. Thirty minutes apart. There was still a long time to go. She decided she should sleep. Once in bed she tossed and turned. Sleep proved to be elusive.

Where was Duncan?

He was supposed to be here. It was after midnight by a few minutes. His promise to her was broken. When the next contraction gripped her, the pain was more intense. They were coming closer together, fifteen minutes now.

It seemed she was on her own in this.

Staying here and having the baby without help was not an option. Quickly, she dressed, donned a warm coat. Johnston wouldn't be here until the morning. She couldn't wait for him.

Heading toward the stables, her water broke. She didn't think she had time to go back to change her gown. The contractions were closer together, more intense. She had to ride to Duncan's parents' home. It would take ten minutes. Prayed they would hear her knocking. Tried anxiously to keep her nerves from unraveling.

This was not supposed to be happening. Duncan was supposed to be here to take care of her.

Half way there, she had to stop. In pain she gripped the horse tightly, desperately trying not to fall, hanging on while she waited for the contraction to finish. She held her breath.

"Oh no, oh no, god no…"

When the pain passed, she urged the horse forward. Another six minutes or so she was at the house. She stopped earlier to let another contraction sweep across her abdomen. Her teeth chattered as she slipped from the horse. They were coming faster and faster now. She was frozen bone-deep and in pain.

Leaning against the door she pounded with the heavy brass knocker. Pounded and pounded. She closed her eyes slipping to the porch floor sure no one heard the noise she made. In any case, she needed to get through the excruciating agony before she tried again.

She wanted to yell. Couldn't because her teeth chattered nonstop.

Needed to curse Duncan for causing this.

Didn't want to have the baby on the front porch.

Suddenly, the door opened.

"What? Who?"

Gordon stood in front of her. "I'm…" She moistened her lips trying to explain what was happening to her. She searched the interior of the house. Warmth, she needed a warm place to rest. She needed to lie down. The devil curse him, she prayed for Duncan.

"Having the baby," he finished for her with a glib smile on his too handsome face. "Seems pretty obvious it's your time. Where is Duncan?"

All she could do was shake her head. Couldn't talk then, as the pain eased, "Not here."

Gordon swore softly, "The bastard."

"Get her inside where it's warm." Sean stood beside her now. The two men helped her to stand, guiding her into the foyer. At least some of these men wanted to help her even if her husband didn't care.

"She's dripping wet...?" Gordon asked, staring blankly at his father as if he didn't have a single idea as to why.

Caro would have laughed at his perplexed expression if she wasn't undergoing the tight pain circling her belly.

"Has her water broken?" Cora was there taking charge as she stepped into the foyer. "Where is Duncan?"

"Seems he didn't make it back in time," Gordon said with a hint of irritation in his words. "He deserves a thorough thrashing."

"Believe I'll be the first in line," Sean said his words grim. "Thought I brought the boy up better than this."

"Come along. No time to waste on technicalities. Get her upstairs into Duncan's old room. I'll fetch a dry nightgown. Find the tarp." After taking charge, Cora set off at brisk pace.

Cora stopped, turning to her husband. "Go fetch the midwife. Tell her it's urgent." She turned to Gordon. "See if you can find your brother. He might be at the townhouse. If he arrived late, he could have decided to stay there until morning. After that, if necessary, go to Caroline's home. I'm afraid you might be on a fruitless mission. However, we have to do everything in our power to alert Duncan to the knowledge his wife is in labor. I know him. He would not break his promise lightly."

"I can wake Johnston too. Have him wait at the house for Duncan to arrive. We all *ken* Duncan was never made aware of the fact his wife moved into the city."

"Hurry. If you can't find him, keep looking. I'm sure he's on his way. He will be here."

Caro wasn't as positive about Duncan as his mother.

Since she woke at midnight, she felt the first flicker of hope that all would be well. Now, before she knew what was happening to her, she was dressed in a dry nightgown and lying on a tarp covered bed. The baby would arrive any time. Duncan wasn't there to hold her hand.

As the hours passed, she wondered if she would survive this ordeal. Cursed Duncan. Her throat scorched raw from the harsh yells. She wanted to hold them back. Tried desperately to keep the cries of pain behind her teeth. Couldn't do that either.

Cora told her to yell and howl as much as she wanted. It was good for the baby. It was also good for her. Cora also told her to curse the father for his absence, for doing this to her. It would make her feel better simply because they both understood her oldest son deserved the swear words.

Finally, by early morning the babe was born. He was the most beautiful baby she'd ever seen. She counted finger and toes. Ran her hands through his thick mat of dark hair. Even while he screamed his lungs out after entering the world, his face red as a beet while his little arms and legs whirled, she thought him beautiful.

"Believe the lad is hungry." Cora helped her as the baby latched on to a nipple.

Her milk let down. Tears slipped along her cheeks. Officially, she was a mother. Didn't have to worry about her sweet *lassie* being ridiculed and tormented. She had a son.

"I know Duncan must have tried like the very devil to get here in time. When he does get home, he'll tell you what happened to him. I know it," Cora told her patting the baby's sandy hair. "Thank you, Caroline. You've given us the most precious gift in the world. I certainly hope my son appreciated the efforts. He should have been here to see what it cost you."

"Caro!" The door burst in, banged against the wall startling all including the baby who let out a howl. "The devil, I tried." Duncan stood at the foot of the bed, his hair a disheveled mess, stubble on his chin, his eyes surrounded by dark circles.

Gordon and Sean stood behind him. It seemed they all waited for the words he wasn't saying.

He hovered over her, his eyes shining with an emotion she'd never seen before. "Not hard enough," she murmured exhausted from the inside out. "You said two weeks if you could. You..." Even while tears spiked her lashes, Cora left the room and closed the door on the eyes prying into

244

the room. "You promised."

"I've an explanation."

"I'm sure it will be very good." She felt certain her sarcasm didn't go unnoticed.

~ * ~

"Those two," Gordon muttered as he stomped down the steps. "What was Duncan thinking? He should have returned two to three weeks ago. There was probably some transaction he couldn't turn down. When I think of all she's gone through all by herself…" Gordon waved his hands through his hair. "I'm going to tell him what I'm thinking as soon as I get the chance. Going to thrash him soundly."

He'd never been able to get the upper hand with his brother. This should be the first time if there was justice in this world.

"You do that," Cora's gentle words startled Gordan from his musings about his brother's behavior.

He looked upward as if asking for divine intervention then back to his mother. He could certainly use help from above. Maybe this wasn't his concern.

"You just remember this when you have a wife and *bairn* on the way. Sometime life puts challenges in your way you can't overcome. Don't judge your brother so harshly. You don't understand what happened to cause the delay."

"He was a selfish bastard," Gordon muttered in an attempt to defend himself. "All of it over making more money none of us need."

"So true. We all understand he didn't need to leave her. Could have delegated to you and your brothers. He has trouble doing that. Always has to have control, to take charge. He needs to accept a new set of values now that he has a wife and son."

"We told him as much. He doesn't delegate. Doesn't know how." Gordon understood his words were bitter toward his brother. What he didn't comprehend was why.

"No, neither do any of the Murray siblings. Again, remember this day for your future. Hold it close to your heart so you will remember how you felt when Duncan failed to be here for his wife."

Gordon sat in front of the fire, watching it crackle and burn. Flames flickered and glowed in the darkened room. He recalled the lump of fear in his throat when he saw Caroline slumped on the porch, her face white, gown sodden. He believed she was dying. With no clue what to do for her, he watched her as if frozen in time.

Thank God for his mother.

He hoped he found a woman as beautiful as Caroline. Also as intelligent, he added with a bitter laugh. In all of Glasgow, he didn't think any woman matched Caro's intelligence. Possibly someone who was creative. A woman who would write poetry to him. The thought that he was abruptly ready to settle down if he found the right woman, a lady who could fill all his dreams, rattled him to no end. The sudden thought both unnerved as well as terrified.

The brandy burned as it made its way down his throat. His father joined him, sitting in the opposite chair. The clock ticked. A baby's cry from above echoed down the staircase. The soft tread of Duncan's booted feet as he walked followed.

He prayed Duncan never discovered the fact that Caroline spent the two months he was in London away from the country home. Minutes later, Duncan appeared in the drawing room sporting a wide smile.

"You have a son," Sean said. "Are you pleased?"

"She wanted a girl."

"Have you named him?" Gordon asked then with the need to bait his brother again, he said, "You could call him Gordon after me."

"Not a chance, little brother." He poured himself a full glass of brandy. "Got caught in two snow storms. Left the carriage half way between London and Glasgow. Had to ride like the devil to get here. Haven't slept in three days. Don't judge me, little brother. I tried my darndest. Now I'm exhausted to the tips of my toes. Can't sleep though. Caro will need me soon."

"Guess that accounts for the dark circles under your eyes," Gordon said blandly still unable to forgive his brother. "You should have started back sooner. Wouldn't have had to kill yourself to keep a promise you ended up breaking."

"You're right." Duncan leaned his head on the back of the chair. Closed his eyes. "I am a bastard. You're also right about delegating. Won't ever leave her again. If she's not with child, I'll take her with me. If she is, I'll stay and send my brothers to do my job. None of this is worth the money earned even though all our individual accounts increased."

"How much did you make on this trip?"

"Until the investment plays out about ten thousand English pounds."

"If you would have sent us?"

"Probably the same." He let the air he was holding rush out of his lungs. "You all are correct. I should have allowed the three of you to make the decisions. After all, I trained you. Need to have more confidence in your collective abilities. Since I'm a father now, I won't have as much time. Got more important things to do."

"Don't suppose you want to share what you're feeling?" Gordon asked believing that maybe he misjudged Duncan.

Perhaps this was a valuable lesson learned maybe for both of them. The problem as he saw it was that the lesson was taught at Caroline's expense.

Duncan shot him a sardonic glare. "No, it's between Caro and myself. What I will tell you is that I was terrified for her as well as our child. When she wasn't at home, I rode back to Glasgow on the rare thought that she disobeyed me. The devil, I knew she was living at her old home across from Miss Scarlett's place. Johnston sent me the message the very day she moved into the city. Well, he didn't come right out and say the words because he promised Caro not to. I've known that man since I was in diapers. He has a way of saying things without actually saying them."

"You weren't furious? I would have thought," Gordon murmured looking on his brother with new eyes. "What happened after you rode back to town?"

"I raced to the townhouse. Should have known better. She would have never gone there. Since I was in the city, I couldn't leave anything to chance. After that I was sure she ran away. Was certain the days we spent together were a sham. No matter where she went, I meant to find her then bring her home."

"We must have just missed each other. I rode all those places on the off chance of intercepting you."

"The second time I put my horse in the stables I was greeted by Johnston. Told me where she was as well as what was happening." He brought me a fresh horse.

"You hightailed it here?"

"Just thinking of the moments when Caro was missing twisted my gut brought my anger to a shimmering crescendo."

"You weren't angry that she moved into town?"

Inhaling a deep breath, he continued, "I don't recall ever feeling so relieved. For a few seconds the terror vanished. When I realized what exactly Johnston told me, the fear I'd been experiencing doubled in moments."

"You love her then," Sean said.

"I do."

Chapter Ten

When he started his trip home, he planned to arrive three days early, eagerly anticipating the birth of his first child. He tried to accomplish his goals two weeks early as he'd hoped. It just wasn't possible. Duncan was proud of himself for getting away before schedule. If all went as it should, he would arrive early, not two weeks but three days prior to the due date. Gave himself a momentary pat on the back. Now, it seemed it was all for naught. He tramped down newly fallen snow just because he had nothing to do while the driver along with several others attempted to dislodge the wheel stuck in a snow-muddied rut.

This was the second time he'd been waylaid by the weather. Damn unpredictable February weather.

The axel was broken. It would take days he didn't have to fix the damn thing. Left with no alternative, he bought a sorry specimen of a horse. Undoubtedly, he would have made better time walking. Every ten miles or so, he changed mounts. By the time he was less than twenty miles from his home, he was finally able to purchase a worthy animal. He pushed the animal hard, praying he would make it before midnight.

Since his vehicle broke down, he'd been riding nonstop. His gut twisted and coiled. Somehow, he understood Caro would birth his child before he arrived. He should have hell to pay.

His promise broken. Breaking vows, especially to his wife, was not the type of man he considered himself to be.

He wanted to be there for her.

Somewhere along the line he came to the conclusion that he more than cared for her. He loved her wit, her mocking words, the way she dimpled when her lips curved in a soft smile meant just for him. How she looked at him her eyes shimmering, taunting him to tell her the truth.

He loved his wife more than he ever believed possible.

Despite his command for her to stay at the manor home in the country, he now prayed she disobeyed him. If she kept to her wayward ways and stayed across the street from Miss Scarlett's home, she would have Torra to help her along with the midwife she would have been seeing in the city. To his relief Johnston wrote to him that she found a very competent midwife.

In the entire two months, she didn't write one word. Johnston told him everything she was doing, some of what she was thinking.

He was pretty certain she must have read every book as well as articles ever published on childbirth. Relief should have been his. A woman shouldn't have to go through labor alone. It seemed she expected to do just that as she prepared for the delivery.

At the moment, Duncan didn't like himself very well. By the time the business deals were completed, he realized any of his brothers would have done fine. It was stubborn pride, coupled with the fear he was growing too close to his wife that had him fleeing the best thing that ever happened to him.

When he arrived at her home, he raced through the house, calling out her name, searching every room. On the off chance she stayed across the street, he pounded on the door until a sleepy-eyed Torra answered.

"You looking for Caro? She's across the street," Torra told him petulantly. "Why didn't you try there instead of waking all of us?"

When he saw the simmer of her eyes, he'd been sure she was lying. "Where? Where is my wife?"

Torra lifted her shoulders as if she didn't know the answer. "Told me she didn't want you to be angry with her when you got home. Might have gone to your townhouse or all the way to the country. At one point she spoke of finding a small out of the way village where you would never find her, probably to the townhouse though. No, I think she went to the country. Why don't you ask Mr. Johnston? She was having pains."

She was having labor pains? "Why would she go anywhere alone when you were here?" The lump in his throat grew to gigantic proportions.

"You'd have to ask her. Just think she was trying to keep you happy." Torra plucked at her robe while she stared at her bare feet.

"She's never cared about keeping me happy. Why would she start now?"

"You don't know your wife at all. Perhaps before you go startin' babies you should find out more about her."

"Well, isn't that just ironic?"

He swiveled on one boot heel. Stomped down the porch to his horse. Knew she went home. Would have had Johnston pick her up. From everything Johnston wrote she confided and trusted him. Why couldn't Torra just tell him and save the time it would take him to reach his townhouse so he could make sure she wasn't there?

So much time.

Immense amounts of energy.

Too many minutes spent searching for her that his body shook with terror. What ifs, compounded in his head?

He needed to reach her.

Where the devil was she?

The second time he handed the reins of his horse over to the stable hand at his country home, Johnston appeared seemingly from nowhere.

Clearing his throat, Johnston accomplished in a brief slew of words that Torra was unable to do, "She's at your parents, in labor. Best you hurry or you'll miss the birth. I'll take care of this animal. Go now!"

Duncan didn't bother with a saddle. Breathing with relief as well as renewed terror, he bolted on his stallion. They raced the wind. Snow fell lightly from the sky. When he reached his parent's home, he saw the light in his old room shining brightly. Saw the silhouette of a woman, his mother, walking across the floor. She held a bundle in her hands.

His son.

Or daughter.

Leaping from the horse his heart pounding, he raced up the steps. He bolted into the room, "Caro! The devil I tried."

She looked at him wide-eyed, accusing eyes. With a wry look in her beautiful, sky-blue eyes, she smiled. He lost his heart anew. He would do anything to see her smile along with her twin dimples.

Gordon and Sean stood behind him. It seemed they all waited for the words he wasn't saying.

He hovered over her, his heart shimmering with an emotion he'd never felt before. Love for his wife and child blossomed.

"Not hard enough," she murmured appearing exhausted from the inside out. Beneath her eyes there were purple smudges. "You said two weeks if you could. You…"

Even while tears spiked her lashes, Cora left the room and closed the door on the eyes behind him prying into the room. "You promised." Her arms holding their baby were shaking.

"I've an explanation."

He knew it was valid. Would she believe him? His heart in his throat he didn't know how to proceed.

"I'm sure the reasons will be very good," she murmured her voice soft.

A lone tear slipped down her cheek.

She sounded exhausted. You fool, of course she was tired. Probably the last thing she wanted to do was talk or argue with him. He was certain she didn't want to hear excuses.

Instead of talking he strode quickly to the bed. Sat down upon the dark blue quilt covering the mattress. She was nursing the baby. Seeing her with his child to her breast was a beautiful sight. He looked at her expectantly as if she could read his mind. Needed to find out if he had a son or daughter. Wished to see the *bairn* closer.

"A son," she murmured crinkling her nose as she whispered. "Do you have an idea for a name. It's something we should have spoken of sooner."

"What name would you like?"

"Where a boy is concerned, I've no preferences. Wouldn't want him named after my father or any of my brothers. What about you?"

"We don't have to decide right now." He watched as she shifted sides, pried his little rosebud lips off her nipple. "Greedy little thing. I *ken* firsthand how you taste. Wouldn't want to let go either."

She flushed.

He grinned. The sight wasn't arousing. Instead, the vision of his wife feeding his son created more startling feelings, warmth, possessiveness, love. He needed to tell her what he realized. The startling conclusions he'd come to over the last few days and moments while he raced to her side. Needing and doing so were two different events. He stroked the dark hair on top of his child's head. "Brown eyes or blue?" He remembered their conversation about different traits being stronger than others. The stronger ones masked the weaker.

"Most babies eyes change color. We don't truly know yet. If they are going to be another color, they change after a few months," she told him. "Do you want to hold your son?"

"I…" He felt damn insecure in this new life he was about to embark upon. "Don't know how." He knew nothing about babies. "I'd feel more at ease if he was turning thirteen."

Her smile stretched across her face. "Best you learn how to hold your son as well as a wealth of other things a proud papa should know. Just make sure you don't let his head flop around. It's heavy. When he turns thirteen, I might give you a bit more say in his rearing.

"There now, very good. Put him on your shoulder. Pat him gently on the back so he can burp." She handed him a cloth to put beneath his bouncing head as he seemed to still be looking for his food source. When he did burp, they both laughed. "Set him in his crib on his back. You can keep hold of his head better when you lie him down."

When he returned to sit on the bed, "We've a great deal to talk about. However…" Perhaps this wasn't the best time to have a lengthy discussion. Her exhaustion was obvious. "Talk later," he said softly.

He was stopped by the knock on the door. Cora stood in the doorway a tray in her hands. "Food and drink. Are either of you hungry?" Then she turned to her grandson. "Don't keep her up. After she eats make sure she sleeps. The lad will only sleep a few hours. He'll be waking you both up before you know it."

"Famished." He turned to Caro. She nodded. "Haven't stopped to eat in three days. Had water only while I rode." He thought on those hours. Hunger pains never materialized for him. While he set his course, all he could think about was Caro.

"I haven't gone as long as that. It's been since last night for me. I was eating cookies and drinking milk in your kitchen, when I realized the contractions were getting closer. Should have left then. The facts of my tardiness, I was too stubborn. Was sure the babe wouldn't be born for quite some time. Poor Dubois, seems I left a mess for someone to clean up."

"I'll send a message he needn't come into work today."

She placed a hand on his arm. "If it's not too much trouble, I'd like to go home this morning. In the carriage the trip will only take a few minutes. We would be there in no time. Truly, I don't want to impose on your family."

Cora was shaking her head no. "The midwife is here to monitor your needs. Duncan needs his sleep also. Here we have several close relatives who would love to help out. At home the two of you will be alone. Well, you'll have Johnston as well as Monsieur Dubois. Doubt if either of those two men will be much help where it comes to the baby. Tomorrow morning will be soon enough for the two of you to venture home."

"What do you think, Caro? We can both relax if we stay here for the day and night. Start getting to learn about our baby. Will the next morning be soon enough?"

To Duncan she appeared wistful. He knew in that moment she would agree to stay. Also knew she still wanted to go home. He spoke to his mother. "It's a good idea you have. One day here will give us both time to recuperate. For me, all I need is a few hours of sleep. Hopefully the young lad will allow that. I'm certain Caro could do with twenty-four hours. Doubt if the babe will go along with something so outlandish."

After Cora left, he slipped out of his clothes. Naked, he brought the tray of food to the bed. "Think you can have a glass of wine now? He asked as he poured her a small portion.

Wistfully, she glanced at the wine, seemingly unsure. "It's not as if the alcohol will go straight to the baby when you feed him." He paused thinking about anatomy and the effects of nourishment. "Will it?"

"Probably not. It will most likely be two or three hours before he needs to eat."

"You don't look too sure."

A soft puff of air left her lungs. "I'm not. However, what you say makes sense to me. Maybe it's wishful thinking. I would love a small glass of wine."

"Don't believe that much wine will hurt the little fellow. Might help you sleep. You look as if you could close your eyes and be dreaming the next second. Sleep for you can only serve to help the baby."

"Yes, you too."

"In my mind, it will all be fine. Finish eating."

Seeing his child invigorated him. His son was very real. When the boy had been inside her womb not so much, at least not until he started kicking.

After two months of sleeping alone, he was pleased to feel his Caro's warmth as she sat next to him. For several minutes they ate in silence, each with thoughts of their own. He needed to explain his tardiness. Now didn't seem the time. Just as returning home would wait so would his explanation. Was it just an excuse to keep the guilt at bay? Perhaps in a day or two she would find it in her heart to forgive him. He could tell her he loved her then. Knew she wouldn't believe him until he returned her possessions.

When he turned his attention back to his wife, her head drooped, her lashes slowly opening and closing as if she tried to stay awake. He picked up the empty plates. Left her half empty glass of wine beside her on the bedside table. Once the food and drink were cleared, he helped her to lie down, pulling the covers up to her chin.

Duncan stepped back, watching her, wondering what the rest of their lives would bring. He still had a few promises to keep. After all, he promised her the research grant. Wondered at this moment with her new responsibilities if she would be able to find the time for this passion of hers. She might no longer care. He doubted that.

When he was in London, besides business he ordered a dozen different types of rose bushes to be planted at the country home. He meant to speak with her about selling the cottage across from Miss Scarlett's. He supposed she would agree if he would promise her the money from the sale.

The devil but he'd acted the bastard where she was concerned. The action did get him exactly what he wanted.

He didn't regret one second even though he was sure that

eventually she would have agreed to marry him. Before he crawled into bed, he checked on his son who was sleeping soundly. Lovingly, he caressed his forehead. If he could, if she could, he wanted at least four children. Laughing to himself, he decided if all she wanted was this child, he'd make do.

He had his heir.

He'd always been the person who wanted more, wanted it all.

Funny how they never spoke of more children. Interesting, how they rarely spoke of anything to do with their future. He knew so little about his wife. Why the devil would she give him input when all he did was command and direct? He had to acknowledge also; he took. It might seem to her that was all he did was take what was precious to her.

If they were to carry on, he would have to change his ways. To do so would be devilishly hard.

He woke to the baby's first cries. While the tiny infant wasn't hollering as he'd heard earlier when he first arrived, he wasn't happy either. Caro slept. He padded to the crib. Found the boy was wet, everything was wet; his clothing, the sheets covering his bed. How the devil did he change him? While he could negotiate deals that doubled his income, he didn't know the first thing about changing a baby's nappy.

Miraculously, his mother peeked inside the room smiling what seemed to be fondly at him. "Do you need some help?"

Duncan understood that she kept her laughter at him from bubbling out. "You heard him cry?"

He was surprised at that. What else would have brought her to the room at this early morning hour? The sun was just now beginning to show itself.

"Truly, Duncan, your boy needs a name. Thought the two of you would have figured something out while you ate last night." Cora set the tray of food she carried on a table near the bed.

"Seems we were both too tired to think. Actually, we know what we don't want."

He had to laugh when his mother arched her brows. Who would ever rule out names first, perhaps only a genius? No, two geniuses.

"What would that be?"

"To begin with we won't name him Gordon as my little brother too eagerly suggested. Neither will we give him the name of her father or brothers. For me, I don't want him to be Duncan the second, or Duncan Junior."

"There is still a wealth of fine Scottish names to choose from. I'm sure he will have a name soon."

"Fine Scottish names," he mused as he stroked his chin foregoing the idea of names for the immediate and pressing problem in front of him. "Perhaps you wouldn't mind instructing me on the best way to change the *wee laddie*."

"Be pleased to show you. When we're finished here, you will have to wake your wife so she can feed him. Surprised the boy has been so patient." Cora stepped back as she gave a few directions as she proudly watched him.

The *wee bairn* let out a loud wail. "No longer." Both father and grandmother laughed.

When he finished and the boy was dry again, he woke Caro. She sat up, sleepily rubbing her eyes. She'd never been more beautiful, her hair tumbling around her shoulders as well as across her breasts. The baby fussed. Made little noises, Duncan assumed were displeasure at having to wait so long for her nipple. He certainly could understand his son's way of thinking.

"Woke you only because the *bairn* needs you. Afraid I can't do this." He spoke while watching her unfasten her gown. Her breasts, swollen with milk, were lovely. After he set the baby in her arms, his little head bobbed around, looking for the nipple. When he found it, he visibly went to work.

"You changed him?"

To his ears, she sounded incredulous.

Duncan knew he was beaming with pride. He puffed up his chest then straightened his shoulders. While he wanted to take all the credit, he understood he couldn't, "I did. Though..."

She appeared surprised yet pleased. "I had no idea you knew how to do something so fatherly. Last night you didn't know how to hold your child. When did you learn?"

"I'll be honest. Mother heard the boy cry. She taught me a few minutes ago." After her changing look of disbelief. "I did the work," he defended himself. "Looks as if mother brought breakfast."

"What time is it?"

"Around six. The little guy slept four hours. Don't suppose he'll sleep longer tonight." He buttered a piece of warm bread for her. "Honey on it?"

"No, too sticky. He probably won't sleep through the night for months," she murmured trying to make herself more comfortable. The pillows behind her back were at odd angles. He adjusted them for her.

He handed her the bread before fixing his own. It was delicious as was the tea washing the bread down. "What do you think of Craig or Malcolm? We could call him Mac."

"I like them both. Believe this one is going to be your decision. You've a *bonny* way with boy's names. Wouldn't give you this much leeway if this child of ours were a girl. I've several picked out."

He arched a brow. "Care to share?"

"No, could change my mind in the interim. Wouldn't want to start an argument if that happened."

For several seconds he tapped one finger on his chin. Thinking back to boy's names. "How about," he paused in thought, "Malcolm Craig Murray."

"Agreed. That's a fine name for this young man of ours. "As you suggested, Mac would suit him best now. When he gets old and stuffy, he can assume his full name, Malcolm."

"Mother will be pleased the *laddie* won't be going into the evening hours without a name. Now, would you consider selling your cottage? I would put the money in a trust for the children."

Duncan thought that a fine idea. Was surprised to see her stiffen. Perhaps the idea wasn't as fine as he thought it to be.

"At least you asked. I *ken* you will do as you please no matter what I say." Her back was rigid as was her words. She remained silent.

Only a few minutes ago he considered giving her back all her possession. What got into him? "I asked because I wanted your opinion. If I didn't, I would have gone ahead, sold the property then told you what

I'd done." Anger began to simmer between them. He wondered if they would ever be rid of the heated emotion keeping the distance separating congeniality in their lives.

To his surprise, she smiled blandly. With a lift of her shoulders, "It's a fine idea. Obviously, I've no need for the cottage. The roses though…"

"Can be transplanted," he said quickly, watching for another reaction besides the stiffening of her body.

"That would be nice. You would have your gardener help my roses thrive in another location?" It seemed she was forging ahead, adapting to this new idea. He was well pleased.

"I would. Would do anything for you."

Now, he should tell her. Let her understand his love for her was more than the baby. He couldn't live without her by his side sharing his life. Making promises to her except for his love and fidelity he wouldn't make. Life had this way of stepping in and blindsiding a body.

When she finished feeding Mac, she handed the boy to him. He walked and burped him. Set him on his back on the bed where they played with him, making faces. Never before had he felt so complete. That very moment, he realized there was more to life than making money. That was totally and unerringly a unique revelation for him. It took him off guard, blindsided him.

Duncan changed Mac several times that day. The next morning the trio ate before he drove them to his manor house. He was pleased with his small family.

They would do well together. She came to his bed day in and day out. He had a devil of a time keeping his hands to himself. Mac was three months old now. The midwife told him he could make love to his wife.

Nevertheless, he hadn't told her he loved her.

Well, she didn't say anything either.

~ * ~

Caro spent the three months wondering if he would ever want her again. Maybe all she'd been to him was a challenge that he easily won.

259

Her body was almost back to normal. Self-doubts exploded swirling dangerously in her head. She watched as her treasured roses were transplanted. When the plants Duncan bought her in London arrived, she threw her arms around him, delighted with the surprise. Even went so far as to kiss him on the cheek. Found that she was disappointed when he didn't kiss her back. All he did was set her on the ground before distancing himself from her.

She didn't know what to do. Three months changed into four. Mac could turn from his back to his tummy. He was a delight to both of them. Duncan played with him every day just to hear him giggle. He no longer rode into the city. His employees came to him. He changed because of the love he held for his boy not because of any great love for her.

He never spoke of love or caring. Never looked at her the way he used to when she knew he wanted her. When she understood in seconds he'd be deep inside her. This wasn't at all as she'd imagined life to be after the birth of their child. Guilt at what she did to him flooded her. He no longer wanted her. That fact should come as no surprise to her.

When she studied her husband, for her the same raw feelings of desire surfaced. If he looked at her, which was rarely, he seemed disinterested. He would always look away as if he didn't want to see her.

It was an hour before Mac's bedtime. Most nights the boy slept through until morning. He was eating some oatmeal and rice cereal. Duncan played with him on the floor encouraging him to sit. That skill seemed beyond the little boy who looked more like his father every day.

For Caro, she tried every ploy she could think of to make Duncan see her differently. Even when she stared at his mouth or his crotch, he appeared unmoved. She supposed there was no longer a challenge in it for him. He was a competitive man.

She gambled on the pregnancy.

He won.

He had his child as well as a wife he could live without. No more simpering daughters presented to him at balls. She was the sacrifice for him to continue on as if she didn't exist. Somehow, she'd become a wife in name only. It was not well done of him. She didn't have a clue how to change his mind.

Disheartened and with a huge sigh, she rose not wishing to watch the tender scene unfold on the floor in front of her. Caro stood to leave the room. For a few days, she thought to move back to the cottage since he'd yet to sell it. If she did, he wouldn't allow her to take Mac. So, she stayed. In all her life, she'd never felt such debilitating despair. Before when she lived with her father, the duke, she expected those feelings. Now that she thought someone cared about her, the happiness she believed would be hers turned to desolation and misery. When no one was around to see, she cried copious tears.

She stood, fiddled with her skirts for a few seconds as she watched Mac slowly fall to one side during his attempt to sit. He giggled. Duncan tickled the little boy. The giggles continued. Since the lad was born, Duncan beamed. His boy seemed to be everything to him.

As she strode to the doorway, she didn't say anything. Didn't believe it mattered to Duncan.

"Where are you going?"

His voice sounded harsh to her ears, gruff as well as annoyed. She didn't understand why he asked.

Slowly, Caro turned. "To look at the roses. Need to see how the transplanted ones are faring. They've been here for a few months. Would like to get to work soon on a new project."

She thought about the grant he promised. Funny, how she no longer cared. Perhaps when Mac was older, she would have the time as well as the inclination to pursue her dreams.

Duncan wasn't very good at keeping promises.

"Do you want company?" He stood bringing Mac with him.

"No, you needn't bother yourself. It's almost his bedtime. I'm sure you would enjoy more playtime with your son."

"We'll come with you. Let me tell the nanny to come get Mac in time for bed."

Caro couldn't figure out how to tell him that she wanted to be alone. Needed to figure out things that mattered to her. Although his presence wasn't as distracting as it used to be, he would be in her way. Tonight, the way he was looking at her, it seemed he had some hidden agenda.

A soft whoosh of air left her lungs then with a slight lift of her shoulder, she said, "Suit yourself, you will anyway."

"I believe I'll do just that." He gathered Mac then strode to the room adjoining the nursery.

She heard the booming of his voice as he gave instructions. Not waiting for them in any case needing the distance, she started down the staircase. She picked up a lightweight shawl. Before she could leave, the two males were beside her.

"You in a hurry?" A questioning tone hovered on his lips.

"No," she said, gently caressing her baby's cheek with the back of her hand. "No, didn't think you cared if I waited."

"You've been distant, Caro. What has you always with that faraway look in your eyes? I'd like to see you smile again. I thought you would be happy now that you got what you pursued so diligently."

She gasped at his cruel words. How did she tell him that he was the one who was different? She didn't know how to explain to him she wanted him to make love to her, to hold her in his arms as he used to do. It was well past time for sex. If he wanted her, he could have her. Certainly, she wouldn't object.

"I smile at Mac."

She kept walking, her head high as she tried to fend off the threatening tears. Caro didn't know what to say to a man who kept her at such a disadvantage she questioned everything he did as well as every word he said.

Stride for stride, he easily kept pace with her.

Answering his question without crying was impossible. She pretended to examine each rose bush. Each new flower blossoming was a thrill to her. By the time the nanny swept Mac off to the nursery, they were at the gazebo. Pillows adorned the benches. A wine bottle sat on a tray that also held two glasses. A single red rose was in a vase. Startled at the romantic scene in front of her, she sipped a tiny puff of air.

"Caro, what's wrong? It's been impossible to talk to you since Mac was born. At first, I just thought your silence was exhaustion holding you back from conversation. Now, I'm worried about you, us." He sounded sincere.

How did she tell him there was no us? "I don't smile except when I play with Mac because I've nothing to smile about." She spoke softly.

It seemed Duncan leaned forward to hear.

"Nothing to smile about?" he asked, appearing confused his brown eyes growing darker with each second of this horrid conversation. "What nonsense are you talking about?" He sounded totally muddled.

The depression that first settled into her heart and soul after Mac was born was hard to describe. For the longest time, she felt hopeless. Since she did keep to herself, maybe all this was her fault. If things could change back, she'd take responsibility. "I don't know how to explain my feelings."

"Try starting at the beginning."

Her breaths quickened as her heart rate sped. Perhaps his hesitancy with her was because of her. "After Mac was born, I didn't feel like myself. Instead of feeling the joy at seeing my child, I always felt sad, felt as if there was a hole in my heart. When you didn't want me after the midwife told us it was safe, the sadness compounded daily. With each new and subtle rejection, despair settled in around me."

She didn't believe she was telling him all this. Her feelings were so private and personal, also embarrassing. For some reason she didn't understand, her words tumbled from her.

"Caro." He held her hands in his, gently squeezed. His warm brown eyes focused on her as he spoke. "Don't ever doubt I want you. Just looking at you, a fever blazes in me. I want to be deep inside you every second of every day. I've waited for you to give some sign you wanted me."

"You haven't kissed me once."

God but her heart pounded. He rubbed tiny circles on the tops of her hands. She supposed it wasn't a kiss. Nonetheless the tiny gesture he now gifted her with stole her breath. Brought memories of the times she climaxed almost the same instant he plunged inside her.

"Because that first time you flinched away, I didn't believe you wanted a kiss from the likes of me, the man who stole your independence." Gently, he touched her cheek with his knuckles. "Believed you were still angry with me. Just because our son was born, doesn't mean our differences have been resolved."

"I did. I do."

She hoped this coldness between them could be bridged with a kiss. She swept her tongue across her lips leaving a trail of moisture. Strangely, he did the same. She'd never noticed before.

"Come here." He didn't wait for her to move closer. His hand was behind her head, the other around her waist drawing her to him. He didn't give her time to protest. Not that she wanted to do anything so very foolish.

A breath of air staggered to her lungs. His lips descended, touching, caressing, before sending the same mercurial heat through her as the contact of his mouth on hers always did. She wrapped her arms around his back, feeling the smooth play of his muscles as his arms pulled ever closer to his big body.

She closed her eyes, memorizing the feel of him. Her body trembled beneath the onslaught of his teeth and tongue. He pulled away, his thumb moving across her lips. She knew they were swollen from his attention.

"I'm sorry, Caro. We should have talked about this sooner. Don't like the idea of your sadness. I might have been able to help. You should learn to confide in your husband. I've only your best interest along with our son's at heart. The two of you mean so very much to me."

His deep brown eyes held a wealth of concern. "It's nothing to worry over now." Now that he kissed her, she found a spark of hope for their future flutter in her heart. "I truly believed now that you had your heir you no longer wanted me. That's the way you acted, all aloof and separate."

"God no, Caro! It took all my willpower to keep my hands to myself. I looked at you and I wanted you. So, I couldn't allow myself that pleasure. Guess I don't have to do that any longer. Do you want me, Caro? God knows I want you."

"More than I've ever wanted for anything."

The groan rumbling from deep inside was all male possessiveness. Warm breezes ruffled the fragrant leaves around the gazebo. Rose scented air swept through her. The earth around her seemed to sizzle with the heat radiating from Duncan. In the distance sounds of animals chattered as the sun began to descend. There was no tempest this evening except the one that was stirred up by them.

His fingers were nimble. His mouth and lips voracious as his teeth closed over the hardened bud at the tip of her breast. She gasped. The sensations over whelmed.

Her clothing fell to the floor.

His followed.

It seemed he touched her everywhere. To Caro who felt long denied the sweet bliss only he could give, it seemed forever since she felt the physical love from her husband.

She arched.

He pulled her closer.

She twisted.

His body filled her, swept into her with the heat and fire she remembered. Spasms began slowly to ignite to an inferno as he moved faster pushing her higher. The end burst inside. The explosion between them dynamic.

"Duncan!" she cried out his name to find his lips closed over her, his tongue thrusting deep. Her nails raked down his back touching on each vertebra.

His seed spilled into her when his guttural cry of pleasure echoed in the small structure where they finally came together again. For a moment, he rested on top of her. Shortly after, he pushed up, moving damp strands of hair from her face. When she calmed, he handed her clothing back to her.

"Please dress. We've something I have to speak with you about. If you stay this way, I'll be inside you again before we can talk. Otherwise..." his voice trailed off.

She nodded despite the fact the tone of his voice frightened her. "If that's what you want."

"Not what I want but the way it has to be before I forget any noble intentions that might surface for a moment. When I look at you naked, all my thought process goes by the way side. Just your gown, sweeting. Don't bother with anything else. Removing them again is not a top priority." He chuckled as he looked at her. "I see you feel the same as I do." Duncan slipped on his trousers leaving his shirt on the floor of the gazebo with her underclothing.

"You look as if you've swallowed a canary," she whispered wondering if she should be terrified.

"Believe I have. *Dinna fash* yourself." He waved his hand in the air. "This should be good news for you. He pulled her onto his lap.

Beneath her derrière she felt his need. Suddenly, she was pleased. He now vanquished her worst fears. "Good news?"

"Yes, just listen to what I've to say."

She squirmed a bit, feeling his deep arousal ebbing through her, heating her anew. This was not something she could do without the incessant need encompassing her. She wanted to straddle him. Bring him deep inside of her. "I'll try."

"To begin with, you truly need to sit still."

"I'll try." She knew this would be difficult. A tiny voice of wickedness inside her told her it might be more fun if she stirred the dragon. She moved as if she tried to do as he said then moved again twisting on his lap, her legs now on either side of his.

He groaned when she shifted position a third time. He gritted his teeth. "Now, when I first discovered your pregnancy, I pulled out every dirty trick I could think of to force the marriage. At the time I didn't regret the lengths I went to secure your acceptance of my proposal. When I look back on the deed, in my eyes the action was necessary. More than necessary." His words were coming out fast, jumbled. Nonetheless she grasped what he tried to say.

"Is this an apology?"

Caro didn't know if she would accept an apology. If he didn't blackmail her into the marriage, she might still be doing this on her own. By her way of thinking this all turned out for the best. She moved back and forth teasing, separated now only by his breeches.

His eyes simmered. She understood he held himself together by a slender thread. "No, never that. What I did that day was necessary for my happiness, yours as well. At least I hope so. I would never do anything different."

"If there is no apology forthcoming, what then?"

"This." From the pocket of his frockcoat, he pulled out three official appearing documents. His hand shook slightly when he handed them to her. She'd never seen him this insecure before. His trousers were unfastened. Flesh on flesh, she felt his hard length against her.

"What are they?"

She looked from the papers to him. Briefly, all thoughts of seduction slipped from her mind.

"I'm sure after you read them you can figure it out without details from me."

A few minutes passed before she finished. She threw herself into his arms, kissing him soundly on the lips. "Is this real?"

"Very much so. I'm praying I don't have to hold your funds away from you to keep you with me. I suppose this is a test of sorts. You now have the money to do and go anywhere you wish."

Her heart pounded, desperate for more than just these documents. For so many months, she'd held her breath hoping to hear genuine words of love. She remembered yelling at him that her baby was only hers. The child was hers, only hers, only Caro's baby. Swallowing hard, "Thank you," she murmured but when she studied his handsome features, looked into those dark brown eyes of his, there was something terribly wrong.

"What aren't you telling me?"

"Caro." He held her hands in his.

"You're scaring me." She tugged on her hands suddenly seeming to need space.

He didn't let her go. "Wish I'd told you sooner. Think I've felt this way for a very long time. Maybe even the first time I saw you with your rouged lips and nipples, other parts too along with that huge pink bow tied around your slender white neck. You were adorable. Think my heart swelled hoping to see you again. Once you left me that morning, I knew I couldn't spend my life without seeing you. Used all my resources to discover where you lived. Once I did, I didn't know what to do with the information. I could hardly storm into your home and carry you out."

"Duncan?" She needed to understand where this was going. "What aren't you saying?'

"I love you, Caro. Don't want to live without you."

God, he sounded so very sincere. She could almost believe him. "You don't? You do?"

"All true."

His handsome features seemed strained. It appeared he wanted to laugh at the strange look on her face. She wished she could hide her happiness until she wholeheartedly believed him. It looked as if he needed to hear the sentimental words returned. "You?"

"Me?"

So stunned by his sudden announcement, she had no words. Thoughts whirled in her head.

"Yes, how do you feel?"

"Me?" dumfounded, she asked again as she tried to get a hold of her escalating emotions.

"Caro, think you *ken* what I'm hoping to hear. If you can't say the words of love I'm looking for, I'll try to understand." It appeared he held his breath behind his teeth. "If you don't…"

"No! I do. Duncan, I love you. Maybe not from that first night we met, made love. Sent me to a pinnacle I never believed existed. Perhaps I did fall in love then. Couldn't stop dreaming about you, about your arms around me. Was that why we couldn't keep our hands to ourselves whenever we saw each other?"

"Maybe. It's an interesting thought."

"What we felt wasn't lust? It was love?" She had been sure all along the feelings between them weren't love. "Is that how love feels?"

"I believe so."

He kissed her hard on the mouth. The sensation was no longer possessive. This time the kiss held a wealth of other emotions. The touch was different, deeper, with more meaning.

When their lips parted. "I do love you, Caro Murray."

With one slender fingertip, she touched his chin. "I love you so much too. I feel as if I've been waiting a lifetime to hear those words."

"Mac isn't just Caro's baby. He's our baby. That makes this all the sweeter."

    In the next moment, he was deep inside her.

Epilogue

Nine years later, Duncan and Caro watched their three boys wrestle on the lawn by the roses. Duncan held their little girl in his arms. She was three months old now. She was the most beautiful baby girl she'd ever seen. Because of Duncan's caring attention to all their children, she no longer cared if the girl child grew up to be brilliant. Much to her surprise she hoped she would surpass both of them with her intelligence, would forge new inroads into the rights of women.

"We finally did it. We've a magnificently intelligent little girl." Duncan brushed the top of her forehead with his knuckles beaming at her as he did so. "In her lifetime, she will never want for love. We will shower love, affection along with more book learning she can ever want upon her. She will grow up with confidence to throttle the world on any level she wants.

"We do. I want her to be just as poised as well as confident as her brothers. She will have to survive her older brothers. Do you *ken* how hard that will be?" Caro watched them roughhouse. Grunts and groans emanated from the yard. Mac tackled his second oldest to the ground. They rolled until their clothing was grass stained. "We will have to make certain they understand that while they can wrestle with her, they will have to make a few concessions."

Duncan barked with laugher clearly amused by the antics of his sons while he was also thinking on the future. "Mac will undoubtedly torment all her possible suitors. He's already told me as much. He says he doesn't intend to let anything bad happen to his little sister. Mac told me that if I lost contact with her anytime, he would be there to follow her." His laughter, the amusement sent heat radiating outward.

"She will never find a moment's reprieve. I already feel sorry for her. She will have to outsmart them on every level to ever have a moment with a suitor."

"She has so many more opportunities than I did, a father to love as well as spoil her. Do you think she'll be a professor or a scientist?" Caro asked as she dreamt of her little girl's future.

They would do everything to secure her place in this world just as they would do for their sons.

"No, I'll teach her all about finances and business. Teach her how to double our fortunes. She will be an unparalleled mathematician. There is no doubt in my mind about this."

Caro punched him on the arm. "We don't need to double anything. We've more than what we can ever want or need. I look at how my life changed when I became your birthday present. That day along with my scheming with Letty's ladies was the best day of my life up to that point. After that it seemed my life grew brighter and brighter so much so that I feel as if the moments behind as well as in front of us rival the sun."

"Especially not our children. Suppose we should try to double them. Nonetheless they do rival the sun in the magical warmth they cast upon us."

As the years passed, Mac along with the other siblings were true to their promise of keeping her safe. The boys attended oxford gaining several degrees in various studies. The little girl decided she wanted to become a physician. That fact terrified Caro, afraid of the diseases that sometimes ran rampant in the cities.

Nevertheless, in her youth along with the courting years, she learned so many different ways to elude her big brothers. Delighted in their frustration when they lost her, she would laugh at their bumbling attempts to keep up with her. They would never know about her first kiss behind the stables from the lad who lived a few miles down the road. Nor would they learn about the time she walked in on Mac involved with a lass, her skirts tossed.

Many of the things she saw would make her mother blush. Her father would take what her brothers did in stride. She would always wonder why it was just fine and dandy for the boys to have sexual dalliances and it was not for her.

All these things we might learn about some we might not. They all might turn up in another story. Perhaps another series involving Naughty Girls.

Coming Soon by the Author
at
Rogue Phoenix Press

Honey
Good Girls Book Three

Glasgow 1824

The day was a lazy April day. While a brilliant sun beat a steady stream of heat onto the land burning the mist hovering as if the grayness refused to depart despite the impetus, the somber funeral continued. In the distance Honey heard the call of a meadowlark. A gray squirrel dashed up a solid oak tree she was standing near. She didn't feel anything for the man who sired her, who made her life a living hell. For some odd reason she couldn't comprehend, she felt drawn to this place of death. Perhaps she just wanted to make certain he was dead. Any other reason eluded her.

While she watched, her father's dark black casket was slowly lowered into the ground. The bastard. No melancholy filled her at his passing. Her teeth grit together, her hands fisted at her sides. She wasn't at all sad to see him gone. During her lifetime, he caused so many problems along with unending heartache. As his bastard daughter, she received no love from him. He tolerated her. That was all.

The earl's five sons gathered around the hole in the ground. The minister read a few words over the grave. Hearing the single word "amen," she understood the ceremony was nearly finished. She hoped she stood far enough away that no one would notice her. There were those in the small graveside group who meant her harm. Shaking her head as if the movement would bring sense to her, Honey MacRae didn't understand at all why she came to the graveside service. Torra along with Muira supported her in this strange endeavor despite the fact they warned her against attending the service. Told her numerous times she would regret the rash action. Torra also told her by coming new wounds would open. Tristan, the escort service's bodyguard, stood a discreet distance from the women.

The earl's oldest son looked in her direction. While shielding his eyes from the glaring rays of the sun, Camdyn seemed to study her for a few terrifying seconds. Honey knew the moment he realized who he stared at. The scowl on his face turned to an evil malicious grin. She gasped in a startled breath of air ready to turn and run. Stopping herself, she decided to meet him if that's what he wanted. Her brother no longer held power over her. All she could hope for was that he wouldn't saunter her way then confront her.

She was nothing to him.

He was nothing to her except nightmares needing to be forgotten.

"Is that your brother?" Torra asked, a tender hand on her shoulder. As if intending to give courage, she squeezed lightly. "Should we leave as it appears he is coming this way? Do you wish to talk with him? You don't have to do so. You know that."

"No, I don't wish to talk to him. However, I will not run from him either. If I did, he would find glee in the fact he still had a hold on me. He doesn't. Miss Scarlet made it possible for me to start a new life." Honey spoke softly reaching to her shoulder to rest her hand on top of Torra's. "With father's death it is only a matter of time he attempts to assert his will on me again. I refuse to show fear. I'm certain he has known where to find me for quite some time. There are few among the gentry, if any, who don't know about Miss Scarlett's place along with the women who reside there."

She touched the rounded curve of her left breast where the horrid tattoo proclaimed her belonging to the evil men's society. When her father was deep in his cups, Camdyn would escort her to whichever home was hosting the meeting. By the time she escaped, they owned a single home where they carried on their lecherous activities.

Thinking of that first time he abused her, her small body shuddered with the renewing despair thoughts of that night generated. The men held her down while the tattoo of the rose and the saber, their motto, was branded into her soft flesh. They weren't gentle, the pain nearly unbearable. Copious tears slipped from her eyes to run down her cheeks. At one point she fainted. The men wouldn't allow her to lose consciousness. She found herself slapped awake each time she slipped away.

After the tattoo was finished, each of Camdyn's five friends took her savagely, Camdyn being the first. With a fist held high in the air, he hooted then bent close to her claiming, "Your virginity is mine. You belong to me, now as well as forever."

The men's association met every week or two at a home the men purchased. Over time, there were more girls initiated into their club. Leaving was impossible; the doors locked, the windows barred. The servants who kept the women fed were all loyal to the men. Besides none of the women had anywhere to go except for her they all were found on the streets. Because of Camdyn's lies about her, she was banned from her father's home.

Torra squeezed her shoulder again as the man drew closer. His long limbed stride, the tilt of his chin, all proclaimed his birth as well as the arrogance associated with aristocratic titles. Honey tilted her chin defiantly, her eyes blazing with the fury she felt for this man. She prayed he wouldn't do anything today. Tristan was here to make certain nothing untoward happened to any of them. Her brother was still tall, muscles rippling as he strode toward them. His expertly tailored jacket fit his broad shoulders perfectly. He was haughty as well as cocky. After all he would inherit the title now as well as the wealth. He would be the next Earl of St. Rose. Nonetheless, he was depraved and evil, an evil man who thought he could take whatever he wished.

Coming here was indeed a foolish endeavor. After the fact, hindsight was often not very useful. She gulped in a smidgeon of air wishing she had more sense than to attend the funeral of a man who despised her. Whatever demons stirred in her soul, to Honey, staying away had been impossible.

"Honey." Camdyn's single word oozed from his mouth. "See you came to pay your respects to our dear father. Nice to see you again, sweetheart. After your sudden departure from my country estate, I didn't believe we'd run into each other again. You didn't have my permission to leave. If I recall correctly, father gave me guardianship over you after he washed his hands of his bastard."

No, she came to put an end to one of her fears. This one man could no longer hurt her. There were others though. Beneath his ardent perusal that seemed to slither down her body, she suddenly realized prudence should have kept her from attending. She'd acted impulsively. Could have witnessed the grave at a different time. Now, she needed to deal with the repercussions.

"No," she said her voice shaking. Her defiance obvious she tilted her chin. "I came to make sure he was indeed gone. As to guardianship, that ended when I turned twenty-one."

"You'd rather the man in the casket was me." Slowly, he reached out to her, touched her cheek with the tip of his finger, his tiger-eyes blazing with lust she'd come to recognize since the first time he accosted her when she was ten years old. That day, he didn't touch her. Instead, he took great delight in humiliating her, stripping her of all her pride.

Flinching away then stepping backward, "Don't touch me!" All too well she understood her command would have no effect on him. He would do as he always did, as he pleased.

"I suggest you do as the lady says," Tristan spoke, his voice harsh as he set Honey behind him. "Ladies, it's long past time to leave. Go to the carriage, now!"

"Ah, a bodyguard for you. How nice for you," he chuckled then, seemingly amused at something. "He called the likes of you three ladies. Whores would be a better description." His smile was an evil leer in his handsome face. "Do you give your sweet charms to this man in payment for his protection? I remember how your breasts taste, just like warm honey. Recall how those small round globes feel in my large hands. Also remember the softness between your white thighs along with the fire of your core."

Tristan's fist hit his jaw. Camdyn stumbled back a few steps while he held his hand to the spot where Tristan punched him. "You'll regret that," he snarled belligerently, his voice low with a wealth of menace lingering with each word.

"Never." Tristan shot him an arrogant smile rubbing his knuckles. "You deserved that and more. In lieu of what I know about you, I found the moment quite pleasant."

Torra and Muria flanking her, they ushered her to the carriage waiting for them. Her breath fluttered through her lungs as she desperately tried to stop the rush of tears threatening. She had hoped to go unnoticed. Obviously, that particular wish didn't happen.

Honey was shaking so hard her teeth rattled in her jaw by the time they reached the carriage. The ladies were right. She was a fool for attending. This was no place for her. Since that time almost two years ago, she'd not seen her brother. Never knowing how she managed the feat, she got away from the home where they were having their weekly debauchery. Honey supposed it was because they were drunk. No, it was also because they found a new girl to initiate into their men's association. Their attention that night was riveted on the poor woman, the branding as well as the rape. The new girl now bore the same mark, the rose and the saber as all the unfortunate women who fell into the path of any of these men.

Just by her appearance here, she understood she would see Camdyn again. He would discover her whereabouts if he didn't already know. After that, well, Honey understood she would never survive the depravity of the men's association if they found a means to force her back. Maybe they wouldn't want her. She was used goods. They liked younger women, those most helpless. Since she wound up at Letty's escort service, she never escorted or slept with a man. She became the downstairs maid. The job was pleasant, the ladies all so very kind. Camdyn didn't know that. She found the home because in her blind rush to escape the country home, she stumbled into the Duke of Southcliff's stables at Southcliff Hall. He discovered her then after hearing her story gave her a place to live.

"He can't hurt you," Muira said encouragingly. "Tristan will protect you as will Bobby and Scarlett. You don't have to worry about ever going back."

"I shouldn't have come," Honey said through strangled sobs. "All of you were right. Should have listened to what you had to say. It's so very strange. I can feel him thinking about me."

"I believe this is something we need to make a bit more public. Next time Bobby and Scarlett visit, I will make sure the Duke of

Southcliff understands what happened here. He needs to understand you are still in a precarious situation."

"Yes, well...I didn't tell him everything that day he found me then brought me here. I couldn't do so. When I think on that time, the shame along with the humiliation is more than I could bear. While I have to endure the memories of what they did to me, I won't allow those days to bring me down. All I can do is put the recollections in the past then move on with my life."

"It's past time the duke is informed of everything. He's a spy. The duke works for the government," Torra said as her mind seemed to drift off to a different time and place. "He believes in protecting women, a rarity from my experiences."

"He has connections," Muria pointed out. "Torra is absolutely right about the last part. He does seem to care about women. Do you think we should send him a message?"

Honey was well aware of Torra's knowledge of Leslie Stewart, the Duke of Southcliff. The duke saved her from a sordid life where she was sold to men for their convenience. Torra didn't object simply because without that man who pimped her out, she was slowly starving to death. Just as Leslie Stewart did with her, he saved Torra's life, in the process giving each of them a place to live along with a means to support themselves.

"Before we begin sending messages to the duke, we should wait to see what my brother will do. He might not approach us." She reminded herself Camdyn wasn't actually a real brother. He was her half brother. Recalled all the times he treated her with the same disdain as her father. As it was, Honey never understood why her father allowed her to stay in his home.

"What if he sneaks into the house and steals you away?" Torra asked, her eyes wide with some emotion she wasn't absolutely certain Torra understood. "He could do that."

"My brother won't sneak. If he wants me, he'll find some time when I'm alone to coerce me or forcibly adduct me."

"What are we going to do then?" Muira asked, her hands fisted on her hips. "He could take all of us if he's a mind to do so. We are exactly the type of women they like."

"No, my brother takes women who are vulnerable, ladies who won't be missed. All of you will be missed. Bobby along with the duke would use all their multiple connections to ruin him. He *kens* that fact. That is exactly why he won't bring me back into the fold." The sudden realization gave her the first ray of hope she felt since seeing his gaze glued to her at the cemetery. "Camdyn won't risk censure of any kind. Since father is dead, he now holds the title. He wants to appear a gentleman. To him appearances are everything. He won't risk his status in the community to take any of us. Not to say the men's association won't continue, it will. Nonetheless, the association will forge ahead with so many destitute vulnerable women they won't have any difficulties finding ladies for their enjoyment."

"What I don't understand is how they continue to hold the women, forgetting locked doors and windows," Torra asked. "Glass can be broken. Most women will fight."

Recalling those times when her brother held another's woman's life in his hands if she refused him, brought back horrible thoughts she prayed she would never have to relive. Her body shuddered with icy fear even though her mind tried to tell her she was safe.

"You're not telling us something," Muira said, her voice so very soft the words could barely be heard. "You're leaving out important details.

She brought a rush of air into her lungs as she roamed to one of the windows in the parlor. Staring outside she tried to compose herself all her nerves stretching as she remembered those terror filled days. Yes, she left a great deal out. How could she explain?

When she turned, "After I was forced, I discovered I wasn't the first woman to fall into their clutches. What the men did to us all was despicable but worthy of keeping all the women at their beck and call, their plan diabolical." She swallowed hard as she tried to give her throat the dampness she needed to continue to speak.

"How on earth?" Torra asked looking more skeptical than ever before. "How could they keep the woman from fighting? That makes no possible sense to me."

"The woman they held over my head was small, petite in every way. Her eyes were the color of a summer sky they were so blue. Her hair was a soft shade of wheat. If I refused to do something they asked, she was punished, horribly so. Sometimes I would hear her scream. Other times, they would punish her in front of me."

"You say the other lady was punished for something you denied them?" Torra poured everyone a glass of wine as she seemed to be mulling over her statement. "Believe I'm going to need this."

"Yes." Honey caught her bottom lip beneath her teeth as she accepted the liquid nourishment from Torra. "Yes...they did cruel things to the woman. Sometimes...no I don't want to go into details. Let it be enough to know they are evil, cruel men, malevolent in every way. I just pray they didn't kill Mary when I left. I had to..." A sob ripped through Honey. "Mary was punished, I'm certain of the fact."

Torra's arm around her shoulder she pulled her close for a comforting embrace between two women. She led her to the sofa. "It's not your fault they are evil."

"Which brings me back to the question," Muira said. "What are we planning to do to keep you safe? I'm not as certain as you that you are not in danger. Other than the women of Miss Scarlett's escort service, who would miss you."

"Beyond any doubt, we need to send for Bobby and Scarlett. Bobby knows men like this. He understands the workings of malevolent men. Didn't he keep Scarlett safe when the underworld threatened her?" Torra said.

"He did," Muira said as she tapped her painted fingernail on her chin. "If I recall at the time, Billy liked our little Honey. Seems he has or had a soft spot for her. We should bring him here also."

Honey gulped back a sob. She didn't want to involve Billy. Yes, he liked her, told her as much but a soft spot? She couldn't be with the man though, couldn't be with any man. Not after what happened to her at the hands of her brother. What does he think of her? She told him how she got the tattoo. Not the rest of what happened to her.

"You think we should send a message to Billy?" Muira asked as she swirled the wine in her glass.

Honey watched with fascinated disbelief. Billy didn't have a soft spot for her. Did he? He did touch a place in her heart that one week he was here when everyone feared for Scarlett. He spent time with her. When he tried to touch her, she recoiled from him. All too well, she remembered how his eyes darkened when he looked at her. She understood he wanted reasons. She'd been unable to humble herself enough to explain.

"No," she quickly spoke up. "Billy is a duke now. What would he have to do with the bastard daughter of an earl? He might be married. Have any of you thought of that? Don't wish to complicate his life with my problems."

"Married or not, the fact doesn't mean he won't help," Muira pointed out. "We should figure out some way to send Honey to him. The farther away from Glasgow the better is what I say."

"What reason would I have to travel to his place in the highlands?" These women were so different when they started scheming. The last scheme was nearly the undoing of the escort service. They presented a friend to the Earl of Downberry as an escort. She wasn't. No, she was a highborn lady who desperately wanted a baby. Well, that was a horrible mistake that actually ended up in a positive way. Camdyn might also be able to ruin their livelihood if he set his mind to the task. Honey didn't want Scarlett's business to suffer because of her.

Torra downed the wine in her glass then grinned over the top. "We will think of something. If you are not here, he won't have reason to visit us. If he can't find you, he won't be able to threaten you or our business."

"She fixes Scarlett's books whenever there is a mistake," Muira said thoughtfully.

"Yes, Honey is a genius with numbers, isn't she? Perhaps Billy will need help with all his books. That's perfect," Torra grinned as if she now had all the answers.

"Why would he need help from me?" Honey asked, her voice a shaky whisper, so terribly unsure of herself. "The man has the groats to buy expert help, the best in the business He doesn't need me. Nor will he want me to muddle up his well-ordered life. He is a duke. I'm a bastard."

"A duke of less than a year. Need I remind you where he came from before that?" She paused seeming to wait for her words to sink in to her head. "Because he will want to see you. Doubt if Billy wants a well-ordered life. He's probably bored to tears. You'll put some adventure back into his life when you show up," Torra said appearing as if a plan was falling into place. "Fetch paper and a pen. I'll start the missive to him.

When he reads this, the man will send for you. I'm positive."

"I don't want to go," Honey said softly. "It wouldn't be right for us to deceive the man." This did not bode well for her. The ladies were insistent. While she enjoyed Billy's company those long ago days, she shied away from him when he thought to even hold her hand. Terrified of men, she would never be able to be with a man intimately. From all that Billy told her, that was the way he wanted her. If she showed up at his door, he would believe she changed her mind.

"We will speak only the truth. What happens after that will be between the two of you," Muira said seeming as enthusiastic about this as was Torra. Holding up her hands, "We are not playing matchmakers even though it might seem that way to you."

"I cannot be what he wants me to be." Honey's voice held a fine tremble as moisture threatened to clog her throat. "If you write to him, you will give him hope for us where there is none." Honey didn't know how to convince these fine ladies that she could not, would not travel to the Duke of Aubrie's estate. After all that happened to her, she could never be intimate with any man, even one as sweet as Billy, Lord William Alexander Cameron, Duke of St. Aubries.

"Bah!" Torra laughed as she waved one hand in the air her grin wide. "There is always hope. I'm certain Lord William would love to pick up where the two of you left off. If anyone could ease your way into lovemaking, he could."

"We did not leave off. We never started anything. I told him no. Explained to him there could never be anything between us. What more is there to say? If you write him, he'll believe I've changed my mind. That would not be fair since nothing for me is different."

"No, he won't. What we are planning is a business arrangement, not a matchmaking scheme," Muira laughed gaily reinforcing an earlier statement. "He will be so pleased to hear from us. I'm just as certain he will be delighted to see you. He is sure to rise to the occasion."

As well meaning as they were, Honey grit her teeth against the machinations of these two women. While she understood protesting overmuch would just set them to a more determined state, she closed her mouth. Warily shaking her head at the two women, she spoke softly, "Do what you will. If he agrees to your enquiry, I will go only because the farther away I am from Camdyn the better I will feel. Even as we stand here speaking, my brother is conjuring plans to get me back in the fold. I *ken* the fact just as I live and breathe."

"Be assured we will," Torra said grinning, an all-knowing smile gracing her delicate features. "By this time next week, you will be on your way to the highlands with all your trunks packed for an extended vacation on Billy's home turf. Think of this as an adventure waiting to happen. Have you ever been to the highlands?"

"I believe Billy's home turf is actually St. Giles Parish in London. He never wanted to become a duke, never wished for the responsibilities associated with the title. Would have been happy staying with Brett MacLachlan. Know he had a girl there he liked. When he became a duke, she didn't want anything to do with him." Honey could not help protesting this debacle. The scheme would more than likely turn out in the very worst sort of way. Something in the back of her head though prompted her to agree with the women. Unable to keep the thoughts of Billy out of her head, she did understand that she would like to see him again. What she didn't understand was why.

"As you recall, just as Bobby didn't have a choice in his future neither did Billy. He is a duke; you are the daughter of an earl. The two of you are perfect for each other," Torra said, her grin wide. "You have the necessary pedigree to make a lovely wife for a duke."

"Bastard daughter," she corrected with a heavy sigh. Honey continued, "At least Bobby remembered his father and mother. Knew who he was along with the fact someday he might be called on to accept the responsibilities he no longer wanted. Billy had no idea who he actually was when the title was dumped at his feet. Why would he accept a bastard for a wife?"

"All true," Torra eyed Muira with a crooked grin, "Should we start the letter to Billy. I don't know, perhaps we should just send Honey to him tomorrow. That way we won't have to wait for a reply. We also won't have to worry about Honey changing her mind. She would be in his protection all the sooner."

"No! Protection? You make it sound as if I'm to be his mistress." Honey stood so quickly she nearly swooned, her head becoming dizzy with the jerky motion. "I will go but not in that manner." She came to the conclusion earlier, simply because she didn't want to see her brother again. "I will go if Billy accepts whatever foolish reason you two come up with to send me to his home. My doing the books as well as some of the paper work I'm certain he is hounded with was a good idea. Nonetheless, I'm convinced he has hired someone for that purpose. He will not have need of the likes of me."

Honey wanted no more of the two women who seemed to take it upon themselves to make all her problems go away. This situation was all her fault, she dispiritedly admitted to herself as she walked up the stairs to her room. Going to the funeral was a colossal mistake, one she might have to suffer the consequences for some time. After she stepped inside her room she wandered aimlessly around, picking up objects then setting them back in their place. She didn't know what to think of this conundrum that she found herself in.

This was the first actual home she ever experienced since her mother died. When she lived with her father, she'd felt out of place, known always as the bastard daughter. Camdyn threw her parentage in her face constantly. He went out of his way to find her alone so he could maliciously taunt her. Not that their father would have ever stopped him if he'd known.

There were so many times. Wrapping her arms around herself in a meager attempt to ward off the horrific memories, she leaned, her forehead against the cold windowpane. Even after the incident with the men's association, in her romantic heart, she still searched for love. Vividly, she recalled the time Camdyn gave her to his friend. He'd told her how much the boy liked her, that all he wanted from her was a kiss. Eagerly, so pleased that a boy liked her, she ran to the stable where he waited for her in an empty stall. Honey knew the moment she saw his eyes shimmering with lust along with the way he grabbed her pulling her to him, he expected more than a kiss. Without warning he stripped her...

Tears slid down her cheeks. Because of the memory a wrenching sob of despair wracked her body. She should not have gone to the funeral. Even if her brother didn't approach her, the sullied memories would have erupted. She despised men and what they could do to a woman. Until Billy, she thought she hated all men as well as what they were capable of doing to a woman.

Billy was different.

Still...the horrible memories haunted her. Even though she understood in the darkest deepest recesses of her brain that Billy would never handle her the way she'd been treated, she didn't believe in a man's presence she would ever be able to relax enough to even allow a kiss. Billy wanted more than a kiss. She wanted more too. Nonetheless, she stopped him every time.

When she told him her feelings, he said she'd thrown down the gauntlet. Told her he had a lot to prove to her. In the telling of that brief story, she challenged him to change her mind. That day had been more than a year ago. He didn't mean what he told her. There had been no letter from him. Nothing to give her hope that perhaps he might want to change her mind.

The ladies could write all the letters they wanted. The messages would be for naught. Billy would never appreciate a visit from her. His life must be running smoothly, without interference from a woman who could never be a woman in a man's arms. He would have other lovers. He wasn't a man who would remain celibate as he thought about another female.

The unhappy fact in all this was that she wished she could go back to those days before she was misused. The days when her dreams revolved around falling in love with a man who would not care about her parentage would never despise her because she was a bastard.

Long ago she resigned herself to the fact that couldn't happen. Her half brother molded her into the woman she was today. Nothing for her would ever vary. She had to admit to herself a change of scenery might be welcome. If nothing else, just to terrorize her, Camdyn would show up at the escort service. Tristan would throw him out, would refuse him entry if he saw him before he strode arrogantly through the impressive double doors on the front porch. Despite his wealth and power, he could not pass the interview given at this place of business to be allowed to pay for an escort. She wasn't an escort. She was the maid.

The quiet tapping on the door surprised her. She figured it must be Torra with the letter to Billy. "Come in."

Torra handed the paper to her while she seemed to be holding her breath. "Thought you might want to read this before we sent it. You should know what we told him."

Honey sat on the chair near the fire, the letter, held in her shaking hands. She read every word. It was just as Torra told her. She mentioned Camdyn along with her fear then asked if he had a safe place where he could keep her from harm. Torra also mentioned her thoughts about the helping with his paperwork. Billy would be overwhelmed by all the details he would have to see to.

"It's everything you said it would be. It's the truth. Billy does have a protective nature where you are concerned." Honey recalled his story about little Piper. He and Bobby protected her with their lives. He would do the same for her. She wasn't certain that she wished for him to put his life on the line for her. Reminding herself she had no reason to believe that might come to pass, she tugged in a breath of air understanding she would go to him if he asked.

"No lies, he should understand your dire circumstance. Don't you think? We both understand he cares for you."

"Cared for me," Honey reminded her friend softly. Yes, once he cared for her. How would he feel now?

~ * ~

Lord William Alexander Cameron Manchester the new Duke of St. Aubries' thoughts were not pleasant at the moment. Where his mind traveled had little to nothing to do with Honey. Because of his title, no other reason, he'd been invited to the Richleigh's ball. Colorful silks and satins twirled by him in a dazzling display of color. A high-pitched giggle caught his attention. He turned to see Lord St. John dance by with Fannie Lipscomb, his dark head bent close to the lady's ear. Billy wondered what outrageous bit of gossip St. John offered or if he seduced her even then. Perhaps there was more to the small flirtation than met the eye.

Negligently, he leaned against a pillar. The balcony outside the ballroom was empty at the moment beckoning him. With a quick look around the room, he escaped to enjoy the chilled night air. None of this year's debutantes caught his eye. When he danced, he always thought of Honey. One time in the upstairs ballroom at Miss Scarlett's home he danced with her. The feeling of her small body pressed against the hard chiseled planes of his hard masculine form infiltrated his head. None of these women would ever do for him. Still, mothers dragging along their daughters for his perusal reminded him constantly, he needed to wed, needed to provide an heir for the dukedom. Unable to stop himself, once again his mind drifted to Honey. When she smiled, her delicate features lit up creating a warm glow around her.

Inclining against the railing on the balcony, his hands clenched tight, his mind wandered to Honey. Her tawny golden curls danced provocatively around her small head. The amber eyes that always seemed to light up when she looked at him reminded him of warm brown honey. She had a pert little nose, the tip of which he yearned to kiss. Ah, there were other parts of her demanding his kisses.

Drawing in a long deep shuddering breath of air, he reminded himself she was afraid of him. That one time he danced with her, felt her slender body so close to his, he felt her shaking. He could never be a part of her fears. When he finally understood she would never give herself willingly to him, he left. Reneging on his promise to write, he spent each day wondering how he could convince her to come to him. One stupid idea after another mucked around in his pathetic brain. After reviewing his deliberations, he understood how faulty they were. She was terrified of men. He didn't have one clue how to change that fact.

"There you are, darling," Della Brown sidled next to him. Her hands around his arm, she leaned into his body, her soft luscious breast pushing against him. Flirting outrageously, she went on to say, "Wondered where you were. Thought you left without dancing with me. Knew you wouldn't do that."

"Needed fresh air," Billy said softly staring out into the darkness of the night. "You know how much I dislike these affairs. Promised though, had to attend at least for a short time."

Della tapped him on the chin, her smile bright. "As do I dislike the crush. We could leave, you and I. No one would be any wiser. Well, the doting mamas who are after you for their daughters would definitely miss you." Slowly, she lowered her lashes, an invitation somewhere in the gesture.

"True, nonetheless I promised Lady Richleigh that I'd dance with her daughter. She's an eye for a title. Nonetheless, she won't become my duchess. The chit is way too young. I'm not about to wed a little girl."

"Ah, you do not care for the simpering little darling. Do believe she just turned seventeen. That isn't old enough for you? No, I suppose you appreciate a woman's charms."

"You're right. I much prefer a woman grown to a girl just out of the classroom."

Della purred softly in the back of her delicate white throat, her tender blue eyes shimmering with raw passion. Billy understood her hunger for sex. The tops of her breasts were framed in black lace. The sight gave Billy reason to smile. Tonight, he would taste her beautiful jewels, explore all the soft curves she possessed. Della was a good lover, as she knew how to please a man. She also understood that sex was all they would share.

Five years ago when she was all but seventeen, she married an old man. Lord Brown was an earl, an incredibly wealthy earl. When he died, Della was left with enough wealth to outlive her. There were no heirs, not unless she sired a child. Della didn't want children, said she couldn't abide them. What would happen to the wealth after that? Billy didn't know nor did he care. Della's wealth was no concern of his.

"How long before you can leave?" she purred eagerly, softly pushing against his body understanding her seduction sent heat straight to his groin.

"Another hour," he told her as he turned pulling her into his arms. Slowly his lips found hers. She opened for him, her tongue sliding into his mouth playing and exploring the inner recesses. He knew she felt his heavy arousal as his large hands closed around her buttocks to pull her against him. She tasted of the sweet wine that was served. Before he stepped into the ballroom, he would have to get his unruly body under some semblance of control. He pushed her away, chuckling at her look of chagrin.

"So soon?" She sighed softly touching his moist lips with one of her fingertips. "Please hurry."

"I'll meet you at the small cottage behind your home in another hour."

"I'll be there."

"What do you have planned this time?" He was never certain what role she wanted him to play. One time she wanted him to be a pirate with a patch over one eye. He was to take her as if she was his plunder from the high seas. Another time, she wanted him to pretend he was a mincing dandy and the control was all hers.

"You'll have to wait to find out. Now, won't you?" She winked tapping him on his shoulder with her fan. "I'll never tell, at least not before you get there. I do believe you'll be surprised. What I've planned is different even for me."

At first the role-playing had been fun. Now, since the newness was wearing off, he grew weary of the pretentious games she initiated. Each time they were together in some physical presentation, he decided that was the last time. Whenever she propositioned him, he didn't deny her the fantasies contrived from her avid imagination. So far there had not been a single role he played he actually enjoyed. He was a tender lover. Inflicting any type of discomfort on a woman went against the grain making his stomach sour with distaste.

Della rose to kiss him quickly on his cheek. "Don't be late."

Maybe that was a clue. She wanted him to be late so she could scold him. Della appreciated arguments. Billy didn't like dissension of any kind, especially not with his women. The way he saw lovemaking was warm as well as extremely willing. He didn't appreciate carnal delights any other way. As she flounced from the room, he did appreciate the gentle swaying of her hips, caught the view of a slender ankle every now and then. A dance with Della might have been nice. Ah, but she had a way of making everything sexual. Billy was known for his zealous lovemaking among the widows in the area. Even he needed to come up for air every now and then.

Lady's Richleigh's daughter, what was her name? Searching his mind for the answer, he stepped onto the floor, his hands behind his back once again surveying the room looking for the girl. Snapping his fingers, as he realized what his problem entailed. He was never very good with names. Noticing Lady Richleigh, her daughter standing beside her, determined to get this dance over with, he strode toward the woman.

The young woman standing beside her mother couldn't have even been seventeen. Her hands clutched tightly together, eyes wide with apprehension, Billy felt certain he heard her knees knocking together.

Good God, what was her mother thinking? She looked as if she were only thirteen or fourteen. Even dressed in silks and satins, her hair wound becomingly on top of her head, he understood she was far too young for the likes of his jaded self. This young woman needed a man who was just as innocent as she was. Pushing thoughts of turning tail in the process avoiding the inevitable, he stepped forward.

"Colleen," He picked up her hand, bending gallantly to place a gentle kiss on the top. Her skin was smooth and soft. He sent her way his most charming smile; at least he hoped the grin would charm some of the terror from those daze-struck eyes. "Would you like to dance?"

"Y-yes." Her small face flushed with the first rush of embarrassment as she looked at him, her eyes huge dark pools of brown. The girl wasn't smiling back at him as he hoped. Instead, she appeared terrified, ready to head in the opposite direction. If her mother didn't stand behind her, Billy felt certain that was what she would do.

Keeping his distance from her slender body, he twirled her onto the dance floor. She didn't look at him as she kept her face straight ahead, focused, he believed on his chest. He wanted to ask her how old she was. Even though she appeared extremely young, he understood she would have to be at least seventeen. It was generally believed a young lady should never be presented to society until they at least came to that tender age. Billy knew he'd never been that young, never filled with innocence didn't think he'd ever been seventeen. His entire life he understood at some time he'd be caught either sent to Newgate to hang or be deported to some penal colony down under.

"Has your dance card been full?" he asked softly innately understanding she was having difficulty speaking. He had no idea what to ask of her. Do you still play with dolls came to mind, as he tossed that absurd notion aside in search of something more appropriate.

She nodded, her gaze still glued to his chest. "It-it's only because of my mother. M-mother made sure I would not want for attention." Her voice shook with the effort to utter those few words.

With that tiny attempt at conversation, Billy decided the fewer words the better. Her stuttering gave him the distinct impression he'd just become a defiler of an innocent. He'd never done so before. So, he didn't intend to start now. For the duration of the music they silently danced.

When the strains of the waltz ended he brought her back to her mother. Thank God he'd done his duty.

Swiftly, he said his good bye to the daughter as well as his host and hostess. Stepping briskly from the doors of the Richleigh home, he breathed in the scent of the daphnia growing by the door. Quick strides brought him to the stable. Strangely, he didn't feel at all eager to see Della. For some reason his thoughts revolved around an amber-eyed temptress who was afraid of him. Well, not just him, she was afraid of all men. Silently, her cursed Camdyn, her half brother, for causing that.

In his phaeton he drove the two matched grays at a spanking pace thinking of the next few hours that Della would spend in his arms. This rendezvous was giving him second along with third thoughts. Della did ease his needs. Other than needing him as an ardent lover, she didn't demand anything of him nor did she expect to become his duchess. He would play whatever role she contrived then he would go home never staying the night. Waking up in a strange bed brought nightmares to his head, reminding him to often of the bitter cruel days he spent in St. Giles Parish.

The crisp cool evening air exhilarated him. His spirits lightened as he made his way down the long curvy road to the cottage. Part of the highlands he loved the most was looking into a velvet black sky to see the stars twinkling as if they were diamonds. All one saw in London was darkness or gray skies during the day. Because of all the smoke there were very few nights a man could see a star. Here the air was fresh, smelling clean when a person inhaled deeply. At times scents of flowers filled the air, along with green grass, heather and pine. For his pleasure he inhaled deeply of all the wonderful aromas he was coming to adore.

A few minutes later, promptly ten minutes late to this meeting with Della, he pulled the phaeton to a stop. Inhaling a long deep breath he gazed at the little cottage while he wondered what the woman had in mind for the evening. A shudder passed through his body. One light shone from the study. Well, that must be where the games would begin. He tied the reins of his horses to the hitching post. Swiping a hand through his hair, he strode up the steps of the front porch.

Slowly opening the door, he peered into a darkened room. The place was not entirely black. One candle burned on a table. The soft scent of jasmine sifted through the air. He stepped toward the study his body strangely tense knowing she would hear his booted steps. He didn't make any attempt to be quiet.

"Come in, I've been waiting for you. You're late, naughty boy." Della's voice sounded small and tight. He heard her giggle. The sound was more like a schoolgirl than a grown mature woman.

What the devil? He stood framed in the doorway, a deep frown forming across his forehead, his nostrils flaring. This was the worst-case scenario. To the tips of his toes, he was disgusted. He would have never imagined she would present herself this way. For a moment he considered bolting.

His breath caught in the back of his throat for several tight seconds while he perused her small form. The sound of his heart hammering in his chest singed his ears. The sight in front of him curdled his innards. Della was dressed as if she was only fifteen. The bodice of the apple green muslin gown ended at her neck. She'd done something to her lush full breasts so they appeared to be nonexistent. No paint enhanced her lovely face. Her long blond hair was braided into two plaits that hung on either side of her head. While she sat on the huge cherry wood desk, flirtatiously she ran her tiny pink tongue along her bottom lip before catching the plump lip between her teeth. After she looked at him, she blinked several times before she invitingly spread her legs.

Deep in the back of his throat he groaned. She did this to point out the fact Lady Richleigh's daughter was no more than a schoolgirl. Single handedly she made it her mission to create beyond a doubt the fact exactly how woefully unsuitable the little girl was for him. Good god, he didn't need her help. When he wed, which he would have to do someday, his wife would never be a debutante.

"What are you doing, Della?" His voice harsh, he strode into the room, ready to tell her he wasn't interested in this ridiculous game. If she didn't justify this in some way, he meant to turn around.

As if she anticipated his revulsion, the bodice of the gown suddenly gave way her now opulent unbound breasts spilling free for his perusal. This was a ploy to keep him interested. His heart slammed against his ribs. The large jewels tipped with tender pink buds sent blood racing to his groin. Clenching his teeth, he held his sexual thoughts in check. The need to taste centered in his brain. All thought of fleeing left his head.

Leaning back on her hands, she moved back and forth, her breasts swinging enticingly to greet his avid gaze. She understood exactly what would get his attention. Yes, Della knew exactly how to seduce a man, how to coax and sweet talk until there was only one thought in a masculine brain. "Papa won't be home for another two hours maybe longer. We can do whatever takes your fancy," she purred as she touched her kissable top lip with her tender pink tongue. As she sat up, her breasts once more caught his attention, the bulge beneath his pants growing harder as he watched mesmerized by her audacity. Della had no shame when it came to her sexuality. She would do as well as risk anything to have her way with any man foolish enough to fall in with her plans.

"Papa? You're not actually going to pretend you're a little girl? You want me to rape a young lady. I can't do that, Della. Not even for you. You will have to change this game you are dancing around me with if you want your pleasure."

She huffed a bit coming out of her role. "You know who I am...now," she spread her legs wider this time, her skirts riding provocatively to her knees then higher. "Just pretend that you don't know I'm not a little girl." She shifted again, her lashes lowering demurely on her shimmering eyes. "I want you, Billy. I've never had a lover. You'll be my first. Take me slow and easy. I'm not a little girl. Nonetheless, I'm a virgin."

Especially a woman such as Della couldn't ignore the bulge behind his breeches. No, she wasn't a little girl. Just as he'd never been a little boy, he doubted if Della had ever been innocent. For an instant much to his chagrin, he wondered at what age she lost her virginity. Unlike this woman, despite the proclivities inflicted on her, Honey was innocent still.

"Della, stop the play acting. When you do so, I'll be more than pleased to see to your woman's pleasure." As he stepped forward, his cravat landed on the floor. He bent over to place a tender kiss on her lush ripe mouth. "I don't like this. It's sordid." His hand cupped one of her large breasts, his thumb brushing tenderly across the hardened tip. Heat flared as her tongue pushed into his mouth.

Pulling his shirttails from his breeches, she ran her hands along his back to his shoulders. A moment later her fingertips sashayed across his nipples. After a harsh gasp of air, he groaned. Her nails scraped down his chest to his waistband to return to the tiny hard buds on his chest. She spread her fingers. Like a wild thing Della twisted beneath his probing caresses. As always if they continued in this manner they would reach the pinnacle all too soon. Billy wanted this to move at a snail's pace not a wildfire. He moved back, his fingers slipping beneath the fabric of her gown, slowly lowering the material to her waist. He needed to savor her ripe woman's body.

"Lift your hips, sweetheart."

She did. Her dress fell in a puddle on the floor of the study. Standing between her spread legs, Billy took his time now, delighting in the silken warmth of Della's skin beneath the palms of his hands. She was lovely yet Billy didn't like the direction of his thoughts, which suddenly centered on Honey. The devil, he needed to get that woman from his mind. She bewitched him all too easily. Honey would never be his.

Della's fingers found their way to his breeches. Billy stepped back for a few seconds struggling with his boots. Stripping the rest of his clothing from his body, he returned to her. Eagerly, she welcomed him between her thighs. He held her hips with his hands. Della's hips began to move in a dance as old as Eve. Almost frantic she pushed up against Billy's hand, her body trembling. Billy smiled knowing she was just about where he wanted her. The next time the dance between them would be slower.

Still, Billy deliberately held back, fighting the screaming demands of his body to take her, to lose himself in the hot, satiny sheathe he knew waited for him. The waiting was an exquisite torture for him, his manhood ripe and swollen with desire. Wanting more he denied them both the immediate pleasure their joining would bring until neither could wait a moment longer. His fingers wound through her braids, unwinding them at a leisurely pace. After he finished, he spread the strands out so they covered the desk.

He watched her eyes shimmering, slightly dazed, her lips wet and parted begging his attention. When he touched her intimately she dripped with her honey. Softly in the back of her throat, she moaned her ecstasy. His hands on her hips forcefully he drove into her silken softness. Her delightful scream sent a wave of power through him. Compulsively, his mouth caught hers, his tongue filling her mouth just as he filled her. She arched to meet the thrust of his body as he plunged deeper into her fiery heat. As her screams of pleasure filled his sense, he released himself inside her.

Thoroughly sated he pulled away. When he looked at her, he admired the way he arranged her loosened hair from the childish braids then spread the long strands enticingly around her ample form. Sitting on the desk, her legs still spread wide, she did present a wanton picture.

"Don't ever do that again," Billy told her as he pulled on his pants then his boots. "Don't ever pretend to be a little girl. If you do, you will never see me again."

"You're leaving?" she asked as she postured in front of him, her breast thrusting forward.

"I've a busy day tomorrow. You'll have to be content tonight with just one time." There were other words Billy thought to use for this joining. In another place and time he would never hesitate to tell her how he felt about this vulgarity. Honey had been little more than fifteen when her brother violated her. This evening's events didn't sit well with him.

Della pouted prettily as she scooted naked from the desk. "It was only a fantasy." As if regretting her game, she found her dress, pulling it over her head. "You should not be so sour. That little chit, Colleen, she's too young for you. I only want to make certain you understood."

"You didn't have to point out something I know. At the moment, I've no intention of courting anyone, especially a little girl straight from the classroom." He was too world-weary for something so vulgar. After tugging on his shirt, he grinned wickedly. "She was terrified of me. I'm a jaded man, yet I didn't appreciate her fear. What mother would wish her daughter thrust into the hands of a man such as myself? No secrets have been kept. Everyone knows where I came from."

Lifting her shoulders, a coquettish smile on her ripe swollen lips, "Who wouldn't be terrified? At the ball, you were scowling darkly at everyone who glanced your way. You weren't thinking about your lost love, Honey, were you?" She placed a delicate finger against her soft pink lips, "Of course, you were. How exceedingly drole."

"What if I was?" Billy cursed the afternoon he confided in Della about Honey. He'd been foxed on brandy, feeling sorry for himself as well as lonely when she flounced into his home looking for someone to ride with her. Later, he discovered he told her far more than she had business knowing. Except for the rare times she spoke to him, his secret stayed behind her lips.

"No reason." She leaned forward scooting from the desk. "You can't wallow in despair over a woman you say you cannot have. Nonetheless, Billy, you could charm a nun into having carnal pleasures. I hate to see you depressed. Get on with your life."

He ran a hand through his hair leaving a disheveled mess behind, one lock falling rakishly over his eye, not wishing to give more of his feelings a way to this woman. The strange thing about Della was that he felt certain he could trust her. Della didn't care about anyone except herself. Nevertheless, she was loyal to him. Neither wished to marry. They understood each other. At least he hoped they did.

"It makes no difference. She is not here and less likely to ever come for a visit. You know of course, I should have never told you about her along with the horrible events that created her life. She fears men including me. If I could find a means, I would change that."

"You could tenderly coax."

"I would always feel as if I forced her. If I ever make love to Honey, it will happen because she came to me. She won't approach me of that I'm certain."

"Don't understand why you've given up so easily. That's not like a man who survived St. Giles. After all the atrocities you've lived through, one would be led to believe you possessed more courage."

No, he supposed it wasn't like him to give up. Where honey's life was concerned, courage eluded him. He just didn't want to force her or coax her into doing something he felt certain she would most likely feel distress. Although a bit of tender sweet-talking might erase some of her fears, she would still say no. "I've thought on all that, nipped every notion in the bud before I could talk myself into doing something I'm certain I would come to regret."

"When will I see you again?" she asked as she walked to the door seemingly ready to leave, her hand on the handle.

"I'll send you a message." What he was actually thinking was not anytime soon. Some of the words she spoke to him tonight about Honey had him thinking of all the sweet possibilities if he could manage what she suggested. Honey only knew degradation along with pain from a man. Perhaps it was possible for him to teach her pleasure from his hands. Maybe coaxing wasn't the same as forcing. Sweet-talking might be the way to show her how he felt about her. Show her he would never harm her. As long as he stopped if she asked. The devil, he didn't understand. He'd never had to charm a woman to come willingly into his arms.

During the trip home, Billy thought more about Della's words. Perhaps a trip to Glasgow would be in order. He would have to put all his business affairs in order before he could leave to reacquaint himself with the tawny haired lady with shocking gold-flecked amber eyes. He grimaced. That feat might take him weeks. What he needed was a competent man who he could trust to shuffle the papers confounding him.

When he walked into his study, he found he was wide-awake. Pouring himself a large drink of brandy he sat down to meticulously go over some of the papers that had piled up on his desk over the long week. The devil, it seemed it had taken him forever to learn to read. When he stared at all the tiny little print, he would inevitably end up with a headache. Massaging his temples he ordered the beginnings of one to leave.

A perfume scented letter sat on top of one of the piles catching his immediate attention. Ah, Jacob, his butler must have thought to put this on top of the stack. For a few seconds, he tapped the envelope on his desk afraid to open the dispatch. Seeing the address was Scarlett's place in Glasgow, he quickly opened the missive hoping maybe Honey was writing to him.

After he read the words written not so innocently on the paper, anger caused him to grit his teeth tightly. Several times he swore while he furiously drummed his fingers on the hard wood of his desk. He had to remain calm. Overreacting would do Honey only harm.

Rapidly, he penned a quick letter, sealed the envelope then set the message aside for his butler to take care of first thing in the morning.

~ * ~

Camdyn sat on the edge of his desk, idly swinging one leg a glass of whiskey in his hand. As he gazed from one man to the next, he felt a moment of pleasure. These friends of his were loyal. He could count on them for anything. His mouth lifted in a half smile of appreciation. Everything in his life had gone his way. Now he was the seventh Earl of St. Rose. Power, wealth, all that went with the title was his. He meant to capitalize in every way possible.

Tipping back the glass of whiskey, allowing the slow glide of heat to slither down his throat then eventually pool in his belly, he thought of Honey, his dear, sweet half-sister. He would have her in his power again. She would be ensconced in the country estate of the Rose and Saber Men's Association before the end of the week.

"What has you grinning shamelessly? Something wicked I hope," Julian Newell asked as he too drank the whiskey. Julian was a tall man, broad of shoulder, lean of hip. Of all his friends Julian was by far the cruelest. His silver-gray eyes gave none of his wickedness away. Women flocked to him, just as they did his other associates. It had been Julian's idea to form the Rose and Saber Association while he carried out the intricate as well as minute details that made the association overpowering. They were a force to be reckoned with.

"My bastard sister," Camdyn murmured a soft expectant purr hummed in the back of his throat understanding he missed her in his bed. She was such a hellish fighter. What Honey didn't understand was that she was his. No longer would he allow the separation from him. He walked to the window overlooking the rose garden. The path leading to the lake and the small gazebo caught his attention, fondly recalling the time he took her in the gazebo. That was just after the forming of the house along with the creation of his stable of women, some of them young girls.

"The one that got away?" Rufus Stanford asked sneering a half mocking smile on his handsome face. Rufus was smaller than the other men although his face was handsomely chiseled. He was still a fine figure of a man. His green eyes seemed to lure women to him. "The only one that escaped you? You scheming to get her back?"

Once again fury rose quickly in Camdyn. The fact Honey got away from him never ceased to be a sore spot for him. Having his friends remind him of that fact didn't sit well. Redeeming himself in their eyes was foremost on his mind. Man or woman, no one else had ever bested him. Behind his back his hands fisted as he whirled to meet his jeering friend.

"I will get her back. Don't any of you ever doubt that fact. She will be in the stable by the end of the week, sooner if at all possible," Camdyn grit out behind clenched teeth.

"Shouldn't be too difficult. I've heard she is whoring for Miss Scarlett. I could use an escort to the theatre. Once in my keeping for the evening, I will joyously hand her over to you," George Wren offered succinctly. He too seemed to be unable to hold his smirk behind his teeth. George was not as handsome as the other two fellows. Though he possessed a brilliant mind. His amber colored eyes didn't miss anything nor did it seem he forgot anything.

"I'll never gain entrance," Camdyn murmured softly as he thought of his friends. Any of them might be able to gain entry to the escort service. Ah, escort service, simply a fancy way of describing a bordello. He didn't like the fact other men were able to buy Honey's favors. Back to his friends, their pedigrees were impeccable as was his. Nonetheless, the women knew who he was. Most likely they heard Honey's version of what happened to her.

"Why ever not?" Nathan Ridgeway asked while he lit a slim black cheroot the soft blue smoke curling upward. Nathan was tall, nearly a stick figure in form. His lips were thin, his eyes narrow as he surveyed the room along with the people he called his friends.

Camdyn sifted in a long breath of air while he decided what he should tell his friends. Of course, his friends knew about the games he enjoyed playing with women. After all, they were part of those sporting diversions all of them willing participants. All of them took Honey that day when he appropriated her virginity. His mocking smile grew. Five men spewed their seed inside her that first day which signaled the beginning of an era.

Clearing his throat, he began in a soft voice, "Saw Honey at the funeral last week. Seems she has a bodyguard." A large man, Camdyn remembered. While he was tall, just over six feet, the bodyguard seemed to tower over him. "I would have to acquire Honey by trickery. I doubt if

I'd ever be allowed in the massive front doors of Miss Scarlett's establishment."

"That bad?" Julian slanted him a mocking smile while he chortled. "You will find a means to circumvent that particular problem. Seems minor to me."

"Yes, with the four of you on my side, I foresee no problems," Camdyn bit out as he thought about Honey's pert little breasts her lush full lips. She was a woman grown now. He wondered if she would taste the same as she did when she was fifteen. He could tell at the cemetery she was no longer a child. Her slender body formed now into delicious curves. He wanted her.

"Hear they interview the men requesting escorts," Rufus offered blandly. "Do you think any of us blokes would pass the test? I for one don't enjoy answering questions about myself. Nonetheless, I'm a damn good liar."

"No one except the five of us know anything about our little peccadillos in the country," George chuckled softly, his gaze wandering absently around the room. "Wouldn't mind having your little bastard sister in my arms again. She always was a feisty little piece of baggage. Enjoyed all that wiggling and squirming. Set me on fire, she did."

"This is all well and good, the remembering along with the joking. Who's going to go to the escort service?" Camdyn asked, impatient to get on with this. Since the funeral he'd been in a state of semi-arousal. Every time he pictured her his blood rushed straight to his groin bypassing every other organ. This second time around would be more pleasant than the first. While little girls proved enjoyable, a full-bodied woman held more fascination. Thoughts of running his fingers through that thick tawny mane of hers sent his body into a tailspin of delightfully carnal thoughts. Even more the possession of her, the scent of her womanly charms, filled his body with need.

"I'll be pleased to offer my services," Julian spoke up. "I've impeccable credentials as you all know."

"I've a different thought." Camdyn placed his hands in a steeple beneath his chin. "Since Honey knows all of us, do any of you believe that we will be able to escort her anywhere? She will have all of you tossed out the door before you are barely inside if you make it that far."

"What do you plan?" Rufus' gaze met his questioning. "What else is there? Since she has seen you, she will be wise to us, especially to you."

"Think..." he paused thoughtfully tapping his jaw as his gaze centered on each of his friends. "We should plant a girl in the little bordello. She will befriend and cozy up to Honey. When we are prepared, she will bring her to us. I want to have a special room made up just for her new appearance. When she is installed, there will be no way for her to break out."

"This new girl..." George inquired solicitously.

"Will be the one she befriends," Camdyn said with a quiet chuckle remembering how she quickly did as he bade whenever the woman only she could protect by her obedience was threatened. "Honey has always been too softhearted. She won't want to see the woman hurt so she will come along with no complaint understanding full well what will happen to the gel if she doesn't cooperate."

"Do you forget the night she escaped she didn't give a fig about the woman who was to receive the punishment if Honey didn't behave. She escaped without a backward thought," Nathan deftly pointed out the fact. "So, why do you think she will cave now? Doesn't seem as if the strategy is well thought out."

"No," Camdyn let out a long slow breath of air. "No, I haven't forgotten a thing about that night. Mayhap we should use that very woman to draw Honey back into our welcoming arms." He thought that a fine idea. "Little Mary suffered some extreme abuse unless I've forgotten. Do believe at least for revenge, she will be more than willing to entice Honey from the safety of Miss Scarlett's into our welcoming embrace. We can always offer a reward, something pleasant for Mary to enjoy when she succeeds."

"For a short time, you could allow Mary to be the woman presiding over Honey. There could be a wealth of tit for tat. Mary could be encouraged to disobey so that we have an excuse to do whatever we want with Honey, not that any of us need an excuse. The act might serve to remind Honey of what her misdeed would inspire if she were to attempt another escape," Julian pointed out with a satisfied sigh.

Several seconds passed while Camdyn considered Julian's suggestion. The plan seemed like a fine one to him. He didn't care if

Honey suffered pain or humiliation at his hands. He so enjoyed implementing the punishment those many years ago. Looking forward to enjoying his bastard sister once more, he downed the remains of his brandy.

~ * ~

More than a week passed before Torra received the message from Billy that gave her reason to smile. He agreed to see Honey while he laid out the facts that he would protect her from her half brother. He knew the entire sordid affair that Camdyn embroiled her in those long ago days. Understood what her brother did to her was the root of her issues with men. All she need do was to let him know when to expect her.

"Well, that's not possible," she told Honey after she gave her the chance to read the message. Torra gave herself time to think on the issue before bringing the information to Honey. "I'm putting you in Bobby's carriage first thing tomorrow morning. I do believe you are packed as well as eager to leave Glasgow behind you for an extended time. Mark my words, Camdyn will have some plot to get you back. Showing up at that funeral was the last thing you should have done."

"He will be surprised. While I don't want to wait, don't you think it's impolite for me to just arrive on Billy's doorstep? I...he is a duke now. He has obligations to fulfill."

"Not impolite but prudent. Billy will understand. Even with their upbringing and sordid past, both Bobby along with Billy are the gentlest men I've ever known," Muira chimed in with an all-knowing grin. "If you give him the chance, he will treat you right."

"What if he's busy or he isn't at home?" While Honey wasn't having second thoughts about this journey or the reason for the hasty departure, she was afraid Billy would believe she had a change of heart about their extremely tame relationship. While she would like to know what it felt like for a man to cherish her, she didn't believe she could ever willingly submit to a man's hungry passion.

"I'm certain he has a butler to take care of unexpected visitors. Your arrival won't be totally unexpected. If you weren't packed as well as eager to leave, I would send a message. Perhaps I will. By horse the message is certain to arrive at his estate before your carriage. I shall think on that."

"That's better. I wouldn't like to surprise him."

Miss May, a small woman with delicate features wrapped a tender arm around her shoulders hugging her close. Her smile broad, "This will turn out for the best. You will be safe from the earl. Billy will protect you."

"I hope so," she murmured, as she seemed to see the hint of amusement shining in Torra's eyes. "I would like to feel protected as well as loved. Except for the women in this house, I've never felt loved before."

"You will see that you will be welcomed by Billy. He will be eager to see you. If you give that man a chance, I'm certain he will love you if he doesn't now."

"Lord William Alexander Cameron Manchester, to be accurate," Miss May said, a twinkle in her expressive eyes. Miss May was always intent on matchmaking. Her mother was a renowned matchmaker in the little village of Selkirk Scotland.

"Now, you go on up to your bedroom. Rest is necessary. The trip will be long as well as tiring," Torra tenderly patted her on the shoulder. Without warning Honey turned pale as death itself. Torra wondered at that. When she saw the new girl walk into the home, that was when her face took on a deathly hue. Despite Torra's valiant attempt to get Honey to speak of it, she was met with icy silence.

Torra had an uneasy feeling about the new girl who appeared skittish as if she hid something about her past. While her story was sad, filled with the same type of abuse all of the girls here experienced in their short lives, there was something sinister in the way she held her body, the way her gaze focused with hatred shining in her eyes when she looked at Honey.

"What do you think is bothering Honey?" Muira asked, concern etched in her voice.

Torra set a finger on her chin watching a woman she'd come to care for a great deal walk dejectedly up the stairs. She looked as if she didn't have a prayer of surviving something. Torra felt certain that her brother caused the desolation Torra read in every line of Honey's slender body. "I don't know. Nevertheless, I mean to discover the truth."

"Seemed to happen when Tristan introduced Mary to us," Miss May said kindly. "Do you think she knows her? Could she be part of the past she came here to forget?"

"I'm certain of that fact. If Honey wasn't leaving first thing in the morning, I would have more concern for the girl's sudden appearance so soon after the funeral."

"You don't think her half brother has anything to do with the girl do you?" Muria asked.

"I'm not putting the thought aside. What we don't want is for Mary to learn where Honey is going. I will inform Tristan he is to set a man to following Mary whenever she leaves the safety of the home," Torra felt such deep seated fear the uneasiness growing the more she thought on the girl.

"There is no denying the bruises or the burn marks on her skin. She's been ill-treated. There is no doubt about that," Muira pointed out as she too stared up the steps toward Honey's room. "Didn't Honey tell us about the burning of the women's flesh when they didn't obey?"

"Some of you don't know Honey's story, at least not in its entirety. I do. If I think too much, damn, I'm certain she lived in the same filthy, despicable place where Honey was mistreated."

"A woman's presence here might be the only way the earl could infiltrate Miss Scarlett's home. Camdyn is after Honey. It's my guess, he's using Mary to fulfill his wishes. I'd bet on that fact," Miss May said, her voice soft yet determined. "Is Mary in her room?"

"Yes, at least I hope so. She's supposed to be enjoying a bath along with a late dinner. I'm going to speak with Honey first."

It seemed Torra's worst fears came true. With Tristan's help along with the carriage driver that Bobby sent, with no one the wiser, they ferreted Honey from the home shortly after midnight.

Other Books by Christine Young
Available at Rogue Phoenix Press

Connal's Eternal Love
Sweet McKenna Book One

A few days shy of All Hallows' Eve Connal McKenna, Laird of Clan Chattan stands on the parapets of his castle. Bonfires line the hillsides while his clan prepares for the upcoming festivities. Drawn by the whispering of the wind, Connal McKenna feels a strange restlessness in his soul. Setting out to discover the wickedness that is calling to him, he discovers his mate. With gentle words and sensuous kisses, the auburn-eyed highlander conquers his mate, the beautiful, defiant Wynnie Adair who he comes upon during an evening ride. She must ultimately put her trust in the only man who can save her from the ruthless plans of her father and succumb to his gentle coaxing.

In Brady's Arms
Sweet McKenna Book Two

Forced to run from the only home she knows, beautiful, headstrong Lillian Townsends seeks shelter in the wild highlands where the McKenna clan live. Trying to avoid a betrothal contract signed by her stepfather to an aging lord, she is desperate to find a means to sidestep the inevitable, including a marriage to the oldest son of the laird. Lilly is enamored of the young lord who pursues her with unrelenting determination flashing his devilishly handsome charms. She is hard pressed to resist.

Besotted from the first moment Brady McKenna sees Lilly, he is determined to find a means to coax her into his arms and bed. With only the promise of carnal pleasure as his mistress, Brady relentlessly pursues the woman who has unwittingly forged a place in his heart. She is like no other woman, proud, defiant and enchanting. Despite his father's advice to stay away from her, he cannot. He boldly seeks her out and makes her his own.

Nobody but Walker
Sweet McKenna Book Three

The Highland Lass...

She was brought up, adored and loved by a doting mother and father ardently protected by her brothers. She was everything sweet and innocent until she was faced with betrayal and an unexpected and out of wedlock pregnancy. When she gave her love to a man who couldn't return her passion and commitment, she was left devastated and furious. Faced with the loss of her child if she didn't comply to his demands, Crissie McKenna followed him to Belfast then on to his country home to discover he was already married.

...The Irishman

Stunned to find out his one and only encounter with the woman he wanted to love forever created a child, Walker Endicott, Earl of Briarwood, claimed his child as his only heir. Walker threatened all her previously held values even while he thrilled her senses. From the moment he first saw her to the second she ran after him begging him to make love to her, his captivating masculinity held her fascinated. In his arms she would know tempestuous passion, bitter despair, and a soaring joy that would humble them both before the power of love.

Roby's Moonlit Night
Sweet McKenna Book Four

Once she'd been a pampered child with high expectations for her future blessed with love. Then she became an innocent pawn in a terrible game of greed and power. Now, with a noose around her neck, Pippa was to hang before she had the chance to unveil the men who drove her from her home, before she had the chance to live.

Roby McKenna was a man blessed with endless charm and wit. While he searched for his eternal love across the Atlantic in a new land, he would have to come home to find her. His silver blue eyes could sparkle with amusement or harden to steel gray with displeasure. He had all the women a man could want or need. As he grew older, mistresses were not enough. A quirk of fate brought him to the gallows, a spark of destiny made him claim the condemned Pippa as his bride.

Made for Houston
Sweet McKenna Book Five

Leah Kennedy is as wary of people as she is strikingly beautiful. However, the shocking death of her father that forever changed her girlhood has left her terrified of the very love she desperately longs for. Only in the untamed splendor of the Scottish crags does she feel safe from the feelings she stirs in men and the cruel mockery of Selkirk's villagers.

Debonair, well-educated doctor Houston Stuart has turned his back on social privilege along with professional honors to set up a medical practice in the lowlands of Scotland. There, serving those who need him the most, he hopes to forget the bitter memories and disillusionment that disturb his days.

Coincidence brings the cultured doctor and this fey mountain girl together. Something as bizarre as destiny disrupts the obstacle of birth and breeding, stubborn pride and fear which has kept them apart...as each seeks to heal the other's wounds with a raw passion neither can deny and all the odds against them cannot defeat.

My Sweet Broc
Bad Boys Book One

He's a bad bad boy...

Broc Wallace is a fun-loving rake who never thought any

beautiful woman could melt his heart. He lives life in the present enjoying the camaraderie of his friends and the pleasures of his mistress. When Bliss races into his life, he is ill prepared to deal with her secrets or give up the tenor of his life. When the truth is revealed, he finds himself unable to forgive and forget the betrayal.

...but she's sweet for him

Bliss MacTavish knows she's playing with fire when she refuses to tell this bad boy her name. He tempts her with sweet whispers of seduction knowing her innocent nature will be unable to refuse all he yearns to give her. Deciding to follow her heart, she finds the repercussions more than she bargains for when she gives herself to this bad boy.

Crazy for Cam
Bad Boys Book Two

He's a bad bad boy...

Lord Cam MacEwen, Viscount of Rosehill, tries his best to be proper and court the lady of his dreams in the acceptable way. The feat proves impossible when the lady in question uses every means at her disposal to tempt him. He fights his jealousy for another man as well as the need to make her his own, finally giving in to her irresistible passion.

...but she's crazy for him.

Chelsea MacTavish wants the bad boy she fell in love with and kissed just before her eighteenth birthday. With feminine wiles and irresistible allure, the sensuous lady plans to best Cam at his game of hearts and make him forget his need to court her properly.

Falling for Flynt
Bad Boys Book Three

He's a bad, bad boy...

Fascinated by Hope's loss of memory yet haunted by her sultry beauty, Flynt is irresistibly drawn to the stoic miss—and into her troubles with the sultan who wants her for himself. When he discovers she is the sister of his best friend, his pride keeps him from pursuing her and making her his.

...but she's falling for him.

Raised in a harem but now penniless, alone and without her memory, Hope must discover a way to remember all that she has lost. She finds a way to continue with her life as a servant in Flynt's home. The first sight of Flynt steals Hope's breath as well as her heart. Can she overcome her fears and give herself to the man she fell in love with.

Dancing With Donal
Bad Boys Book Four

He's a bad bad boy...

Once a bad boy always a bad boy, Donal Chamberlin's carefree ways come crashing down around him when he meets the ravishingly beautiful Daryl MacTavish, the innocent little sister of one of his best friends. He is determined to win her heart as he sets his sights on marriage and an heir. His past gets in the way of his quest when a woman he once loved threatens Daryl's life.

...but she's dancing with him.

Daryl has seen the control her sister's husbands hold over them. She yearns for a life where she makes decisions for herself. No man will have power over her. But no man kisses her the way Donal does. No man can make her forget all her goals leaving her helpless to give up her dreams. Yet Donal is determined to dance through all the barriers she thrust in front of him, pursuing her until she says yes.

Loving Leslie
Bad Boys Book Five

He's a bad bad boy...

Leslie Stewart, Duke of Southcliff is stoic, set in his ways, a spy who is used to having his life well ordered. He expects life to continue on in this perfectly conventional fashion. He assumes his bad boy status while keeping mamas and debutantes at arm's length. An heir is needed but Leslie has every intention of finding a woman who doesn't covet his wealth and tittle. He is irresistibly drawn to the headstrong young lady who becomes more beautiful as she develops into a woman.

...but she is loving him.

When Leslie kisses Lacie MacTavish, she knows even at the tender age of fifteen this is the man of her dreams. Forced to wait until she comes of age, Lacie withdraws into herself. Now she is eighteen and Leslie has returned from a mission for the British Government ready to claim her as his bride. She refuses him and he must find a way to seduce her and in the process create a burning passion within her, which she cannot deny.

Pleasing Arie
Bad Boys Book Six

He's a bad bad boy...

Arie Demir has never been denied anything in his life. He takes what he wants. What he undeniably yearns for is the beautiful redheaded spitfire he sees in a restaurant in Glasgow. At every turn, she confuses him by disputing his power over her. Alison refuses to accept the fact he owns her. While Arie tries desperately with patience and tenderness to drive her wild with new sensations, his scorching kisses ignite the fires of her very soul to make her understand he is all she will ever want.

...but is she pleasing him?

Alison Fletcher never expected to find herself kidnapped and sold to a whorehouse then bought by a Turkish sultan to become his slave. She vows to never surrender to the arrogant man who believes he owns her. She is stunned by the magnificently handsome man who awaits her compliance. Unexpectedly, she finds Arie the lesser of all the evils. The hidden depths of his mesmerizing dark brown eyes hold her into their power; his muscular embrace makes her weak with desire. She is his to do with as he wishes.

Graham's Wicked Kiss
Bad Boys Book Seven

He's a bad bad boy...

Graham Chamberlin is stunned to find three young boys dangling from the trees lining the drive to Runningmead Manner. On further inspection, he is astonished at their obsession to protect a young woman who has been brutalized by her pimp. The woman he discovers hiding in a third-floor attic room is gravely injured. He takes the silver haired stowaway under his wing. Clearly, Graham's new guest is a lady with many secrets. He is determined to unlock all the mysteries surrounding her.

...But she can't resist his wicked kiss.

The years since Ria left the convent where she was raised have been a nightmare. Her secrets are dangerous—as is the powerful man determined to find her. Handsome Graham Chamberlin is clearly a gentleman with secrets of his own, but staying with him could mean the difference between life and death for Ria. With each passing day, her handsome host turns Ria's convalescence into an increasingly sensual escape. Now her greatest challenge may be imagining anything less than a future in his arms.

Feeling Etienne's Love
Bad Boys Book Eight

He's a bad bad boy...

Etienne Dubois is the son of a wealthy vineyard owner who craves the excitement of putting his life on the line. Working with the French government and as a confidant of King Charles X give him reasons for living. An encounter with a beautiful young woman in a plush bordello in Paris has him rethinking his roguish ways. Etienne never expects to become a father especially from one encounter with an innocent prostitute who whispers his name and has him rethinking his well-ordered life.

...But she can't help feeling his love.

Elisa Moreau, the only daughter of Angelique Moreau, the owner of an exclusive bordello in Bordeaux, France, has loved Etienne Dubois since she was six. Unfortunately, until an unexpected encounter at a brothel in Paris puts the two of them in the same room, Etienne doesn't even know she exists. Confused but wanting Etienne and this chance meeting to never end, Elisa gives herself to the man who has held her heart in hands for what seems like her entire life.

All I Want Is Link
Bad Boys Book Nine

He's a bad bad boy...

Merry Stewart is wildly unpredictable. Left alone to run wild over the Bordeaux and Scottish countryside she becomes impetuous and daringly bold. Over the years, she's found she can bedevil her softhearted brothers into allowing her exploits to go unnoticed. As a young woman she has learned she can do as she pleases when she pleases. Now, Merry has set her amorous sights on the Duke of Weston—a man she has never met but has every intention of marrying. No other suitor will satisfy her— especially not the exceptionally striking, horse breeder, Devlin Mathews.

...she's the woman of his desires.

Posing as commoner Devlin Mathews to escape a potentially fatal confrontation, Devlin is enthralled and infuriated by the audacious, duke-hunting dark haired vixen. Bedeviled at every opportunity, he finds dealing with the tiny she-devil exasperating as well as intriguing. Without revealing his true identify, the infamous rogue pledges to thwart Merry's plans to wed the man of her dream-never imagining the bewitching strategist would turn out to be the only woman he would ever dream of marrying.

Devlin's Angel
Bad Boys Book Ten

He's a bad bad boy...

Merry Stewart is wildly unpredictable. Left alone to run wild over the Bordeaux and Scottish countryside she becomes impetuous and daringly bold. Over the years, she's found she can bedevil her softhearted brothers into allowing her exploits to go unnoticed. As a young woman she has learned she can do as she pleases when she pleases. Now, Merry has set her amorous sights on the Duke of Weston—a man she has never met but has every intention of marrying. No other suitor will satisfy her—especially not the exceptionally striking, horse breeder, Devlin Mathews.

...she's the woman of his desires.

Posing as commoner Devlin Mathews to escape a potentially fatal confrontation, Devlin is enthralled and infuriated by the audacious, duke-hunting dark haired vixen. Bedeviled at every opportunity, he finds dealing with the tiny she-devil exasperating as well as intriguing. Without revealing his true identify, the infamous rogue pledges to thwart Merry's plans to wed the man of her dream-never imagining the bewitching strategist would turn out to be the only woman he would ever dream of marrying.

Foolish for Piper

The pickpocket...

Piper has spent her life surviving the streets of St. Giles Parish in London, a den of iniquity and crime. Masquerading as a boy she escapes the whorehouses the young girls are sent to as they come of age. The day she encounters Brett MacLachlan begins the same as every other one. When she picks his pocket, she has no idea her life is going to change irreversibly.

...and the mark

Handsome aristocrat Brett MacLachlan has come to London for his amusement only to find his world turned upside down by a thief and her dog. From the moment he spots her, Brett knows there is something intrinsically wrong. In his arms, Piper discovers passion and joy. Yet secrets of her past haunt her, and a scar will tell the true tale as well as her identity.

Taylor's Destiny

She traveled to another time and place to change destiny...

Enjoying a day of sailing, Taylor Maxwell never expected after a suffering a concussion she would wake up in another century. A resilient independent woman in the twenty-first century, the blond beauty is ill prepared for life in the 1800s. Her first sight of the naval captain who rescues her makes her heart stop, giving her hope for her future.

His life is transformed by a woman who appears from nowhere...

Born to a life of ease, Reid Stewart defies the dictates of those born to aristocracy and chooses a life of adventure in the navy and as a spy for the crown. When he discovers a nearly naked woman on the bow of small sailing ship, his heart warms. His love for Taylor and his need to protect her from a man who pursues her might cost him his life as well as hers.

Caitlin's Duke

She played a fiddle in an Irish pub...

Caitlin O'Shea Is the most beautiful woman Roc Leighton has ever seen. With her blue violet eyes and long black hair she captivates him. In turn he mesmerizes Caitlin. Caught in the power of his gaze as he watches her, she is wise enough to know he desires her but will never give his heart to her. Caitlin has vowed to never be any man's mistress.

And fell in love with an English Lord...

Roc knows the first time he watches her play the fiddle and dance around the pub, she will be his next mistress. Despite her protest, he will find a way to convince her that her place is with him. While Caitlin's determination to keep her vows, fate takes a cruel turn and she is forced to seek refuge with Roc.

Catching Meara
Book One in the McKenna Clan Series

Meara Thorton was a feisty, world-class computer hacker—cornered by the FBI and shockingly given the chance to be their newly acquired technical analyst. Brilliant and intuitive, yet aching with the loss of everyone she has cared about, her restless heart led her to discover a love she fought and a world she didn't know could possibly exist.

Sweet Sexy Sadie
Book Two in the McKenna Clan Series

From the first time Sadie's eyes met those of Brody McKenna in the hot Sierra Madre Mountains, theirs was a potent attraction—not gentle, slow, and easy, but hot, hard, and all-consuming. The daughter of a dysfunctional family, Sadie had dreams no man could wrench from her with hot sex and an all-consuming passion. She'd challenge this alpha male with all the strength she possessed. But her red hair, fiery temperament, and indomitable spirit obsessed Brody...and he knew he had to find a way to show her he was more than he appeared and convince her to make a life with him.

Sweet Misbehavin'
Book Three in the McKenna Clan Series

Cast adrift after fleeing the home of Jokul, the ice demon, Atantsi, a firestarter, grew to womanhood as she moved through time to keep the demon from finding her. Though stubborn and courageous, she was ill prepared to use powers she had not been taught. Her first sight of the intoxicating Carr McKenna left her breathless, and her second encounter gave her hope for a future she never thought she had.

A playboy, a second son and a shifter, a man who thought his life would be carefree, Carr McKenna was shocked to discover the woman he'd paid as an escort is a firestarter who is running for her life. He is the leader of all the McKennas around the world and that he has multiple powers. His passion for Margo and the need to defend her might cost him his life as well as hers.

Sweet Talkin' Sugar
Book Four in the McKenna Clan Series

Lyonesse McKenna, was dreaming, or was she? From the instant Lyn saw Deacon McClain across a black jack table in a crowed Las Vegas casino the unmistakable attraction sent Lyn's senses flying into overdrive. Her family of shapeshifters believed in soul mates. She'd always been skeptical yet she couldn't help but question the way her heart sped when he looked at her.

When Deacon appeared in Las Vegas he knew his first job was to save Lyn from a Sea Demon, but the next order of business was to convince her he would someday mean more to her than she'd ever expected. But her stubborn nature and unbendable spirit consumed Deacon...and he had to chase away all the demons real and imagined in order to win her heart.

Sweet Surrender
Book Five in the McKenna Clan Series

Ripped from her family at the top of Infinity Cliff, Kimi McKenna finds herself thrust somewhere into the future. Dark elements threaten to destroy the earth unless Kimi can work together with the white witch to stop the destruction. Confused by her mate's role in the conspiracy, she refuses to acknowledge the connection. But amidst raging fire and attacks on the people she is coming to hold dear, she allows Maska O'keefe into her heart.

Maska O'keefe has loved the beautiful shapeshifter for years. Unable to save her life years ago, he vows to watch over her as he is given a second chance to convince her that even though he is a witch and not a shifter, they are indeed soul mates. Kimi's divided loyalties between her family and the cause she is now a part of will determine their relationship. Only the part she plays as the messiah can bring this to a conclusion in the final battle.

Dakota's Bride
The first book in the Lakota/Pinkerton Series

When Emma St. John received her brother's letter imploring her to escape her stepfather's vengeful scheme and to trust Dakota Barringer with her life, she was willing to chance it. But the handsome, brooding riverboat owner Emma found in Natchez a danger of another kind. For Emma soon found herself surrendering to an unrelenting desire.

Raised by the Sioux when his parents were killed, Dakota had been betrayed once before by a white woman. He wasn't about to trust another, especially one claiming that her stepfather, a powerful U.S. senator, had framed her as a murderess. But he couldn't let Emma's intoxicating effect on him. Now Dakota would risk his very life to protect the innocent beauty who had seduced him with her tender love.

My Angel
The second book in the Lakota/Pinkerton Series

A BEAUTY IN BUCKSKINS

When her father decided to send her to a finishing school back East, Angela Chamberlain refused to be confined to stuffy drawing rooms. Instead, the daring spitfire who could shoot like a man and ride like the wind longed for a life of adventure and romance—and she knew exactly who could give it to her. Devil Blackmoor was a hired gun with a dangerous reputation. But Angela was willing to go to the ends of the earth to capture the handsome devil's heart.

A DEVIL IN DISGUISE

He'd come to America looking for excitement, but Devil Blackmoor got more than he bargained for when he encountered a beautiful rebel who answered his kisses with a wild innocence that touched his very soul. Yet standing between them were more obstacles than either ever dreamed. For Devil had strapped on a gun for the wrong man. And that made Angela his enemy. Now he'll have to choose between his duty and the woman he loves more than life.

The Locket
The third book in the Lakota/Pinkerton Series

The year is 1894. Seeking revenge for crimes against his family, Misha Petrovich follows a path that leads straight to Ariel Cameron's boarding house in Mist Harbor, Oregon. A family heirloom in Ariel's possession leads Misha to believe she is guilty. The locket has been handed down to the oldest girl in the Petrovich family for generations. Ariel is innocent of wrong doing, but her father is not. Misha is torn by his feelings for Ariel and his need for restitution against her father. Knowing that the relationship between them is fragile, Misha does everything in his power to protect Ariel's father. His efforts are to no avail when her father is shot. Ariel comes to realize Misha's steadfast courage and determination to protect her and her father despite what has happened to his family. Ariel's love and devotion heals Misha's heart.

The Talisman
The fourth book in the Lakota/Pinkerton Series

Running from a marriage that lasted one night, Dr. Moriah McKeown discovers the land she has settled on is coveted by determined and lawless men. Yet the proud young woman who once vowed never to abandon her home has second thoughts when her adopted children are threatened. Her only recourse is to enlist the aid of a dark, dangerous gun for hire.

Haunted by the past and a betrayal he will never forgive, Ian Civanovich uses his fast gun and his reckless courage to forget the faithlessness of a woman in his past. He will trust no female—nor will he rest until the threat hovering over Moriah McKeown is put to rest.

Forever His
The fifth book in the Lakota/Pinkerton Series

Struggling to come to terms with the part she played in Jacob St. John's death, Etta Barringer resigns from Pinkerton Agency and seeks peace and solace in a Rocky Mountain Cabin.

Jacob has vowed to discover the reason Etta has betrayed him, sold him out to his enemy and left him for dead.

Isolated in their cabin, they discover their love for each other and learn to trust. But the trust is shattered when Jacob learns she is married to his sworn enemy; the man who left him in the desert to die.

Allura's Secret
Twelve Dancing Princesses Book One

Allura McClellan is horrified by her father's decision to take out an ad in the Times awarding her to the man strong enough and smart enough to win her hand and uncover her secrets. She's an intelligent young woman who takes great delight in the freedom allotted to her by her father. She's well aware that marriage would effectively curtail the adventures she's shared with her sisters and cousins.

Hunter Gray is nothing like the other men who've arrived to vie for Allura's hand in marriage and everything that goes along with it. However, he is the first to refuse to concede defeat and pursue her despite her attempts to disguise her true appearance. It's her temperament that is of more concern to him than her looks. Hunter has worked all his life with the hope of someday owning his own land. Now that it looks like there's a very real possibility that everything he's ever wanted is within reach nothing is going to deter him – including Miss Allura's disagreeable disposition.

Amorica's Wager
Twelve Dancing Princesses Book Two

Amorica Hepburn was sent to London to find a husband. Finding a man was the last item on her agenda. With her two cousins, Amorica wagers she can dissuade her suitor before the others. Despite her efforts she discovers a chemistry that cannot be denied. Suddenly she is the arrogant man's wife, pledged to a marriage neither desire. But swept off to his ancestral home above the Dover cliffs and into his strong embrace, Amorica is soon possessed by a raging passion for the husband she had vowed to despise...

Damian Andrews couldn't afford to trust the emerald-eyed spitfire who happened upon his secret. Amorica's hatred of all men of his kind only inflames the war that rages between them. Still, he can not control the intense desire his stubborn bride inspires, or make her surrender to his will until he has conquered the headstrong beauty on the battlefield of love...

Ravyn's Marriage of Inconvenience
Twelve Dancing Princesses Book Three

A REGAL BEAUTY

When the duchess decides to wed her to a wastrel and a fop, Ravyn Grahm takes matters into her own hands and declares her engagement to another man. Instead of fessing up and telling her great aunt what she has done, she goes through with the pretense. Ariec Lakeland is the bastard son of an earl and has a dangerous reputation. But Ravyn is willing to do most anything to keep the duchess from discovering the lie.

A DEVIL-MAY-CARE SMUGGLER

He'd bought land in America, looking to put down roots and end his life of adventure, but Ariec Lakeland got more than he bargained for when he encountered a beautiful heiress who made a promise she didn't want to keep. But the promise could not be undone and standing between them were more obstacles than either ever dreamed. Ariec had made plans to spend the rest of his life in America and that was at odds with Ravyn's plan of living in England and running her father's estate. Now, he'll have to choose between his dreams and the woman he loves more than life.

Christel's Sunrise
Twelve Dancing Princesses Book Four

He Made Her An Offer...

Life has thrown Christel McClellan some experiences that could have devastated a less determined woman. Beautiful, self-assured and fiercely independent, she is trying to forget the loss of her stillborn child. But is the child alive?

She Couldn't Deny...

Life is carefree for Ryder MacLaren who loves to see what is on the other side of the sunrise. Laird of Clan MacLaren, he is wealthy, handsome and happily unencumbered...until stunning Christel McClellan enters his life. When he hears her story, he believes the child she thought dead has been sold to a wealthy buyer.

Storm's Passion
Twelve Dancing Princesses Book Five

SHE MADE A PROPOSAL...

Life strikes Storm Graham a shattering blow when she learns her father has bartered her to a man she detests. Storm is beautiful, self–assured and fiercely independent, and refuses to be a pawn in her father's schemes, yet she can find no way out of this bargain made in hell. Going on the offensive she asks the wealthiest man on the eastern coast of England to marry her, never believing she might fall in love.

HE TRIED TO REFUSE...

For Hadden Johnston life has provided everything he ever wanted, including a sanctuary for homeless children. He is wealthy, handsome and happily unencumbered...until stunning Storm Graham marches into his life and proposes a marriage of convenience. Yet this type of marriage to a woman who inflames his senses is far from acceptable. If he's going to be tied down, he will move heaven and earth to have this woman warming his bed.

Gotta Have Fayth
Twelve Dancing Princesses Book Six

A regal beauty with raven hair and piercing blue eyes, Fayth Graham is unwilling to parade herself in front of the wealthy Lords of England during the season. Seeking a means to dissuade any man wishing to wed her, she seeks a way to ruin herself for marriage. When she unexpectedly meets a man with sparkling gray eyes and an infectious grin, she decides this is the man who will keep her from agreeing to obey.

He returned from six months at sea, looking for a few nights of pleasure with a willing lass, but Jarret Kinsley got more than he bargained for when he met a beautiful debutant who responded to his kisses with a wild innocence that touched his heart. Yet the obstacles looming between them might rip them apart. Both had vowed never to marry, so when consequences of their dalliances got in the way, Jarret would have to choose between the life he's always desired and the woman he loves more than life.

Ella's Pleasure
Twelve Dancing Princesses Book Seven

A WHISPER OF PLEASURE
Ella Hepburn was an auburn haired debutant from the harsh Scottish coastline—a wild innocent to be seduced and tamed. A spirited beauty, she captivated Drake Montgomerie's jaded heart—while succumbing to the smoldering desire she felt for her unyielding suitor.

A WHISPER OF DANGER
In Drake Montgomerie's glittering world of money and privilege, young Ella discovered passion and desire could overcome everything she'd been taught to resist—entangling Drake, the heir apparent, in a lethal coil of aristocratic family intrigue. But grave peril would only nurse the sparks of a love that knew no limits and a magnificent ecstasy that would not be denied.

Eveleen's Seduction
Twelve Dancing Princesses Book Eight

A WHISPER OF SEDUCTION
A brutal attack on Eveleen Hepburn's cherished island off the Scottish coastline leaves her shattered and bewildered. Learning a man she once trusted can kill as easily as he can breathe even though the deed saves her life, creates questions that need answers. An innocent beauty, she enchants Logan Maxwell's cynical heart—giving in to the raging passion she feels for her mysterious suitor.

A WHISPER OF INTRIGUE

In Logan's Maxwell's world of espionage and privilege, young Eveleen discovers truths about herself she never expected, and a need for passion and love can overcome all her fears if she learns to accept certain truths. She finds herself entangled in a lethal battle for land that was once owned by French nobility, taken from them during the revolution and sold to Maxwell. But grave peril would unleash the flames of love that simmers, creating a magical union that cannot be refuted.

Tavia's Deception
Twelve Dancing Princesses Book Nine

WHISPERS OF DECEPTION

When her father decides to send her to London for her season, Tavia Hepburn resolves to see the world instead. The raven haired beauty decides to disguise herself as a lad and find employment on a ship bound for Barcelona as a cabin boy. But she never bargains on finding passion and love to a red haired sea captain who rescues her from certain death.

WHISPERS OF MURDER

For James Macmurra, the world is black and white until he meets a young debutante, who turns his world upside down. He's unable to deny Tavia's intoxicating effect on him. In a match tense with obstacles, unwillingness to divulge secrets, and unforeseen peril, irresistible desire and passion grows into undeniable love. James would risk his life to shelter and protect the innocent debutante who seduces him with her sweet love.

Larena's Fascination
Twelve Dancing Princesses Book Ten

WHISPERS OF FASCINATION

Fiery, free spirited Larena Graham never wanted to marry a duke.

She is thrilled to be in love with the fourth son of an aristocrat, Gavin Broon. But when it seems Gavin ignores her, she set her sights on politics and bettering human life. Unsuspecting intrigue and a plot against her, she continues her dangerous plans despite Gavin's wishes.

WHISPERS OF TRUST

Gavin has every intention of properly courting the beautiful Larena until he must leave the city in order to put his affairs in order. Returning to London, he finds the woman he means to make his own is embroiled in political protests that could lead to a prison ship. Larena must learn to trust the handsome Scotsman whose most pressing mission is to protect her and keep her from harm.

Tira's Education
Twelve Dancing Princesses Book Eleven

WHISPERS OF EDUCATION

Learning how to build ships is Tira Hepburn's only dream until she meets Jamie Lundin and her world is turned upside down. With her raven black hair and vivid green eyes, she tempts Jamie and pushes him to defy his vows. She never bargains on finding an irrevocable love and a passion to a man who cannot fulfill her dreams despite his burning desire for her.

WHISPERS OF A BARGAIN

Arrogant and self-assured Jamie is brought up short when Tira captures his heart. All his carefully made plans are put to the test when he decides to teach her the art of ship building if she will spend a week with him alone on his ship. He is unable to deny Tira's intoxicating effect on him. When Tira leaves him behind unwilling to live with him without the benefit of marriage, he races after her. Jamie will risk everything to shelter and protect the innocent debutante who seduces him with her sweet love.

Aidan's Love
Twelve Dancing Princesses Book Twelve

Whispers of Love

Aidan McLellan has loved since she first set eyes on him as a young girl. Spontaneous, wild and eager to grow up, Aidan haunts his waking thoughts day and night, insinuating herself into his life. With her fiery red hair and sparkling sapphire eyes, she seizes Blade's heart even while he tries to resist the innocent child until she becomes a woman.

Whispers of Courage

Blade has waited what seems a lifetime to claim the woman who captures his heart as a little girl. Claiming his inheritance before his younger brother takes what is rightfully his, Blade must convince Aidan of his sincerity after years of avoidance and wed her before his father dies so he can return home, securing his rightful place. Everything is put to the test when his life as well as Aidan's is threatened by the man who once called him brother.

Don't Hustle Letty
Good Girls Book One

She's a good girl...

As tempted as Scarlett was, she had too many secrets to let someone enter her world—secrets that would send any reasonable man to the farthest ends of the earth. Bobby was far from reasonable and despite her desperate attempts to hold him at bay, he would not let her past destroy their future. With her escort service, Scarlett used men and their insatiable lust for women to capitalize on the means to survive and prosper. She vowed to never wed, to never put herself in the control of a man.

...nonetheless he has other ideas.

Lord Robert Munroe, with his newly acquired title of marquis goes to Scarlett's for training on how to comport himself. The marquis, better known as Bobby, knows how to pick a pocket as well as get into a bloke's home to steal them blind. What he doesn't know is how to be a gentleman. When he sets his sights on the prim Miss Scarlet, Letty, to his way of thinking, he decides she is the woman he wants to call his wife. He tempts all that she is with sweet words and tender coaxing until she is unable to refuse all he hopes to give her.

Twelve Days to Love

When Archer Steele shows up at Calanthe Durand's failing plantation with an alligator over his shoulder, Cali thinks she's never seen a more handsome man. During the war she had to defend herself and her servants from both union and confederate soldiers. Independent and self-sufficient, she vows to never marry.

But Archer Steele has different ideas. The first time Archer sees Cali in town, he feels an instant attraction. He decides he will do everything and anything to convince the beautiful Miss Durand he is worthy of her love. During the weeks leading up to Christmas, he gives her twelve gifts in hopes she will fall in love with him. Yet they are faced with challenges they must overcome before Cali can commit to a marriage.

Door to Heaven

Jessica Lawrence is the stepdaughter of a woman born in the twentieth century transported back in time to the year 1868. An acclaimed suffragette, she raises Jessica to believe in the equality of women. Jess Law believes everything she was taught, and when the time is right she becomes a private investigator. Courageous and impetuous, Jess finds danger in her quest to save all women from white slavery. Her passionate mission results in a wedding to Roc Newman, a man she knows can steal her heart...

Roc can't trust the sapphire-eyed spitfire who invades his home in search of secret papers and knocks him flat with her karate moves. Jessica's refusal to obey his wishes serves to inflame the war between them. Still, he cannot control the intense desire his reluctant bride inspires, or make her surrender her independence, until he has conquered the headstrong beauty on the battlefield of love...

Rebel Heart

HER REBEL SPIRIT DEFIED HIS OUTSIDERS SOUL...She was velvet and silk, eyes the color of a summer storm and amber hair. Victoria DeMontville, because of a promise and a codicil to her father's will, was forced to marry one man to protect her from another. She hated Cameron Savage with a fierce passion. But to hold on to her genetic research and find a cure for the deadly Signe virus, she must pretend to love the enemy at her door, come with weapons of fire to melt her icy heart...

HIS OUTSIDERS TOUCH IGNITED RAGING PASSIONS... He wore a mask, disguised as the Phantom, a true legend come to life. Even as war and debate over new genetic research engulfed them all, he would find his greatest adversary in the beauty who'd branded him an outsider and barbarian, the woman he was born to possess, his soul mate.

Safari Moon

Solo St. John, a wildlife photographer, is preparing for a trip to Alaska. Suddenly, Solo finds women of all sorts invading his privacy, his home and his office, all cooing nonsense words and blatantly throwing themselves at him. Solo doesn't know why, and he has no idea how to rid himself of the persistent women. He finally decides to beg a favor of his best buddy Nyssa Harrington.

In love with Solo for the past ten years and knowing he doesn't return her feelings Nyssa doesn't want to talk to Solo. She knows if she accepts his phone call, she will not be able to resist the temptation to hope again.

Straight to Heaven

Running from demons, Alexandra McMurdie stumbles into Forbidden Ground where up is down and elements of nature are contested. Though a strong independent woman in the twenty-first century' she is unprepared for life in the 1800s. Her first site of the formidable James Lawrence makes her heart skip a beat, giving her cause to reconsider her desperate need to find a way home.

Born with a silver spoon, James' life was torn apart during the War Between the States. Moving west he vows to put the life he once knew in the past. When he discovers a half-frozen woman near Gold Hill, his heart begins to thaw. His love for Alexandra and his need to keep her from a man who has pursued her through time might cost him his life as well as hers.

A Valentine's Anthology

The Lending Library-a fantasy by Christie L. Kraemer
Faeries try to fit into the human world when the forest where they make their home is destroyed by a mysterious enemy.

Chasing Rainbows-a contemporary romance by Genene Valleau
An eccentric aunt, an inventive uncle, a mother who wears poodle skirts, and a brother who wears pearls provide a hilarious backdrop for the courtship of a young woman who yearns for a "normal" family.

The Gift-an historical romance by Christine Young
A man and a woman on opposite sides of the Civil War get a second chance at love after one final battle returns soldiers to their war-torn homes to rebuild their lives.

A St. Patrick's Day Tale
Christine Young, C. L. Kraemer, Genene Valleau

Tumble through time...

...to Ireland in 1817, when tensions are high between Protestants and Catholics and fae people guide the fate of villagers. A lovely Catholic lass stumbles upon the weakly ritual fisticuffing between Irish lads. She falls into the lap of a handsome young Protestant. Family ties, grudges, and two conniving faeries threaten their budding love. But the faeries outsmart themselves when they hijack a time machine that has mysteriously appeared in their forest and are whisked to...

...Eugene, Oregon in the 20th century, amid a property feud between the local faeries and night elves. The conniving faeries from Olde Ireland try to stir up more mischief. However, a warrior gnome convinces the magic folk to control their own destiny, and forces the intruding faeries to take refuge in the time machine again, spinning their way toward...

...A modern day castle in western Oregon. An eccentric inventor is determined to reclaim his wayward time machine and save his beloved wife from her latest misadventure. If only they can travel safely past the black hole...

a May Day Anthology
Christine Young, C. L. Kraemer, Rosemary Indra, Genene Valleau

Highland Miracle — Christine Young
HURTLED THROUGH TIME, Sean Michael Sterling, landed in the midst of a May Day celebration he didn't understand, assuming the role of Laird Sterling.

ILLIGITAMATE CHILD OF NOBILITY, Reagan Douglas searches for a way out of her half brother's house.

Defying the Odds — C.L. Kraemer
The night elves on the hill aren't happy without their magic. They

concoct a plan to punish those who were involved in the act that rendered them almost human. Meanwhile, Uther, the rogue night elf, has returned to woo the Librarian to be his eternal mate.

Love in Bloom — Rosemary Indra
When childhood friends reunite it takes two fairies and a matchmaking daughter to help them admit their true love for each other.

No More Poodle Skirts — Genie Gabriel
After drifting for years in the innocent age of the 1950s, a woman struggles to join today's world by finding a career and a new love, with some help from her zany family.

Once Upon a Christmas Moon
Christine Young, C. L. Kraemer, Genene Valleau

TWELVE DAYS TO LOVE
When Archer Steele shows up at Calanthe Durand's failing plantation with an alligator over his shoulder, Cali thinks she's never seen a more handsome man. During the war she had to defend herself and her servants from both union and confederate soldiers. Independent and self-sufficient, she vows to never marry. But Archer Steele has different ideas. The first time Archer sees Cali in town, he feels an instant attraction. He decides he will do everything and anything to convince the beautiful Miss Durand he is worthy of her love. During the weeks leading up to Christmas, he gives her twelve gifts in hopes she will fall in love with him.

BOOTS AND BLADES
An ancient evil from the old country has arrived in the high desert of Oregon. Gnome children are vanishing then re-appearing, showing various stages of traumatization. Tiamoon, warrior gnome, will put her skills to use alongside Killian, a handsome warrior, also in need of a cause.

CHRISTMAS PAWSIBILITIES

With their world destroyed and their space ship malfunctioning, the dogizens of Planet Canid have little choice but to crash land on Earth. They face tortuous experiments at the hands of the Geeks in Green...or they can trust an eccentric inventor and his zany family to deliver the Canine Queen's puppies and help them celebrate new lives.